"NIGHT HUNT"

by Liam Stuyvesant

For Logan and BB,

my brothers in spirit and fellow fang-fans

Author's Note

Although this is a work of fiction, my goal has been to make this story as real as possible.

To that end, all of the bars and restaurants mentioned herein actually existed in New York City in 1979, many of which I frequented when I first set foot in Greenwich Village in 1981. The two major exceptions are the Acropolis Diner and the Pot Shop, both literary conceits on my part, as are Lamont & Ellis, McCambridge & Blair, and the Holloman Funeral Home.

While I didn't initially set out to include them, several events in this narrative did take place in mid-Summer 1979: the premiere of the film "Dracula" starring Frank Langella, the protests at the location shoots of "Cruising," and the conviction of Ted Bundy in Florida.

Thanks to conversations with associates, along with the invaluable search engines provided by Google and Bing, I was able to further my commitment to verisimilitude and accuracy in what I wrote insofar as New York City hospitals and cemeteries are concerned.

For where I failed in that, please accept my apologies.

HE KNOWS THE MOMENT HE ENTERS THE CROWDED, SHADOWY BAR in Greenwich Village that he'll score tonight.

He steps into the refreshing air conditioning and leaves the balmy heat outside. Even at night, the summer months in New York City are sweltering, oppressive. Letting his eyes adjust to the dark, he takes in the lay of the land. The air is a haze of cigarette smoke, lending an ethereal, multi-hued glow to the flashing disco lights. Bodies undulate on the dance floor, each offering its own evocative interpretation of the flavor-of-the-month hit—Donna Summer's "Hot Stuff," at the moment—every square inch of exposed flesh glazed with sweat despite the artificially cooled air. He can smell the hunger in the room and savors the potent aroma. As usual, the music's volume is pumped so high that he feels the bass in his chest.

Or is that his heart? Difficult to tell. Being on the prowl always spikes his senses and his pulse rate. He never fails to delight in the rush.

He smiles—a cynical smile with self-aware amusement—noting that he could very well be in any gay club in New York. All over the city, this exact scene is playing itself out at this very moment, the only variations being the different actors portraying the same roles in the nightly tragic comedy.

But isn't that part of the allure? he asks himself. *Maybe the* whole *allure?* All the players know the script of this two-act farce by heart. Act One in the club, Act Two to be brought to life in some other, equally random setting. And after the curtain call, no cast party, no fond farewells, no promises to always stay in touch. Each will go his own way, secretly hoping not to cross paths again.

At least he knows the score, as well as why he is here. One coin, two sides. Not to mention, it's less obvious than the baths. He actually enjoys the façade of seemingly being out only for a drink, maybe a dance or two, and playing along with the false serendipity of leaving with someone. All part of a game he shamelessly relishes playing, especially since he plays it rather well.

As he makes his way through the clusters of men, he stealthily scans the crowd, waiting for his instincts to tell him he's found what he came for. Summer nights in the Village offer a veritable smorgasbord; it's simply a matter of deciding which selection will satisfy his appetite. The bar is packed with men, many of them clones of one another: muscled torsos encased in form-fitting tank tops in an array of colors, bubble butts that had been poured into well-worn Levi's or snug basketball shorts, bulging biceps sporting the occasional leather armband, a rainbow of bandanas—color-coded to communicate assorted interests and predilections—hanging from back pockets, two out of every three guys proudly displaying a mustache identical to the one on the Winston man blowing smoke rings from the billboard above Times Square.

Yes, he thinks, *quite the delicious selection.*

He sidles up to the bar and orders a beer he has no intention of drinking, wanting only the prop as he continues his search. Bottle in hand, he finds a spot from which his vantage point allows him to take in the whole room, and he leans casually against a wall away from the entrance.

As he expects, it isn't long before eye contact is made, and he immediately knows he's found what he's come looking for. Leaning against the opposite wall, in almost a mirror of his own faux-casual pose, is a man who appears to be in his mid-twenties: well-toned body, dark hair not unlike his own, piercing eyes that seem to defy the pervasive shadows.

He walks with a purpose as he crosses the room and leans against the wall next to the object of his desire. Without maintaining the eye contact that had been established from twenty feet away, he disinterestedly observes the dancing bodies.

"Crowded tonight," he says, as if to no one in particular.

"Yeah," replies the stranger, who, like himself, is idly watching the room as if still on the prowl.

"Wanna get outta here?" he asks. His tone implies that if he were answered in the negative, he wouldn't much care. Why should he? The place is packed with options, each as anonymous as the next.

Thus is the game of the hunt.

"Sure."

Without further conversation, they make their way to the door and step back into the sultry night, each intent solely on satisfying his own desires.

CHAPTER ONE

JAKE'S HEAD WAS POUNDING as he parked his car on the one-way street and got out.

The prior night's revelry with Tommy and four of their friends had left Detective Jake Griffin with a massive hangover. The fact that his partner of five years, Detective-Sergeant Frank Prentiss, had woken him just after dawn with a most unwelcome phone call did not help.

He'd picked up the bedside phone less out of interest in the call and more to stop the incessant ringing. "Yeah?" he'd said by way of answering it, his hoarse voice barely audible.

"Who the fuck is calling this early?" Tommy grumbled from beside him, his head buried in the pillow.

"Shh," Jake hissed at him, his hand cupped over the receiver. "Yeah, I'm here," he said into the phone. "No, I'm alone. What's going on?"

Tommy grunted his disapproval into the down pillow.

Frank's news was more unwelcome than the painful noise that had woken him moments before. Despite the crushing agony behind his eyes, Jake found himself suddenly lucid. "Gimme twenty minutes," he said, his tone now all business. "I'll meet you there."

Shit, he thought. *Not again.*

TWENTY-FIVE MINUTES LATER, Jake emerged from his car, having flashed his badge to the uniforms affixing the bright yellow "Crime Scene" tape to whatever was available.

He was already prepared to lie to his partner about the five-minute delay. The truth was that Tommy had been giving him grief about leaving for work hours ahead of his shift on Tommy's day off, but Jake wasn't about to share that with Frank.

A decade had elapsed since Stonewall, and while there was some minor progress being made here and there for gay men in New York City, being out of the closet in the N.Y.P.D. was not included on that rather brief list.

"Sorry I took longer than expected," he said as he approached Frank at the entrance to an alley on West 10th Street. "Couldn't get outta my own way with this hangover." Prentiss snorted his empathetic understanding.

Okay, Jake thought, *not a* complete *lie.*

"Whadda we got here?" he continued before Frank could comment on his impaired state.

"Schwartz called me. Looks like another fruit loop," Frank said without malice. He ran his hand over his closely cropped Afro and exhaled a ragged sigh, always a dead giveaway to Jake that his partner was troubled by a case. "Ripped the fuck up like the other two. Garbage man phoned it in around oh-five-hundred. Found him behind the Dumpster. M.E.'s back there now."

Fruit loop, Jake's mind echoed. Far from being an asshole, Frank was nonetheless guilty of the careless epithets that Jake found degrading, ones that Frank would find equally degrading were they about blacks. Jake had never heard the words "fag" or "queer" pass Frank's lips, but he still bristled inwardly at his partner's comments nonetheless. This was exactly why he kept his private life to himself, even with Frank, whom he'd otherwise trust, unequivocally, with his physical life.

"Same M.O.?" Jake asked, although he was sure he already knew the answer. Over the course of almost two months, starting Memorial Day weekend, two other young men had been found in the West Village, their throats viciously slashed. In both cases, they'd last been seen at one of the area gay bars. In both cases, theft wasn't the apparent motive since the victims still had their wallets and jewelry. In both cases, the only wound had been the ravaged throats with no head trauma or bruising on their torsos or limbs. And in both cases, they'd been murdered elsewhere and dumped where they were later found.

They knew this had to be so, because in both cases, the autopsies revealed that the vics had been drained of blood, yet none was to be found at the scene. Easy math for even a rookie in Homicide: no blood in the body and no blood on the scene meant a dump job.

"Same so far," Frank confirmed and flipped open his pad. "Vic's name is Cody Fischer. Age twenty-eight, lived up on West 12th. Still have to retrace his movements last night to find out if he was at a meat rack. I sent a unit to his place to secure the scene, in case he's got a, umm, roommate." The hesitation was Frank's way of saying what needed to be said without having to say it, another indication of his discomfort with the situation. "They're gonna radio back when they know more. They took the vic's keys, just in case."

Jake left Frank and digested this as he made his way into the alley, passing the chief medical examiner as he headed out. "Talk to me, Ruiz," Jake said to the M.E. as he flipped open his own pad.

Miguel Ruiz shook his head in weariness and lit a cigarette. Jake surmised that he, too, had been roused earlier than he'd planned. "Apparent C.O.D.'s exsanguination," he said in a raggedly tired voice through a plume of exhaled smoke. "No defensive wounds, no petechial hemorrhaging, and, obviously, no lividity, 'cause there ain't no blood. I put the time of death between eleven P.M. and three A.M. based on rigor, but even that's hard to say with this heat. Won't know more 'til I get him on the table, but he looks enough like the other two that it's a safe assumption to say they're related. I'll send you my report by the end of the day." Ruiz continued on his way, stopping to confer for a moment with Frank before disappearing from Jake's view.

Turning, Jake approached the crime-scene unit gathered around the Dumpster. As with the other two cases, there were no evidence markers on the ground since there was a complete absence of physical evidence, aside from the corpse. The Dumpster obscured the view of the body from the sidewalk, so there was no need to discreetly drape it with a sheet. Jake looked down at the remains of Cody Fischer.

Wedged between the trash and the bricks of the building, the lifeless young man looked like a rag doll that had been hurled in anger against a wall by a petulant toddler. The ashen pallor of his face was a stark contrast to the gore beneath his chin where the front of his throat had been less than twelve hours before. His eyes, wide and staring, registered the horror he'd experienced in the final moments of his young life. Averting his gaze from the carnage, Jake took note of everything below the lethal wound. Royal blue Izod, the collar blood-soaked, gold Star of David pendant resting on his chest where the shirt was unbuttoned, gold watch, faded Levi jeans, Adidas sneakers. His muscular arms and chest indicated a disciplined workout regimen, as well as the likelihood that he could have fended off an attack if given the chance.

The other two vics had had similar builds, making Jake wonder if they'd been blitzed or if, perhaps, he and Prentiss were looking for more than one perp working as a team. It didn't make sense that such physically fit young men would be so brutally murdered yet show no signs of a struggle prior to death.

"Griff," Frank called from where Jake had left him. His initial assessment complete, Griffin made his way back to his partner. A crowd had formed on the sidewalk on the opposite side of 10th. He could see that the looky-loos were talking to each other, their heads quite animated, but their gazes remaining fixed on the mouth of the alley.

"Unit radioed in," Frank said when Jake reached him. "Fischer lived alone, had a studio in a subdivided brownstone. Other than a dime bag of weed, a bong, and some poppers, nothing outta the ordinary. At least, nothing in plain sight. They secured the scene until we can get there."

"Ruiz is gonna send us his report later," Jake said, knowing that Frank most likely already had this information. "Not much more we can do here. Why don't we go check out the apartment?" Jake, being the junior partner, always deferred to Frank's judgment even when he knew his own to be sound.

"Sounds good," Frank said, giving Jake a brief glance. "You look like shit, man. I'll drive."

ONCE THE UNIFORMS HAD BRIEFED FRANK, he retrieved the keys to the apartment and sent them back to the alley. He and Jake then set about giving the studio a thorough examination, gloves on, notebooks in hand, evidence bags at the ready.

Cody Fischer's studio occupied the front half of the top floor. While the space was small, Fischer had made optimal use of the room, decorating it with style and keeping it relatively tidy. On the walls were several frames of various sizes: a couple of Erté reproductions, eight-by-ten photos with what Jake assumed were friends, a "Welcome to The Pines" flyer from Fire Island, Playbills from recent hits on Broadway, and what appeared to be a Robert Mapplethorpe original, albeit a small one. Dominating the space between the two windows was the six-colored flag that had only just come on the scene the year before to celebrate Gay Pride.

A sofa bed, the single upholstered seat in the studio, took up most of the wall under the flag and the windows, which offered a view of 12th Street and the brownstones across the way. In front of the sofa bed was a square coffee table. The dirty plate and empty glass told the detectives that this also served as Cody Fischer's dining room. Next to the dishes were the bag of pot and the bottle of poppers the uniforms had reported, along with an ashtray. The bong was on the floor underneath. A rabbit-eared television sat a few feet away on a battered cart, and mismatched, second-hand bookcases lined the wall behind it. Jake perused the volumes arranged on the shelves. Art books, celebrity biographies, a wide array of Agatha Christie in paperback, a couple of Armistead Maupin's "Tales of the City" collections, a smattering of classics, both modern and 19th-century. *No red flags here*, he thought.

In the corner between the sofa-bed and the bookcases were an impressive turntable and amp situated on an upended, open steamer trunk, a collection of records inside the chest, speakers flanking it. The albums were as uninformative as the books: show tunes, disco. Jake knew that Frank would have viewed this as a cliché, and he was loath to admit that he was inclined to agree. There was also some jazz, some classical, some rock, both old-school and current. But the majority of the collection was show tunes and disco. *C'mon, Cody,* Jake thought, *help me out here. And while you're at it, try not to be so predictable.* Before moving on to join Frank across the room, he noted the small stack of Blue Boy and Mandate magazines next to the steamer trunk.

Opposite the makeshift library and media center was Fischer's workspace. A high-end draftsman's table with a matching stool were next to a desk fashioned out of a wooden door, the knob removed, atop two short, mismatched filing cabinets. Tucked under the door was a metal folding chair.

Used bookshelves, an old TV, a desk made out of a door; and then a finely crafted draftsman's table and state-of-the-art stereo? Fischer was an artist and a music lover. A cursory look of the items on the desk was all they needed to confirm the former: the deceased had been a graphic designer employed by an ad agency uptown. His datebook, laying open on the desk, yielded little information, aside from a few random notations about lunch plans, work deadlines, a dentist appointment, and other minutiae, none of which offered any leads.

Neither did his address book, since none of the entries, with the exception of "Mom & Dad," indicated the nature of the deceased's relationships with the names listed, of which very few included surnames. Mr. Cookie-Cutter, as Jake was beginning to think of the late Mr. Fischer, was shaping up to be a stereotype, and not a very flattering one.

Frank checked his watch and picked up the address book. "Ad agency should be open by the time we get uptown," he said. "Let's start there, and then see what we can turn up from these." He slipped the address book, along with the date book, into a plastic evidence bag. To those he added a five-by-seven black-and-white photo of the deceased, having removed it from a frame. "Add this to file," he said by way of explanation.

They locked the door and affixed "Crime Scene" tape across it. That completed, they made their way down the two flights of stairs and emerged onto the street.

CHAPTER TWO

"HE DID IT AGAIN," Tommy LaRosa complained into the phone.

He was still in Jake's bed, the receiver from the nightstand in one hand, a cigarette in the other.

"What do you expect?" his sister asked, her tone not at all challenging. In fact, it imparted empathy and understanding, for Jake as well as Tommy. Even if she were inclined to be impatient with him—which, for the record, she wasn't—she was at her desk in the public defender's office where she worked as a paralegal. Not unlike Jake, she had her own unique need of discretion.

Three years his senior, Cara was Tommy's regular sounding board, as well as his personal voice of reason. Most recently, they'd had a variation of this very conversation less than a month prior in the apartment they shared on Grove Street. In the days before the annual Gay Pride Parade in Greenwich Village, Jake had refused to join Tommy and their circle of friends—*Tommy's* friends—for the festivities. It was Cara who'd helped Tommy begrudgingly accept that Jake couldn't risk being seen and recognized by one of the many N.Y.P.D. uniforms patrolling the streets to ensure order, especially in his own precinct.

It was apparent to Cara that her little brother had forgotten that conversation in the thirty or so days that had elapsed since then.

"What I expect is to be acknowledged," he shot back. "Look, I get it, he can't come out of the closet at work, but c'mon! To deny that I'm even *here*? That shit's just insulting! It's like there are whole parts of his life where I don't even exist!"

"I understand," she said. "You feel demeaned. That's legitimate." She continued, choosing words that Tommy might hear. "Put yourself in his shoes, though. You told me the call woke him up and that he was hungover. Half-asleep and in pain isn't a good combo when coming up with a believable lie, especially since there was a crime scene he had to get to."

"But—"

She cut him off with a bright tone. "I have an idea," she offered. "And it's a good one."

Tommy waited a moment, taking a drag off his cigarette before biting at the bait. "Okay," he conceded. "What is it?" He knew in advance that it would indeed be a good idea, most likely a *very* good one. Such was her gift.

"Call the precinct and leave a message for him to call you when he gets back there," she began. "Don't let on that you know he isn't there. And keep it professional, maybe say, I don't know, that he gave you his card in case you had any info on an investigation he's working. Don't sound personal or familiar."

"With you so far," he said. To Cara's well-trained ears, his voice didn't sound like he was one hundred percent on board yet, but getting there. "Then what?"

"Get yourself together," she continued, pressing what she knew to be her advantage, "and when he calls you, ask him when he expects to be home. Tell him you're gonna make a late lunch or early dinner or whatever, depending on when he'll get there. Tell him you want to make his day a little easier. Then get busy in the kitchen."

"And then?"

"Relieve *his* stress before bringing up your *own*," she counseled. "And I don't mean in bed." She heard Tommy snort a laugh, a sure sign she was making headway. "It's that simple, little brother. It's what couples do. Let him vent, and you listen. Attentively."

"Isn't that a little manipulative?" he asked, a hint of suspicion in his voice.

"Only if you're doing it with an agenda," she pointed out. "If it's sincere, then no, it's not. Do you sincerely want to relieve his stress? Or is this only all about you?" She knew her brother well enough to predict his answer.

"You don't have to ask that," he said. "Yes! Are you happy? Yes, I want to help him leave the work bullshit at work." He hated when she was right and, in these matters, she usually was. Probably why he always called her instead of one of his bar buddies who'd stand in solidarity with his indignation.

"Besides," Cara added, well into the homestretch, "he may very well bring it up before you do. Tommy, he's not oblivious to you and how you feel about all this. He's walking a tightrope, and I don't envy him, but he cares a lot about you and wants to make you happy." She paused a beat for effect. "Why not give him the chance to do that?"

CHAPTER THREE

"RIGHT THIS WAY, DETECTIVES," the Lamont & Ellis receptionist invited warmly, leading them down a short corridor and into a smartly appointed conference room. Frank, having appraised her figure from behind, shot Jake a lecherous glance, as if to say, "Go for it, partner!"

Fuck, Jake thought, remnants of his hangover gnawing at the edges of his patience. *I hate when he does that shit.*

A dapper, smiling executive in his forties stood as they entered. Jake adjudged that his designer suit cost more than the ones he and Frank were wearing, combined and doubled. "Thank you, Gretchen," the exec said to the young woman, who recognized her cue to leave, which she did. "Have a seat, detectives," he continued. His demeanor was slick and affable. Jake had no trouble envisioning him pitching the firm to prospective clients over cocktails, and then picking up the tab to close the deal. On the corporate card, naturally.

They took two of the leather-upholstered armchairs, sitting side by side, and the executive sat back down at the head of the table in a matching, though slightly grander, chair. Jake and Frank pulled out their notebooks and pens. "Gretchen told me you have a few questions about one of our employees," he said, his expression now appropriately, if artificially, concerned. "You mind me asking which one?"

"Not at all, Mr. ...?" Frank responded with a question, one to which he already knew the reply. Best to start off establishing who did the asking and who did the answering, a tactic Jake had long ago learned working beside him.

"Damn, I'm sorry," the suit said, extending a hand in which a business card had appeared as if by some feat of legerdemain. "Pete Lamont, one of the partners here. Marty—Martin Ellis, that is, he's the other partner—is out of town this week."

Frank accepted the card, slipping it under a paper clip in his notebook, before shaking Pete Lamont's hand briskly. Jake was already scribbling notes in his own pad.

"I'm Detective-Sergeant Frank Prentiss," he said. "This is my partner, Detective Jake Griffin." He acknowledged Jake with a nod as brisk as the handshake.

Lamont looked down at the two business cards on the table before him, cards Gretchen had provided when she informed him of the detectives' presence. "So I saw," he said, lifting one up. "It says here you're with

Homicide, which concerns me, naturally. Which employee are you here about?"

"Cody Fischer was found murdered this morning in Greenwich Village," Frank stated, subliminally reclaiming control of the interview. Jake was familiar with his partner's technique: hit them cold with a harsh fact right out of the gate and gauge the reaction.

Lamont's was immediate and unmistakable: shock, with heavy shades of denial. "What?" he stammered. "I don't understand." Frank's assessment was that the executive was sincere, not that he'd really thought this guy had been prowling the Village, slaughtering homos.

"He was found in an alley by some garbage men," Frank continued, "and we're now trying to establish his movements prior to the attack. Was he in the office yesterday?"

"Yes," Lamont replied, still registering the news. "Let me think. I saw him late in the afternoon, around four or so, and reminded him of an upcoming deadline on an account he's heading up." He paused and swallowed. "*Was* heading up, I guess." He reached for the glass of water on the table, his hand trembling as he took a sip before clearing his throat.

"Who left first?" Frank continued. "You or him?"

"I did," the exec replied. "I had a dinner meeting with a client. I left shortly after Cody and I talked."

"So, you have no idea how late he worked?"

"No clue," Lamont said. "The security guard in the lobby would probably know."

Jake noted this, however unnecessary it was. Questioning security in buildings like this was S.O.P.

"He say anything about where he might have been headed last night?" Frank pressed, not unkindly, after Lamont set the glass back down. "You know, anyone he might have had plans with? Maybe dinner reservations? Theater tickets? Anything like that?"

"No," he replied. "We just talked about the campaign, and briefly at that. Cody is—*was*—one of our best graphics men. Needed very little hands-on management. Gifted artist, impeccable vision." He took another swallow of water. "Fuck," he whispered. "This is unbelievable."

Lamont's repeated use of the present tense suggested to the detectives that, prior to their visit, the executive had no clue that his employee was dead.

"Were you two close at all?" Frank asked.

"If you mean were we friends, the answer is no," Lamont said. "Other than after-hours mixers with clients, I make it a point not to involve myself in my employees' personal lives. Makes the business more efficient. Removes any expectations that can come with fraternizing."

"Anything you might be able to tell us about his, uh, personal life?" Prentiss continued. "You know, anything he might have mentioned in passing?"

"If you're asking if I knew he was gay, detective," Lamont replied, his shoulders and his tone stiffening just enough for Frank to take note, "yes, I knew. It's not an issue in our industry, thank God. Not that it should be an issue in any field. When I hire someone to do a job, all I care about is their ability to do that job, and how they can benefit L&E. I don't give a shit who they fuck."

"Are you gay, Mr. Lamont?" Frank was ready with this question the moment the ad exec had finished speaking.

"What the hell does that have to do with anything?" Lamont protested. "I don't see how—"

"Until we know more about Mr. Fischer, sir, we don't know *what's* gonna be relevant to the case. Please just answer the question."

"No, I'm not," Lamont said, appearing a bit insulted.

Not an issue, but you're pretty damn offended by the suggestion, Jake thought. *Typical.*

"So you and Mr. Fischer weren't …?" Frank let the implication of the question dangle in the air.

"I already told you that Cody and I had no personal relationship whatsoever," Lamont replied, his tone now strictly business. "Of any nature. He was my employee, he and his work will be sorely missed, but beyond that, it doesn't really affect me. Is there anything else, detectives? Replacing him is going to be a tall order, and I really need to focus on that right now. Especially with deadlines coming up."

From everybody's best friend to hostile witness in less than five minutes, Jake thought. *Frank hasn't lost his touch.*

"You know if he was involved with anyone else here?" Frank asked, changing the aim of his questions, however slightly.

"No, I don't know," Lamont said curtly. "Romantic involvements between the employees are strongly discouraged, for obvious reasons."

Frank took his time making note of this. "That's it for now," he said after letting Lamont stew for a moment, his tone slightly more congenial. But only slightly. "You mind if we look through his workspace before we go?"

"Of course," the executive said, matching Frank in the de-escalation. "Miss Mills will show you."

Miss Mills? Jake wondered. *Guess we're off first-name basis, even with Gretchen.* His slight amusement helped the hangover, at least.

He and Frank stood to leave. "Again, I'm really sorry for having to bring you this news," Frank said. "And for your loss. The firm's loss, I should say." The junior partner silently noted that the apology didn't extend to the questions about Lamont's personal life. Every case was a master class with Prentiss. "If you think of anything, even if it seems insignificant to you, call one of us. You have our cards."

"Of course," Lamont said for the second time in less than a minute. "Naturally."

"And thank you for taking the time to talk to us."

Frank always tried to end things on a cordial note.

THE SEARCH OF CODY FISCHER'S CORNER OF THE LARGE OFFICE proved as uninformative as the one at his apartment, if not less so. At least, insofar as the case was concerned.

Jake found it interesting that, even in a field where homosexuality wasn't an issue, as Lamont had indicated, Cody had no traces of his personal life on his desk. A surreptitious glance around the open area told him that the deceased had been an exception here. Various desks sported framed photos, small placards suggesting that passersby should "Live! Laugh! Love!" and "Take it Easy!," even an "Elect Ed Koch" bumper sticker from almost two years prior. In general, assorted expressions of the occupants' lives and philosophies.

But in Cody's workspace, nothing but the job, a stark contrast to the apartment where he'd expressed himself so freely all over the place.

His assessment of the area and the employees also told him that word about their late coworker was already spreading. Across the expansive office, several of the clustered women had tissues in hand, the men looked grim, all were sneaking subtle glances at Jake and Frank, if not unabashedly staring.

The large blotter-style calendar on Cody's desk listed only deadlines, office meetings, and other business-related dates, along with phone numbers under account names in the margin. No reminders of after-work plans, no mention of the shows he must have seen, if the framed Playbills at his studio were any indication. *All work and no play*, Jake mused.

But Cody Fischer *did* play. His apartment, if nothing else, was proof of that. And if this homicide was committed by the same perp who'd killed the other two vics, which seemed likely, Cody had been at a gay bar last night.

So, no, Cody Fischer worked *and* played. The two just didn't seem to overlap.

Jake felt an unwelcome kinship with the deceased young man. Even in a much more open-minded field, Cody, too, felt the need to hide his true self in the workplace. If that poor kid stayed even partially in the closet in this industry, what hope could Jake *ever* have in his own?

"Griff?" Frank said, a slight edge in his tone.

"What?" Jake answered, coming back to the present moment.

"Where'd you go, man?" the senior partner asked.

"No place," Jake replied. "Just seeing what pieces might fit together."

"And?"

"I got nothing. So far, anyway."

Frank turned his attention to a rather efficient-looking woman who had just left the crowd across the room and returned to the desk next to Cody's. "Okay if I use Cody's phone to call the precinct?"

"Certainly," she replied, her business demeanor giving way to subtle flirtation as she offered Prentiss her best smile. It was brief, though, and she caught herself, remembering the solemnity of their visit. "Just dial 9 for an outside line," she said, turning her full attention to her own work.

Jake shook his head. For all the assumptions and stereotypes that straights have about gays, they're just as guilty of always being on the prowl. Probably more so because they can do it wherever they please.

Frank took a step closer to the woman's desk. "Mind if I ask you a few questions first, ma'am?" he inquired, making the most of her apparent attraction by offering a winning smile.

Looking up from her work, her own smile restored, she said, "Anything I can do to help, officer."

"Actually, it's detective," Frank said, pulling a business card from his wallet and handing it to her. "Detective-Sergeant Frank Prentiss, at your service, Ms. ... I'm sorry, I didn't catch your name."

"Gail," she said. "Gail Krasinski, Detective Prentiss." She slipped his card into the corner tab of her desk blotter. "And it's Miss," she added to make a point.

Could she be any more obvious? Jake silently asked himself.

"I see you worked right next to Mr. Fischer," he said. At this, her smile appropriately disappeared.

"Yes," she said, her tone a touch too tragic.

"I'm sorry for your loss, Miss Krasinski," Frank offered with sincerity. He was always sensitive to the grief, either real or feigned, experienced by the survivors of the vics that wound up on his caseload.

"Thank you, detective," she said.

"Were you two close?" he asked. "As in, did you socialize outside the office?"

Gail Krasinski was eager to be of help to Detective Prentiss. "Oh, yes," she said, immediately animated.

"Go on," he prompted.

"Oh, you know," she hedged. "Drinks after work now and then, things like that."

"Things like that?"

Gail let out a nervous laugh. "Oh, lord, no," she sputtered. "We were just friends." She paused for effect. "I'm single."

Frank pretended to note this in his pad. "Well," he said, "we're already aware that Mr. Fischer was a homosexual, so I wasn't assuming anything."

"Oh," she said, somewhat taken aback. Prentiss took mental note of her reaction, always the chess master in these situations.

"He ever mention any boyfriends to you?" he asked, pressing his advantage.

"Oh, you know, the usual." Gail lied effortlessly, if not unnoticeably. "This and that. 'Girl talk,' I guess you could call it." Her laugh was more nervous than light-hearted.

This chick knew nothing about him, Jake thought, losing interest in the exchange. He turned his attention back to Cody Fischer's workspace, opening for the second time the top drawer of the desk. He noticed something he'd missed before when he'd allowed himself to get lost in thought.

Almost completely hidden beneath an interoffice memo was a matchbook. Pulling it out, Jake saw it was from the Ninth Circle, a meat rack on West 10th. While he'd never been inside, he knew the place by reputation and the occasional times he'd passed it with Tommy. It was hardly a dive, but there was no glitz to the Circle; it was just a dimly lit neighborhood bar catering to an ever-growing clientele of gay men. It didn't have a dance floor, owing partially, Jake assumed, to the surcharge by the liquor-licensing board that would deem it a "cabaret" if dancing were allowed. Mostly, he surmised, it was a matter of not trying to pretend to be something that it wasn't.

He respected, even envied, that.

Opening the matchbook, Jake found all of the matches unused, as well as a name—Kyle—followed by a seven-digit phone number. Whether it was a home number or an answering service remained to be determined, but the absence of an area code was a strong suggestion that it was in Manhattan, not Jersey or one of the other four boroughs.

He was slipping it into a plastic evidence bag as Frank returned. Without comment on his interview with *Miss* Krasinski, the senior partner took a seat at the desk, lifted the receiver and, after pressing 9 as he'd been instructed, dialed the captain's direct line in Homicide.

"Prentiss here, Cap," he said. "After the crime scene, we searched the vic's apartment and just finished questioning his boss at this ad agency." He paused, listening. "Yeah, my thoughts too. We'll be there as fast as midtown traffic allows." Hanging up without a "Goodbye," he turned to Jake. "Okay, partner, let's head back and start the paperwork."

Stopping in the lobby, it took Frank and Jake less than five minutes to ascertain from the Security desk that Cody Fischer had left the building at seven on what would be his last day of work. That accomplished, they headed out.

CHAPTER FOUR

THE BOLD PURPLES, BLACKS, AND GOLDS OF THE LARGE ABSTRACT PAINTING stood out in stark and dramatic contrast to the blindingly white wall on which it had just been hung.

As the workmen stepped aside, Sandrine Delacroix stood immobile, scrutinizing the effect of the artwork opposite the entrance to her gallery. It was imperative that visitors be stopped in their tracks, however momentarily, upon opening the door. The twenty feet between the entrance and the painting offered a perfect distance from which to take in—and, more to the point, feel—its impact.

Satisfied with the result, she offered an efficient nod of her head and a curt "*Merci*," thereby dismissing the hired help. The two men smiled, a gesture Sandrine did not return. They left the gallery, but not without assessing the owner's figure no less intently than she'd appraised their work. Once they were past her sightline, of course. They may not know shit about art, but a sexy woman in a tight skirt, silk blouse, and "fuck-me" pumps was well within their expertise.

Sandrine was fully aware of their gazes, even if she didn't see them. She wasn't oblivious to the effect her appearance and bearing had on people, men and women alike. At forty-two, she had the figure of a woman half her age, but the youthfulness of her physical charm was balanced by a sophistication and business sense envied by people on four continents, many of whom several years her senior.

This combination of attributes, honed over more than two decades, had opened countless doors, quite a few of them leading to bedrooms, all leading to furthering her presence in the international art world.

The task at hand complete, Sandrine locked the front entrance to the gallery. The glass double doors, as well as the large windows on either side, were completely covered in brown paper, blocking any view of the interior from the busy street. In elegant lettering, a sign in each window informed passersby that Galerie Delacroix would soon unveil its debut exhibit, listing the date and time of the event. Already, she'd had several requests for interviews from various newspapers and magazines eager to get a jump on the competition in profiling her. None of the requests, however, had been accepted as of yet, but that would change in short order.

The grand opening and reception were still more than two weeks away, and she was happy to note that she was, as usual, ahead of schedule. It had been less than three months since she'd taken ownership of what had been an industrial building on Houston, a prime piece of real estate. The expansive main floor had been converted into a luxurious gallery with several viewing rooms separated by movable walls. Like all aspects of her life, the entire design was realized according to her precise specifications. The second floor was still under construction, being subdivided into studio spaces for emerging artists, while the third was being converted into three apartments. The fourth, and top, floor had been completed on the same schedule as the gallery level, providing Sandrine with an elegant living space, allowing her to relocate from her suite at the Plaza.

The basement, too, had been finished at the same time, but by a different contractor, one able to meet her stringent needs and whose expertise met the demands that came with a 19th-century foundation. Moving her base of operations from Europe to New York City had been no whimsical decision, but once made, she knew exactly what she wanted and needed.

In her experience, the two didn't always align. But when they did?

"*Magnifique*," she whispered as she descended to the cellar of her building, ignoring the phone ringing in her office, allowing her answering service to field the call.

ALEX MAYHEW HUNG UP THE PHONE AND SIGHED, noting on his pad the latest unsuccessful attempt to reach the owner of Galerie Delacroix.

He was determined to get this interview, if only to prove to his editor at *The Village Voice* that he had the tenacity to cover actual news, *real* news, and not fill the Arts Section with puff pieces. Word on the street was that this Delacroix woman hadn't responded to any of the papers, and he'd made it his personal mission to get an exclusive or, at the very least, scoop the competition.

"Son of a bitch," Brian Trent exclaimed from across the abutted desks that he and Alex occupied, the phone pressed to his ear. The two, close friends as well as colleagues, spent their time in the office facing one another, often to their mutual amusement.

"What?" Alex whispered, but Brian waved him off, a clear signal that Alex and his curiosity would have to wait.

"Okay," Brian said into the phone, now wedged between his ear and shoulder as he searched his cluttered desk for a fresh pad. "Gimme what you got." His pen poised, Brian's face registered an expression of annoyance.

"Well, what *can* you tell me?" he demanded. Immediately, he began to nod, his pen flying over the blank page.

"Okay, thanks," he said after only a few minutes. "Of *course* I know not to name you as my source. You think I suddenly forgot that? Jesus Christ, how long we been doing this?!" He paused to listen, then said in a more patient tone, "Well, thanks. You know I appreciate it. And be sure to tell me anything you hear, got it?" He hung up and cradled his face in his hands, his elbows on his desk and his fingers pushing into his blonde hair, leaving it tousled, as he thought.

Seeing Brian's familiar habit made Alex wonder what it would feel like to be able to do that. A black man, Alex kept his hair close-cropped and fashioned his personal look after that of Victor Willis, the cop in the Village People. He hit the gym religiously to keep his slim-framed body well-toned, defined, and ready, at a moment's notice, to make the most of a snug wifebeater.

"What is it?" Alex asked, his voice at a discreet, conspiratorial volume, but Brian only shook his head, his face still hidden from view. "C'mon, don't do this to me! Is it good?" Alex loved gossip.

Brian sighed into his palms and lowered his hands. Alex saw at once that it was anything *but* good.

"Tell me," Alex said, his voice now softened with concern for his friend.

Brian gave a quick look around the newsroom and said, "Let's go get lunch. We'll talk while we walk."

Once on the sidewalk and out of earshot, Brian filled in his fellow reporter.

"That was my contact at the 6th Precinct," he began. "There was another one last night."

Alex stopped walking momentarily; he didn't need to be told more. Brian had covered the two slashings that had taken place since Memorial Day and, while he dreaded the precise nature of the work, he'd taken pride in giving the crimes more extensive coverage than had the *Times*, the *News*, or even the *Post*.

Still, despite that, the last thing that Brian wanted was another one of these murders to cover. No byline was worth that.

"From what Nico heard, it's just like the other two," Brian said after telling Alex what little information he'd obtained. Alex had never met Nico and knew him only by his first name. Brian was very serious about protecting his sources.

He and Nico had shared an apartment ten years earlier, while Brian was at Columbia and Nico at John Jay. A "Roommate Wanted" flyer in a pizza joint had brought the two together and, despite one being gay and one being straight, one training to be a journalist and one training to be a police officer, a deep and abiding friendship had been born.

And, once each had found gainful employment, that friendship included the occasional anonymous tip from cop to reporter.

"He told me the same two detectives are handling this one, so at least I can reach out and they already know me," Brian said. Alex noted that the advantage added no hint of consolation to Brian's demeanor.

Wanting to change the subject, at least until he started making calls, Brian asked, "What about you? Right before my phone rang, you looked like somebody pissed in your Mimosa. What's that about?"

Alex grunted. "I have no right to bitch after what you just told me," he said. "Not with the pissant bullshit I cover."

"C'mon," Brian cajoled. "Distract me with your pissant bullshit. Besides, nobody bitches like a first-class bitch, bitch!"

Alex gave him an appreciative smile. "Still can't get through to that gallery chick on Houston. The French one. But you know me. I won't give up until I can pin her down for an interview."

Brian snorted a laugh. "I'm glad you said, 'For an interview.' I don't see you pinning any woman down, unless it's for fashion tips."

They both welcomed the momentary humor as they entered Gray's Papaya on 7th Avenue to get gyros for lunch.

CHAPTER FIVE

FROM LAMONT & ELLIS, FRANK DROVE SOUTH to West 10th Street so Jake could retrieve his car from where he'd parked it hours earlier.

After meeting up in the precinct parking lot, they entered the building carrying, along with the evidence bags, the take-out sandwiches and bottled soda they'd picked up at the Acropolis Diner across the street.

The partners made their way upstairs to the large, open squad room occupied by the Homicide Division and deposited their lunches and the evidence bags on their desks. Jake grabbed the pink "While You Were Out" slip that was taped to his phone before they headed to the captain's office and was tucking it into the pocket of his jacket, unread, as Frank lightly rapped his knuckles on the glass of the open door.

Captain Eddie Young looked up from the paperwork in front of him and, seeing who it was, waved them in. Their pads in hand, Frank and Jake seated themselves in the two wooden chairs in front of the desk.

Far cry from the chairs at L&E, Jake thought. Still, though, he found this seat to be infinitely more comfortable.

"Okay, guys, whadda we got?" Young asked, neatly moving the case files to the side.

"So far, it looks like we've got a third gay slashing," Frank said. "Ruiz is gonna fax us his report by the end of the day, so we'll know more then. Otherwise, everything at the scene matches the other two." He ran down the list of similarities: condition of the body, lack of evidence at the crime scene, victim profile, et cetera. "Still trying to establish his movements after he left work last night."

Young removed his bifocals, leaned back in his chair, and stared up at the ceiling, considering this news before responding. He let out a long breath as he put his glasses back on and, having reestablished eye contact, said, "Well, boys, it's not officially a case until you start the report, so that's the next order of business. Lemme know when it's done."

Jake and Frank retraced their steps to their desks and sat down, ready to begin the tedium of paperwork, an aspect of the job neither relished.

"Frank?" Jake said, a pensive look on his face.

"What's up, partner?"

"You ever study statistics? In college, I mean."

"Can't say that I have," Frank replied. "Why you ask?"

Jake shifted in his seat, leaning a bit more in his partner's direction. "Well, where the laws of statistics are concerned, the pattern of a sequence isn't established until the third instance."

"And you're saying that today's vic officially makes this a pattern? We already kinda suspected that."

"Yeah, but now it's statistically official," Jake said. His brow furrowed, he paused a moment before continuing. "You think maybe we got a serial killer on our hands here?" He hadn't wanted to say it aloud.

While it had been bandied about within the inner sanctums of law enforcement for some time, it wasn't until the arrest and subsequent conviction of David Berkowitz some thirteen months prior and the coverage of Ted Bundy's trial, currently underway in Florida, that the term "serial killer," and all it implied, had penetrated the public consciousness.

It had only been about two years since Berkowitz's arrest, ending his twelve-month reign of terror as the Son of Sam. For as much as the city had managed to return to something resembling normal after his capture, there remained an undercurrent of nervous apprehension that hadn't been there prior to the murders. The media attention being paid to Bundy had only fueled that.

A lifelong New Yorker who'd seen his city at its best and its worst, Prentiss couldn't begin to imagine the damage that would be done to the Big Apple's spirit if there was another serial killer on the loose, especially so soon.

"Another serial?" Frank asked, however rhetorically. "Jesus, I fuckin' hope not." He tossed his pen onto his desk. It had occurred to him in the alley, but he'd pushed the thought aside, as if he could negate the possibility by force of will.

"You and me both, man," Jake concurred. But his gut was telling him it was false hope.

Reaching into the file drawer of his desk, Jake withdrew the forms awaiting his attention. At the adjacent desk, Frank pulled on a pair of gloves and extracted Cody Fischer's address book from one of the evidence bags. He flipped through it until he found the page he wanted.

"I hate *this* shit more than the goddamn paperwork," he said.

Jake looked his way and, seeing the book, realized that his partner was about to make a phone call that would shatter Mr. and Mrs. Fischer's world. He pressed his lips together and gave Frank a slow nod to show his empathy and commiseration. Seeing Prentiss lift the receiver of the phone reminded him of something, and he reached into his pocket for the message.

"Tommy LaRosa" was neatly written on the top line, and, beneath the name, it said, "Has info on a case, says you have the number on file."

Jake assumed Tommy was still at his place, and was grateful that he'd been so discreet, not giving the desk sergeant the number, which could have been recognized by anyone who might have read the slip on his desk.

As Frank began his conversation with Cody Fischer's father—he heard him say, "Mr. Fischer?"—Jake picked up his own phone and dialed the number he knew by heart.

Tommy answered on the third ring. "Hello?"

"It's me," Jake said. "What's up?"

"Any idea when you'll be able to get home?"

Jake shut his eyes, imagining the pressure Tommy was about to put on him. *One step forward, two steps back*, he thought. "No clue. Why?"

"Well," Tommy said, "I wanted to have food ready for you. I know today's been rough so far and it'll probably stay that way until you can get outta there, so I just wanted to help make it a little easier. It doesn't matter how late, just gimme an idea so I can have everything ready when you walk through the door."

Wow, Jake thought, *one step forward, and then two* more *steps forward.* He admonished himself for assuming his boyfriend was going to make a hard day harder.

"Honestly," he said, "I don't see me being able to get outta here before my shift starts at three. That won't get me home 'til around midnight. I don't wanna make you wait that late to have dinner." This last was said at a much lower volume than what had come before it.

"Midnight it is," Tommy said cheerfully. "I really don't mind, babe. And that gives me almost twelve hours to get it right." He laughed. "What kinda animal you wanna eat?"

Jake was gladly warming to the direction the day had suddenly taken. "Beef. And preferably Italian."

Tommy laughed again. "I meant for dinner, sexy."

"You decide," Jake said. "You know the things I like and the things I don't. Surprise me." He lowered his voice again and added a flirtatious hint of a growl. "Just make sure I get my Italian meat."

"You can count on *that*, sweetie." He blew a kiss into the receiver.

"Right back atcha," Jake said. "And thank you."

"Well, you haven't eaten the dinner yet. Save the thanks until you taste it."

"I don't mean that," Jake said. "Well, yeah, I do. Thank you for that. But I meant the message you left. I want you to know how much I appreciate how you handled it. I *mean* that."

"No problem," Tommy said. "And *I* mean *that*. I love you."

"Same here," Jake said. "I'll see you later."

After they said their goodbyes, Jake hung up.

Frank had already finished his unfortunate task and smiled at his partner. "You got yourself a lady friend you ain't told me about, man?"

"What?" Jake asked, not because he hadn't heard, but in an effort to buy himself a moment or two before replying. With yet another lie.

"That call," Frank said. "It sounded like a date."

"Oh, that," Jake dodged. "No, not a lady friend. Just a friend. Who happens to be a lady. Nothing romantic."

Frank was smiling and nodding in amusement. "Yeah," he teased, "let's see how long it stays that way with midnight dinners."

"Shut the fuck up," Jake said, laughing. "Lemme get started on this shit." He waved a hand over the blank forms on his desk. "We got a report to file."

CHAPTER SIX

DANI KRAMER FISHED A COMPACT OUT OF HER LARGE, SAC-LIKE PURSE and checked her hair as soon as she emerged from the subway.

Her sable brown curls were pulled back sleekly into a ponytail but were allowed to spill loosely past her shoulders. It was the best she could do with the intense New York City humidity. Her lustrous mane could be unruly, even on the most temperate of days. *Good,* she thought, *neat and professional, but still a touch bohemian.* Her makeup was subtle and understated, as was her usual style.

It was her outfit that worried her: a peasant skirt, a scoop-neck blouse, and sandals. A third-year student at Parsons, after rent and her phone bill, the majority of her waitressing tips was spent on art supplies, leaving little else for her wardrobe. Dani rarely felt hindered by this; when she wasn't covered in paint or ink, she was in her uniform for the diner.

But today was different. Today could well be one of those days that marks a major life change.

She took a deep breath and walked the two blocks from the station to Galerie Delacroix, praying that the oppressive weather wouldn't wilt her appearance and bathe her in a sheen of sweat. Her appointment was for two o'clock and a brief glance at her wristwatch reassured her that she was fifteen minutes early, as she had planned.

Arriving at the front of the gallery, she checked her reflection in the glass of the door and read the sign in the window. The grand opening reception would also launch Colin Davenport's first North American exhibit. Dani had never heard of him, but that wasn't unusual for a smaller gallery, however chic it might be.

She was just about to knock when she heard the lock being disengaged and the door was opened. Before her stood a breathtaking woman in a snug designer skirt, an emerald-green silk blouse, and gorgeous black heels. Her shiny auburn hair was upswept into an elegant French twist. Any satisfaction she'd mustered with her appearance for her interview was gone.

"Ms. Delacroix?" Dani asked.

"*Oui,*" Sandrine replied with a warm but professional smile. "Are you Mademoiselle Kramer?"

"Yes," Dani said. "Yes, I am. I'm here for my interview." She was self-consciously aware that her own Long Island accent was a far cry from the elegance of Sandrine's. Where the Frenchwoman purred her "R"s, the Long Islander dropped them altogether.

"You're early," Sandrine observed without checking the gold watch she wore. "An enviable quality in an assistant. *Entrez-vous, s'il vous plaît.*" Sandrine stepped aside, holding open the paper-covered door.

Dani stepped in, grateful for the air conditioning, and she looked around in wonder at the interior design, gasping when she saw the painting. "Oh, my god," she said softly. "That's amazing."

Sandrine was pleased to note that the first person to enter the gallery since the abstract had been hung had registered the desired reaction.

"It is, isn't it?" she said, stepping beside the girl.

"May I?" Dani asked, looking at Sandrine with a slight gesture toward the artwork.

"Please."

The art student slowly approached the painting, moving from side to side to view it from different angles. Sandrine watched her, watched how she seemed to be forming a relationship with the work. She already liked Dani.

"Is this one of Mr. Davenport's?"

"*Oui.* He calls it 'Mourning Becomes Electric.'"

Dani gave a subdued, intelligent chuckle. "That's good," she said. "I like that." She took a step back to broaden her view of the painting. "The way he swirls the moody purples and blacks, and then lights them up with the gold. Beautiful."

Dani didn't know it, but the fact that she understood the title's reference to the O'Neill play had earned her even more points with Sandrine Delacroix.

"Shall we go into my office, Mademoiselle Kramer?"

"Yes, please," she replied. "And, please, call me Dani."

Dani followed Sandrine through the other, smaller viewing spaces and into the "Employees Only" rear of the building. The gallery owner's office was compact, but comfortable. Dani took a seat in an antique Queen Anne armchair with deep crimson velvet upholstery, and Sandrine took her place behind the desk, also a Queen Anne.

"As I told you on the phone, Dani," Sandrine began in her mellifluous accent, "I'm looking to hire an assistant. Someone I can depend on to complete tasks efficiently, but who also knows art. I believe in using my business to cultivate young talent, but not just the *artistes*. The work of running a gallery can be demanding, but I believe the right person will thrive here.

"Tell me about yourself," she said.

Dani had to work hard not to be effusive, preferring to leave a highly professional impression. If she landed this job, she could very well be interacting with some rather sophisticated people, and she didn't want her prospective employer to see her as a flighty, artsy college girl.

She told Sandrine about growing up on Long Island, roughly ninety minutes from Manhattan, and about her first visit with her mother to the Museum of Modern Art uptown. She'd been nine at the time, and the whole trip home on the LIRR, she solemnly told her mother, in detail, all about the career she knew she'd have as an artist known all over the world.

"And then I got accepted at Parsons," she said, "and finally got to move into the city. For the last two years, I've been working as a waitress in a diner. The hours work well with my class schedule, and the tips are good. But with my junior year about to begin, my advisor suggested I start working in the art field in some capacity. When I saw a new gallery was opening, I took a chance and wrote to you." She smiled at Sandrine. "And here I am!"

"I've looked over the résumé you mailed me," Sandrine said, "but I'm not much concerned with where you've worked. What I need in an assistant can't be typed onto a piece of paper." She returned Dani's smile with sincerity. "When can you start?"

"Oh, my god, Ms. Delacroix!" Dani had to restrain herself from jumping out of the chair. "I can't thank you enough! I promise you won't be sorry!" The college girl had come out in full force, and Dani collected herself. "I'm sorry," she said with more composure. "This is a dream come true for me."

Despite her European sophistication, Sandrine was thoroughly enjoying Dani's enthusiasm. She, herself, had once felt it, even if through a different continent's filter. Sandrine knew in the front of the gallery, while the girl was looking at the painting, that she was going to hire her, the interview at that point being only a formality. She was confident that Galerie Delacroix would be a perfect fit for the young woman, and vice versa.

"When can you start?" Sandrine repeated. "Your next semester won't begin for another month, from what you wrote, but what about your other job?"

"I'm giving them two-weeks' notice tonight. I only work there evenings, so until the two weeks is up, I can be here during the day. Every day if you need. And then, once the diner job's done, I'm all yours."

"*Magnifique*," Sandrine said with sincerity. "We open in two weeks, and a great deal still needs to be done. Having you here to help during the mornings and afternoons will be *my* dream come true. Tomorrow morning will be perfect."

She stood and extended her hand across the desk. "*Bienvenue au Galerie Delacroix!*"

CHAPTER SEVEN

JAKE LEANED BACK IN HIS CHAIR AND RUBBED HIS EYES. His jacket was off, his sleeves rolled up, his tie loosened. Looking up at the clock on the wall of the squad room, he groaned.

Two-thirty. In half an hour, his regular shift would begin and he'd already put in almost a full day's work. At least the hangover was long gone, but the eye strain from the paperwork had replaced it. While he'd been busy with that, Frank had pulled the files on the other two open cases and was looking for similarities of a less obvious nature.

Jake pushed away from his desk and stood, coffee mug in hand. "Refill," he said to his partner as he made his way to the coffee pot across the room. Without looking up from the files covering his desk, Prentiss held his empty mug aloft. Jake retrieved it in passing.

Returning a few minutes later, he handed Frank the full mug. "Anything?" he asked as he sat back down at his own desk.

"Nothing's jumping out," Frank conceded. "Aside from the obvious shit we already know."

Jake considered this as he took a sip. He set his mug down and said, "Well, that's enough to start with." He stood, picked up the pile of papers from his desk, and headed for the captain's office.

Knocking lightly on the open door, he asked, "Cap? You got a minute?"

Young was just hanging up the phone and waved him in. Jake shut the door behind him.

"Everything okay, Griff?"

"Yeah," Jake replied. "Preliminary paperwork's just about done." He paused and gestured toward one of the wooden chairs. Young nodded. As he sat, Jake said, "Something's eating at me and I wanna run it by you."

"I'm listening."

"This is the third homicide in two months with a pretty much identical M.O."

"Okay, that much we already know."

"Seeing as all three vics were gay men in the same age range," Jake began, "what do you think the chances are that we might have a serial killer on our hands here?"

Young's response was to not respond. He sat, seemingly impassive, and chewed on this. After about a minute, he asked, "Prentiss on board with this theory?"

"You'd have to ask him that yourself, sir," Jake sidestepped. "I'm not gonna speak for him."

"Okay," the captain said. "Other than what we've already gone over, did you turn up anything new? Any of the vics know each other? Have a common ex? Belong to the same goddamn barbershop quartet? Anything at all in common besides being queer and how they died?"

"Nothing like that, sir. Not that we've uncovered, anyway."

"All right," Young continued. "I'm not telling you to rule out the possibility, but keep it between you, me, and Prentiss. Until we know more, let's just leave the words 'serial killer' out of every conversation since we don't have any evidence that's what this is. Last thing we need is the fairies all screaming that we're not protecting them from Son of Samantha."

Disappointed, but not at all surprised, Jake stood, saying, "Understood, captain."

"Appreciate it, Griff," Young said. "Would you mind shutting the door on your way out?" He already had the phone in his hand and, as Jake pulled the door closed, he was dialing. Although Jake didn't know it, the captain was calling the chief of detectives, hoping to avoid a full-scale shit storm.

By the time Jake got back to his desk, he was doing a slow boil. Young was a good cop and a solid captain, so why couldn't he see what was right in front of his nose? Maybe he did, but the victim profile wasn't making him lose sleep. His casual use of the words "queer" and "fairies," and his ignorant assumption that they'd all shared sexual partners were enough to tell Jake everything he needed to know.

"You okay?" Frank asked, picking up on Jake's vibe as he sat down.

"Yeah, fine," he lied. For now, this was a possibility he was keeping to himself, beyond what he'd already said.

"I gotta go get some air," Frank said, his knees audibly cracking as he stood. "Jesus, I'm getting old." He made his way toward the stairs and was gone.

Jake picked up his phone and, using the eraser of a pencil, stabbed the buttons seven times. It was answered promptly.

"Ruiz? It's Griffin," Jake said. "We know anything yet on the vic from this morning." He listened, jotting a couple of random thoughts he'd get back to later. "Okay, man, I appreciate it. I'll keep my eyes open for the fax around five? That work for you?" Brief pause. "Great. Thanks."

He hung up but hadn't removed his hand from the receiver when the phone rang. Lifting it, he said, "Sixth precinct, Homicide, Griffin speaking."

"Detective Griffin?" asked the voice on the phone. It sounded vaguely familiar, but Jake couldn't place it. "This is Brian Trent with *The Village Voice*. We met last month concerning the Curtis murder."

"What can I do for you, Mr. Trent?"

Brian dove right in. "I got a tip that there was another slashing this morning," he said. "Can I get a comment from you?"

"I'm not at liberty to—" Jake began, but stopped himself. "Listen," he said. *Shit*, he thought, *what the fuck am I doing?*

He did it anyway.

"Where are you right now?" His volume was considerably lower.

"In the newsroom. Why?"

"Meet me at the McDougal Café in thirty minutes," he said and hung up.

CHAPTER EIGHT

"THAT CUTE BRUNETTE?" TOMMY ASKED, INTERRUPTING HIS CHOPPING.

The chef's knife and carrots forgotten, he gaped at his friends. Dmitri and Steven were nodding.

Along with Rich and his boyfriend Vinnie, the two had been at Jake's the night prior for what had come to be known as S&M Night, which stood for Snacks & Music, along with copious amounts of beer and tequila, and whatever party game amused them. Last night, it had been Celebrity.

At the moment, the trio was in the kitchen, surrounding the butcher-block island in the center of the room. Tommy had the day off from the boutique in the Village and he didn't have a job that night with his side-gig as a cater-waiter. His friends stopped by, at Tommy's request, before heading to work at Uncle Charlie's, the Upper East Side bar where they worked as go-go boys.

"Just like those other two," Steven said, clutching at pearls that weren't there. A tall, toned black man with a gleamingly shaved head and expressive, sparkling eyes, he was the more flamboyant of the two.

"And you said this happened last night?" Tommy asked. In truth, he hadn't been giving them his full attention, more focused on the *boeuf bourguignon* he was preparing. He'd taken Cara's advice to heart and was intent on serving up a feast for Jake.

"Yeah," Dmitri said, flicking his cigarette into the ashtray with one hand and raising his wine glass with the other. "I heard they found him around dawn. In an alley a few blocks from the Circle." A study in opposites compared to his best friend, Dmitri was fair, blond-haired, and blue-eyed. An inch or two shorter than Steven, he was muscled and solidly built.

"Fuck," Tommy said. "I wonder if that's the call Jake got this morning."

"I bet it was," Dmitri offered. "You said he and his partner worked the other two, so it makes sense."

"He's gonna be a mess when he gets home," Tommy said. "The other two really ate at him. I've never seen him so fucked up by a case he was working." He paused and frowned. "And I was such a dick this morning when he had to leave." He didn't mention that he'd been a dick more because Jake had told Frank he was alone and less about his unexpected, early departure.

"Oh, sweetie," Steven said, reaching across the butcher block to pat Tommy's hand. "Don't beat yourself up. How could you have known?"

"He's right, Tommy," Dmitri concurred. "And look," he added with a sweeping gesture to indicate all the ingredients on the island. "When he gets home, you'll have a beautiful dinner ready and waiting for him. He's lucky to have you, and I'm sure he'd agree with me."

"Well," Tommy said, "I guess I won't be bringing up what I was pissed about this morning. Not after the day I'm sure he's having."

"Probably a good idea," Steven said. "He won't need more shit to deal with."

"Who told you about Cody?" Tommy asked.

"Garrett," Dmitri replied. "He went out this morning to get milk and walked past the crime scene. He recognized one of the paramedics from the baths. He told Garrett it was Cody."

"Isn't that against some kinda rule?" Steven asked.

"Honey," Dmitri, said, "with shit like this, we gotta make our *own* rules. Nobody's looking out for us." He turned to Tommy. "No offense to your man, but the cops ain't done shit to find this guy."

"No offense taken. He'd agree with you anyway," Tommy said. "He's been pissed as hell that nobody in the department is making it a priority." He sat on the stool next to him, topped off his half-empty wine glass, and lit a cigarette.

BRIAN TRENT WAS ALREADY SEATED WHEN JAKE ENTERED THE MCDOUGAL CAFÉ. A cigarette was resting in the ashtray and a half-empty coffee cup was next to it.

"You beat me here," Jake said, sitting in the chair opposite the reporter.

"I try to be a day early and a dollar ahead," Brian said.

"Wish I could be," the cop said with a disheartened sigh.

Brian waved the waiter over. "What'll you have?" he asked Jake. "You look like you could use something from the bar."

"Can't," Jake said. "Still on duty." To the waiter, he said, "Cup of coffee. And a plate of fries."

Once the waiter had departed on his assigned task, Brian leveled a gaze at Jake and asked, "Whadda ya got for me?"

Jake took a deep breath and slowly exhaled. "Okay," he said, "first of all, you know I'm breaking every rule in the fucking book just being here with you, right?"

"I figured as much."

"But the brass ain't doing shit on this. If this perp was wasting pretty white coeds, they'd be all over it. But who cares that a bunch of fags are getting hacked to shit? Fucking pisses me off."

"I'm right there with you, man," Brian commiserated. "Even though it's a feather in my cap, I guess, how do you think I feel? *The Voice* is the only rag in town giving this any column inches. And forget the TV news. I'm ashamed of my so-called colleagues." He took a drag off his cigarette and a gulp of coffee while Jake digested this. "So, what're you and me gonna do about it?"

"I WISH THERE WAS SOMETHING WE COULD DO ABOUT IT," Steven said.

"Like what?" Tommy asked. "Get out our superhero capes and fly into action?"

Dmitri laughed so hard he almost spit wine out his nose. "As long as you have matching tights," he said.

"I'm serious," Steven defended himself. "Who's more gossipy than queens like us? Nobody blinks when we start asking personal questions. It's when we *don't* that they notice."

"Ain't that the truth," Tommy said.

"Between the three of us," Steven continued, "and God knows how many others, I bet we could turn up more inside info than the cops and the newspapers combined." Something delicious occurred to him. "We could be like 'Charlie's Angels'!" He clapped his hands, palms flat and fingers straight, before striking a pose with an invisible handgun.

"He's got a point," Dmitri conceded, tipping his wine glass in Steven's direction to punctuate his statement. "Well, except for the 'Charlie's Angels' thing."

"Okay," Tommy allowed. "Go on. Where do we start?"

"LET'S START AT THE BEGINNING," BRIAN SAID, "and work forward."

"Okay, the first vic was Gil McCandless," Jake said, referring to the notes he'd scribbled into his pad, transcribing pertinent details from the case files before he left the precinct. "Age 29, Caucasian, last seen at the Ninth Circle around one A.M. Saturday, May 26th. Found at nine-thirty the next morning in Washington Square Park. Throat ripped open, no blood in the body, no blood at the crime scene, obvious dump job. Nobody saw him leave the Circle with anyone. In fact, nobody even noticed him leave. We interviewed the two guys he went there with, friends of his. They both said they'd lost track of him around midnight or so. Bartender was the last to place him there at one A.M. None of them remembered seeing him talking to anyone in particular, nobody knew if he left alone or with somebody. From there it went cold."

"That's pretty much what I got when I covered it," Brian said. "Other than what you and Prentiss gave me at the time, only ones I interviewed where the friends, the bartender, and a few patrons. Nobody knew anything."

"YOU KNOW ANYTHING ABOUT THE FIRST GUY?" Steven asked. "That was Memorial Day."

"No," Dmitri said, "but I know people who did. Guy, or Gil, something like that."

"We can start there," Steven said. "Talk to them, the people you know. See what they remember. How about Billy?"

"Good luck with that," Tommy said.

Billy Curtis was the second victim, killed over Father's Day weekend. A regular on the bar scene, everyone had known who Billy was, but none of them were close to him. Like many guys who devote a considerable amount of time to working out and staying impeccably groomed, he was aloof and distant. He knew everyone wanted him. He also knew he'd never condescend to give them a taste.

No tears were shed when he was murdered.

"We can work with that," Dmitri said. "Get people gossiping about him. There's bound to be something useful in all the trash they'll talk." He turned to look directly at Steven. "Just don't believe everything they say."

Raising his right hand in a Boy Scout salute, Steven said, "I swear I'll be the soul of skepticism."

"What about me?" Tommy asked. "Want me to see what I can get out of Jake?"

"Hold off on that," Dmitri cautioned. "Especially if he's trying to leave his work in the office. If he offers something, great. If not, don't push it. If he catches on to what we're doing, he might get pissed off at you. You just keep him happy at home." He cast his glance pointedly, complete with one arched eyebrow, at the ignored carrots.

"Gotcha," Tommy said and resumed slicing.

"And now with Cody," Steven said, "I'm kinda scared to go out to the bars."

"Tell me about it," Dmitri said. "Whoever woulda thought that you could die from a one-night stand?"

"Miss Thing clearly hasn't read 'Looking for Mr. Goodbar'," Steven said to Tommy. He glanced at his watch and addressed Dmitri. "And on that note, we should get going. I want to stop on the way to work to get a new pair of sneakers. These things have no arch support when I dance. And we need to grab some dinner."

"YOU SURE YOU DON'T WANT TO ORDER SOME DINNER?" Brian asked.

"I'm sure," Jake said. "These fries'll hold me over. A friend's planning a late supper at my place when my shift ends."

"Nice," Brian said, smiling. "Back to business. Victim number two: Billy Curtis."

"As we both know," Jake said, "pretty much the same as McCandless. Caucasian, same age range—he was thirty-one—good physical condition. Only real differences were that Curtis was at the Ramrod, not the Circle, and his body was found down by the Christopher Street piers. Everything else is a carbon copy."

"Another difference," Brian said, "is that Curtis was as disliked by the barflies as McCandless was popular."

"And with good reason, from everything Prentiss and I were told. That actually threw us off," he went on. "So many people couldn't stand him, we had to rule out a scorned boyfriend or a jealous lover of one of his pick-ups, something like that. But the M.O. and C.O.D. were identical, which brought us back to square one."

"Correction: it now brings us forward to victim three."

"Cody Fischer," Jake said with a weary sigh. "Other than it looking like the same perp—or perps—there's not much I can tell you. Haven't even seen the M.E.'s report yet." Jake went on to share his observation that all three victims, based on their physiques, should have been able to fend off an attack or, at the very least, put up one hell of a fight. In addition, the autopsies on McCandless and Curtis didn't reveal an inordinate level of alcohol or narcotics in their systems, so their reflexes shouldn't have been impaired.

"And there were no defensive wounds on Fischer either?"

"No, none that I could see. Don't know if Ruiz'll turn up anything."

"I see why you think there could be more than one assailant."

Jake signaled for the waiter to refill the coffee cups, wishing he were off the clock and could order a Scotch. "What I'm about to tell you is strictly off the record," he said to Brian. "At least until further notice."

"I'm all ears," the reporter said, making a show of putting his pen on the table.

Leaning in and lowering his voice, Jake said, "I can't shake the feeling that this could be a serial killer, targeting gay men."

"Already had that thought myself, man," Brian shared in an equally hushed tone. "Why off the record, though?"

Brian explained the statistical theory of patterns, adding, "I wanna see the M.E.'s report on Fischer first. No sense in panicking the public prematurely. But here's the thing: my captain won't even entertain the suggestion, and that scares the fuck outta me. Look how fast Son of Sam was national news. And even *with* that media spotlight, he still managed to keep finding victims. If this is another serial, he'll have free rein if it's not put out there."

"Your captain isn't behind your 'serial killer' theory, and you're telling the press?" Brian said with a shrewd look in his eyes. "Now I get your *real* reason for wanting it off the record." He paused a moment. "Okay," he conceded, "off the record it shall stay. For now." He withdrew a *Village Voice* business card from his wallet.

"I still have your card in my Rolodex," Jake said.

Brian was writing on the back. "This is my home number and my answering service," he said. "I want you to be able to reach me day or night." He handed Jake the card.

"Fair enough," Jake said, and did the same with one of his own cards.

"For now," Brian said, "I'm gonna run the story on Fischer's murder, hopefully in Monday's edition." The *Voice* hit the streets weekly. "I'll cite 'an anonymous source within the N.Y.P.D.' I'll mention, but only in passing, the other two killings, probably in the closing graph, and finish with something like, 'Officials have yet to determine if there's a connection between the crimes.' Does that work for you?"

Jake mulled it over briefly and replied, "Sounds good." He reached for his wallet.

"No, no," Brian said. "This is on me. I already owe you big time."

"Tonight's the end of my work week," Jake said as he stood. "Barring the unforeseen, I'm off tomorrow. I'll call you then. Easier to talk from home."

"I'm looking forward to it," Brian said, extending his hand.

They shared a firm shake, which Jake refused to release. "Let's make this worth the risk I'm taking here," he said.

"That's the plan," Brian assured him.

CHAPTER NINE

DANI ARRIVED AT THE ACROPOLIS DINER twenty minutes before her shift started at four.

In the time between her interview at Galerie Delacroix and reporting to work, she dashed home and typed up a letter of resignation, having to restrain her elation in order to remain focused on the wording. Throwing on her uniform, she dashed off again.

Stavros Karolis, the Greek-born owner-manager, barely acknowledged the formality, mumbling in a heavily accented voice, "Just be sure you give me the two weeks. And you better turn in your uniform."

Like I'd want to keep this polyester shmata, she thought.

Her happy task completed, she went back into the kitchen, hanging her purse on one of the coat hooks. She noted with joy that she'd only be hanging her purse on these damned hooks nine more times. After that, she'd be stowing it on the arm of an antique Queen Anne chair or an equally beautiful piece of furniture.

Turning, she found herself face to face with Iggy, a classmate at Parson's and a busboy at the diner, a position he'd obtained when Dani had referred him to Karolis. He was oblivious to his surroundings and almost stumbled into her with a loaded bus pan. She grabbed it before it and its contents crashed to the floor.

"Whoa, Iggy," she exclaimed, "watch out!"

"Sorry, Dani," he said distractedly.

"My fault," she said cheerfully. "I wasn't paying attention. I have big news to—." She noticed for the first time that Iggy's eyes were red-rimmed and moist, and the chocolate-brown skin around them was puffy.

She took the bus pan from him and set it on a counter. "Ig," she said, her tone concerned, "what's wrong?" Knowing Iggy, it could be anything from a lousy grade on an assignment to the global economy.

"It's Rembrandt," he said, referring to the graphic artist who guest-lectured at Parsons the prior spring.

Oh, no, she thought, *Iggy got dumped.*

Less than five minutes into that lecture on career options in the art field, Iggy had been smitten. At the end of the class, he'd approached the speaker, ostensibly with art-related questions, and had achieved his true mission: they'd exchanged phone numbers. Far from the "happily ever after" fairy tale her hopelessly romantic friend had envisioned, it had been a casual fling, with dates being planned sporadically over the last four months. Still and all, Iggy had grown quite fond of him and, while the affair remained low-key, the affection had been mutual. She couldn't remember the guy's name since Iggy always referred to him as Rembrandt, usually with a wistful, dreamy expression.

That expression was nowhere to be seen now, gone forever, Dani feared.

"He's dead," Iggy said, the tears flowing freely once more. It was the first time he'd said it aloud since learning the devastating news only an hour earlier.

"Oh, my god!" Dani gasped, chiding herself for assuming Iggy's distress was the result of something so trivial by comparison. "C'mere." She encircled his shoulders with one arm and led him into the storage area which doubled as a break room. "Sit down, sweetie."

Once they were seated on the metal folding chairs—Karolis spared no expense—she asked, "What happened? Was it some sort of accident?"

"N-no," Iggy stammered, trying to abate his stifled sobs. "He was murdered." Speaking the word unleashed a torrent.

"Holy fuck," she said, hugging him. "A mugging?"

"I d-don't know," he sobbed against her shoulder. "I called him at the office and the receptionist told me. The c-cops were there this morning, asking questions." Something occurred to him. "You think I should call them?"

"No," she advised, lifting his head so she could face him. She wiped the tears from his cheeks with the pads of her thumbs. "What I think you should do is take care of yourself first. You're still in shock, Ig. You need to worry about you before you do anything else. I'm sure they'll be looking into all his associations and your name is bound to come up. They may find you before you reach out to them."

"Okay," he said, his sobs reduced to sniffles and small hitches in his throat. "You said you had news. I hope it's better than mine." He tried, unsuccessfully, to chuckle. Iggy was known for his dark wit.

"Well, shit," Dani said. "I'd feel like a jerk sharing it now."

"Please," he said. "I could use it."

"Well," she began, "it *is* better than yours. *Much* better." She reminded him of the interview—an appointment he'd known about but understandably had forgotten—and told him of its successful outcome.

"Dani," he said, mustering what heartfelt enthusiasm he could, "that's incredible. I'm really happy for you, even if it means I won't see you here anymore. You keep me sane in this asylum."

She knew his happiness on her behalf was sincere even if his weary tone suggested otherwise.

"Tell you what," she said. "After our shift, let's go to my place. We can celebrate while you decompress. Then you're crashing there, I don't want you to be alone tonight."

Iggy managed a smile and said, "You know, I really love you, Dani."

"Right back atcha, kiddo," she said softly before fully embracing him.

CHAPTER TEN

JAKE ARRIVED BACK IN THE SQUAD ROOM JUST BEFORE FIVE-THIRTY. Prior to heading out, he'd told Frank that he was meeting with a C.I.—confidential informant, in cop-speak—and would return immediately afterward.

While Jake had been meeting with Brian, Frank was working his way through Cody Fischer's address book, cold-calling the various entries. The responses he'd gotten had ranged from unbridled histrionics to "Cody who?," covering the full spectrum in between. As Frank had anticipated, a decent handful had been no-answers, along with two or three that were disconnected.

Apparently, the late Mr. Fischer hadn't stayed on top of keeping his address book up to date. Frank couldn't help wondering how many of these numbers had been entered in the directory, but never dialed.

By the last few calls, it was obvious that the news had begun to spread along the grapevine: on three occasions, upon identifying himself as a police detective, Frank was informed by the person on the other end of the line that he already knew about Cody's murder. It became increasingly difficult to maintain the "I ask, you answer" tone that Frank liked, so numerous were the questions he had to field, all of which were answered, "I can't comment on that."

"Get anything useful?" he asked when he saw Jake enter.

"Nothing we didn't already know," Jake replied. He wasn't comfortable with how much he was lying to his partner today. First covering about Tommy—this morning on the phone and then at the crime scene and then later after the call from the squad room—which wasn't all that major, and now about his meeting with Brian. He'd entered another realm of dishonesty altogether with that, one that troubled him greatly. "At least I got out of the squad room for a couple hours."

"I don't wanna hear it," Frank said with only the merest trace of ironic humor.

Jake felt chagrined by his conversational misstep. "Sorry," he offered. "How about you? The address book turn up anything?"

"Zilch," Frank said. "You wanna take a crack at it? I'm about done with breaking the bad news."

Jake was poised to oblige his partner when Walt Friedrich hollered from across the room. "Hey, Griff, you got a fax."

Saved by the bell, Jake thought. Aloud, he said, "That better be the M.E.'s report."

Friedrich had the flimsy papers in his outstretched hand when Jake reached him. He tossed the cover sheet in the trash and was relieved to read "Office of the Medical Examiner" emblazoned across the top of the second page. By the time he returned to his desk, he'd already absorbed the salient details.

"Well?" Frank asked as he hung up the phone.

"Same as the other two." He wished he had a nickel for every time he'd uttered that phrase since waking up. "As we expected, C.O.D.'s exsanguination. Wound was inflicted by something resembling a claw, probably metal, definitely multi-pronged. No defensive wounds. Blood-alcohol level was below the legal limit. Gotta wait on the tox screen for traces of narcotics. We already know he'll test positive for pot."

Prentiss once again ran his palm over the top of his head. Jake noticed how much more gray there was at his partner's temples. "When we gonna catch a mother-fuckin' break, man?" Frank held out the address book. "Here. Take this shit off my hands. I gotta piss."

As he stood, Frank remembered something. "By the way, that was Curran on the phone. I got him and Schwartz to start their shift a few hours early so we can get the fuck outta here by eight. This day's been too fuckin' long already," he said. "At least there's that." Having imparted a tiny shred of good news, he headed in the direction of the men's room.

Jake sat at his desk, the address book open before him and his notepad next to it, a blank page on top. He prepared himself with a deep breath and picked up the phone. He didn't dial the next number in the book, though. He'd fished the business card out of his pocket and dialed Brian Trent's answering service, leaving a brief but intentionally cryptic message.

"Call me at home after eleven. It's on the record."

He next dialed his own number. Tommy answered almost immediately.

"Hey, it's me," he said impersonally.

"And it's me," Tommy answered. Jake could hear the smile on his boyishly handsome face. That put a smile on his own.

"Just wanted to let you know that the eleven-to-seven guys are coming in early," he said. "I'll be home by nine. That work for you?"

"Like a charm," Tommy said. "I can't wait."

"Neither can I. After this cluster-fuck of a day, I really need a drink, a good meal that I don't have to cook, and your company. Not necessarily in that order."

"Well, you called the right guy. All three will be ready and waiting for you. Want me to have a hot shower running?"

Jake was touched, but chuckled. "I think I'll be able to work a faucet." He dropped his volume. "But if you're waiting in the shower, I won't complain."

"I'll do you one better," Tommy flirted. "I'll make sure the soap's already good and slippery so I'm bound to drop it."

The unexpected erection forced Jake to shift uncomfortably in his seat. "Baby, you sure know how to improve a cop's day. Lemme get back to work here. I'll see you around nine."

"Jake?" Tommy said.

"Yeah?"

"I love you."

Jake paused a moment. "Same here," was the best he could do. That he couldn't do better pissed him off.

Frank returned from the men's room just as Jake was hanging up. He noticed his partner's frown.

"No luck either?" he asked.

It took Jake a moment to realize what Frank meant; he was still wishing he'd said, "I love you too." "No," he replied, grateful that it wasn't technically another lie added to the day's mounting list. "Lemme try the next number." Also the truth.

The two got to work, Jake making his way through the address book, Frank cross-referencing the autopsy report on Cody Fisher with the two already on file. After about an hour, Frank heard Jake say, "And what time was that?"

Prentiss turned his attention to his partner's desk, eager to learn what he'd found out.

"Did you see him talking to anybody?" Jake asked, then listened to the reply, scribbling on the pad that until two minutes prior contained only doodles. "Thank you," he said. "You've been a big help." He then dictated his direct line in the squad room, saying, "If you think of anything else, please call right away. If I'm not here, someone will give me the message. Again, thank you." With that, he ended the call.

"Well, Frank," he said, "we got that break you asked for." He recounted the call, from which he'd learned that Cody had been at the Eagle's Nest the night before—not the Ramrod or the Ninth Circle like the first two victims—arriving when they opened at ten. However, he'd left unobserved. "Last time his friend saw him was just after midnight. That's when Fischer's friend met a guy and headed to one of the back rooms." He noticed Frank shift ever so slightly in his seat. *He must be picturing what happened next*, Jake thought. *Well, too damn bad.*

"Okay," Prentiss said. "I guess I know where we're heading now."

THE EAGLE'S NEST AT 11TH AND 21ST WASN'T YET OPEN FOR BUSINESS when Jake and Frank arrived, but their repeated knocking, along with their badges, gained them entry when a bartender opened the door.

"I got two cops here," the bartender told the manager from the entrance to his office.

"Jesus Christ," the manager muttered, "what the fuck now?" Heaving a resigned sigh, he added, "Let 'em in."

Once inside the small office space, Frank introduced himself and Jake.

"Sal Giordano," the man behind the cluttered desk said. His voice hadn't warmed any.

"May we sit?" Frank asked.

"Have at it," Giordano said. It was clear from his tone that he knew he had little choice in the matter. "You's want anything? I know you're workin', so I won't offer nothin' from the bar, but I could have one of the boys bring some coffee or sodas."

"No, thank you," Frank said. "We're fine."

"Suit yourself." Giordano then dove into the deep end. "So, what're you boys here about? We got all our permits up to date, ain't had no fights or nothin'. Fill me in."

"One of your patrons was murdered after leaving here last night," Prentiss told him. "A Cody Fischer."

"God damn," the manager said. "You said *after* he left, right? So it didn't happen *here* or nothin'?"

"That's right, Mr. Giordano," Frank said. "At least as far as we know as of now."

"'Cause if anything like that happened here, I'd know about it," he said. "And call me Sal. Or Sally. The boys here get a kick outta callin' me that, like I'm a chick or somethin'."

"We wanted to know if we could talk to your staff," Frank said, deliberately choosing not to use any of the options for a name. "Find out if anybody remembers Mr. Fischer being here, maybe saw him talking to someone or leave with him."

"Sure, sure," Sal said. "Anything you need. Always happy to help the boys in blue."

Jake involuntarily remembered the Blue Boy magazines at Cody's apartment and pictured his partner in a photo spread. He had to stifle a laugh, masking it as a cough.

Giordano picked up his phone and stabbed three buttons with a fat index finger. After only a moment he said, "Round up everybody here and come to my office. Pronto." He hung up without saying anything more. "They're on the way," he told the detectives.

In less than three minutes, four young, attractive men, including the one who'd allowed them entrance, appeared in the doorway. "We ain't open yet," Sal informed the cops, "so's this is all the staff I got here now. They're all yours, boys."

After introducing himself and his partner to the assembled workers, Frank said, "As we told Mr. Giordano, one of your patrons was murdered after leaving here last night." He produced the photo of Cody that he'd taken from the apartment. "Any of you remember seeing this guy? Name's Cody Fischer."

They passed the photo among them. Three were shaking their heads in the negative when the fourth said, "Yeah, I remember him."

Jake and Frank exchanged glances, communicating their shared excitement at finally having a lead.

"You three can go," Frank said to the head-shakers. "Your boss will have my number in case you remember anything." He turned to the fourth bartender. "But you stay. We want to ask you some questions."

Sal Giordano leaned back in his chair and laced his fingers behind his balding head, clearly pleased that he'd been of help. The pompous gesture left his comb-over in disarray. Jake noted his self-satisfaction and thought, *You didn't do shit, you smug S.O.B. Stop patting yourself on the back.*

"Have a seat," Frank suggested to the bartender, who took the only remaining chair in the cramped office. "First off, what's your name?" he asked after the young man was seated.

"Chris," he said. "Chris Albright."

"Okay, Chris," Frank proceeded. "What can you tell us about Mr. Fischer?"

Chris glanced at his boss, who nodded his permission to continue. "Well," he said, "I thought he was hot. *Really* hot. I was hoping to score his number, but no luck. He was kinda standoffish, and then he was totally into this other dude. Talked to him the whole time."

Jake felt his pulse spike at this piece of information and noted from the look on his partner's face that Frank's had as well.

"What can you tell us about him?" Frank asked the bartender. "The man Mr. Fischer was talking to."

"Well," he said, dragging the word out into three syllables. "He was cute, but not my type. I could tell just by looking at him that he's a bottom, and *I'm* a bottom, so I'm only into tops."

Jake took note of Frank's discomfort at this, a shift in attitude on which neither of the other men picked up.

"I mean," Frank said, "can you give us a physical description of the man?"

"Oh. He was young, like about my age," the bartender recounted.

"And how old are you, Chris?" Frank asked.

"I'm 29," came the reply, "but I tell people I'm 25. I mean, hey, look at me. I can get away with it."

Even when we're out of the closet, we keep living lies, Jake thought with some degree of disgust, a portion of which was for himself.

"Yes," Frank agreed, "you surely can." Jake knew that Frank hoped his flattery would grease the wheels with the bartender, who, in his opinion, could easily pass for thirty-two, if not older. On a good day.

"Thank you, officer," Chris said, blushing.

"What else about the man Mr. Fischer was talking to?" Frank chose not to correct the witness about his actual title. More wheel-greasing. "What I mean is, what did he look like?"

"Oh!" Another three-syllable word. "I get it. You mean like for a sketch artist." He had a sudden thought and became even more animated, improbable though that may have seemed to Frank, if not Jake. "I can come to the station to do that if you want me to."

"We'll set that up," Frank assured him, "but for now, can you give us a general description?"

"He was, I don't know, maybe six feet or so?" Chris said, clearly excited to play a role in a real-life investigation. "I didn't really pay much attention to him because, as I said, he wasn't my type."

"Go on," Frank prompted.

"And thin. Almost skinny, I'd say. Another turn-off for me. I like men with some meat on their bones." He eyed Frank's stocky physique in a rather unsubtle manner.

"Okay," Frank pressed on. "Six feet tall, thin. What else? Hair color? Was he black? White? Spanish?"

"Oh, he was white," Chris replied, as if this was a given. "And brown hair. Straight." He giggled. "His hair, I mean. Not him." The giggle became a laugh. Giordano shook his head in annoyance, but Jake and Frank remained impassive.

"Did he have a beard or anything?" Frank asked.

"A beard? Here?" Chris said. "Honey, the guys who come to the Nest are well passed needing a beard."

"Chris," Sal said firmly.

"Oh, he means on his face? Oh, my god, I'm such an airhead sometimes! No, no beard. Or mustache. No facial hair. A real baby face. Another turn-off—." He interrupted himself when he saw Giordano's stern look. "No, no facial hair."

"Okay," Frank said, weary of the bartender's effusiveness, a sentiment only Jake could perceive. "Caucasian male, late twenties or early thirties, roughly six feet tall, slender, straight brown hair, no facial hair." He looked at Chris. "Anything else? Did you see them leave together?"

"Well, I can't see the door from the bar I was working last night," he said. "They were there and then they weren't. But I can tell you that I didn't see them part ways. The last time I saw either of them, they were still together."

"Did you interact with either of them at any point?"

"The guy whose picture you showed me ordered himself a few drinks," Chris replied. "But the other guy? No."

"Did Mr. Fischer say anything about where he might be headed afterward?"

"No. He just ordered his G&Ts and that was it. Didn't order anything for the other guy either. After they started talking, I mean."

Frank glanced at Jake, his silent way of communicating, "Anything you wanna ask?" Jake shook his head.

"Okay, Chris," Frank said. "You've been very helpful. You, too, Mr. Giordano. Chris, we'll be in touch to arrange for you to meet with a sketch artist at the precinct. Okay if we leave a message for you here or is there another number you'd prefer we call?"

Without hesitation, Chris grabbed a piece of paper and a pen from his boss' desk and scribbled. "This is my home number. If I'm not there, it goes to my service."

Jake and Frank pulled out their business cards for both employer and employee and imparted the usual "If you think of anything else" speech before excusing themselves. Giordano told Chris to let them out. From the office to the exit, the bartender chattered at a nervous pace and Jake intuitively sensed his fluster, wanting to flirt with Frank but afraid to openly do so. The junior partner was relieved once they were back on the muggy sidewalk and the door to the Eagle's Nest was closed and locked.

"Holy shit," was all Frank could say.

Welcome to my world, his partner thought.

CHAPTER ELEVEN

AT A QUARTER TO NINE, JAKE PARKED IN THE GARAGE ON AMSTERDAM AVENUE where he rented a space and walked around the corner to his brownstone on 75th.

The night was still warm and several people were strolling the sidewalks. He took in the view of the row of brownstones, each looking pretty much like the next, their façades identical. The only real variations were the ones where the residents had placed potted plants on the front steps. Other than that, any of them could easily have been the ones on either side.

He'd lived here for more than a decade and it was the only home he'd ever had for that long. Growing up an Army brat, he was a world traveler before hitting puberty, hopping from base to base around the globe with his parents and older brother.

His father was a hardcore drill sergeant, in essence if not in rank, who tolerated no hint of weakness from his sons. Not that he was abusive; he was just rigidly strict with high, exacting, though not entirely unreasonable, expectations. Ever the dutiful 1950s-era wife, Jake's mother almost never imposed herself on her husband's demands on the boys. As such, Jake grew up knowing what was expected of him, which basically boiled down to "be a man."

And that could never leave room for being a gay man.

By the time Jake was ready to enter high school, Lieutenant Timothy Griffin took a post at Fort Belvoir in Alexandria, Virginia, commuting regularly to the Pentagon. This had turned out to be a permanent location for the family.

Having known nothing but military life, it was a foregone conclusion—for Jake, if no one else—that he'd enlist after high school rather than take his chances with the draft. His brother had opted for college and was therefore deferred, but Jake wanted to follow in his father's footsteps, even knowing that he could never acknowledge his sexuality. But he was willing to make that sacrifice.

For Jake, "being a man" meant, above all else, helping and protecting those who couldn't do it for themselves. For all his demands, Lieutenant Griffin had been a devoted husband and father, always putting the welfare of his wife and sons above his own. This was the example Jake had hoped to emulate.

Unlike his dad, however, the branch of the armed forces that Jake had chosen was the Marine Corps. After basic training on Parris Island, he'd been stationed at Camp Pendleton in Southern California, but when Lyndon Johnson deployed U.S. troops to Vietnam in 1965, his had been among the first boots to hit the ground and defend the defenseless. Unlike his boots, he remained deep in the closet since that was a necessary part of the package.

He'd only been in Nam about a month when he'd become friends with one of the guys in his barracks, Private Larry Wagner from just outside Pittsburgh, who slept in the bunk next to Jake's. Often, they'd sat up late shooting the shit about life back home before the war, what they hoped to do when they returned there, all the usual, "let's not get too personal" topics. But, despite the conversational distance, their chemistry had grown substantial roots.

One night, after they'd smoked a rather potent strain of weed with some of the other jarheads, Larry had looked at Jake across the small space between their bunks and, in their usual hushed tone, had said, "I think you and me got a lot more in common than we know."

"How do you mean?" Jake had asked.

Larry had looked into his eyes with a deeper intent and said, "I think you *know* what I mean."

Jake had been dumbstruck. He'd had a crush on Larry for some time by that point, but between the fear of a dishonorable discharge and his certainty that his friend had to be straight, he'd done what he'd spent his entire life doing: ignoring who he was and not pursuing anything.

But the look Larry had given him that night was unmistakable, and equally irresistible, like a planetary gravitational pull. Jake just hadn't known how to proceed.

After a minute or two without a response from a dumbstruck Jake, Larry had said, "Look, buddy, I gotta go see a man about a horse. If you wanna continue this conversation, you know where to find me." With that, he'd gotten up off the bunk and headed for the latrine.

Jake had realized that he had a "now or never" situation on his hands.

He'd chosen "now" and, after an amount of time that wouldn't raise suspicion, had followed Larry to the john.

That had begun what would be Jake's first relationship with another man, and the two had remained inseparable until fate decided otherwise.

In the region of South Vietnam where their platoon had been deployed, the Viet Cong had taken a village. Jake and Larry had been among the Marines ordered on a reconnaissance mission in preparation for a full-scale assault. Under the cover of darkness on a moonless night, they'd hidden themselves among the foliage about a hundred yards from the village. The relative silence was broken when the jarheads heard the voice of a terrified girl crying out in Vietnamese. Their senses suddenly on high alert, they discerned the shapes of three vee-cee dragging the petite form of a struggling girl.

"Fuckin' Charlie's gonna rape that girl!" Larry had whispered.

From behind him and Jake, Tomlinson whispered, "Think they'll share?"

"Shut up with that shit!" Jake spat in hushed tones. No longer in view, the girl's cries had given way to screams.

"Ain't nothin' we can do about it," Tomlinson had said.

"The fuck there ain't," Larry had muttered and stood up, his M16 at the ready.

"Larry, what the hell?!" Jake had said, forgetting to keep his volume in check.

"Relax," Larry had assured him. "I'm just gonna fire off a few rounds. Let 'em know they got company."

He'd advanced about ten yards out of the brush when the night was split open by the explosion of the land mine.

"No!" Jake had screamed. He'd jumped to his feet to dash from the safety of cover, but Tomlinson and the two other jarheads got hold of him, dragging him deeper into the forest.

"Get the fuck offa me!" he'd protested loudly, but his battle buddies took no heed.

The three vee-cee had reappeared in the clearing, having forgotten their young victim, guns poised.

"He's gone, man," Tomlinson had barked at Jake. "We ain't got no back-up. Ain't nothin' any of us can do for him now." Jake had tried to pull away, but they held firm and dragged him deeper into the forest, heading toward base.

After Larry's death, Jake had gone deeper into himself than he'd ever been before, going through the motions of his duties, not allowing himself to connect with anyone, and certainly not sharing his most guarded secret with another living soul.

He'd gained a deeper fear than the shame of a dishonorable discharge.

After his tour had ended, he'd had no interest in re-upping. He'd found that his father's footsteps could not be his, and he returned to the States. At about the same time, his maternal grandmother had experienced a decline in her health. Knowing that Jake had no solid plans for his immediate future, his mother had suggested that he move in with his ailing relative in New York City, not so much to be a caregiver, because she wasn't gravely ill, but to be an extra pair of hands and be present should an emergency arise.

It had made sense to Jake, especially since New York City was a far cry from an almost rural part of Virginia. He also wondered if his mother had sensed something in her younger son that he couldn't pursue under his father's nose. Upon moving into his grandmother's brownstone, he applied to the New York City Police Academy, hoping to parlay his military experience into a worthwhile career. As he had in the service, Jake excelled at the academy and was graduated with honors. His parents, brother, and grandmother had all been there, cheering from their seats. The family then took him to Luchow's for a celebratory dinner, followed by a comfortable visit at the brownstone before heading back to Virginia.

Although he had moved to one of the world's most bustling metropolises, he'd maintained his pattern of absolute discretion where his personal life was concerned, only venturing into a few of the city's gay bars, and very rarely at that. Mostly, he'd been a tourist, observing a life he hadn't thought would ever be available to him. He'd go, have a few beers, maybe talk to a guy or two and, on almost nonexistent occasions, accompany one of them home.

It wasn't long after he'd been assigned to a beat in the 6th precinct that his grandmother's health had taken an unexpected turn for the worse and, in less than three months, she had died. Jake had been devastated by the loss, feeling once again, however irrationally, that he'd failed to keep someone he loved safe from harm.

But he was more thunderstruck to discover that she'd left the brownstone to him in her will.

Even now owning a home of his own, his personal life had remained unchanged. While the threat of a dishonorable discharge no longer hung above him like a sword of Damocles, he'd known that his life on the job would be a living hell if he ventured forth from the closet, especially with the raids on the gay bars that were regularly taking place at the time. Hence, Jake had gone to work, done his job, and come home to an empty house. It was only when the longing had become unbearable that he ventured out, as far from his precinct as he could, to find a gay bar. And maybe more.

And then came Stonewall.

Jake had been all too aware of the anti-homosexual agenda that the N.Y.P.D. had undertaken, under the guise of a crackdown on the Mafia, which operated many of the establishments. He'd only had to raid bars on two occasions and had felt like shit afterward. But the riot that weekend in June of 1969 was a whole new arena of self-loathing for him. He'd had no choice but to join his fellow officers in attempting to stave off the protestors, having to get aggressively physical with more than a few.

When it was over, he'd used the personal time he'd accumulated to stay drunk for almost a week.

After his binge of self-hatred, he'd returned to work, where he'd discovered a higher level of disgust with gay men. His fellow officers now saw this faction of society as more than loathsome perverts; they had become the enemy.

It was then that Jake had installed a deadbolt on his closet door. And there it remained for eight years. In that time, his performance on the job had led to promotions and, ultimately, a position in Homicide.

Eight years after he'd installed the impenetrable lock, Celeste, the captain's secretary at the time, had a birthday. He'd always enjoyed an effortless, comfortable rapport with her, and he'd suspected that she might have known his secret, although she never hinted at it. He'd wanted to do something special for her.

Having gotten to know the Village from his time as a beat cop and, later, working Homicide, he'd decided to see what he could find for her in one of the many, slightly over-the-top boutiques on his next day off. After having ruled out the stationary store, a shop that sold only scarves—hundreds, if not thousands, of them—and, God forbid, a boutique specializing in sex toys, he'd found himself frustrated beyond belief. Not with his lack of success in shopping; he'd been frustrated that he couldn't give her something outlandish, something he might have given her had he been open about himself, something you'd give a friend who knows, and protects, your deepest secret.

Wanting a break from his fruitless search, he'd stopped into Marie's Crisis on Grove to get a drink. Since it was mid-afternoon, there had been no one at the piano—the establishment's primary identity was that of a piano bar—and the place was fairly empty. He'd taken a seat at the bar and ordered a Johnny Walker Red, neat.

"Rough day?"

He'd turned in the direction of the voice and saw an attractive young man seated four stools down, a hamburger platter on the bar in front of him.

"You have no idea," Jake had replied after thanking the bartender for his drink. "I'm trying to find a birthday gift for a lady I know. Someone I work with. I want to get her something unique because we click really well. But she doesn't know I'm gay and everything I can think of that I'd like to get her screams, *'Homo!'*"

The young man had laughed, a refreshingly sincere and unguarded sound to Jake's ears. "Been there, done that, my friend," he'd said. "Lemme ask, does she like art and stuff like that?"

"I don't know," Jake had replied. "She wears some pretty funky jewelry. It looks handmade. Maybe?"

"Tell you what," the guy had said. "When I'm done with my lunch break, why don't you come back to where I work. We sell handmade pottery. Maybe you'll find something for her there."

"That's the best offer I've had all day," Jake had told him. "And since you're about to make my life so much easier, I suppose I should introduce myself. My name's Jake."

With a mouth full of hamburger, the young man had said, "I'm Tommy."

JAKE LOOKED UP AT THE FAÇADE OF HIS HOME FROM THE BOTTOM OF THE STEPS.

What a fucked up day, he thought. *But*, his higher self whispered internally, *it's about to get better.*

He climbed the stairs, feeling twenty years older than he was, and slipped the key into the door. Once it was open, he was greeted by the most enticing aromas wafting from the kitchen. Candles had been placed and lit on every available surface.

And he could hear the shower running on the second floor.

He climbed another flight of stairs, feeling considerably younger than he had moments before.

HE AND TOMMY SLOWLY MADE LOVE IN THE CANDLELIT BATHROOM, the hot water jetting out of the showerhead and onto their joined bodies. Jake hadn't even waited for Tommy to deliberately drop the pre-lathered soap.

Afterward, they toweled each other dry and headed downstairs to eat, not bothering to put on clothes.

"Baby, this is incredible," Jake said, speaking around the *boeuf bourguignon* in his mouth. "You really made this?"

"With my own two hands," Tommy said, holding them aloft as if Jake didn't know what hands were. "And it's Julia Child's signature recipe. I had Dmitri pick up the Julia cookbook from my place and drop it off."

"You're amazing," Jake said, leaning in to kiss him. "And this wine! You paired it perfectly." Between the day's long hours, starting with a hangover, and then the nature of the work he'd been doing, the Scotch waiting on the bathroom counter, and now the wine, he was feeling more than a little buzzed.

He didn't mind at all.

"And you haven't even had dessert yet!" Tommy said.

"I thought I did. Upstairs. Before dinner." He gave Tommy a smile that was equal parts lust and love.

Just as Tommy was serving the *mousse au chocolat*—another recipe from the same cookbook—the phone rang, eliciting a groan from Jake.

"Don't answer it," Tommy beseeched.

"You know I have to, baby." Jake stood, crossed into the living room and picked up the receiver. "Hello?"

"Jake? It's Brian Trent. Talk to me."

His sudden rise and walk to another room had let Jake know that he was indeed feeling the Scotch and the wine. "Listen," he said, "what're you doing right now?"

"Nothing. Just watching TV. Why?"

"I gotta tell ya, Brian," Jake said, hearing the slightest of slurs at the edges of his voice, "this day has royally kicked my ass and I'm half-drunk right now. Any chance you can come over my place? I don't think I can have this conversation on the phone."

"For a story like this, I'd walk to Jersey. Where do you live?" Brian asked. "And please tell me it's not in Jersey. That was just a joke."

"No," Jake said, laughing, "it's not in Jersey." Having given Brian the address and hung up, Jake resumed his seat at the dining room table. "I hope you don't mind," he said to Tommy. "It's this reporter from the *Voice*. Trust me, it's important. You'll understand when I tell him what I have to."

"It's about the call you got this morning?"

"Yeah," Jake said, his elevated mood dropping a few floors.

"I think I already know," Tommy said, saving his boyfriend the ordeal of recounting it. He told him about his visit with Dmitri and Steven, leaving out the part where the trio decided to play "Charlie's Angels."

"So you already know," Jake said. "You weren't friends with this Fischer guy, were you?"

"No. I only knew him in passing," Tommy assured him, sensing Jake's concern. "We never actually met, but I knew who he was."

Jake reached over and took Tommy's hand. "Baby, please be careful. I can't lose you too."

"I'm very careful," Tommy said. "Besides, it's not like I'm out looking for one-night stands or anything." He paused, registering Jake's comment. "And what do you mean 'too'? Who else did you lose?"

Jake cursed the Scotch and the wine. "Somebody a long time ago," he allowed. "I'll tell you the story another time. I just don't have it in me right now."

"Your grandmother?"

"Yeah," Jake lied.

"I'm all ears whenever you're ready," Tommy said. "And no pressure. I can wait."

"You know I love the hell outta you, right?"

"You better," Tommy said. "Now eat your mousse. I didn't slave away in the kitchen all day for nothing!" He laughed. "And then we should probably put on some clothes."

CHAPTER TWELVE

SINCE THE ACROPOLIS DINER WAS OPEN TWENTY-FOUR HOURS A DAY, Dani and Iggy didn't have to concern themselves with any closing duties. When their shifts were over, they were done and gone.

Dani's small studio apartment was a short walk from the diner, and the night was nice. The ever-present NYC humidity had mercifully lifted, so the heat that lingered wasn't suffocating. She and Iggy strolled in silence. She wanted to let him grieve on his own terms, not insinuating herself into his moment, only taking his hand in a comforting gesture.

She and Iggy were the exact same height, although his frame was much more muscled. As a result, holding hands had always been very comfortable with neither having to adjust for a height difference.

"It's not like we were living together or anything," he said after a block and a half, "or even dating exclusively. It was just a now-and-then kinda thing. I shouldn't feel this way."

"Ig, you should feel however you feel," Dani said. "If you try to squash down something that's legitimately inside of you, you'll destroy yourself."

"It's just so unreal," he said. "I saw him last week. And now he's dead."

"Honey," she said, "you're in shock. That's natural. You have to allow the process to play itself out. Just remember that, no matter what you're feeling, I'm here for you. Always."

"Always?" he challenged her. "Until you leave me for that French cunt and her fancy gallery."

To an outsider, his tone would have sounded bitchy and hurtful, but Dani knew better. She laughed and put her arm around his waist as they walked. "I'd never leave you for a French cunt, sweetie," she said. "Now a Danish cunt? You might have to worry about that! Whole different accent."

Iggy stopped walking and turned to face her. "What would I do without you?"

"The same thing I'd do without you," she replied, also having halted in her tracks. "Curl up and die! Now let's get back to my place and unwind."

"Speaking of which," he said as they resumed walking up 6th Avenue, "you got any grass at your place?"

"Am I ever without?" She answered his question with one of her own, rhetorical though it was.

"And cocoa," he said, sounding a bit more like his usual self. "I want cocoa."

"In this heat?"

"What can I say, I like chocolate."

SANDRINE LOCKED THE FRONT DOOR OF THE GALLERY and headed for the stairs leading to her apartment on the fourth floor.

Colin had a key, so he could let himself in when he finally decided to return from wherever he was off carousing. With the opening only two weeks away, she wished he'd spend more time painting in his studio and less time pursuing other passions. But it wasn't like she could dictate his movements. In a sense, she worked for him as much as he worked for her. Without him, she'd have no opening to plan.

But without her? Where would he *be?*

The thought troubled her.

She reflected on their first meeting some years prior. She'd been an assistant curator at a small gallery in the south of France and he'd been traveling the continent, having left his native England behind in search of new adventures. He'd stopped in one night when the gallery was open late.

"This is fucking amazing," he'd said, admiring an expressionist piece by a local artist. "Look at those lines, the way they intersect. Fucking mind-blowing."

She'd found the traces of a Cockney accent immediately charming. As she had his vocabulary. It had been quite refreshing to hear someone express himself so freely without any filter. Many of the visitors to the gallery carried a *bourgeois* air of pretense.

"He lives in the area," she'd told him. "I could arrange a meeting if you'd like."

"You're French!" he'd said, then rolled his eyes. "Well, of course you are. This is France after all." He'd laughed at his own folly without a trace of self-consciousness.

Sandrine had suspected the young man was a bit high or drunk. Still, though, she'd found him completely engaging. Almost entrancing even.

"*Oui*," she'd confirmed in her native tongue. "*Je suis tres français.*"

"*J'amerais l'être aussi*," he'd said, telling her that he wished he were as well.

"Oh, so you speak French?" she'd said, not in English.

"Of course," he'd replied in the same language. "What self-respecting Englishman doesn't?"

While she'd found his Cockney accent charming earlier, having it layered onto his French had been completely captivating for reasons she couldn't quite identify.

"Are you an artist?" Sandrine had asked, reverting to English.

"Yes. Well, trying to be. No, I am. Yes, I'm an artist."

She had found everything about this young man to be like a gentle breeze on a day that was only a bit too warm.

"What kind of work do you do?" she'd asked.

"Mostly abstracts," he'd replied. "I like to just explode onto the canvas and let the colors say what I'm feeling. The people who see it later can just suss it all out. Fuck 'em anyway. Most of 'em are just bleedin' wankers pretending to know shit about art."

Sandrine had known the type and shared his opinion of them.

"We close in twenty minutes," she'd said impetuously. It hadn't been Sandrine's nature to be impulsive. Nothing about her life was spur of the moment, so focused was she on rising in the art world and increasing her presence and power therein. But something about this young man had brought it out in her. "Would you like to join me for a coffee or a drink? I would very much like to talk more."

"That sounds ducky," he'd said with enthusiasm. "I got me no plans so I'm all yours, mamselle."

As she climbed the stairs to her apartment, Sandrine wondered how different her life might have been had she not asked Colin to join her at the café that night. By the time she reached the top floor and opened her door, she realized she was beyond caring about that.

"GIMME A MILLER LITE, ON TAP," Alex told the bartender at Uncle Charlie's Downtown on Greenwich Avenue.

As always, the music was pumped to an almost deafening level. *Why is that necessary?* he wondered. *It's not like there's even a dance floor here.*

Beer in hand, he found himself a spot from which to view the room. Maybe he'd connect tonight. God knows, he could use it. Between his frustrations over not being able to reach that Delacroix bitch and then the news that another guy had been killed, he needed a good fuck. Especially one he didn't have to worry about calling tomorrow.

One hour, and three Miller Lites, later, Alex Mayhew called it a night. A night as unproductive as the day had been. *Maybe tomorrow,* he thought. *Fridays are always better.*

As he set the empty glass on the bar and headed for the door, he failed to notice the young, brown-haired guy in the shadows staring at him intently with piercing, hungry eyes.

CHAPTER THIRTEEN

"BABE, CAN YOU GET ME A REFILL?" Jake asked Tommy, holding his empty coffee mug aloft. He then turned to Brian. "You want another beer?"

Without looking up from his pad, Brian said, "Yeah, that'd be great."

Brian Trent had arrived at the brownstone just before midnight, eager to find out what Jake had for him, whereupon Jake had introduced him to Tommy. The couple had thrown on clothes, Jake in shorts and a tee shirt, Tommy in shorts and remaining topless.

"You look familiar," Brian had said to him. "Have we met?"

Tommy had glanced nervously at Jake. "I don't know," he'd said, hoping they hadn't been a one-night stand for each other. "Wait!" he'd added, having thought beyond the carnal and clandestine. "I work up the block from your office. Maybe we've seen each other around the neighborhood."

"Where do you work?" Brian had asked.

"The Pot Shop," Tommy had replied.

"That must be it," Brian had said. "I stop in there now and then when I need a gift for someone."

Tommy had smiled, relieved that they hadn't fucked, and looked at Jake, taking his hand. "That's how we met actually," he'd said. "Jake was shopping for a birthday present, and here we are!"

He'd then offered their guest a serving of chocolate mousse and disappeared into the kitchen. Jake led Brian into the living room.

"'Friend,' huh?" the reporter asked his host.

"Yeah," Jake answered a touch too quickly, prompting his astute visitor to arch one eyebrow. "Well," he dared, "more than that." He'd felt himself blushing and had turned his attention to the couch, as if choosing a place to sit.

"Nice," Brian had said, taking the information in stride without hesitation. "Okay," he'd continued, "first things first. You said it's on the record?" They hadn't even yet seated themselves before official business commenced.

"Yep," Jake had replied, grateful for the change of subject, as they sat down, he on the sofa and Brian in a wingback chair, the coffee table between them. "I got the M.E.'s report and it was basically a Xerox of McCandless and Curtis. I already knew in my gut that we had to go public, but I needed something to nudge me off the diving board. The autopsy did it."

Tommy had returned with a chocolate mousse for Brian, a wine glass, and a bottle of burgundy, the same vintage he'd served with dinner. Brian had asked if there was any beer, eliciting a look from Tommy that said, "Beer? With chocolate mousse? Philistine!"

"Hey," Brian had said with a smile, "I happen to like beer."

"Baby, I'll have coffee, if you don't mind making it?" Jake had said. "I've already had too much booze tonight."

Tommy had leaned down and given him a kiss. "I already turned Mr. Coffee on," he'd said.

"Watch it," Jake had cautioned playfully. "You're about to turn Mr. *Griffin* on."

"All in a day's work," Tommy had said before returning to the kitchen.

"He's cute," Brian had shared.

"Yeah, he is," Jake had said, smiling and still looking in the direction Tommy had gone, although he was no longer in sight.

"Nice muscles too," he added appreciatively.

"Yeah, he works out a lot," Jake said. "Sometimes I go with him, but not as often as I'd like. I'm usually at work when he hits the gym."

"How long you two been together?" Brian had asked, taking a spoonful of mousse.

"Two years now," Jake had replied. "It's not always easy, but it's always worth it."

"How is it not easy?" Brian had asked, ever the reporter.

"He's out of the closet and I'm not," Jake had stated. "It's not usually a problem, but when it *is*? Man, it can be a *big* one." Although Brian had understood without needing to be told, Jake had elaborated on the necessity of staying under the radar at work.

"I envy you," he'd concluded, "working where you do. It must be so, I don't know, liberating to not have to lie all the time. And then *remember* the fucking lies." He paused and lowered his volume. "Plus, I wouldn't have to make Tommy feel like a dirty secret. I know that hurts him."

"I can imagine," Brian had said. In his experience, he'd encountered relationships like this before. They usually didn't end well.

He'd noticed the U.S.M.C. tattoo on Jake's forearm, a body part that hadn't been exposed when they'd met at the café. "You served?" he asked, nodding toward the ink.

Following Brian's gaze, he said, "Yeah, one tour in Nam. One was enough."

"Damn straight," Brian said.

Tommy had returned with a small tray bearing a bottle of Heineken and a coffee mug. "Sorry to keep you waiting on your beer," he said, "but I wanted the coffee to finish dripping first." He set the tray on the table and took a seat next to Jake.

"Tommy," Brian had said as he finished the last of the dessert, "this mousse is amazing. If I knew my way around a kitchen, I'd ask for the recipe!"

"Thank you, kind sir," Tommy had replied.

Noting the crystal ashtray sparkling on the coffee table, Brian had asked, "Okay if I smoke in here?"

"Why not?" Jake had replied. "This one does all the time." He'd leaned over and kissed Tommy on the cheek before he could balk at the comment.

"Thanks," Brian had said and pulled a box of Winstons from his shirt pocket.

"Okay," Brian had then said to Jake once he'd lit up, "let's get to work." He'd gone on to inform Jake that he'd already filed the story on the Fischer murder. "It'll be in Monday's edition," he said. "Where, I don't know. I'm' hoping for the front page, but who can tell." He'd then told Jake that he'd followed through on his promise to minimize the connection between the murders, making only a passing reference in the final paragraph of the article. Jake had expressed his appreciation for that.

"But if I'm gonna write a piece on a possible serial killer," Brian had continued, "I'll have to hustle to meet the deadline on Sunday." He'd glanced at his watch, seeing it was now after twelve-thirty in the morning. "Which means I'm gonna be working around the clock on this one."

"Join the club," Jake had said. "Let's get started then."

"Quickly begun is quickly done," Tommy had interjected, quoting "Mary Poppins," his favorite movie.

"He's adorable," Brian had said to Jake, who'd returned the reporter's smile.

"Tell me something I *don't* know."

THEY SPENT THE NEXT HOUR SCRUTINIZING PAPERWORK. Jake had brought home Xerox copies of all three autopsy reports, as well as the details of the crime scenes. Brian had provided the articles he'd written on the first two murders, along with his copious interview notes, all photocopied in duplicate so Jake would have a set.

While they reviewed the documents and took notes, Jake brought Brian up to speed on the investigation, primarily the visit to the Eagle's Nest after they'd parted ways at the McDougal Café.

When Jake asked Tommy for a refill—his third mug—Brian was ready to interview the cop, however informally.

"Do you mind if I get this on tape?" Brian asked, pulling a cassette recorder from his leather messenger bag and placing it on the coffee table between them.

"Not at all," Jake said. With that, Brian depressed two buttons, a blank cassette already in the machine. "Just don't let anyone but you hear it," he added. "Can't risk somebody recognizing my voice."

"Trust me, this is for my ears only," he told Jake.

Jake thanked him, knowing in his gut that he could indeed trust Brian's integrity without hesitation.

"Before we start," Jake had said. "You told me you got an anonymous tip about the Fischer murder. Considering when you called me, it had to be somebody from within the department, probably from the 6th. Can you tell me who that was?"

"Sorry, man," Brian had said. "I don't reveal my sources. Hope you understand."

"Yeah," Jake had said. "I do. No worries." In truth, he'd been less curious about a possible leak in the department than he was to learn who else at the 6th might be gay, since he'd assumed that was the common denominator at play here.

Into the recorder, Brian said, "Interview with anonymous source with the N.Y.P.D., Friday, July twentieth, nineteen-seventy-nine." With that, he proceeded with the interview. "Why do you believe this is the work of a serial killer?"

"Because it fits a pattern," Jake replied. "Look at the victim profiles and the M.O.s. You don't need an advanced degree in criminology to see it. All three victims were the same basic type, they'd all been at a gay bar prior to being murdered, they'd all been drained of blood and dumped in another location. And nobody remembered seeing any of them leave the bars with anyone."

"You mentioned that a bartender at the Eagle's Nest had seen Fischer talking to somebody," Brian stated. "What can you tell me about that?"

Jake recounted Chris Albright's description of the unknown male. "He'll be coming into the precinct in the next day or so to work with a sketch artist. I'll make sure you get a copy. Don't know if it'll be in time for this, but I'm guessing you'll be doing a follow-up or two."

"Or three or four," Brian amended.

Tommy sat silently beside Jake, almost mesmerized by what was unfolding before him. He'd never actually observed his lover at work, nor had he ever seen a journalist ply his craft.

He was also taking mental notes on anything he could pass along to Dmitri and Steven.

"And you told me that the higher-ups at your precinct won't entertain the possibility that this is a serial?"

"You can't print that," Jake said firmly. "Young is bound to read this and he'll know I'm your source."

"Understood," Brian deferred. "Moving on."

He proceeded with several questions about the specific similarities between the three murders, mostly forensic details that would be lost on the average reader. Finally, he got to what he'd hoped would be the thrust of the article.

"Tell me why you feel it's important to share this speculation with the public. Especially since it *is* just speculation at this point."

"Jesus, man, look how fast Son of Sam was on every front page!" Jake said with fervor. "Every fuckin' paper and TV station in the city was profiling the vics and warning young brunette women to be careful, even if they didn't come out and say so." Jake was on a roll, finally giving voice to things that had been gnawing at his gut like a rat living in his intestines trying to work its way out. "Okay, to be fair, Berkowitz was writing to the papers, giving you guys grist for your mill. But, c'mon, Brian! We've got three homicides now with identical M.O.s, but because the vics are queer, nobody's willing to go on record and call this what it is." He grabbed the wine bottle and poured some into the glass Tommy had intended for Brian. Tommy looked at Brian with concern. After draining it in one gulp, Jake said, "Nobody official gives a shit about us. That's the bottom line." He fell back against the couch cushions.

"Sweetie," Tommy said, placing a hand on Jake's thigh.

"I'm sorry," Jake fired back, rousing himself. "Wait," he added, changing course and surrendering to both his emotional weariness and the alcohol he'd consumed. "I'm not. I'm not sorry. I'm not one goddamn bit sorry. Somebody's butchering us," he said to both of them, getting heated once more. "And nobody cares!" He'd long forgotten that every word he uttered was being recorded.

"Jake?" Brian said, his tone having shifted from that of reporter to newfound friend. "I feel your frustration. I have to deal with it too. But we're *doing* something here. We're *gonna* make a difference."

"He's right, baby," Tommy concurred. Turning his attention to Brian, he said, "I think he's pretty much shot. Do you have everything you need?"

Between the long hours and nature of the day, then the Scotch and wine, and finally the unleashing of what had been a torrent, internal up until the last few minutes, Jake was indeed shot. He once again slumped back on the sofa, spent and exhausted. And more than a little bit drunk.

Brian helped Tommy hoist Jake off the couch and lead him upstairs to bed. Having deposited the incapacitated cop on top of the quilt, they returned to the main floor, where Brian put all his belongings into his messenger bag.

"He's internalizing all this too much," he observed.

"Tell me about it," Tommy said, sounding almost as weary as Jake. "He was bad with the first two, but now it's like a dam breaking."

Having packed up his gear, Brian pulled a business card out of his wallet and handed it to Tommy. "Jake has my home and service numbers," he said. "Call me anytime if you need to." Pulling Tommy into a chaste embrace, he added, "As a friend if you need one. I'm not always a reporter."

"I appreciate that," Tommy said before showing Brian to the door.

Once he'd locked everything up, loaded and started the dishwasher, and turned off all the lights, Tommy made his way upstairs to undress Jake and tuck him into bed before joining him.

Thank God he's off tomorrow, he thought as he climbed beneath the covers. *Frank better not fuckin' call.*

CHAPTER FOURTEEN

FRIDAY'S SUNRISE BROUGHT WITH IT THE RETURN OF THE HUMIDITY that had been plaguing the city for weeks.

As Tommy had hoped the night before, Jake's bedside phone did not ring. Choosing to let his boyfriend sleep in—because, God knew, he'd earned it—Tommy slipped from beneath the sheet at eight A.M. and went about getting ready for work. After showering and dressing, being careful not to rouse Jake, he ate a light breakfast and left a note on the kitchen counter.

> *Hey, handsome!*
>
> *Mr. Coffee is ready and waiting for you, just turn him on! (But not like you turn me on! Haha!)*
>
> *Call me at the shop when you're awake and let me know you're OK. I love you lots & lots!*
>
> *—T.*

Tommy took the #1 train from 72nd to the Christopher Street station and ascended to the already balmy sidewalk. Once inside the Pot Shop, having let himself in with his key, he was greeted by Fuchsia Lammé, née Dwayne Jarvis of Biloxi, Mississippi, the six-foot-two, 275-pound, black drag queen who owned the establishment.

"Lord almighty!" Fuchsia exclaimed, her hand dramatically poised at her throat. "Did you hear the terrible news?"

That's all *I heard about for a whole* day, Tommy thought. "Yeah," he told his boss, being intentionally succinct. As much as Tommy had shared with Fuchsia over the last three years in her employ, he'd never betrayed Jake's confidence when it came to his police work, so he did not elaborate on how he'd learned of Cody Fischer's murder or the extent of his knowledge.

"Chil'," Fuchsia said, "I been worried sick about all our peoples." With that, Ms. Lammé swept into the back room, her voluminous caftan swirling behind her like the paisley wake of a ship.

Tommy made sure everything was as it should be in the shop before unlocking the door for business at ten o'clock. As was usually the case, foot traffic was light before noon, so he busied himself by pulling a legal pad from the shelf beneath the counter and jotting down everything he remembered from

Jake's conversation with Brian, intending to pass the information along to Dmitri and Steven. Around eleven-thirty, the phone rang.

"Good morning, the Pot Shop," Tommy answered. "How may I help you?"

"You can come back here and get in my bed," Jake said, his voice sexy even though resembling death warmed over.

"Baby, you sound like shit," Tommy said with sympathy.

"I sound worse than I feel," Jake replied. "I'm just tired. No hangover today, thank God."

"Well, that's nothing short of a miracle," Tommy said.

"I know, and I'm not complaining." Jake paused. Tommy could hear him swallowing and hoped it was the coffee he'd gotten ready before he left the brownstone. "I'm just tired," Jake repeated. "And missing you. I got your note. You asked me to call, so I'm calling. What's up?"

"Nothing," Tommy replied. "I just wanted to hear my man's voice and know he was okay. Especially after yesterday."

"I'm fine. Really," Jake said. "At least, as fine as I can be with all this shit going on."

"Understandable," Tommy said.

A beep intruded on the conversation. Fuchsia had added Call Waiting, Ma Bell's latest high-tech gadget, to the account.

"I've got a call coming in," Tommy informed Jake. "Lemme call you back after lunch, okay?"

"Sure thing, baby."

"And rest," Tommy commanded before depressing the disconnect button on the phone to switch over to the incoming call. "Good morning," he said. "The Pot Shop. How may I help you?"

"Hey, it's me," Dmitri said. "Just touching base."

"And I'm so glad you did," Tommy told him with enthusiasm. He then recounted a nutshell version of Brian's visit to the brownstone the night before. "Can you meet me for lunch?"

"Yeah, no problem."

"And bring Steven, if he's awake."

They made plans to meet at the Riviera Café on 7th Avenue at one and said their goodbyes.

"AND HE'S REALLY GOING PUBLIC WITH THIS?" Dmitri asked.

Tommy had brought him and Steven up to speed by the time the waiter had brought their lunches. Steven eyed the server with obvious hunger.

"Well," Tommy answered, "not officially. As in, he's not being named as the source. But yeah. It'll be in Monday's *Voice*, hopefully."

"Your man is really stepping up, girlfriend," Steven said, sipping his iced tea with the requisite raised pinky. "Is that waiter new?" he asked, changing the subject.

"Steven," Dmitri chided, "stay focused."

"But here's what's important to *us*," Tommy continued. "Cody was at the Eagle's Nest the night he was killed, and a bartender talked to him and saw him with another dude. The bartender's name is Chris Albright," he said, checking his notes. "Either of you know him?"

Dmitri and Steven exchanged looks before shaking their heads.

"You know how to reach him?" Dmitri asked. "The bartender?"

"No," Tommy replied. "Jake didn't say his number out loud. Just let Brian copy it from a piece of paper. But we know where he works. He should be easy enough to find."

"We're both dancing all weekend, honey," Steven said. "We won't be able to hit the Nest until Monday." Dmitri was nodding.

Tommy chewed on this information, his eyebrows knitted. "Jake and I don't have any set-in-stone plans for tonight," he said, evolving an idea. "I could go to the Nest myself and call you both tomorrow."

"That sounds good," Steven said. "And be careful, honey!"

"One more thing," Tommy added. "If we're gonna be Charlie's Angels, *please* let me be Farrah."

BACK AT THE SHOP AFTER LUNCH, TOMMY CALLED VINNIE at his office.

"Hey," he said, "what're you and Rich doing tonight?"

"Nothing definite," Vinnie answered. "Figured we'd go out to a bar. Just don't know which one."

"Come with me to the Eagle's Nest," Tommy said.

"Okay," Vinnie obliged. "Sounds like you're on a mission. Anything you wanna tell me? Are you leaving Jake for somebody with less baggage?" Vinnie wasn't Detective Griffin's biggest fan.

"No," Tommy asserted. "Jake and I are fine. I just wanna raise a little hell is all."

"Fair enough," his friend said. "What time?"

"Let's meet up outside around ten. I wanna get there when it opens."

"It's a date," Vinnie told him. "Ten it is." He hung up.

Pulling the business card out of his wallet, Tommy next dialed Brian's number at the *Voice*.

"Brian Trent. Talk to me."

"Hi, Brian, it's Tommy. Jake Griffin's boyfriend?"

"Oh, hey, Tommy," Brian said, his official "journalist" tone gone. "What's up? Everything okay?"

"Yeah, everything's fine," Tommy replied. "But I have a favor to ask you."

"What do you need?"

"Yesterday and last night really kicked my ass," he said, "and I hate to say it, but I need a break from the intensity. I know, I know, I'm a shitty boyfriend." He said it before Brian could.

"Okay. With you so far," Brian said, ignoring Tommy's self-deprecation.

"But I don't want Jake to be alone tonight. Is there any chance you could call him and ask to get together? I don't know, maybe to talk more about what's going on?"

"Actually," Brian said, "I wanted to meet up with him again anyway. This could work for both of us."

"Oh, my god," Tommy gushed. "Thank you so much."

"And Tommy?" Brian said. "Don't ever feel guilty about needing a break from things like this. The work Jake and I do can be heavy, and the people in our lives shouldn't have to take that on themselves. You did the right thing, calling me. You'll get the break you need, but you made sure your man was taken care of first. That's not being a shitty boyfriend."

"Thanks for that," Tommy said. "It means more than you know."

TOMMY WAITED UNTIL THREE TO CALL JAKE BACK, hoping that Brian had reached out by that time.

"Hey, honey, it's me," Tommy said when Jake answered the phone. "How's your day going? I hope you've been taking it easy."

"I take it any way I can get it. You of all people should know that by now," Jake said, with a chuckle. The relaxed tone was music to Tommy's ears.

"About tonight," Jake continued. "Brian called and wants to meet up, talk more about his story on the murders."

"Okay?" Tommy said, hoping his exhilaration wasn't audible.

"Would you be pissed if we didn't get together this evening?" Jake asked, sounding almost contrite. "I just don't wanna make you sit through all that again."

"Baby," Tommy assured him, "this is huge for you right now. As long as it doesn't wear you out even more, I'm on board with whatever you need."

"Tommy boy," Jake said, "you're the best. Really. Thank you for understanding. And I promise, I won't let all this shit bring me down."

"I just want you to be okay," Tommy said. "I know how important your work is to you, but I hate when I see it weigh on you so much. Please take care of yourself."

"I will," Jake promised. "So," he continued, changing the subject, "what're you gonna do with a suddenly free Friday night?"

"I don't know," Tommy lied. "Maybe I'll call Rich or Vinnie and see what they're doing. Or maybe see if Cara wants to go to a movie. The Frank Langella 'Dracula' opened today." He and Jake had seen the actor play the role on Broadway before it was adapted for the screen. "If all else fails, there's always a rerun of 'Dallas.'"

"That sounds fun," Jake said. "But whatever you wind up doing, though, please be careful. There's a lunatic out there and I don't want him finding you."

"I promise," Tommy said. "And you and Brian go fight the good fight. I'm really proud of you for what you're doing."

"Thanks," Jake said, meaning it. "I can't just sit back and do nothing, even if it puts my ass in the wringer at work. I appreciate your support 'cause Christ knows I won't get any at the precinct."

"You always have it. You know that."

"I do," Jake said. "I love you."

"I love you too," Tommy replied, and they ended the call.

CHAPTER FIFTEEN

ALTHOUGH IT WAS HIS DAY OFF AS WELL, Frank Prentiss arrived at the 6th Precinct around one.

He'd called Chris Albright from his home in Queens that morning, leaving a message with the bartender's answering service. The young man had called back within fifteen minutes.

"Good morning, Detective Prentiss," Chris had said, sounding groggy but eager. "What can I do for you? I'm at your disposal."

Frank had chosen to ignore the obvious subtext. "Good morning, Mr. Albright," he'd replied. "Listen, if you're available this afternoon, I'd like you to come into the station and meet with our sketch artist. So far, you're the only one who saw Mr. Fischer with anyone on the night in question and having a sketch of this guy to work with would be a big help."

"Anything I can do to be of assistance to you, detective," Chris had said, his eagerness apparent in his voice. "What time do you want me?" More subtext.

Frank had instantly calculated his own journey into Manhattan, as well as what he'd like to accomplish before heading in. "Does one-thirty work for you?" Frank had asked. "I know you're a busy man."

"One-thirty is perfect," the bartender had replied. "That'll give me time to make myself beautiful, but it's early enough that I can get to work by four."

Frank had given Chris the address of the precinct and ended the call.

AT ONE-FIFTEEN, FRANK'S PHONE RANG. It was Hagerty, the desk sergeant downstairs.

"Prentiss," Hagerty said, "I got a … What'd you say your name was?" Frank could hear someone speaking in the background. "A Chris Albright down here. Says you're expecting him."

"Great," Frank said. "I'll be right down."

Three minutes later, the detective appeared in the lobby, right hand extended as he approached the front desk. "Chris," he said as they shook hands, "thanks for coming in. I don't think this'll take too long. Your memory seems pretty sharp."

"It is, detective," he said. "I'm more than happy to help."

"The squad room is right up these stairs," Frank said, gesturing toward the flight he'd just descended moments before. "After you."

As Chris started toward the stairs, Frank and Hagerty exchanged glances, the desk sergeant punctuating his with a limp-wristed gesture, making Frank chuckle.

Frank escorted Chris into an interview room where Greg Evanick, the sketch artist, was waiting for them. After introducing them to one another, Frank took a seat, allowing Greg to take the lead. Once they got started, Frank observed how much more detailed Chris' description of the man at the bar had become since the day before. He hoped that, in his exuberance, the bartender wasn't adding false flourishes that would make the composite useless and thereby fuck up the investigation, always a risk with an over-eager witness.

As Chris chattered and Greg sketched, Frank was struck by the irony that Evanick was creating a composite of a man who may have murdered a fellow artist. He made a mental note to share this tidbit with Greg after this fairy had left.

It took about an hour to complete the sketch, with Chris regularly saying, "No, not quite like that," over some detail of the face taking form on Greg's pad. At last, the bartender was satisfied and exclaimed, "Yes! That's him!" He looked to Frank and added, "Of course, the bar *is* kinda dark."

Jesus Christ, Frank thought, *just get the hell outta here already!*

"As long as you're pretty sure this looks like him," Frank told Chris, "you've given us a lot to go on." With that, the detective stood up. Greg Evanick recognized this as his cue and left the interview room, the sketch on the table. "I don't want to keep you from your day, Mr. Albright."

"Oh, you're not keeping me from anything," Chris said, not rising from his chair.

"Well, then," Frank amended, "I guess I should say I don't want to keep *me* from *my* day. I'll show you out."

As he had when their roles were reversed at the Eagle's Nest, Chris chattered incessantly as they made their way to the exit. What he said, Frank wouldn't be able to repeat later because he wasn't listening at all. Having seen the bartender on his merry way, he turned and gave Hagerty an exasperated but slightly amused look.

"Takes all kinds, man," Hagerty said, shaking his head in bewilderment.

"That it does, my friend. That it does."

Frank returned to the squad room and ran off several photocopies of the composite, placing one in each of the three case files and neatly piling the rest in the wire basket atop his desk. One last order of business: he wanted to call Jake before he headed home to Queens.

"We got ourselves a sketch, partner," he said when Jake answered his phone.

"Perfect," Jake said. "Where're you at? Tell me you didn't go into work today."

"Unfortunately, I did. But only to meet with Albright and Evanick. That's done and I'm headin' home to Loretta. Just wanted to call you first so you could drop by and pick up the sketch if you wanted. I made copies for all the case files. I'll leave one on your desk."

"Sounds good, man," Jake said. "Now get the hell outta there!"

Frank Prentiss didn't need to be told twice.

AFTER GETTING OFF THE PHONE WITH TOMMY TWENTY MINUTES LATER, Jake walked around the corner to the parking garage.

The traffic at that hour wasn't too bad, especially in midtown where it was often the most congested, and he made it to the precinct in less time than he'd expected. Parking his Civic in the lot, he almost ran into the station and up the stairs to Homicide.

As Frank had promised, the composite sketch was waiting for him on his desk. Jake sat down to examine it. *Is this our guy?* he wondered. If so, it didn't help the situation enormously. The face he was looking at could be any one of thousands of men. Still, though, it was a start. If nothing else, it ruled out guys who weren't white, as well as blonds and redheads. *At least there's that.*

He made four additional Xerox copies, slipping one into a manila envelope and the rest into a file folder, and headed back downstairs, the envelope in his hand. If he delayed leaving much longer, he'd wind up hitting midtown just in time for Friday rush-hour traffic, and that wasn't an option he was willing to entertain. Pulling out of the lot, he waved to the pretty brunette waitress he'd gotten to know at the diner across the street as she and a guy entered the Acropolis to start their shift.

CHAPTER SIXTEEN

"I'LL BRING THE BEER, YOU ORDER THE PIZZA," Brian said to Jake when he called him before leaving the newsroom.

"Works for me," Jake said. His day off had done wonders for him, and he was revived, renewed, and ready to plow ahead with this covert collaboration, especially since they were now armed with the composite sketch.

"At this hour," Brian said, "the One's gonna make every stop." Unlike the express Numbers Two and Three trains, the One was the local on the Red line that traveled underneath Broadway. Also unlike the Two and Three, it was the only Red train that stopped at Christopher Street, necessitating Brian's use of it. "I'm hoping to ring your doorbell by six, but plan on six-thirty just to be safe. I fuckin' hate cold pizza."

"You got it," Jake said. He laughed unguardedly, surprising himself. The day off hadn't been the only tonic for his spirit. This new friendship—at least, he hoped that's what this was—was a very welcome and refreshing turn of events in his life.

Aside from Tommy's friends, who were a mixed bag, he had no other gay men in his personal circle. He found himself looking forward to cultivating something with Brian. The reporter's questions the night before about his relationship with Tommy was the first opportunity Jake had ever had to share his feelings about his intimate personal life with someone whose prejudices didn't require redaction, editing, or the changing of pronouns. It was only in retrospect that he'd realized how good that felt.

Yes, he thought, *I hope Brian and I remain friends after this shit is done.*

TOMMY GOT HOME FROM WORK AT SIX-FIFTEEN, surprising Cara with his entrance into the Grove Street apartment.

"Oh, my God," she said. "You're actually gracing your own home with your presence?"

She was seated on the sofa, chopsticks in hand, Chinese take-out on the coffee table in front of her, watching Eyewitness News on Channel 7. Bill Beutel was informing the viewing audience about the latest developments in the Iran hostage crisis since there were New Yorkers among the captives.

"Yes," Tommy said, "I'm here in the flesh."

"No plans with Jake tonight?" she asked. "Everything okay with that?"

"Uh huh," he assured her, "everything's fine. He's meeting with somebody about a work thing, so I'm gonna go out with Vinnie and Rich."

"Oh, okay," she said. "How did your dinner last night go? Dmitri left me a note saying he'd let himself in with his key to pick up a cookbook. What did you make?"

"Miss Julia's *boeuf bourguignon*, if you must know," he said as he sat next to her and picked up the container of pork fried rice and a plastic fork. "And, naturally, it was wonderful." He shoveled a heaping forkful into his mouth.

"And after?" she pressed. "Did you two talk?"

"We didn't really have the chance," he said, chewing the rice. "This reporter from the *Voice* came over. They were discussing the murders that've been happening."

"Are you okay with that?" she asked. "I mean, I know you really wanted to talk to him. Air things out."

"Actually, I am," he said, setting down the container. "The call he got yesterday morning was about the murders. There was another one. Now I understand why he had to fly out of there so fast." Cara knew about the first two crimes, so further clarification was unnecessary. "His boss isn't making them a priority, I guess, so he called this reporter. His name's Brian. That's who he's getting together with tonight. He's feeding him anonymous information."

"Wait," she said. "Back up. There was another slashing?"

"Yeah," Tommy told her. "And I'm worried about him. I never saw him like he was last night. This is eating at him like crazy. I hope what he's doing with Brian helps."

"And Jake is working with the press?" On more than one occasion, she'd heard him gripe about the media sticking its nose into police work and complicating investigations.

"Yeah," he said. "Imagine that." Remembering her job with the Public Defender's office, he caught himself. "You don't have to say anything about that, do you?"

"You got any cash on you?" she asked.

"Yeah," he replied, clearly confused. "Why?"

"Gimme a dollar," she said. "Or whatever. Even a quarter. I don't care."

Looking at his sister like she was crazy, he fished a coin out of his pocket and handed it to her.

"There," she said. "You just paid my retainer. Attorney-client privilege now applies." She gave him a grin, one that he returned.

"But you're not an attorney," he pointed out.

"Stop splitting hairs or you'll go bald," she playfully chided.

"God forbid!" he exclaimed. He looked at his watch. "And speaking of my flawless beauty," he said, "I want to take a nap and do a deep-pore scrub before I leave to meet Vinnie and Rich." He leapt from the couch and dashed down the hall toward the bedrooms.

BRIAN TRENT PRESSED THE DOORBELL TO THE BROWNSTONE AT SIX-THIRTY-FIVE.

Before Jake even answered, Brian was joined on the front steps by a delivery boy bearing two pizza boxes. "Perfect timing," Brian told him as the kid referenced a slip of paper and glanced at the address.

The door was opened and Jake said, "Wow, perfect timing!"

"That's what he just said," the delivery boy pointed out disinterestedly before telling Jake what was owed on the pizzas. As Jake fished out his wallet, the young man eyed both the other men with an appreciative, knowing stare, noting for the first time the two six-packs of Heineken in Brian's hands. Once he was paid and handsomely tipped, he handed the boxes to Jake and said, "Thanks. And you two have fun tonight." He grinned and winked.

As the young man descended the stairs, Jake and Brian exchanged a look and laughed.

"If only he knew," Brian commented.

"I know," Jake concurred. "And I see you come bearing gifts! Excellent."

"Absolutely," Brian said. "Can't have New York pizza without the appropriate libation."

Pizza boxes in hand, Jake stepped inside, allowing Brian entrance, and closed the door with his hip.

They set up shop on the dining room table, which allowed ample room for a meal as well as the paperwork they both had at the ready. Before digging into their makeshift dinner, Jake slid a large manila envelope across the table to Brian.

"Is this what I think it is?" he asked.

"Open it and find out."

Without hesitation, Brian pulled back the flap on the envelope and withdrew the photocopied composite sketch, which included descriptive details of the suspect across the bottom of the page. "Person of Interest" appeared above the drawing.

"Well, shit," Brian said, sounding somewhat crestfallen. "This could be anybody at the bars. For all I know, I might have slept with him."

"Damn, man," Jake said, "don't say shit like that. You coulda been one of his victims if you did."

"You know what I mean, Jake," Brain responded. "I'm just saying that so many guys on the scene look the same. It's like they've all been cloned. I was hoping there'd be something unique about this one."

"Tell me about it," Jake commiserated. "At least we can rule out the ones who *don't* look like him."

Brian carefully returned the sketch to its envelope and slipped that into his messenger bag which he'd set on the chair beside him. "Okay, man," he said, his tone now more enthusiastic, "I'm fuckin' starving. Let's get some food and drink in us."

As Jake opened the first pizza box and Brian the first two beers, the reporter asked, "Where's Tommy tonight?" He knew what he believed to be the real reason for his absence, but was curious as to what had been said between the two.

"After you reached out to me, I called him at the shop," Jake informed him. "I didn't wanna make him sit through another work session, so I begged off getting together tonight. He understood."

"Great," Brian said. "I mean, great that he understood, not that you cancelled on him."

They continued with their meal, keeping the conversation pointedly away from the reason for their meeting, sparing their digestions the stressful topic. Brian asked Jake if he was a native New Yorker, to which the cop replied in the negative.

"I didn't think so," Brian commented, eliciting a puzzled and curious expression from Jake. "No telltale accent," he elaborated.

"Oh, gotcha," Jake said. "I don't really have *any* sort of accent." He went on to explain his global childhood, pointing out that he was never in any one place long enough to acquire a dialect, not to mention that the majority of his interactions had been with other Americans. From there, he told him about his tour in Nam, elaborating on the brief answer he'd given the night before.

Brian listened with interest, nodding understandingly at the more horrific details of the story.

"I've interviewed a lot of Vietnam vets," Brian said. "Even have a few friends who served there. I was lucky. Being in college, I managed to not get drafted. My heart goes out to all of you."

As he reached for another slice of pizza, Jake felt a sudden spark of intuition. Placing the food on his plate, he looked at Brian. "Can I share something with you that I've never told anyone?"

"Sure," Brian said, putting his own slice down. "Anything. I've been hoping that this is a becoming a friendship and not just a professional thing."

"I thought the same thing," Jake said. He looked down at his plate. "Something happened over there, something I kinda need to talk about."

From his experience speaking with other vets, Brian could only imagine the battlefield nightmare his new friend was about to reveal. "Go on."

To the reporter's mild surprise, Jake didn't bring up the horrors of war.

He told him about Larry.

When he reached the point in his narrative where Larry had stepped on the land mine, Brian reached over and held Jake's hand on the table. It was a gesture of familial support, not one of romance, a subtle distinction immediately felt by Jake.

He finished by sharing that he'd chosen not to re-up when his tour was over, citing both Larry's death and the realization that was indeed not cut out to be like his father, and how that decision had ultimately brought him to the city.

"You okay?" Brian asked, his tone softened by the nature of what he'd just been told.

"Yeah," Jake said, giving Brian's hand an appreciative squeeze before releasing it and taking a hearty bite of pizza. "Guess now you understand a little better why I'm so deep in the goddamn closet," he added with a mouthful of food.

"Yeah," Brian said. "It certainly adds some perspective to it all." He paused. "You do realize, don't you, that he probably saved the girl's life, right?"

"Only for a few hours," Jake muttered, his disgust plain. "Once they knew we had 'em in our sights, they used flame-throwers on the whole village. And the villagers."

They ate in silence for a few moments. Returning to the subject with delicacy, Brian spoke. "Can I ask why you haven't shared this with Tommy? I mean, you said you'd never told anyone about you and Larry until now."

"I don't know," Jake replied, pausing to mull over what he might say next. "I guess it's just that, after Larry, I figured I can handle things better if I keep them to myself."

Brian regarded the cop before commenting. "Yesterday morning, when the garbage men told the beat cops about Fischer's body, what's the first thing the uniforms did?"

Jake looked at him with a puzzled expression. "Called for backup. Why?"

"Because we all need backup from time to time," Brian said. "Some things aren't possible until we work as a team."

Jake considered this, opting to change the subject. "As for Tommy, he knows I was in the Corps in Nam and that I grew up an Army brat, just not about Larry. I was hoping that would be enough to help him understand why I'm so secretive about who I am."

"And did it?"

"Somewhat," Jake replied. "But it's not a life he's ever had to really inhabit. The only repercussions he's ever had to deal with, where coming out is concerned, are with his parents."

"What happened there?"

"The disowned him," Jake said bluntly. He wasn't being callous; the elder LaRosas' reaction left him disgusted and he wasn't shy about expressing that. "But that relationship was already strained, so he just moved on. Still and all, I know it bothers him on some level, especially when his sister goes to visit them in New Rochelle."

"They live that close?"

"Yeah, but they never come to the city. They avoid the reality of Tommy's life at any cost."

"I gotta give Tommy credit," Brian said. "It takes a lotta guts to live your own truth and accept the losses that come with that."

"I agree. Maybe that's part of why he gets so frustrated with me."

"It's a strong possibility," Brian concurred. "From his perspective, you're scared." He laughed. "Imagine that. A big, tough Marine-turned-cop scared."

"I guess we all have things that frighten us," Jake said before draining his beer bottle. "What frightens you?"

Brian considered this. "Well," he said, "snakes, for one thing."

Jake laughed. "That's not what I meant, asshole."

Joining in the much-needed levity, Brian said, "I know what you meant." He paused a moment, his expression pensive. "Secrets, I guess."

"Should I take that personally?"

"No, not at all. No judgments here," Brian assured him quickly. "I'm talking about the secrets that can hurt us from the outside. You know, all the shit that 'The Man' keeps from us that we should probably know about."

"Now you're sounding a little paranoid. Have you been reading '1984' lately?"

"Maybe we should *all* be a little paranoid," he said, opening another beer for each of them. "I mean, and I know this isn't the same thing, but look at what's going on right now. Don't you think the guys hitting the clubs, bars, and baths should be a teeny bit paranoid? It might keep some of them from going home with this guy, whoever he is."

Jake chewed on this. "I see you're point," he said. "Speaking of which, why don't we clear the table and get to work?"

"Exactly what I was thinking," Brian agreed, standing and grabbing an empty pizza box.

CHAPTER SEVENTEEN

TOMMY ARRIVED AT 21ST AND 11TH FIFTEEN MINUTES AHEAD OF THE APPOINTED TIME and positioned himself on the corner, not knowing which direction his friends would approach from.

He hadn't expected it, but now that he was here, he found himself to be quite nervous. Talking about digging up dirt on a serial killer is one thing when you're safe at home and drinking wine. It's quite another when you're dressed to attract would-be admirers and you're about to enter the club where the last victim probably met his killer. If the other two Angels were with him, he might feel better, but Vinnie and Rich were oblivious to the real nature of his plans and therefore wouldn't be watching his back.

He lit a cigarette with shaking hands and looked in all directions of the intersection. It wasn't long before he caught sight of them walking his way on 21st. They, too, were dressed to impress.

"You got here early," Rich observed, kissing him on the cheek.

"Yeah," Tommy said. "Guess I'm anxious to catch a little night fever. It's been a while since we went out and cut loose and I'm overdue." He took a drag.

"Your hands are shaking," Vinnie observed. "What's up? Did you and Jake have a fight?"

"Not a big one," Tommy said, his fingers mentally crossed behind his back. "I just hate when he lies about me to his partner, and he did it again. I'll be fine once I get a few cocktails in me."

Vinnie and Rich exchanged a look. "Tommy," Vinnie said, "you deserve a boyfriend who's proud to be with you, not one who drags you into the closet with him."

"Can we please not talk about it?" Tommy asked, not wanting his cover story to take on a life of its own with his well-meaning friends. "I'm out tonight to forget about that for a while, not relive it over and over." He felt guilty making Jake the villain of the piece. Vinnie already had a low opinion of him, and Tommy didn't want to make it worse.

"Fair enough," Rich said before his boyfriend could put in two more cents. "Whadda ya say we go raise a little hell?"

Once inside the club, Tommy excused himself, saying he needed to use the bathroom and suggesting that they go order drinks and he'd meet them at the bar. When they were headed off on their assigned task, Tommy found an employee, a muscled bar back in tight shorts and a wifebeater.

"Hey," he said, hoping he sounded as casual as he intended.

The bar back looked him up and down. "Hey, yourself," he said in a deep voice, a flirtatious smile playing around the corners of his mouth.

"You know if a bartender named Chris is working tonight?" he asked. "I think his last name is Albright or Albert or something like that." He knew the name very well but was trying to create a casual vibe about the inquiry.

The guy looked disappointed, and his tone reflected it. "Yeah, he's working," he said. "Upstairs at the main bar." He gave Tommy a look of disdain. "But good luck with him, honey. You got bottom written all over you and so does Chris. Unless you got a double-headed dildo hidden in your pocket, you and him won't have anything to discuss." He went about his business, leaving Tommy where he stood.

I happen to be versatile, thank you very much, Miss Thing! he thought before heading to the stairs.

There were two guys working the main bar and Tommy found himself grateful for the bar back's snide comment. Of the two, one was clearly a top, which meant the other one had to be Chris. Tommy made his way through the crowd, sparse though it was, cash in hand, and caught Chris' eye, summoning every ounce of his inner macho man in the hopes of maintaining his attention.

"What can I get you?" Chris asked.

"Anything you want," Tommy replied, dropping the register of his voice a touch. "But I'll start with a—" He was about to order a Sea Breeze but thought better of it, thinking something more manly might fit the bill. On the fly, he said, "Gimme a Jack Daniel's and ginger ale." He flexed his biceps in the sleeves of his snug tee shirt, hoping it was subtle.

Chris gave him a smile and said, "Comin' right up." He returned almost at once with the drink and Tommy paid him, adding a two-dollar tip, causing Chris to raise his eyebrows. "Thanks," he said with a smile.

Tommy decided to linger at the bar and lit a cigarette. Since the Nest had only just opened, it wasn't yet crowded, most guys usually arriving closer to midnight when things started to bustle. This worked well for him, leaving Chris with more time to talk than he'd have in about an hour.

"You good here?" he heard. Turning, he found Chris, ready to offer a refill.

"Yeah, still working on this one," he said. He wasn't overly fond of whiskey, so he was taking his time, wishing he'd ordered a butch drink made with vodka. If there *was* such a thing. Looking around, he said, "Kinda quiet, huh?"

"It's still early," Chris said. "Plus the fucking heat. People don't wanna leave their air conditioning long enough to get where they're going."

"I guess," Tommy said noncommittally. "And with everything goin' on right now."

"What do you mean?" Chris asked. "What's going on?"

"The three guys that got killed?" *Jesus*, he thought, *Jake didn't mention that this guy was an idiot.*

"Oh, yeah, that," the bartender responded as if it was some unsubstantiated rumor making the rounds. "Hey, you know, the last guy that got killed was in here that night." He was eager to capitalize on his status as a star witness.

"Holy shit, man," Tommy said, trying to butch it up a little. "Get the fuck out!"

"Uh huh," Chris preened. "And I *waited* on him. G&Ts, that was his drink."

"So you actually *saw* him?" Tommy asked, another question to which he already knew the answer.

"Yes, sir. And I saw the guy he was talking to. The cops think it may have been the killer." This last he stage-whispered. He was making the most of it.

"Wow," Tommy said and downed of mouthful of his drink, trying his best not to grimace.

"The cops even had me go to the precinct and help a sketch artist," Chris continued bragging. He leaned over the bar and lowered his voice, at least as much as was realistic with music playing and people talking. "From what they told me, I'm the only witness to see the killer."

Tommy noticed that Chris had already promoted the guy from suspect to convicted murderer. He felt pangs of empathy for his boyfriend if this was the kind of witness Jake had to deal with on a regular basis.

"*There* you are! We thought you fell in! What're you doing up here?"

Tommy turned to find his friends approaching him, carrying their drinks, Rich holding his own Sea Breeze plus one for Tommy. Thinking on his feet, he said, his voice still deepened, "Guys, this is Chris, my newest friend."

They eyed the bartender with suspicion. They eyed Tommy with even more.

Addressing Chris, he said, "This is Vinnie, and this is Rich. We came here together."

"I'd ask what I can get you," Chris said, "but it looks like you got that covered. You even have a back-up already," he added to Rich. The other bartender—the top—called to him and he excused himself.

"Okay, give," Rich said immediately. "What the hell is going on here?"

"Nothing," Tommy said. "I was just flirting. That's all."

"With *him*?" Vinnie commented. "He's not your usual type. And what's with the voice? You go through a second puberty or something?"

"So maybe I need to shake things up a little bit!" he defended himself, ignoring the comment about his voice. "It might do me some good to spread my wings."

"Honey," Rich said, "it's not your *wings* that you're trying to spread." He glanced in Chris' direction. "He doesn't strike me as a top, but you never know."

"Who says I can't top once in a while? For the record, I'm not *all* bottom!"

Vinnie looked at Rich and said, "That must have been one hell of a fight!"

TOMMY REMAINED AT THE BAR CHRIS WAS WORKING, but Vinnie and Rich excused themselves to go make use of one of the back rooms.

Chris continued to provide Jack and gingers, much to Tommy's dismay, and after an hour or so only charged him for every other one. Apparently, he wasn't half bad at playing detective and going incognito as an aggressive top. The thought amused him, especially given the liquid lubrication. The latter had also soothed his nerves, for which he was grateful.

In between other customers, Chris stayed near Tommy, eager to enjoy his newfound celebrity as the N.Y.P.D.'s star witness. Tommy continued to pump him for information on the suspect, working hard to maintain an air of morbid curiosity and capitalizing on Chris' swelling ego.

After a few hours of this, Chris came over and said, "I got a break coming up. You wanna get outta this noise and talk more about it in private?"

Tommy froze. He hadn't anticipated this scenario and was unprepared. "Uh, yeah," he managed to say. "Sure. Where do you take your break?"

"Anyplace I want," Chris replied and winked.

Five minutes later, Chris led Tommy through a door marked "Employees Only" and down a dimly lit corridor. Tommy realized they were in the service hallway behind the infamous back rooms.

"Not much of a break area," he commented, feeling himself beginning to sweat. His heart rate had increased, and his stomach was churning, partly from nerves, partly from Jack.

"Where do you think you are, sexy?" Chris teased him. "Studio 54?"

He pulled Tommy through another doorway and into a small dark room, a carpeted banquette lining one wall. Chris was immediately kissing Tommy, his hands fumbling with Tommy's belt and fly.

Tommy pulled away and said, "Whoa, slow down."

"Can't," Chris replied. "I only got half an hour." He leaned in to continue what he'd been doing, but Tommy put a hand on his shoulder, stopping him.

"I thought we were gonna talk," Tommy said, trying to still sound flirtatious.

"We can talk after you fuck me, stud," Chris said, stating his terms. "Don't you wanna give it to a local celebrity?"

It was clear to Tommy that Chris, despite his ego, had only one agenda, and if he had any hope of further achieving his own, he'd have to step up. Perhaps he'd overstated things earlier, mentally to the snarky bar back and aloud to his friends, because "*step* up" and "*get* it up" weren't the same thing. He opened his own belt and jeans, pushing them down. "Why don't you show me what you can do with that pretty little mouth besides talk," he commanded.

Chris gave him a salacious smile and dropped to his knees.

Forgive me, Jake, Tommy thought.

To Tommy's surprise, Chris was eliciting quite a response from him. After only a few minutes, Chris looked up at Tommy and breathlessly said, "Looks like you're good to go." With that, the bartender stood up, pulled some lube out his back pocket, and handed it to Tommy. Undoing and lowering his own pants, he turned to face the wall and braced himself against it with his hands.

Tommy was grateful it was so dark; at least he could try to pretend this was Jake. Fortunately, Chris' need to always be talking abated once Tommy entered him, his entire vocabulary reduced to grunts, moans, and the occasional "Oh, fuck yeah!"

Being annoyed with how things played out also worked in Tommy's favor. He channeled it completely into what he was doing, in effect making this idiot pay for backing him into a corner. He didn't realize he could be so aggressive in this role and found himself surrendering to a side of his personality he hadn't known existed before tonight.

After they both climaxed simultaneously, crying out in unison, they pulled their pants back up and refastened them. Tommy handed the lube back to Chris, wondering how often he made use of it on his breaks.

"Holy fuck," Chris said, his breathing still ragged. "You're amazing! When I first saw you, I thought you were a bottom like me, but damn! You're all top!"

"You oughta be careful," Tommy cautioned.

"With what?"

"How do you know that the guy you saw wasn't just some innocent bystander and that I'm not the real killer?"

In the shadows, Tommy heard Chris gasp. "You're not, are you?" he asked.

"Of course, I'm not," he said, not hiding his impatience. "But *you* didn't know that?"

"Oh, thank God," the bartender said, letting out his breath.

Tommy sat next to him on the banquette, being careful to avoid the spot where Chris had made his deposit, and lit a cigarette. He offered one to Chris, but the bartender declined it. "How long before you have to get back to work?" he asked.

"Another fifteen minutes or so," Chris replied. "Why? You wanna go again?"

Tommy laughed. "No," he said, "I don't think I could after that." It was probably the most truthful thing he'd said all night. "I just wanted to sit here a while. You said you'd tell me more about how much you've been assisting the cops." He deliberately couched it as an ego-stroke.

"Well," Chris said, stepping gladly back into the spotlight. "I thought about it a lot today, ya know, after they had me come in to help, and I realized that I do remember seeing them leave together that night. It was around one-thirty, I think, and I had to go find a bar back. I walked downstairs and I saw them by the door, heading out." Something occurred to him. "You think I should call the police? The cute one, the older black guy, he gave me his card." He made a face. "The other one did too, but he's kinda a douche, if you know what I mean."

If we went again now, you asshole, I'd fuck you right through this goddamn wall. Head first.

"You wanna exchange numbers?"

Acting on impulse despite the anger he was feeling, Tommy agreed, hoping that Chris would tell him if the dark-haired stranger returned to the Nest.

His mission accomplished, he told Chris he'd see him around. He then went in search of Vinnie and Rich, hoping he'd find some way to deal with a very guilty conscience.

CHAPTER EIGHTEEN

BRIAN HAD BEEN AT THE BROWNSTONE UNTIL AFTER MIDNIGHT, discussing various strategies that might help them in their covert operation.

At Jake's insistence—and on Jake's dime, also at his insistence—Brian took a cab home to his apartment in Chelsea. It wasn't necessarily that much quicker than the subway, especially at that hour, but it was far more comfortable and peaceful, and for that Brian was grateful. Upon arriving home, he walked Woodward. His pug was named after Bob Woodward, he of Watergate-scandal *Washington Post* fame. Brian chose that name over Woodward's partner in crime-exposure, Carl Bernstein, because, as he liked to joke, "I don't want people to think my dog's gay *and* Jewish."

After the nightly man-dog constitutional, Brian crashed and crashed hard.

It was Woodward who woke him up around seven on Saturday, wanting to go out again on his own personal schedule.

"Okay, okay, buddy," Brian groaned as his canine companion licked his face. "I guess I owe you after I left you alone all day yesterday." The afternoon prior, when he knew he wouldn't be home until late, he'd called his neighbor, Mrs. Martinez, who had a key, and asked her to walk the dog around dinnertime. Mrs. M. was happy to oblige, she and Woodward being close pals. But Brian felt guilty having deprived his faithful sidekick of his attention for a full day, so he hauled himself out of bed, pulled on shorts, a tee shirt, and sandals, and grabbed the leash.

By the time they got back to the apartment, he was too awake to go back to bed, so he made a pot of coffee and hit the ground running. He had a lot of work ahead of him if he hoped to have his "serial killer" article ready by the Sunday noon deadline for Monday's edition.

He sat at his small dining table and pulled out a blank legal pad.

BEFORE NOON, BRIAN HAD WRITTEN THE FRAMEWORK OF HIS ARTICLE and had committed it to paper. At the same time, about twenty blocks south, Tommy was roused from a deep sleep by repeated knocking on his bedroom door.

"Are you *alive* in there?" Cara asked sharply.

Why the fuck did I order whiskey? he asked himself as he lifted his lids with a bit of pain. His eyes opened only to slits, he was disoriented and confused. "Um," he said, his voice gravelly, "I think so." He cleared his throat. "Whadda ya want?" His tone made it clear that he wasn't happy with the intrusion.

"His majesty has guests seeking audience," she replied. "Get your royal ass out of bed. It's almost noontime anyway."

As he groped, almost blindly, for his clothes, he was praying it wasn't Vinnie and Rich. He'd jumped through hoops the night before to avoid their prying questions in the short walk between leaving the Eagle's Nest and parting ways at the corner. He wasn't yet coherent enough to maintain the charade.

Tommy was just buttoning the fly of his jeans—the only garment he'd bothered with—when he entered the living room to find Dmitri and Steven engaged in animated conversation with his sister.

"The Prodigal Son Also Rises!" Steven exclaimed upon seeing him. His friend had curiously, and incorrectly, combined Hemingway and the Bible. Tommy didn't notice, the other two let it pass.

Rubbing his left eye with one hand and unsuccessfully attempting to tame his auburn curls with the other, Tommy asked, "What's up? Why're you two here so early?"

"Early?" Dmitri snorted. "Looks like somebody had a late Friday night."

"Mm-hmm," Steven concurred with a knowing nod.

"We came to take you out to brunch, you ungrateful S.O.B.," Dmitri said and, glancing briefly in Cara's direction, added with meaning, "We wanted to talk to you about something."

Tommy was tired, but not comatose, and he read between the lines without effort. "Sounds fun," he managed without enthusiasm. "Lemme go put on some clothes."

He returned to his bedroom and finished dressing himself in whatever he could find, not caring a whit about fashion.

Twenty minutes later, they were once again seated at the Riviera Café, mimosas before them. Tommy was grateful for the hair of the dog in a flute glass.

Dmitri and Steven had waited until they'd all placed their orders to interrogate Tommy and, as soon as the waiter—not the one Steven had been eyeing the day before, but no less cute—turned his back on them, they could wait no longer.

"Okay, give," Dmitri began. "Were you able to find anything out?"

If there were any two people on the planet Tommy could confide in about his clandestine tryst with the bartender, it was these two. So, he did.

Steven groped for his invisible pearls, his signature gesture. It was Dmitri who spoke.

"And how are you this morning?" he asked. Tommy had never once cheated on Jake, a fact they both knew. Dmitri's desire for information on the killer put aside, he was concerned about his friend.

"Does 'guilty as fuck' cover it?"

"Oh, honey," Steven said. "I can't begin to imagine. Being backed into a corner like that? And then having to be a *top*?!"

As open as the trio always was with each other, Tommy chose not to share the unexpected exhilaration he'd felt giving voice to his usually suppressed dominant side while with Chris. That would be another conversation when this whole mess was over.

"But you said he told you something new, right?" Dmitri asked, redirecting the conversation back to the matter at hand. "What did he say?"

"It wasn't a whole lot," Tommy replied, "only that he remembered seeing Cody with the stranger as they were leaving. It's not really much." *Certainly not worth what I had to do to get it.*

"But it's something," Dmitri said. "Now we have to see if we can find out if Cody went there with anybody. You know, friends. Maybe one of them saw Cody and this guy together in between the bartender waiting on him and the two of them leaving."

The waiter returned with their orders, blatantly cruising Dmitri as he placed the plates on the table.

"Honey, that boy was checkin' you *out*!" Steven said when the waiter had left.

"I know," Dmitri said off-handedly, although he'd shown no sign of noticing while the cruising took place. "I'll get his number later."

They began eating, silently reaching a consensus to put their "Charlie's Angels" conversation on hold until they were properly fed.

AFTER MORE REWRITES AND EDITS THAN HE COULD COUNT, Brian was at last satisfied with his article.

He grabbed a quick lunch—bologna and mustard on whole wheat with a large glass of ginger ale—and asked Woodward, "You wanna go out before I head to the office?"

As always, Woodward was on board as soon as he heard the word "out."

Brian took his buddy for a leisurely stroll around the neighborhood—much more lengthy than the one they'd taken earlier—before they returned to the apartment. The article written, the reporter felt much less burdened than when he'd woken up, and wanted to enjoy this time with his closest companion. Finally, when both man and dog had had enough of the heat and humidity, they headed home. Brian wanted to get to the office to enter his article into the new, state-of-the-art typesetting machines the *Voice* had recently acquired.

He got to the newsroom around one-thirty and set the coffee and Danish he'd picked up at the corner bodega on his desk. He placed his handwritten pages in the copy holder attached to the side of the monitor and was about to start typing when Alex entered.

"What brings you in on a Saturday?" he asked his friend.

"This place is air conditioned and my apartment isn't," Alex replied.

"That's a good enough reason," Brian said, laughing.

As he took his seat across from Brian, Alex said, "Also, I'm pretty obsessed with getting an interview with this Delacroix woman. I figured if I could actually talk to her in person today, I'd rather be in front of the keyboard than scribbling on napkins at home. Scribbles I'd only have to type up tonight or tomorrow morning."

"Makes sense," Brian said, looking at his own scribbles before him.

"How about you?" Alex asked. "How come you're here?"

Choosing to be discreet, though not suspiciously so, Brian only said, "I interviewed somebody last night after hours. Wanted to file it before the day was out."

Alex was nodding empathetically. He'd had similar situations when he'd covered Friday night openings, spending the next day in the newsroom writing his review. Sunday deadlines really fucked up weekend plans.

"Okay," Brian said, "let's use our time well. Wanna grab an early dinner when we're done?"

Alex agreed without hesitation, only suggesting that they change their clothes in between. Brian glanced at his own casual attire, and they made it a plan.

"What about after?" Brian asked. "Any plans for tonight?"

"Thought I'd hit the bars," Alex said. "Solo. I've been restless lately. If I was into hustlers, I'd just pay somebody to fuck me. But what can I say? I'm a hopeless romantic." The irony was lost on neither. "So, the bars it is!"

Without further conversation, they got to work. Simultaneously, Brian's hands hit the keyboard as Alex's hand reached for the phone, which had rung at precisely the same moment.

CHAPTER NINETEEN

"MR. MAYHEW?" DANI SAID AFTER THE REPORTER ANSWERED HIS PHONE. "I'm so glad I caught you in the office. This is Dani Kramer, I'm calling on behalf of Sandrine Delacroix. I'm her personal assistant."

Friday, Dani's first day of work at Galerie Delacroix, had been mostly consumed by Sandrine familiarizing her new employee with the facility. What time was left after that, before Dani headed off to the Acropolis Diner, was spent with manual labor: preparing various pieces of Colin Davenport's work to be hung, rearranging the movable walls to Sandrine's precise specifications, various minutiae that comprise an assistant's "To Do" list.

This morning, however, Sandrine had tasked her with responding to the numerous requests she'd had for features on the gallery. The only reporter she'd chosen to grace with a personal interview prior to the opening was the one from the *Voice* since, as Sandrine had put it, "The Village is our neighbor. We should start there."

"Oh, my God," Alex said into the phone, not bothering to conceal his excitement. "Thank you for calling me back."

"Of course, Mr. Mayhew," Dani replied, sounding like a seasoned executive. "Ms. Delacroix would like to grant you an exclusive prior to the gallery's opening. When can you be available?"

Sandrine was standing in the doorway to her office, listening intently. She was pleased with what she heard. *I was right to choose her*, she thought in her native French.

"I can be available at whatever time works for Ms. Delacroix," Alex said. "You tell me when and I'll be there."

"Please hold," Dani told him and covered the mouthpiece with her hand. To Sandrine, she said, "He says he can be available whenever you want. When would you like me to schedule him?"

"Tell him tomorrow at ten," Sandrine advised her assistant. "In the morning, not at night."

"Does tomorrow at ten A.M. work for you?" Dani asked into the phone. "I know it's the weekend and short notice, but—"

Alex cut her off. "Ten is perfect. That gives me time to make my deadline for Monday's edition." He was almost gasping. "Thank you so much,

Ms.— ... I'm sorry, what did you say your name was?" He was clearly flustered.

Dani laughed unguardedly. "Kramer," she said. "Dani Kramer. And thank you Mr. Mayhew. We'll see you tomorrow at ten. You know the address?"

Alex did. He'd committed it to memory. They ended their call.

"He'll be here tomorrow morning," Dani said from her seat at Sandrine's desk.

"*Parfait*," Sandrine said, her voice not revealing her pleasure with Dani's performance.

They spent the next few hours attending to other details of the upcoming opening—arranging a caterer and the wait staff, lining up a bartender, making sure invitations would be sent out in Monday's mail to all the appropriate dignitaries, such as they were, as well as the press.

At two-fifty, there was a knock on the front door. Sandrine nodded to her assistant, indicating that she should tend to it.

Dani peeled back the brown paper on the glass of the entrance and discovered Iggy standing outside. She'd asked him to drop by on his way to work so they could walk to the diner together.

She excitedly unlocked and opened the door, eager to show her friend the gallery.

"Holy shit, Ig! What did you do?!"

"I needed to shake things up, try and get out of this funk," he said. "Do you like it?"

He'd been to his hairdresser. His Afro, which he'd always allowed to grow about an inch from his scalp, had only been neatened up. But it now featured a platinum blonde streak that had been bleached, front to back, along the right side of his crown.

"Well, it certainly makes a statement," she said. "But if it helps you feel any better, then I'm all for it!" She looked at her watch and said, "You got here early. We don't have to be at the diner for another hour."

"I know," Iggy said. "I wanted to check out your new digs without rushing through it."

"And who is this?" Sandrine asked in a welcoming voice as Dani admitted him into the gallery.

Dani turned, her nerves apparent. "This is Iggy," she said. "He's a classmate at Parsons and we work together at the diner. At least until I'm done there. He wanted to see the gallery." She paused. "I hope it's okay?"

"Of course, Dani," Sandrine said, smiling, ever her gracious self. "Are you an artist as well?" she asked Iggy

"Of a sort," he said. "I'm studying fashion design."

"Also an art," Sandrine assured him. "Some of my clothes are masterpieces!"

Iggy quickly assessed her outfit. Even though she was in attire suited for manual labor, she looked flawless. He said, "I can imagine. You look amazing, Ms. Delacroix."

"*Merci*," she said.

"Is it okay if I show Iggy around?" Dani asked her employer.

"*D'accord*," she replied, using the French phrase for "Of course," one which Dani had already come to understand after only two days in Sandrine's employ.

"*Merci*," Dani said, doing her best to become part of Galerie Delacroix in every way.

Sandrine stepped aside, enjoying the pride that her new employee took in displaying the gallery. Once again, she felt justified in choosing Dani and she didn't hide her enthusiasm. She watched the young woman, smiling with pride as a doting parent would observe a favored child excel in their field.

However, in the windowless storeroom behind the back most gallery, in the deepest shadows between two large, upright crates, someone else was observing the scene, and with far less enjoyment than Sandrine was exhibiting.

Colin Davenport found himself seething, noting the joy Sandrine was taking in her new protégé. That was *his* position and God help anyone who dared encroach on the territory he'd claimed. He'd find a way to make this stupid girl sorry.

IT WAS NINE O'CLOCK WHEN SANDRINE FELT SATISFIED WITH THE DAY'S WORK and turned off the lights in the gallery. In only two days, Dani had proved to be an enormous asset, not only to the gallery, but to Sandrine's peace of mind. As if they were two separate entities.

She saw in the girl a younger version of herself: passionate about her field, driven to succeed, possessing all the attributes that would aid her in both areas. It hadn't been since she'd met Colin, all those years ago, that Sandrine felt such exhilaration in cultivating young talent.

As she opened the door to the stairwell, she was interrupted by a voice.

"I don't like 'er," it said.

Turning, Sandrine noted Colin's shape in the shadows. After all these years, she'd come to know his silhouette, even in the darkest shades of gray.

"That is not my concern," she said, the steel in her voice conveying her resolve. "She is my assistant for the gallery. It is none of your affair."

"The gallery *is* my affair," Colin asserted, advancing into the relatively more illuminating light spilling from the stairwell. "What you do affects me."

"I have honored our agreement," Sandrine asserted, striding toward him with confidence. "I have brought you and your work to America. The rest is up to you. What I do about my own business is simply that—my *own* business."

She turned toward the door to the stairs, but Colin grabbed the bend of her elbow, turning her toward him roughly. "Just make sure that your business and my business aren't at cross purposes, love," he snarled in a Cockney accent by which she was no longer charmed. He shoved her arm away from him.

Feeling emboldened, Sandrine turned to fully face him. "And what about your business?" she challenged. "How much time have you spent painting? You still have to finish your 'Sins' collection, yet every night you're out prowling the streets to satisfy your appetites. What about *my* needs?" She placed a hand on his cheek, making sure that the tips of her manicured nails impressed upon his skin. "*Mon cher*," she said softly, but with a slight edge in her voice, "if *I* fail, *you* fail."

Having made her point, she turned and ascended the stairs, neither waiting for nor wishing a reply.

AS SANDRINE LOCKED THE DOOR TO HER APARTMENT BEHIND HER, Jake and Tommy exited a movie theater on Broadway.

"I don't know," Tommy said. "I think I liked him more on stage."

"C'mon!" Jake countered. "That closeup where we thought he'd bite her neck and then dragged his lips on her skin? That never coulda been done so well in live theater!"

They'd just seen Frank Langella in "Dracula." Tommy knew when they'd spoken the day before that his only plans for Friday night were to hit the Eagle's Nest in search of information. His mention of going to the movies with Cara was nothing more than the fleshing out of his alibi.

But once he'd mentioned it, he knew it would make a perfect Saturday night date, especially since he and Jake had seen the Broadway production almost two years prior, shortly after it opened at the Martin Beck. It had been one their first extravagant dates.

He just hadn't anticipated the guilt he'd carry with him into the cinema.

The movie helped, though. He was reminded of an earlier time in their relationship when the schism over Jake's being closeted—not to mention the very recent addition of his own infidelity—weighed on the unique and precious chemistry they shared, one which blossomed when they enjoyed impromptu outings. Such as tonight's movie.

He pushed aside thoughts of Jake's lies to Prentiss and his own visit to a back room with Chris. He committed himself to enjoying the moment.

As they walked, both secretly wishing to take the other's hand and cursing the fact that they couldn't, Jake asked, "You wanna head home? Or grab a bite?" Tommy thought this over and, in that brief moment, Jake sensed an opportunity. He dove ahead. "Or find a bar?"

Tommy looked at Jake. "Really?" he asked.

"Yeah," Jake said. "Not down in the Village, obviously. But maybe someplace up this way. Don't Steven and Dmitri work uptown?"

"Are you sure?" Tommy asked with sincerity. His sudden deference to Jake's "closet" status surprised him, but it was genuine, nonetheless.

"Completely sure," Jake said with equal conviction. "I wanna share a drink with my boyfriend, and kiss him if I want, and in someplace other than my living room."

Tommy was dumbstruck, but even more in love. His guilt forgotten for the moment, he said, "Let's do it!"

He had no idea, but Jake was as surprised by his off-the-cuff suggestion as he was. Opening up to Brian the way he had the night before had helped him realize how much of his life he was missing out on, and that was something he'd vowed to change.

JAKE AND TOMMY HAD JUST ORDERED A FOURTH ROUND and had slipped dollar bills into Dmitri's and Steven's jock straps, laughing the entire time, when Dani and Iggy finished their shift at the Acropolis.

Emerging from the air-conditioned diner, Dani said, "Why in God's name is it so hot fucking at this hour?"

"It's NYC, girlfriend," Iggy said.

"You seem a little better tonight," she observed as they began their walk. They hadn't gotten to talk much since their short trip from the gallery, Saturdays being busy at the diner.

"I don't know," he said. "Maybe. Not really sure where I'm at."

She could tell something was on his mind, and had a feeling it wasn't about Cody. "What're you thinking?" she asked. "You've been distracted all evening."

"You probably won't like it," he said.

"Try me."

"Well, with you quitting the diner," Iggy began, "I think I will too. It just won't be the same without you there, and we both know Stavros isn't gonna put me on the wait staff. I think it's time for me to find something else."

"You wanna crash at my place again?" she offered. "We can talk more about your options."

"Actually," he said, "I think I need a little 'Iggy' time, if that's okay." His look to her requested her permission; her look in return granted it. "I thought I might go out for a drink. Remind myself that life is still waiting for me out there."

"You're sure?" Dani asked. Her unneeded permission notwithstanding, she worried. She was, after all, a Jewish mother in training.

"Yeah," Iggy said, his voice carrying a note of conviction, one that she welcomed. "Who knows?" he added. "Maybe I'll meet a guy who makes me forget all about Rembrandt!"

They both knew him forgetting about Cody was an impossibility, at least so soon, but they silently agreed to the conceit and went their separate ways at the next corner.

CHAPTER TWENTY

JAKE AND TOMMY STAYED AT UNCLE CHARLIE'S UNTIL TWO IN THE MORNING. Jake's sense of abandon once inside the bar surprised Tommy, Dmitri, and Steven, but it had surprised Jake even more.

Jake did indeed kiss his boyfriend in public, several times, in fact. They also danced and were quite boisterous when stuffing dollar bills into Steven's and Dmitri's jock straps. Tommy had never seen his boyfriend like this.

After taking a cab back to the brownstone, Jake started kissing Tommy and removing his clothes the moment the front door was shut. By the time they entered the living room, they were both naked. The sex wasn't slow and sensuous, as had been the case in the shower two nights prior. The unguarded freedom Jake had felt at the bar was still present, leading to passion that bordered on animalistic.

Tommy felt it too. Not wanting to admit to himself that his encounter with Chris had added a bit of fuel, he surrendered to the moment and was as enthusiastic as Jake.

Their passion took them from the living room to the dining room and, ultimately, to Jake's bed. It was here that Tommy was the one to make a surprising suggestion.

"Let me top you," he said as they fell onto the mattress in each other's arms.

"Really?" Jake asked, his smile lascivious.

"Really," Tommy asserted, moving above his boyfriend and pinning his arms to the bed.

Jake was loving this. "What's got into you?" His tone was playful and eager.

"It's not what's got into *me*, detective," Tommy said, sounding more dominant than Jake could ever remember hearing him. "It's what's *gonna* get into *you*."

"Then get to it, mister."

What followed was the most mind-blowing sex they'd had in ages and by five o'clock, they were dozing in each other's arms.

"I oughta suggest we go to a bar more often," Jake murmured into Tommy's hair as they fell asleep.

THE UNEXPECTED EXERTION OF THEIR MARATHON LOVE-MAKING, combined with the stress of the few days prior, had left them exhausted and they slept until noon on Sunday.

As they awoke, Jake asked Tommy to give an encore performance, and he was glad to oblige. Instead of providing Jake with another taste of his newfound dominance, this time Tommy was slow and tender, and they luxuriated in making it last.

After, Jake lay there gasping. "Oh, my God," he said. "I think I like this new side of you."

"Good," Tommy said, nuzzling Jake's neck, "'cause he's here to stay."

Jake turned and kissed him, and then said, "Unfortunately, I can't lay around with you all day, much as I want to. I gotta get my ass into the shower and get ready for work."

"No problem," Tommy assured him. "While you do that, I'll make us lunch."

"Don't bother," Jake said as he stood up. "I won't have time to eat it. I'll grab something from the diner across from the precinct. Wanna do something after my shift?"

"Can't. Got a cater-waiter gig tonight. It'll probably run late."

Jake looked disappointed. "I guess I can wait to get some more of *that*!"

Tommy laughed and watched his naked lover disappear through the bedroom door and down the hallway.

BY THE TIME HE PARKED THE CIVIC IN THE PRECINCT LOT AT TWO-FORTY, Jake felt like Superman, ready to leap any tall buildings he encountered.

He picked up a Spanish omelet from the Acropolis and headed into the station. Frank was already at his desk when he entered the squad room. His expression was grave.

"What is it?" Jake asked, setting his lunch onto his own desk.

"Patrolman just radioed in," he said. Jake felt his gut sink. "They found another body. Let's go."

Jake's omelet would go uneaten, but he didn't care. His appetite was gone.

JAKE AND FRANK ARRIVED AT THE CRIME SCENE ON THE WEST SIDE HIGHWAY and approached the uniforms, one of whom, Officer Sean Flanagan, walked toward them.

"That was fast," he said to Prentiss.

"Yeah, well, what can I say?" he replied. "Guess I couldn't wait to see your smiling face. You know I got the hots for you."

The young officer laughed, despite the circumstances.

Jake didn't show it, but he was annoyed by his partner's use of homosexuality as a punchline.

"Whadda we got?" Frank asked.

"Lady walkin' her dog saw a bum crouched over a body down by the water, started screamin' her fuckin' head off. That's when me and Sanchez came runnin'. Bum tried to flee, but he was too drunk and tripped over his own feet. Sanchez has him detained over by the squad car. Scene's secured, but the M.E. ain't here yet. Bum says he found the vic already dead, was just seein' what was in his pockets. Whadda ya want us to do with him?"

"Keep him where he is for now. Where's the witness?"

"Givin' a statement to one of the other guys."

"Good," Frank said. He turned to Jake. "Okay, let's see what we can see." The three of them headed toward the river. Frank and Jake were pulling on latex gloves.

Among weeds tall enough to block the view from the highway was a tableau they'd seen three times before with only slight variations. Sprawled face-down was another man with a good physique, arms flailed on either side, legs bent at the knees. Unlike the prior three victims, however, this one was black.

"The bum find him like this or turn him over to get at his wallet?" Frank asked.

"Said this is how he was," Flanagan replied. "Anyway, he threw the wallet into the river when he saw us comin'."

"Goddamn it!" Frank spat out.

Jake noted the van with the crime scene unit pull up and nodded in their direction, alerting his partner to their arrival.

"Okay, Griff," Frank groaned, running his hand over the top of his head. "Let's give the body a look. Then we can let the crime scene guys take over." To Flanagan, he said, "Let us know the minute the M.E. gets here, and I wanna talk to the dog-walker before she leaves."

With that, they approached the body and squatted beside it. Even with the victim face down, the savage slashing of his throat was visible from the side. They weren't expecting to see any blood pooled there, and they were proven to be right. Without any I.D. to work with, this one was going to be even harder.

DANI RUSHED INTO THE ACROPOLIS DINER FIFTEEN MINUTES BEHIND SCHEDULE having come straight from the gallery. She had practically run the whole way and was out of breath, as well as distracted by not arriving on time.

"You're late!" Stavros Karolis barked from behind the register. "And where's your friend? He's not here yet either!"

"You mean Iggy?" she asked. The question was unnecessary since she wasn't friends with anyone else who worked there, at least not outside the diner.

"Yeah, him! Your little colored friend, the *poustis*," he said, using the Greek word for pansy. "When he don't get here with you, he's always early. He's a no-show so far."

Dani thought back to their conversation after work the night before when he'd told her he was thinking about quitting. But it wouldn't be in Iggy's nature to just abandon a job without letting the boss know. Besides, he'd said he didn't want to work there without her, and she still had a week and a half to go before her last day.

"Okay if I use the phone to call his place?"

"Already done that. No answer."

"Well," Dani speculated, "maybe he got tied up and he's on his way."

"He better be!" Karolis barked as he headed toward the door to the kitchen.

Please get here, Ig, she thought. *I don't want you getting fired.*

By the time the dinner crowd, what there was of it, started filling the booths, Iggy still hadn't shown up for his shift. Karolis shot daggers at Dani every time he passed her, but she averted his angry gaze. It's not like she was Iggy's keeper.

Still, she was getting more worried with each passing minute.

HAVING FILED HIS STORY SATURDAY AFTERNOON, Brian didn't go into the newsroom on Sunday. Instead, he slept in late and took Woodward to Central Park for a run after lunch.

He considered calling Alex in the newsroom before he and the dog headed out. He was curious, mostly about Alex's interview at the gallery, but also to see if he'd been able to get his itch scratched the night before.

Woodward whined his impatience, prompting Brian to grab the leash. "Okay, buddy," he said as he hooked the leash to the dog's collar. "I'll call Uncle Alex tonight. Now let's go find a canine-loving cabby."

It was after two when they entered the park. Being out with Woodward like this was one of his few indulgences that effectively banished all thoughts of work. After a run, they played fetch with a tennis ball they'd brought along, and then just lazed in the grass. Brian removed his T-shirt, now rather sweaty, and soaked up some late-afternoon sun, all the while discreetly checking out the other topless guys working on their tans.

They didn't get home until almost seven. After feeding the dog, Brian called his service.

"You only have one message, Mr. Trent," Charlene told him. "It's from Griff, he wants you to call him at the office. Didn't leave a number, though."

"I have it," Brian told her. "Did he say anything else?"

"If he did, it's not written down," she said. "I didn't take the message, so I don't know."

"Okay," Brian said. "Thanks, Charlene. You have a good night."

"You do the same, Mr. Trent."

Brian was a little surprised that there wasn't a message from Alex. He usually wanted to gossip after a night of carousing. *Maybe he didn't get lucky*, he thought, *and is licking wounds.* Still, after his relentless pursuit of the gallery interview, it was a bit surprising he hadn't called about that.

He kept Jake's numbers on a pad next to his phone and dialed his direct line at the precinct.

"Homicide, Detective Griffin," Jake said.

"It's me, returning your call," Brian said. "What's up?"

He had to wait for Jake to reply and assumed that he was making sure he wouldn't be overheard. "I'm taking a dinner break at eight," he said at a much lower volume. "Can you meet me?"

"Absolutely," Brian said without hesitation. "Same place?"

"I can't be away from the squad room that long this time. Meet me at the Acropolis Diner across the street from the precinct."

"Isn't that a little too close to home?"

"I'll have to take that chance."

"Something happened, didn't it?"

"I'll tell you when I see you, but yeah."

AT SEVEN-FIFTY, BRIAN ENTERED THE DINER AND ASKED FOR A BOOTH away from the front windows. He was shown to a table in the back corner by an ill-tempered Greek man.

Jake arrived promptly at eight, looking nervous, and spotted Brian quickly. He waved off the owner, pointing to the back table, and headed in that direction.

"I got us a table away from the door and the windows," Brian said, who already had two menus for them.

"Good thinking," Jake replied.

A waitress appeared, pad in hand, and asked, "Are you ready to order?"

Jake turned and started to ask for more time, but said, "Oh, hi, Dani."

The waitress said, "Hi, detective," without her usual cheerfulness.

Sensing something was amiss, Jake asked, "You okay tonight?"

"I'm fine," she said, "but my friend's not. He didn't show up for his shift and didn't call. He's probably gonna get fired. Stavros is pissed off big time."

"I hope things work out for him," he said.

"So do I," Dani replied. "You guys know what you want, or do you need more time?"

Jake decided not to wait. He was familiar enough with the Acropolis menu to place his order, and Brian glanced at it quickly and selected the first thing that looked palatable. He wasn't here to eat.

"I'll be right back with waters and coffees," she said, tucking her pad into the pocket of her apron.

"Talk to me, man," Brian said once she'd stepped away.

"Number four was found today."

"Jesus Christ," Brian muttered. "Where?"

"West Side Highway, opposite Perry Street, near Pier 49."

"That's not too far from where Curtis was found," Brian noted.

"I know," Jake said, and paused as Dani approached with two cups of coffee and two glasses of water on a tray.

"Here you go, guys," she said as she placed the beverages on the table and departed.

Jake gave Brian a quick run-down of the crime scene, noting that, unlike the first three victims, this one was black.

"How's that fit with our 'serial' theory?" Brian asked.

"No idea," Jake said. "But it's gotta be the same perp. Except for his race, it was just like the others." He drank some water. "What really worries me," he continued, "is that we only found Fischer three days ago. There was about a month between each of the first three, and now only three days? Either he's escalating, or he was hunting outside the 6th Precinct in those interim periods."

"What's your money on?" Brian asked.

"I wish I knew," Jake said, dumping two packets of sugar into his coffee. "I'd like to think we would have heard if vics matching the M.O. were found in one of the other precincts, even in one of the boroughs, but with the way the department's been handling this, who the fuck knows?"

"What can you tell me about this victim?"

"Not much. A bum was robbing the body when a lady walking her dog screamed. Bum threw the vic's wallet into the Hudson, so we've got no I.D. Crime scene looked just like the others, but we won't know anything specific until the M.E. can get him on the table in the morning."

"Well," Brian said, "obviously it's too late to include him in tomorrow's story, but I can start working now on a follow-up for next Monday's edition." He thought of something. "Oh, yeah, I forgot to tell you. The composite is gonna run with the article tomorrow."

"Let's hope it does some good before we find number five," Jake said, reaching for more sugar packets.

Dani returned with their dinners, and they ate and talked strategy for the next half-hour.

"What would you think if I leaked this to one of the local news stations?" Brian asked.

"I thought of that too," Jake admitted. "Let's wait until after tomorrow."

"Why?"

"Because I wanna see what kind of a shit storm your article is gonna stir up in the department before we take it further," he said.

"Fair enough," Brian conceded. "Just keep me posted. I've got contacts at all three networks, plus Channel 5. We could have that sketch on every TV in the city by midweek."

When Dani came back with the check, Jake took it.

"Any word on your friend?" he asked her.

"No," she said. "When I take my break, I'll call his apartment."

"I'm sure everything's fine," Jake assured her.

"Thanks, detective," she said before returning to the kitchen.

"I got this," he told Brian, holding up the check. "You picked up the last one."

"And I'll get the next," Brian said. "And maybe it won't be a work meal."

Jake smiled, although it was weary. "That would be nice."

JAKE AND BRIAN LEFT THE DINER SEPARATELY TO AVOID BEING SEEN TOGETHER should anyone from the 6th be stepping out at the wrong moment.

"There you are!" Frank exclaimed when Jake entered the squad room. "We lucked out, man."

"How so?" Jake asked as he sat at his desk.

"We got an I.D. on our vic."

CHAPTER TWENTY-ONE

FRANK FILLED JAKE IN ON THE LATEST DEVELOPMENT.

Immediately before Jake entered the squad room, after his dinner with Brian at the Acropolis, Frank had gotten a call from Barry Thompson, the M.E. who covered for Miguel Ruiz on his days off. Frank had told him at the crime scene that the vic was a John Doe.

"Rather than wait for Ruiz to get in tomorrow," Frank said, "he took the prints off the body and had some people in his office get to work. Turns out our vic had a record."

"Damn," Jake said. "That was fast."

"He had a scar on the pad of his left thumb. Made a match easy."

"Who was he?"

"Name's Kenneth Wilson," Frank said, reading from his notes. "Age 29. Got picked up during the Stonewall bullshit for resisting arrest, but got charged with underage drinking. Don't have a current address on him, but that won't take long now that we have a name."

Jake knew what that meant: coming in early on Monday, when government offices were open, and getting on the phone.

"How early you wanna start on this tomorrow?" he asked, almost dreading the answer.

"Ain't nothing we can find out at nine that won't still be there at noon," Frank said. "You wanna take the DMV and I'll hit up Social Security?"

"Whatever you want, Frank," Jake agreed, grateful for the three-hour reprieve he'd been granted in the morning.

Frank glanced at the clock on the wall, double-checking it against the Timex on his wrist. "Curran and Schwartz'll be here in a couple hours," he said. "Let's take our time with the crime scene report and call it a night."

"Sounds good," Jake said and pulled the forms out of his desk.

DANI ARRIVED AT THE GALLERY AT TEN ON MONDAY, not having slept well.

She'd called Iggy's apartment during her break at the diner and then again when she got home, getting no answer. She continued trying him until exhaustion overtook her and she begrudgingly went to bed.

Upon letting her in, Sandrine exclaimed, "*Ma chérie*, what is wrong?"

"Do I look that bad?" Dani asked.

"*Non, pas mal*" her boss replied, waving a hand to dismiss the inference. "You just look like you haven't slept. That is all."

In brief, she told Sandrine about Iggy's absence from the diner and her inability to reach him by phone, adding his connection to Cody and what had happened to him. "If it's okay with you," she said, "I'd like to take a break at some point and go to his apartment. See if he's there and just not answering his phone."

"*D'accord*, Dani," Sandrine readily agreed. "Would you like to go now?"

"No," Dani said. "I want to feel like I've accomplished something worthwhile first, and I have a feeling that I'll only be able to do that here."

Sandrine understood. Many times over the years, the only place she felt valid was in a gallery or an artist's studio.

"Then come along, *cherie*," she said, putting an arm around Dani's shoulders. "We have plenty that we can accomplish together."

She led Dani into the back room where work, along with coffee and croissants, awaited.

BRIAN WAS ALREADY AT HIS DESK WHEN ALEX GOT TO THE NEWSROOM, takeout coffee in hand.

"Hey," he said. "Good morning."

Alex just grunted, which confirmed Brian's suspicion that Saturday night's quest had been a washout.

"How was your weekend?" Brian asked.

"No comment," he said. "Other than *finally* getting to interview Sandrine Delacroix—who is *divine*, by the way—and tour her gallery, the weekend was a disaster."

"No fun Saturday night?"

Alex looked at him with the deadest of deadpans. "Do I look like I had fun?"

Brian laughed, but not unkindly. "Hang in there, sport," he said, "it'll find you when you least expect it." Yes, it was a platitude, he conceded to himself, but not an entirely unfounded one.

"But Sunday made up for it," Alex said. "Sandrine showed me the upper floors under construction. *And* I got to meet the artist." Brian raised his eyebrows, impressed with his colleague's coup. "He wouldn't consent to an interview, but I got to meet him at least.

"And get this: he said he was checking me out at Uncle Charlie's last week!"

"Damn," Brian said, "look at you go!"

"How about you?" Alex asked. "How was your Sunday?"

"Rejuvenating," Brian said. "Woodward and I went to Central Park, and then I had dinner with a friend."

"Oh?" Alex's curiosity was piqued. "How close of a friend? Do tell!"

"Just a friend," Brian assured his co-worker. "Somebody I met working on a story. We enjoy each other's company. Nothing more." Seeing Alex's titillated expression, he added, "He has a boyfriend! Whom I met. Knock it off! You work at the *Voice*, not the *Enquirer*!"

They both laughed and got to work.

About fifteen minutes later, a delivery man entered the newsroom pushing a hand-truck stacked with the new issue. Brian made a beeline and grabbed a copy as soon as the binding on the papers had been clipped. He was disappointed that his story didn't make page one, but took consolation in the fact that it filled page three which, in the news trade, is like a second page one.

The composite sketch was in the center of the copy with "Murders Could Be Work of Serial Killer" across the top. He'd incorporated his coverage of Cody Fischer's murder into the larger article, making it the lead and then expounding on the possible—make that *probable*—connection between the crimes.

"Let me see one," Alex, suddenly at his side, demanded. Brian pulled a copy off the pile and handed it to him. Alex rifled through the pages until he found his feature on Galerie Delacroix. He'd brought a staff photographer with him, so the story featured a shot of Sandrine in front of "Mourning Becomes Electric." He wasn't surprised to note that she looked fabulous.

"See?" he said, holding his copy open for Brian to view. "I *told* you she was divine!" He then scanned the story and was furious that the editor had cut a third of what he'd written.

Brian was oblivious to Alex's rant. Looking at page three, he realized that he and Jake had passed the point of no return with this.

"CAN SOMEONE TELL ME WHAT THE FUCK THIS IS?!" Captain Eddie Young screamed across the squad room, a crumbled copy of the *Voice* clenched in his upraised fist.

Everyone present looked at him with blank expressions and he stormed back into his office, slamming the door behind him hard enough to make the glass rattle. Reemerging only a moment later, he yelled, "Griffin! Get in here!"

Jake and Frank had only been at their desks for about fifteen minutes when Young had his meltdown. Looking at Frank with an expression that said, "My guess is as good as yours," he approached the captain's office. He took a mental, if not physical, deep breath.

"Sir?" he said from the open doorway.

"Get in here," Young repeated and Jake obliged. "And shut the door.

"Is this your work?" the captain demanded the moment the door was closed.

"Is what my work, sir?" He silently cursed himself. Being a detective, he was well aware that a response of this nature was a red flag to interrogators.

"This!" Young yelled, hurling the *Voice* onto his desk. Page three stared up at them.

Taking time to give the impression that he was reading an unfamiliar headline, he said, "Shit. But I'm not sure what you mean, cap." It was an evasion, Jake knew, and he leaned in to read the article for the third time. He'd picked up a copy from the corner bodega on his way in and read it twice before tossing it into a trash can on the sidewalk.

"No?" Young said loudly. "You come to me with a bullshit theory on Thursday, and on Monday it's a headline in the *Voice*?"

"I'm not sure what to say, sir," Jake replied. "They've been covering these murders from the start. Maybe the reporter drew the same conclusion. Or, I should say, speculation."

"It says 'anonymous source within the N.Y.P.D.'! Tell me that's not you!"

"It's not me, sir. The only people I've discussed these cases with are you and Prentiss. But, to be fair," he continued, "we're not the only ones at the 6th who know about them. Lots of the guys are talking. For all we know, the 'anonymous source' is a kid in the mailroom or a secretary. You know what the media's like, they'll quote anybody if it sells papers."

"Well, I better not see anymore shit like this in print, you hear me?"

"I hear you, sir, loud and clear, but I'm not the leak. There's not much I can do."

Young didn't seem satisfied, but he had no proof. "Get outta here," he barked.

"Yes, sir." Jake left the office and returned to his desk. He'd dodged that bullet, but wondered how long his luck would hold out when Brian published more stories.

He and Frank spent the next hour on their phones. Like many New Yorkers, Kenneth Wilson didn't have a driver's license, but Social Security was able to provide them with his place of employment—he'd been a junior trader at a lesser brokerage firm downtown—as well as a home address on East 132nd Street. Frank dispatched a unit to secure the location until they could get there.

As they were about to leave, Frank's phone rang. Grabbing it, he said, "Homicide. Detective Prentiss."

"Detective?" the voice on the other end said. "This is Martin Ellis, with Lamont & Ellis? My partner, Pete Lamont, gave me your card and told me to call you. We're all broken up about Cody. What can I do to help?"

Frank made a gesture to Jake, indicating that their departure would be delayed, and sat down.

Twenty minutes later, he hung up.

"That was Lamont's partner at the ad agency," he told Jake. "He got back into town last night and Lamont filled him in this morning."

"And?"

"And nothing," Frank said. "Couldn't tell me anything more than Lamont did, which was also pretty much nothing. Let's head to Wilson's office and then up to Harlem. Then I figured we could make the rounds of the gay bars with the sketch. The ones that're open, anyway."

THEIR VISIT TO KENNETH WILSON'S OFFICE proved as uninformative as had their interview with Pete Lamont. Wilson had been a hard worker, reliable and responsible, and an asset to the firm.

Jake and Frank didn't need to be told that "asset to the firm" meant he made them money.

Unlike Fischer, though, Wilson was not out of the closet at work. The news of his sexuality took his supervisor, Zachary Hoffman, by surprise, causing him to adopt a look of disgust.

"Surely this crime was related to … *that*," Hoffman said, not troubling himself to mask his distaste, "and nothing to do with the firm."

"It's still too soon to say, sir," was all Frank said by way of reply.

Likewise, their search of the deceased's office yielded nothing that could be of use to them. After speaking briefly with two of Wilson's co-workers, they headed uptown.

THE SUPER IN KENNETH WILSON'S BUILDING GREETED THEM AT THE MAIN DOOR. The uniforms who'd secured the scene had apprised him of the situation, making that an unnecessary task for Frank when they arrived.

"Kid never gave me no trouble," the super said as they climbed the stairs to the second floor. "Nice kid. Little fruity for my taste, but the world's changin', brother. Guess us old-timer's just gotta keep up." Jake adjudged the super to be nearing seventy and wondered how Frank, only fifty this past June, felt about being called an "old-timer."

Still, it was clear to Jake that the super was attempting to bond with Frank over their shared ethnicity more than the implication that they were of an age, so to speak.

"But these kids," the super continued, shaking his head, "they's fightin' the same battles we been fightin' for years. I feels they pain, brother, I feels they pain. More power to 'em, is what I says. You and me, we knows what them struggles is like."

They reached the second-floor landing and the super groaned. "I's gettin' too old for these stairs. Arthritis gettin' to me somethin' fierce. Guess it won't be long 'fore I gotta give up the job." Catching his breath, he proceeded down the hall.

Unlocking the door to Wilson's apartment, he stepped aside to allow them entrance. "Y'all needs me for anything," he said, "I'm in apartment 1B. Jus' knock. Name's Jerome. Jus' lemme know when y'all leave so's I can lock up." With that, he headed back downstairs, taking his time in deference to his knees.

The apartment reflected the moderate success its occupant had been enjoying in his career.

Unlike the mix-and-match décor of Cody Fischer's studio, Wilson's two-bedroom home looked as if he'd hired a first-class decorator. The living room furniture all matched and was complemented beautifully by the carpet and the artwork, all of which were original paintings and not prints or reproductions. Small pottery lined the marble mantlepiece, interspersed with framed photos, most of which were of the deceased and another young black man, the others included an elderly woman. Jake surmised from the poses in the former that Wilson might have had a boyfriend, especially since two of the framed photos included all three. A thriving potted ficus plant stood in one corner, and crimson-hued velveteen curtains adorned the two windows overlooking the street.

"Looks like Mr. Wilson was doing alright for himself," Frank observed.

The second bedroom served as Kenneth Wilson's home office, and that's where the detectives started. What this location *did* have in common with Cody Fischer's apartment was the focus of their search, which quickly yielded both a personal calendar and an address book, two items which would aid them in the investigation. Wilson's personal planners were rather more informative that Fischer's had been, including numerous notations of gatherings with an Aunt Thelma, as well as quite a few plans with someone identified only as "O." Given the varied specifics of these notations, Jake surmised that the "O" was the young man in the photos on the mantle. By process of elimination, the elderly woman must be Aunt Thelma. While the two may have died under similar circumstances, Wilson and Fischer had clearly lived much different lives.

While Frank looked through the drawers of Wilson's desk, Jake, acting on his hunch, flipped through the address book, searching for anyone whose first name began with the letter O. Near the end of the book, he found what he was looking for. Owen Toussaint was entered, listing an address in midtown and phone numbers for home, work, and answering service, along with a marginal notation of a date some four years prior, punctuated by an exclamation point. Jake surmised that it was the day Kenneth and Owen had met.

"I think I got something," he said. Frank interrupted his search and turned his full attention to Jake.

"You saw all those entries in the datebook mentioning an 'O'?" Jake asked.

"Yeah?"

"There's an Owen Toussaint in here," Jake continued. "I think it may have been Wilson's boyfriend."

"Good work, partner," Frank said. "I ain't found shit in this desk. Let's check out the rest of the place and track down this Owen. Maybe he can tell us who the next of kin is."

The rest of their search was completed rather quickly. Kenneth Wilson's life had apparently been very straightforward and, his lifestyle notwithstanding, traditional and ordinary. With only the datebook and phone directory encased in evidence bags, Frank and Jake left the apartment. Frank went downstairs to summon the super.

Once the super, whose surname was Givens, had locked the door, Frank and Jake provided him with their cards, asking that he call if he remembers anything or notices something suspicious. They affixed the yellow "Crime Scene" tape over the door to Wilson's apartment and headed back to the station.

CHAPTER TWENTY-TWO

AS FRANK DROVE BACK TO THE PRECINCT, he suggested to Jake that they hold off on making the rounds of the bars until after the dinner hour and focus on their one lead so far in the Wilson case, namely Owen Toussaint. As always, Jake deferred to him.

Once in the squad room, Frank handed Jake the address book. "Why don't you handle the call," he said. "You've got a lighter touch than me."

Jake wasn't sure what, if anything, that meant. Nevertheless, he obliged.

Flipping open Kenneth Wilson's address book to the pages headed "S-T," he located Owen Toussaint's work number and dialed.

"McCambridge & Blair," a woman's voice answered with efficiency. "How may I direct your call?"

"Owen Toussaint, please," Jake said.

"Certainly," she replied. "Just one moment."

Jake heard the generic "hold" music and then ringing.

"Owen Toussaint," the voice answered.

"Good afternoon, Mr. Toussaint," he began. "My name is Jake Griffin, I'm a detective with the N.Y.P.D."

"Yes?" Owen said, a distinct hint of apprehension in his voice.

"I was wondering if you'd be available for my partner and me to come by your office this afternoon."

"My schedule's open, but may I ask what this is in reference to?"

"I'd rather explain that in person," Jake said. "Where is your office located?"

Owen Toussaint provided an address in the west forties, not far from Times Square. "Our law offices occupy the entire fourth floor, so you won't have any trouble finding us." He paused. "Should I be concerned, detective?"

"We just want to ask you a few questions regarding a case," was all Jake would allow.

They agreed on four o'clock and hung up.

After being told what time their appointment was—unnecessary because he'd been listening—Frank excused himself to use the men's room. Jake took advantage of a moment alone and dialed Brain at the *Voice*.

"We've got an I.D.," Jake said in hushed tones as soon as Brian picked up.

"Okay," Brian said, "I'm ready."

Jake told him Wilson's name, as well as his place of employment.

"Thanks," Brian said. "Keep me posted."

"Will do," Jake replied and hung up.

THE RECEPTIONIST AT MCCAMBRIDGE & BLAIR escorted Frank and Jake to Owen Toussaint's office. Judging from her voice, it was the same woman Jake had spoken to earlier.

"Have a seat, detectives," Owen said, standing to greet them, hand extended. They presented their cards and, after Owen shook hands with both, they took seats. The attorney closed the door to his office and sat behind his desk.

"Mr. Toussaint—"

Owen interrupted Frank with his voice, as well as a raised hand. "Please, before we go any further, tell me what this is in reference to." Owen, an associate at the firm, handled tax law and their cards said Homicide Division, so he knew this wasn't regarding a case he was representing.

Frank glanced at Jake, handing off the baton. It wasn't often that Frank let Jake take the lead when questioning a witness. Not relishing the task, Jake said, "I believe you were acquainted with Kenneth Wilson?"

"Yes," Owen said, "we're … friends. Why? What's this about?" Having been focused on the necessary discretion of his answer, the wording of Jake's question only then hit him. "And what do you mean 'were'?" he asked, clearly agitated.

"Mr. Toussaint," Jake said gently, "I'm sorry to inform you that Mr. Wilson is dead."

"What?" Owen gasped. "What do you mean? He can't be." Jake could see the attorney's eyes begin to fill with tears and his Adam's apple bobbing up and down.

"I'm sorry, sir," Jake repeated. "He was found yesterday afternoon just off the West Side Highway. He'd been murdered."

"I can't believe this," Owen said. It was clear that the man was in shock. "Was it a mugging?"

"We're still not sure. If it's okay," Jake continued, pulling a pad and pen from his pocket, "we'd like to ask you a few questions."

Not yet completely focused, Toussaint nodded his consent.

"Can you tell us," Jake continued, "when was the last time you saw Mr. Wilson?"

"We had lunch on Saturday and then did some window-shopping."

"And where was this?"

"Fifth Avenue," Owen replied.

"And you didn't have plans Saturday evening?" Jake asked.

"No," Owen said. "I had to be in court first thing this morning, so I had to spend all day yesterday preparing. Kenny and I said goodbye before dinner. I made an early night of it."

"Can anyone verify that?" Frank interjected.

"Am I a suspect?" Owen asked, disbelief written all over his face and saturating his tone.

"It's just procedure, sir," Jake said.

"I don't know," Owen said, clearly searching his memory. "I was on the phone with one of the partners here from eight until around ten or so."

"Can you give us his name," Jake asked.

Owen did so. Jake wrote the name Eli Mirisch in his pad, and Frank did likewise.

"Do you know if Mr. Mirisch is in the office today?" Frank asked.

"I believe so," Owen replied.

"And then?" Jake asked. "After you finished your phone call with Mr. Mirisch?"

"And then I went to bed," Owen continued.

"Alone?" Frank asked, not harshly.

"Yes, detective," Owen said, his indignation evident. "Alone."

"Do you know what plans Mr. Wilson might have had for Saturday evening?" Jake asked, reclaiming the reins of the interview.

"He didn't mention anything specific. Usually, if I have to work on a Friday or Saturday night, Kenny just bar-hops."

"Alone or with friends?" Jake asked.

"Both, depending on who's around," Owen replied. "I still can't believe this." Jake could tell the attorney was struggling to control his emotions. He imagined Owen Toussaint, Esquire, would lock his office door when they left and have a good cry. He felt for the man.

"Did Mr. Wilson have family here in the city?"

"Just an aunt, but they were close," Owen said. "His parents were killed in a car accident ten years ago. Miss Thelma raised Kenny after that. He lived there while he put himself through City College.

"She lives a couple of blocks from his place," he continued. "When he got settled in his job, he moved out, but he wanted to stay close." He gave Jake the woman's address. "If it's not against protocol, I'd like to be the one to tell her. It might be easier coming from me. She's almost eighty."

Jake glanced at Frank, who nodded. "That'll be fine, Mr. Toussaint," Jake said.

"How did you and Mr. Wilson meet, if I may ask?" he continued.

"Through work," Owen replied. "I was representing a partner at his firm."

"Don't they have in-house counsel?" Frank asked.

"They do," Owen explained, "but this was a matter of his personal taxes. That's all I can say. Privilege applies." Looking back to Jake, he went on. "Anyway, that's how we met. I had been visiting my client at the firm and someone introduced us." He glanced at Frank, then back to Jake. "In passing."

"And how long ago was this?" Jake asked.

"A little more than four years," Owen said. "May of seventy-five. Saigon had just fallen. I remember we talked about that a lot on our first—" He glanced briefly at Frank and returned his attention to Jake. "The first time we met for dinner. Socially."

"Mr. Toussaint, what I'm about to bring up is somewhat delicate," Jake said, to which Owen nodded his consent, but not without apprehension. "It's the matter of identifying Mr. Wilson's remains."

"I see," Owen said.

"You mentioned an aunt," Jake continued, "but given her age, it might be too much for her. Considering you were close with him would you be able to do that?"

The attorney's eyes once again moistened. "Yes, detective," he said. "No need to put Miss Thelma through that ordeal."

They made arrangements for Owen to visit the coroner's office after he left work that evening.

Jake set his pad and pen on the desk and pulled a handkerchief from his jacket pocket. After blowing his nose, he said, "Again, Mr. Toussaint, I'm very sorry for your loss. You have our cards. If you think of anything, no matter how small, please call us. And please give our information to Mr. Wilson's aunt and ask her to do the same."

"Certainly, detectives," Owen said as if an automaton. "Let me see you out."

He escorted them back to the lobby and they were about to leave when Jake said, "Damn! I left my pad and pen on the desk." To Owen specifically, he asked, "May I go back to get them?"

"Of course, detective," Toussaint said.

"While you do that," Frank interjected, "I'll follow up with Mirisch."

Owen led Jake back to his office, retracing their steps down the hallway.

Once inside, Jake turned to the attorney. "Look," he said hurriedly and in a hushed tone, acting solely on an unexpected impulse. "I know you and Mr. Wilson were involved, and I also know you can't say so. I'm in the same boat, so I get what you're having to deal with, believe me." He grabbed his pad and pen, which he'd deliberately left behind, and scribbled his numbers onto a page before ripping it out and handing it to Owen. "Call me if you remember anything you don't want on the record," Jake said. "Or just if you need to."

"Thank you, Detective Griffin," he said, not bothering to hide the depth of his appreciation as tears spilled from his brimming eyes. "For the offer and for your discretion." He offered his hand, and this shake was noticeably less routine.

"And let me say again," Jake offered, their hands still clasped, "how truly sorry I am for your loss."

"Thank you." It was clear that there were many levels to Owen's statement, and nothing more needed to be said.

"You stay here," Jake suggested. "I can see myself out, and you probably want to be alone."

Owen Toussaint thanked him again and sat down at his desk, looking numb. The detective closed the door as he left the office.

As Jake made his way back to the lobby and Frank, it occurred to him that his impulsive admission, veiled though it was, marked the first time he'd come out to anyone outside his immediate circle of acquaintance, his begrudging admission to Brian a few nights prior notwithstanding.

Rejoining Frank, they left the offices of McCambridge & Blair.

ONCE BACK IN FRANK'S CAR AND HEADED SOUTHBOUND, the senior partner suggested they grab a bite in transit and then make the rounds of the bars in the Village.

They had burgers at a diner in Chelsea.

"You did good back there," Frank said. "But how come you didn't ask Toussaint about the nature of their relationship?"

"Didn't have to," Jake said. Seeing Frank's raised eyebrows, he added, "Did you get a look at the photos on the mantle and how many times 'O' was in the datebook? And then the way he reacted to the news? C'mon, partner, you trained me better than that."

"Okay," Frank said with a satisfied smile, dipping a French fry into ketchup. "Just wanted to make sure." He shoved the fry into his mouth. "And yes, I did see the photos and the datebook. *And* his eyes."

"I feel for the man," Jake dared saying. This was the first of these homicides that involved a boyfriend and, as such, the first time on this case he'd had to witness that particular brand of grief, not to mention the fucked-up filter through which it had to be expressed.

"Yeah, I know what you mean," Frank said, surprising Jake. "Guy looked devastated. So far on this case, I only had to break that news over the phone. Always sucks to see 'em react. Can't imagine what I'd do if some cop came to my door to tell me Loretta was dead. Guess it ain't all that different."

Although he didn't know it, Frank had just earned himself a little more respect from his partner.

After finishing their meal, they headed to the Village and parked in a lot. "I'll submit an expense report," Frank told Jake as he pocketed the receipt.

Jake noted Frank's discomfort being inside the bars when patrons were there, doing the things patrons of such establishments do. They visited more than half a dozen such places, all with the same result: either no one remembered anyone who looked like the sketch, or they knew several people who did. Frank and Jake collected names and, when possible, phone numbers and-or addresses of the associates whom the witnesses allegedly recognized from the composite. Not surprisingly, this information was scant, bordering on non-existent.

Jake had taken note of something else, something far more unsettling to him. At each of their stops, he observed men connecting and leaving in pairs, sometimes in trios. While Jake was far from being a barfly, he clearly recognized one-night stands in their larval stage.

Someone's been killing us, he thought, *finding us in these bars. And all of you are still going home with total strangers.*

"Whole lotta nothin'," Frank groused as they headed back to the parking lot. "Whadda ya bet none of these names lead to anything?"

"I'd bet a lot," Jake said. "And I ain't a betting man."

THEY ARRIVED BACK IN THE SQAUD ROOM AROUND NINE-THIRTY, leaving only ninety minutes of their shift remaining.

Once seated at his desk, Jake picked up the phone and dialed Tommy's number at his Grove Street apartment.

"Hey, it's me," Jake said.

"Hey, handsome," Tommy replied.

"Wanna come over tonight after my shift? I could pick you up."

"Totally," Tommy said.

"One thing, though," Jake went on. "Do you mind if I invite our friend over? Only for a little while."

"I guess not," Tommy conceded, understanding that Jake was choosing not to say Brian's name aloud in the squad room. "But not another really late night, okay? I want some time alone with you."

"I haven't even called him yet," Jake said. "Wanted your 'okay' first. And I promise. Not too late." He gave Tommy a nutshell version of the latest developments. "Thanks for understanding."

They said their goodbyes and, using his finger to depress the disconnect button, Jake called Brian at home.

"Hey," he said when Brian answered. "It's me."

"Hey, you," Brian replied. "What's up?"

"Just wondering if there's any chance you can come up to my place tonight. I know it'll be late for you. I just wanted to bring you up to date, and not over the phone."

"Sure," Brian said, "I can do that. What time you want me there?"

"Well, I can actually pick you up, if you want. I'll be getting Tommy on Grove Street, so we'll be passing right through your neighborhood."

"That works," Brian agreed and gave him the address.

Jake hung up and noticed Frank looking at him. "Was one of those phone calls your mysterious lady friend?" he asked.

"No," Jake said without lying, a welcome change. "Just a couple of buddies." He realized Frank could overhear his conversations and found himself not caring. Well, caring a little *less*, to be precise.

"Well, we all gotta unwind however we can," Frank said. "Me? I got Loretta."

"And you're a lucky man, Frank," Jake said, wishing he could speak Tommy's name with the same freedom and affection.

CHAPTER TWENTY-THREE

ON WEST 23ᴿᴰ STREET, TOMMY GOT OUT OF THE CIVIC so Brian could climb into the backseat.

"How was your weekend, Tommy?" Brian asked once he and his gear were situated, and Tommy was back riding shotgun.

"It was nice," Tommy replied, understanding that Brian was curious if his break from the investigation had served its purpose. "I went out with friends Friday night, and on Saturday, Jake and I saw 'Dracula.'"

"I knew about the movie," Brian said. "He told me last night at dinner."

Tommy cast a look in Jake's direction.

His eyes on the road, Jake sensed Tommy's glance. "We met at the diner across from the precinct," he said. "I wanted to keep him in the loop with the fourth victim."

"Were you able to come up with anything?" he asked. "Anything new, I mean."

"Not really," Jake allowed. "That's why I asked if you minded Brian coming over tonight."

"Well," Tommy said, "I hope you have more luck this time."

As Jake drove uptown, he told them about his visit to McCambridge & Blair, including his private conversation with Owen Toussaint before he and Frank made their exit.

"That poor man," Tommy said. "How was he when you left?"

"Like you'd expect," Jake said, sounding weary. "He just found out his boyfriend had been murdered, and then had to play along with the bullshit of not showing his true reaction. I actually wanted to hug him."

"You did the next best thing," Brian assured Jake. "You came out to him, letting him know he wasn't alone."

"I'm really proud of you for that," Tommy said. "You took a chance— a *big* one, for you—to help somebody who needed it."

"That's the finest of New York's Finest, my friend," Brian said from the backseat, reaching forward to give Jake's shoulder a squeeze.

"It's just that, sitting there looking at him, I saw myself," Jake said. "There he was, having to squash down all this pain just to keep up this stupid façade. If he'd been in a straight relationship and we delivered the same news, he would have been free to express himself." Jake paused. "It wasn't a mirror I enjoyed looking into."

Tommy reached past the stick shift and placed a hand on Jake's thigh. "I repeat," he said, "I'm really proud of you."

"So am I," Brian added, his hand still on Jake's shoulder.

Jake realized he'd never felt such a sense of community, being comforted by the physical touch of his lover and his newfound friend. But with that sense of community came the almost unbearable realization that he had the same connection with the four victims, as well, and owed them no less than he'd provided Owen Toussaint.

Something occurred to him. "Brian, what would you think," he began with caution, "if we brought Owen in on what we're doing?" Before either could respond, he continued. "Hear me out. He's a lawyer, which suggests he thinks like we do. Okay, he handles tax law, but still. Plus, he's already involved, however tangentially, and has a vested interest."

Brian mulled this over. "Well," he said, "you met him, I didn't. If you think it wouldn't muddy the waters, what with his emotional involvement and all, I trust your judgment."

ONCE THEY'D ARRIVED AT THE BROWNSTONE, Jake pulled out a folded piece of printer paper. He'd photocopied the page of Kenneth—make that *Kenny*—Wilson's address book that included Owen Toussaint's information.

He dialed the phone.

"Hello?" Owen Toussaint sounded like someone who'd been through several wringers.

"Mr. Toussaint," Jake said. For all his usual professionalism, the nervousness he was feeling was evident in his voice. "This is Detective Griffin. I'm sorry to call so late. I hope I didn't wake you."

"Oh, hi, detective," he replied. "No. Don't know how much sleep I'll be getting now. Is there a development?"

"No, unfortunately," Jake said. "And I understand. About you not sleeping." It was clear from his tone that he meant it.

"Thank you again," Owen said. "For this afternoon, I mean. You didn't have to tell me what you did, and I want you to know how much it meant. I really appreciate that." He started to cry. "I can't believe he's gone. I feel so alone."

"You're not alone, Owen," Jake said, acting on instinct. "That's why I called. If you need to go right now, I understand. We can talk another time."

"No, no," Owen said, getting his grief under a modicum of control. "What did you want?"

Jake went on to explain the alliance that he'd formed with Brian in an effort to shine a light on what they believed was going on.

"I'm in," Owen said without equivocation and before being asked. "When do you want to get together? I'll make myself available day or night."

"Well," Jake said, not sure if he should broach it, "Brian's here at my place right now."

"What's the address?" Owen asked, the resolve in his voice squelching his grief. "Not like I'm gonna be sleeping anyway."

TWENTY MINUTES LATER, JAKE'S DOORBELL RANG.

Owen Toussaint looked like death warmed over, but under the heavy veil of sorrow was a determination that was palpable. Jake introduced him to Brian and Tommy, who instinctively hugged the attorney. Owen returned the embrace and said, "Thank you."

Moving to the dining room table, they all took seats and Jake brought Owen up to speed on what they'd done so far. Brian slid a copy of the *Voice*, opened to page three, to Owen, who told them he'd read it that morning.

"When I read this, I had no idea it had already affected me," he said, dazed by the realization. "It's good," he continued, reigning in his emotions. "Ballsy." He looked to Jake and said, "I'm guessing you're the 'anonymous source'?"

"I am," Jake admitted.

"You should be honored," Tommy told the latest addition to their circle. "Today when Jake talked to you alone? You're the very first person he's ever come out to that wasn't already a friend."

Owen looked at Jake. "I get that," he said. "And I am. Honored, I mean."

"I had to say something," Jake shared. "I was watching you having to hide your feelings, and I was having to hide my understanding. All because a straight guy was sitting there. I couldn't leave without talking to you alone."

"Sometimes the worst things help make the best things happen," Owen mused. "I'd do anything to have Kenny back, but I'm glad that something good could come of it." They could all see that he wasn't glad about anything, but respected his statement.

"If you're not up to talking about it, I understand," Jake said with caution. "You visited the morgue?"

"Yes," said Owen, the memory of the event clear on his face. "It was Kenny."

Jake already knew this, the scarred fingerprint having confirmed it.

"And his aunt?" Jake continued.

"Miss Thelma's a force to be reckoned with," Owen shared. "It was obvious that it devastated her, but she stayed firm. More firm than I did. She wound up comforting me. I can't tell you how much I admire that lady."

"Owen," Jake continued, "was Kenny local? What I'm asking is, will his funeral be here in the city?"

"I believe so," Owen said. "He grew up in Harlem. His parents are gone, as I mentioned in the office, but that's the only home he's ever had." The reality hit him. "I guess it'll be up to me to make the arrangements. I can't put that on Miss Thelma's shoulders, at least not solely." He started to cry softly. Brian, seated next to him at the table, slid a sincere and comforting arm around his shoulders. Jake reached out and held Tommy's hand, and the three allowed Owen his expression of grief.

"I'm sorry," he said, at last collecting himself. The other three spoke at once, all assuring him that he owed no apologies.

"Thank you all," Owen said. "Like you," he told Jake, "I'm not out to many people. If you hadn't called, I wouldn't have been among friends tonight."

Jake was struck by his comment. Yes, he realized, we're all friends here. A community. Last Wednesday, two of these men wouldn't have been sitting at his table, and yet here they all were, united in mutual support and a desire to do something that no one else wanted to do.

"The reason I asked about the funeral," Jake said, "is because I'd like your permission to have undercovers there. A lot of times, a spree killer will attend the services to get an added thrill." He went on to explain that the first three victims had all been buried out of town, making Kenny's services the first that would be local.

"Anything you need, Jake," he complied. "If it helps, I'm on board. I know Miss Thelma would agree."

"Might be a good idea if you don't tell her about the undercovers," Jake said. "The fewer people that know, the better."

"I completely understand."

"Okay, moving on," Jake said, trying not to sound insensitive. "Owen, you bring a new perspective to this group. As a lawyer, what're your thoughts?"

Happy to be actually doing something, Owen said, "I'm not sure what my expertise can offer. I only come into the picture once someone's been charged. But I'll do what I can. For Kenny." He paused. "For all of them."

"For all of *us*," Brian amended.

DESPITE JAKE'S PROMISE TO TOMMY, IT WASN'T A SHORT MEETING.

During the course of their brainstorming session, Jake brought up his observations at the bars earlier that night while questioning potential witnesses with Frank.

"It's probably like most other things," Brian said. "People know about something, but secretly believe it won't happen to them." He lit a cigarette and laughed. "Case in point."

At around three, Tommy went into the kitchen to make more coffee and see what snacks were available. He called to Jake.

"Baby," he said, "can I see you a second?"

Jake excused himself from the table and headed to the kitchen.

"I know, I know," he was saying as he entered. "I promised it wouldn't be a late—"

Tommy interrupted him. "Don't worry," he assured him. "I'm fine. Especially after meeting Owen." He took a deep breath and looked Jake in the eyes. "There's just something I need to tell you."

"What?" Jake asked.

Tommy let him know about Charlie's Angels and their secret mission, omitting the back room with Chris Albright.

"Are you *crazy*?" Jake blurted out. "You coulda put yourself in danger!"

"I'm fine," Tommy assured his boyfriend. "Really." He went on. "But I wanted you to know about it, now that there's a fourth victim and you brought Owen into this." He looked at Jake. "Maybe we could all work together?"

Jake started to object, but Tommy cut him off. "Babe, there's nothing official about us. If you or Brian or Owen ask questions, people see a cop or a journalist or a lawyer. They shut down. But us? We're just gossipy queens."

Tommy's point wasn't lost on Jake, a fact he hated admitting. Although a decade had elapsed since Stonewall, the memory was still fresh in the minds of many gay men, resulting in a deep-seeded mistrust of law enforcement.

Furthermore, not only was he lying to his partner and his captain, he was now involving civilians. It didn't sit well, but what sat even worse was the realization that it made sense.

Jake glanced at his watch. "Any chance you can reach them now?"

Tommy kissed Jake tenderly and reached for the wall-mounted phone in the kitchen. He called Uncle Charlie's, knowing they were just closing up, and got Dmitri on the line.

"Come over to the brownstone when you leave there," Tommy said with an authority Jake noted.

"Umm, okay?" Dmitri replied. "What's going on?"

Tommy filled him in briefly and hung up.

"They'll be here soon," he told Jake.

EVERY SEAT AT JAKE'S DINING ROOM TABLE WAS FILLED.

After returning from the kitchen, Jake had made Tommy tell the other two what was going on, including the undercover operation he'd launched with Dmitri and Steven.

"And that's why you wanted Friday to yourself?" Brain had demanded. "Why didn't you tell me the real reason? I woulda talked you out of it!"

"Exactly why I didn't tell you!" Tommy had retorted.

"Wait," Jake had said. "What're you two talking about? You were in on this?" The last question had been aimed, with sniper precision, at Brian.

"Tommy here called me Friday and asked me to make plans with you that night," Brian had said. Looking at Tommy with admonishment, he'd continued, "Told me he needed a night off from the stress of the case." His look and tone had elicited no response. "Thanks for being honest with me, Tom!"

"Guys, c'mon," Owen had interjected, not having the emotional strength for the tension. "I think one thing we all have in common is having to be dishonest when it's needed."

The other three had completely understood what he meant and put the confrontation aside.

It wasn't long before Dmitri and Steven arrived, filling the last two empty seats at Jake's dining room table. He realized it was the first time since he owned the brownstone that it was fully occupied.

After introductions were made and refreshments, such as they were, had been served, all cards got put on the table.

The most salient point was that Tommy had learned that Cody Fischer and the unknown suspect had been seen leaving the Eagle's Nest together the night of the murder.

"Did Kenny go to the Eagle's Nest?" Jake asked Owen.

"Not that I'm aware of," he replied. "He's—" Owen corrected himself. "He *was* more into the bar scene that I am. I know he liked to bar-hop with his friends. But he never mentioned the Nest. His favorite was Marie's Crisis. It's a—"

"We're familiar with it," Jake said, exchanging a look with Tommy and taking his hand, reminded of what matters by the mention of the bar where they'd first met.

"Okay," he continued. "So, none of the four victims had been at the same bar the nights they were killed."

He asked Owen to give him the names and phone numbers, if he knew them, of Kenny's bar buddies, which the attorney provided, adding that he'd already called them with the news of his murder.

"So, where do we go from here?" Dmitri asked.

They all looked to Jake. "I wish I knew, man," was all he could offer them.

Before everyone left around five, they'd all exchanged numbers. In the foyer of Jake's brownstone, a spontaneous six-man hug occurred.

From the huddle, Tommy gasped. "Oh, my god!" he exclaimed. "This fucks everything up!"

"What are you talking about?" Jake asked.

"Well, there's six of us now," Tommy said. "And there are only three Charlie's Angels! What are we *now*?"

Brian took inventory of the group, noting that he was a blonde, Jake a brunette, and Owen a black man. "How about Charlie's Angels meets the Mod Squad?"

Still with their arms around one another, everyone shared a much-needed laugh.

"Sounds good," Owen said. "Now let's kick some ass."

CHAPTER TWENTY-FOUR

WHEN DANI ARRIVED AT THE ACROPLIS DINER ON TUESDAY, she was immediately tasked with training a new waitress.

"If you're gonna leave me high and dry," Stavros barked, "you can train your replacement."

Margareta Codrescu, a young, Romanian-born refugee, was starting her new life in a free country by working as a diner waitress. Despite her preoccupation with Iggy's continued status of being off the radar, Dani rose to the occasion and took Margareta under her wing. The distraction was welcome.

"Have you ever been a waitress before?" she asked.

"Not really," Margareta admitted in heavily accented English. "I serve the dinners in my home, but I never have job in restaurant."

Dani sighed. "Okay," she said, "let's start with the basics."

Per Karolis' instructions, not that Dani needed them, she had Margareta shadow her throughout her shift. Her first order of business was to have the trainee on point with refilling water and coffee, tasks that required minimal interaction with the patrons but taught her to be constantly aware of their needs.

Around seven, the nice detective from the 6th Precinct came in for dinner and requested the back corner booth. He was shortly joined by another man, the same one he'd eaten with a few nights prior. Dani took their orders and had Margareta deliver the coffees and waters. She noticed that they immediately spread out their work on the table, including photographs which, even from a distance, looked rather grisly.

"Go refill their coffees," Dani instructed Margareta after about twenty minutes. The new hire approached the table and began pouring.

Margareta suddenly gasped, spilling coffee onto the table. "*Strigoi!*" she shrieked, pointing at the photos with the hand not holding the coffee pot. "*Strigoi!*" Brian and Jake were scrambling to pick up the photos before they were damaged by the spill.

Dani rushed over. "I'm sorry, detective," she said to Jake. "She's new. I don't know what happened."

Jake was less concerned with the mishap than he was with the waitress' reaction to the photos. "What's *strigoi*?" he asked Margareta, doing his best to repeat the word she'd used and placing the pictures back on the dry spots of the table.

"*Strigoi*," was all she could utter, her voice strained, her skin ashen. Her eyes, reeking of terror, were fixed on the photos.

"Dani, do you have a break coming up soon?" he asked.

"In about fifteen minutes," she said with a brief look at her wristwatch. "Why?"

He glanced in Margareta's direction—she was frozen, staring at the black-and-white photos that were once again spread across the table—and said, "I'd like to talk to her, if that's okay."

Not sure what was going on, Dani said, "I guess I can make that happen."

Looking at Margareta but addressing Dani, he said, "See if you can calm her down. Don't wanna give Stavros ammunition against a new hire." He was smiling, and Dani responded in kind.

"Thanks, detective," she said.

"What's going on?" Brian asked once the waitresses had left.

"Not sure," Jake said. "But something."

IN THE SAME ROOM WHERE DANI HAD COMFORTED IGGY ONLY A FEW DAYS BEFORE, Jake asked, "What's *strigoi*?"

Margareta, still visibly shaken, said, "Is legend my grandmother told me. *Strigoi* rip open throat and drink the blood. Those pho-to-graphs"—the word was clumsily broken into syllables—"they look just like drawings in the books *a bunicii mele*." In her distress, she'd reverted to her native Romanian. Realizing this, she said, with some effort, "Am sorry. In my grandmother's books." Dani was standing beside Margareta's chair, attempting to comfort her with an arm around her shoulders.

Jake shot Brian a concerned look.

"So this is all just a myth?" Jake put forth.

"No!" Margareta protested with vehemence, her spine stiffening. "*Strigoi* are real!"

"Okay, okay," Brian assured her, his hands extended in a calming gesture. "What can you tell us about them?" he asked, speaking slowly to bridge the language barrier as well as her distress.

"They hunt at night!" Margareta said, still quite agitated. "And they *kill*! They rip open throat and drink the blood! *All* the blood!" She had begun crying, making the end of her reply not much more than a wet garble.

Jake and Brian exchanged another look.

"I thought I left this behind," Margareta said, sobbing into her hands. "In America, these things do not happen! My *bunicii mele* tell me so!" Dani embraced her against her hip.

"Our break is almost up, detective," she said, "and I'm gonna need a few minutes to help her get herself together."

"Understood," Jake said. Turning to the new waitress, he added, "Please make sure Dani has a number where we can reach you. You've been a big help."

Back at their corner booth, Brain asked, "What the fuck was that?"

"I don't know," Jake admitted. "But you saw her. She was terrified. And not like the average person would be, seeing those pictures. Something rang true for her. Something that runs deep. And I wanna know what that is."

He told Brian to find out everything he could about the legend of the *strigoi*, and they agreed to meet again the next night for dinner at the Acropolis.

THAT MEETING NEVER HAPPENED. The filming of an upcoming Al Pacino movie had instigated protests within the gay community, and Brian had to cover the latest demonstration.

The actor had been in the city filming the movie "Cruising," a flick about an N.Y.P.D. detective who goes undercover in the city's gay leather bars to track a serial killer. Outraged by the film's depiction of homosexuals in the Big Apple, New York gay men took to the streets, protesting at location shoots.

Brian called Jake at home on Wednesday before he left for the precinct to let him know he'd have to cancel. However, he also informed him that he'd spent the morning at the New York City Public Library finding out everything he could on the Romanian legend of the *strigoi*.

"It pretty much boils down to your garden-variety vampire," he summed up. "Just a lot more gruesome. What the movies have given us is a romanticized version. The *strigoi* were known to rip open the throats of their victims, not seductively bite their necks while wearing a tuxedo. And then they drain *all* the blood.

"I gotta tell ya, though," he went on, "the drawings, like the ones Margareta mentioned, and the descriptions written in the books sounds exactly like the wounds on our victims. Gave me fuckin' goosebumps, man."

"You're not suggesting we have a gay Count Dracula here, are you?"

"Look, I'm not suggesting anything. I'm just telling you what my research turned up. I made photocopies of all of it—several copies, in fact. I'll bring everything with me the next time we meet up."

Vampires? Jake thought as he hung up the phone. *Gimme something I can work with, man.*

Margareta's words from the night before came back to him: "In America, these things do not happen!"

CAPTAIN EDDIE YOUNG HAD BEEN CHILLY SINCE MONDAY'S CONFRONATATION with Jake over the story in the *Voice*, and today was no different.

Jake knew he'd placed himself on thin ice with his C.O., but he couldn't allow second thoughts. Meeting Owen on Monday had changed a lot for him, not the least of which was his determination to stop the killing spree.

Young had argued on Tuesday that Kenneth Wilson's race broke the pattern of victimology. Jake had anticipated he would and nodded when appropriate until the captain's harangue had ended. He could have pointed out that Fischer having been Jewish could imply the same, but he didn't. That would only add fuel to Young's conviction that this wasn't a serial killer.

At about four on Wednesday afternoon, Jake's phone rang.

"Hi," the voice said after he answered. "It's Owen."

"How are you holding up?" he asked.

"I wish I could tell you," Owen said. Jake could hear the weariness, as well as the sorrow, in the other man's voice. "I took personal time this week. I couldn't face the office. Not with having to keep up the pretense that this wasn't personal. Plus, I needed to make the arrangements."

"That must have been rough," Jake said.

"You have no idea." Owen paused. "I wanted to give you the details so you could arrange undercover officers to be there. At the funeral home and the cemetery."

"I'm ready when you are," he said, and Owen dictated the information, which Jake notated on his pad. The viewing would be Thursday and Friday at a funeral home in Harlem, with the burial Saturday morning at Calvary Cemetery in Queens. Kenneth Wilson would be laid to rest with his parents.

"I gotta ask this," Jake said, not comfortable with the question that was to come. "Will most of the mourners be black?"

"Mostly, I guess," Owen said, clearly puzzled by the question. "Why?"

"It'll help the undercovers blend in if they look like everyone else. Sorry for having to ask that."

"No apologies needed," Owen said. "It makes sense."

Jake went on to explain what Owen should expect with undercover officers at the funeral home, most notably not to acknowledge Frank. Owen understood.

"In the meantime," Jake continued, "is there anything you need? I'm here until eleven, but Tommy's free after six. Please don't hesitate to call him, even if it's only just to talk."

"I really appreciate that, Jake," Owen said. "I do. I wish you and Kenny had met. I think he would have admired you." He started to cry softly.

Jake wasn't sure how to take that comment. He was just doing his job. And didn't feel particularly admirable lately.

No, an inner voice said, it's more than that. Doing his job would mean maintaining the department's party line and not going rogue.

"Well, I'm just doing what I can," he said to Owen.

"And that's more than a lot of people do," he replied, collecting himself. "Don't sell yourself short."

"Do you have any more arrangements to make today?" Jake asked, changing the subject.

"No, that's all done."

"Then why don't you try and get some rest. You don't sound like you've had much sleep since Monday."

"I haven't," Owen admitted. "Maybe I will. I don't know. I don't seem to know what I'm doing from one minute to the next."

"That's understandable," Jake said. "But try, okay? Kenny wouldn't want you to burn yourself out, so try for him."

"That wasn't fair," Owen said, no malice in his voice.

"I know," Jake replied. "It wasn't meant to be. Did it work?"

"Yeah," Owen admitted. "It did. I'll try. Fair enough?"

"Fair enough. And remember, call Tommy if you need."

"I will," Owen said. "And Jake? Thank you. For everything. I mean that."

"Not a problem, my friend," he said. "How is Kenny's aunt holding up?"

On the other end of the line, he heard Owen laugh, the kind of laugh only those in mourning ever display. "Man, I wish I had half that lady's guts.

"By the way," he continued, "did you see the news last night or read the papers today?"

"No. Why?"

"Ted Bundy got convicted," Owen informed him.

"Of course he did. He killed pretty, white coeds." Jake did nothing to mask either his bitterness or his disgust.

"I hear you, man," Owen said. "I still thought you'd want to know."

"Well," Jake said without malice, "score one for the good guys."

After saying goodbye, they ended their call.

Jake got out a Manhattan Yellow Pages and looked up the number for a florist in Harlem. He then called the business and placed an order for an arrangement to be sent to the funeral home, with a card reading "Jake and Tommy."

His next order of business was to call the Pot Shop and the *Voice* to let Tommy and Brian know the details on the funeral arrangements. He left a message for Brian, but was able to speak with Tommy directly. While he had him on the line, he also informed him that he'd told Owen to reach out should he need to.

"No problem," Tommy said. "I'll do whatever I can."

Fortunately, Frank had been away from his desk, so Jake wouldn't have to explain the personal nature of the calls. He'd promised himself to stop speaking in hushed tones in the office and just let the chips fall where they may. Still, though, dealing with the follow-through wasn't topping his list.

When Frank returned to the squad room, Jake gave him the particulars on Kenneth Wilson's funeral, as well as his plan to have undercovers in attendance and the need that they be black.

"Can't hurt," Frank said. "Let's see who we can get. We got me, for one. I'll see who else is available."

Jake's phone rang.

"Homicide, Griffin," he said.

"Jake, it's Miguel," the M.E. said. "I've got something unusual here."

"Talk to me," Jake said.

"I picked up something when I did the autopsy on Wilson," Ruiz told him, "so I went back and ran tests on tissue samples from the other three."

"And?"

"There are traces of human saliva in all the wounds."

CHAPTER TWENTY-FIVE

"THERE ARE *WHAT?*"

"Traces of human saliva in all the wounds," Jake repeated.

"You've gotta be fucking shitting me!" Brian exclaimed, loud enough for Jake to pull the phone away from his ear.

"I shit you not, my friend," Jake said.

Jake had called Brian's answering service in the hopes that he'd check in while he was covering the protests at the film shoot. Apparently, he had, because at roughly ten o'clock, he'd called Jake in the squad room. From the background noise, he could tell that Brian was still on the scene of the protests, calling from a sidewalk pay phone.

"Okay, okay," Brian said, digesting this new piece of information. "What're your thoughts?"

"I wish I fuckin' knew, man," Jake said. "If I believed in all this vampire shit, I'd say Margareta was right."

"Lemme think," Brian said.

"Think away."

After a few moments, Brian spoke up. "You free after your shift ends?"

"Yeah," Jake answered. "Why? You wanna get together?"

"That's what I'm thinking. Don't involve the others, though."

"Well," Jake said, "Tommy'll be at my place already. I'm not gonna send him home."

"No, you shouldn't," Brian allowed, "but nobody else. Not until we can sort through all this."

"I hear you," Jake said. "Don't need everybody thinking we're crazy." He heard a sudden commotion from the other end of the line.

"Look," Brian said, "I gotta go. I'll meet you at your place at midnight."

"Sounds good," Jake said before hanging up.

The last hour of Jake's shift was uneventful and was filled mostly with paperwork and watching the clock. When eleven rolled around and Curran and Schwartz showed up for their shift, he made tracks and headed home.

When he opened the door to the brownstone, he heard laughter. And smelled pot.

Shit, he thought. *I should have called ahead and made sure he was alone.*

Entering the living room, he found Tommy and Dmitri lounging on the couch, passing a joint.

"Oh, my god!" Tommy exclaimed, jumping up from the sofa, "You're home!" He ran to Jake and kissed him.

"You two look like you're having fun," Jake observed.

"Maybe a little," Tommy said and burst into giggles.

"You *do* remember I'm a cop, right? And that you're breaking the law in my living room?" He couldn't resist giving Tommy some good-natured shit.

"Maybe you'll have to cuff me, detective," Tommy teased before kissing him again.

"Hey, Jake," Dmitri said dreamily, his head lolling back onto the cushions.

"Hey," he replied. "No work tonight?"

"Nope. Steven's shakin' his groove thang, though."

"Okay, here's the deal," Jake informed them. "Either you two need to straighten up or you have to take this party upstairs to the bedroom."

"Why? What's up?" Tommy was suddenly as serious as Jake had been.

"Brian's coming over," he told them. "Something's come up with the case and if you wanna be part of the conversation, I can't have you being all silly and shit."

Tommy looked at Dmitri. "Whadda you think? Can we pull it together?" His tone was comically militaristic.

Having heard what Jake had said, Dmitri was already on point. "Hell, yeah," he said. "We didn't smoke that much." He then dissolved into laughter.

"Get some coffee in him," Jake said to Tommy. "And you too, while you're at it."

By the time Brian rang the doorbell, Tommy and Dmitri were both lucid.

"I see we have company," Brian said as Jake escorted him into the entry hall, the living room visible from where they stood.

"He was here when I got home," Jake said.

Brian sniffed the air. "Are they in any shape for this?"

"They're fine," Jake assured him.

"If you say so," Brian said before making his way unescorted to the dining room table.

Once all four were seated, Jake said to Tommy and Dmitri, "What we're about to tell you is gonna sound completely off the wall. If you think you're gonna get silly, now's the time to leave."

Tommy and Dmitri looked at each other. Tommy spoke for the both of them. "We're fine," he said. "This is important. We want to help."

"Okay," Jake said, taking Tommy's word for it. He then told them about Margareta Codrescu and her reaction to the crime scene photos.

"Shit," Dmitri said. "Sounds like she totally wigged out on the two of you."

Jake handed the narrative off to Brian, who recounted the results of his research at the library. Tommy and Dmitri sat silently, unable to respond.

"And this evening," Jake said, "I got a call from the M.E. telling me he'd found traces of human saliva in the wounds on all four victims." He let Tommy and Dmitri digest this information. "I'm not saying we have a vampire, because that's just crazy. But I think we have a perp who *thinks* he's a vampire." He looked to Brian for corroboration. The reporter was already nodding.

"Wait," Tommy said. "Back up. Why would that be crazy?"

"Why?" Jake asked. "Tommy? A *vampire*? That shit just doesn't exist."

"How do we know that?" Tommy countered.

Jake started to reply, but Tommy cut him off.

"You believe this place has a ghost, right?"

Jake looked at Dmitri and Brian, mostly Brian. "What's that got to do with anything?" he asked Tommy. It was clear that he was embarrassed to have this piece of information announced publicly.

Since his grandmother's death, Jake had often attributed creaking floorboards and unexplained drafts to an unseen presence, occurrences which Tommy had also witnessed.

"Just answer," Tommy pressed.

"Well," Jake stammered, "yeah," He averted his gaze and shifted in his chair, making his discomfort evident to everyone.

"Then you admit that you believe in things that a lot of people would call 'crazy'."

"I guess," Jake conceded, his unwillingness to do so quite clear.

"Then why is this any different?"

"Are you suggesting we arm ourselves with crucifixes and garlic?" Jake balked.

"No," Tommy said, sounding firm and rational. "What I'm suggesting is that you allow yourself to consider things you're inclined to call 'crazy.' Nothing more."

"Wait," Dmitri said, "this place is haunted?"

"Shut up, D," Tommy chided. "You need more coffee."

"Okay," Jake said, "just for the sake of argument. Suppose we consider the possibility that our perp is a *strigoi*. What then?" He looked from one face to another.

It was Brian who spoke. "I don't know, Jake," he said. "I've encountered some pretty outlandish stuff in my time. And, like you, I've had experiences with spirits. There's a lot of shit in this world that science and common sense can't explain."

"Don't tell me you're buying into this," Jake said.

"I didn't say that," Brian responded. "It's just that I'm not dismissing it either."

"Does your ghost talk to you?" Dmitri asked.

"It's a good thing you're cute," Brian said. "And so well built." He gave Dmitri's biceps an appreciative squeeze.

Tommy looked at Jake. "I'm sorry, babe," he said. "I gave him four cups."

"Okay," Jake said. "So, what're we thinking?"

"Honestly," Brian said, "I say we don't rule anything out. Especially after Margareta's reaction and my research at the library. So far, that's the only stuff that lines up."

"Which makes us all officially insane," Jake said. He leaned back in his chair and took a deep breath. "Okay, Brian, show us what you got."

Brian handed out the copies of his research and they all began reading.

AS BRIAN HAD SAID EARLIER, everything he'd been able to find on the *strigoi* was a match for the four murders.

Despite all the vampire legends, mostly established in movies, there was no mention of crucifixes or stakes through the heart. The only references to disabling the creatures involved silver, while destroying them completely required decapitation or fire.

"I can't believe we're actually considering this," Jake said, still unable to wrap his mind around the concept.

"Has any other theory made this much sense so far?" Brian asked.

Jake looked at him and exhaled. "No," was all he could muster.

"Oh," Tommy interjected, addressing his boyfriend, "I forgot to tell you. Owen called me this evening."

"And?"

"He just wanted to talk," Tommy said. "So I listened. Guy's a mess. I was gonna invite him over so he wouldn't have to be alone, but he said he was going to bed. I hope he's getting some sleep."

"That reminds me," Jake said, turning to Brian. "I left a message for you in the newsroom, but since you're here I may as well tell you." He gave Brian the details of Kenny Wilson's funeral.

To Dmitri, he added, "Make sure you pass that along to Steven, okay?"

"Definitely," he said. "We should all go together. Show of solidarity for Owen."

"Good idea," Brian said.

Tommy noticed a slight shift in Jake's demeanor at the suggestion. "What is it?" he asked.

Jake looked up. "I don't know if I can," he said. "We're gonna have undercovers there, keeping their eyes open for anyone suspicious. Frank'll be one of them. I figured I'd go too, since I'm working the case, but to show up as part of a group ..."

"Gotcha," Brian said before Tommy could comment.

Jake still looked troubled. "But Dmitri's right," he continued, playing devil's advocate with himself. He blew out a breath. "I don't know. Lemme think about it when I'm not so tired."

"Speaking of which," Brian said, "whadda ya say we call it a night?" He turned to Dmitri. "Where do you live?"

"Barrow Street," he replied, naming one of the quieter spots in the Village.

"I'm in Chelsea," Brian said. "Wanna share a cab downtown?"

"Sounds good."

After they left, Jake pulled Tommy into his arms and just held him, standing silently in the front hall.

"You okay?" Tommy asked, his cheek against Jake's shoulder, his voice soft.

"Not sure," Jake said. "Not sure of anything lately." He kissed the side of Tommy's head. "Except you. I'm sure of you."

Tommy's mind flashed back to Chris Albright. He knew he'd have to confess it all to Jake at some point, but now was clearly not the time.

CHAPTER TWENTY-SIX

WITH THE GRAND OPENING ONLY EIGHT DAYS AWAY, Dani
arrived at the gallery early on Thursday morning.

She still hadn't been able to track down Iggy, and she was beside
herself with worry. In addition to repeated phone calls, all of which had gone
unanswered, she'd stopped by his apartment more than once, finding only an
ever-growing pile of mail outside his door, but not her friend. She'd also
reached out to their mutual acquaintances, all fellow students at Parsons, but
none of them had seen or heard from him either. Naturally, everyone was
concerned and asked Dani to call the minute she knew anything, promising to
do the same should they hear from him first.

Dani had to draw on everything she could to remain focused while at
work. All the paintings for the exhibit had been hung, with the exception of the
"Seven Deadly Sins" series; Colin's procrastination on those works had
Sandrine quite annoyed, and she vented to Dani on the subject daily.

"*Regardez!*" she said, telling Dani to look at the empty walls in the
middle space, adding an emphatic sweep of her arm. "He has given me
nothing! *Rien!!*"

Dani realized there was little she could say or do that would be of any
tangible help in the matter, so she just listened, allowing Sandrine to get it out
of her system.

Hoping at last to redirect the conversation toward a possible solution,
Dani asked, "And there's no chance I can meet him before the opening?
Maybe I might be able to encourage him to get the paintings done. You know,
flatter him and let his ego do the rest."

"I am afraid not, *chérie*." Sandrine had told on her first day working at
the gallery that Colin enjoyed remaining something of a mystery, an enigma,
unveiling himself and his work simultaneously. "*C'est vrai*, he does have quite
an ego, but he would not be susceptible to your feminine charms. You lack
certain, shall we say, attributes." Sandrine was not going to tell her assistant
that the artist had been harboring a deep resentment for her. What good would
that do?

"Understood," Dani said, excusing herself and heading into Sandrine's
office, where she retrieved a file from an upright rack. In the workroom, she
took a seat at her own desk, an addition to the space that Sandrine had made
after Dani had been there a few days. It wasn't nearly as grand as her
employer's in terms of size, but equally lovely.

"I wish I could give you an office of your own," Sandrine had said the prior Monday as two deliverymen carried in the antique.

"Don't be silly," Dani had replied as she marveled at the beauty of the desk and chair. "This is gorgeous. Thank you so much, Sandrine."

"*Ce n'est rien*," her employer had said, a smile on her face.

Opening the folder, she called to Sandrine. "We've gotten quite a few responses to the invitations already." They'd gone out in the mail early Monday and by Wednesday, the phone at the gallery had begun ringing. In addition to Alex Mayhew, all the other papers in town would be sending art critics, and Dani had fielded all the calls, promising each that she'd arrange for Sandrine and Colin to be available for interviews the week after the opening and mollifying those who felt miffed that the *Voice* had gotten an exclusive.

In addition to having worked as a *de facto* press representative for the gallery, she'd also booked a caterer to supply hors d'oeuvre as well as a wait staff, and a bartender who'd set himself up in a corner of the front room, providing Champagne and an assortment of wines. At Dani's suggestion, Sandrine had given her seal of approval to the addition of live music and was delighted when Dani not only put forth the idea of a harpist but was able to book one for the night.

In short, aside from fielding responses to the dozens of invitations, everything was in order for the gala opening. Everything, that was, with the exception of Colin's missing seven paintings.

Sandrine had entered the workroom and was observing Dani at her desk. It was clear to her that she was still very burdened by her missing friend, despite the girl's impressive productivity.

"Dani?" Sandrine said softly. The assistant turned in her chair. "Is there any word on your friend Iggy?"

"No," Dani replied, tears springing to her eyes.

"Have you considered going to the police?"

"Yes," Dani said. "I just kept hoping that he'd turn up with some explanation. Even a ridiculous one. But it's been almost a week. I wouldn't even know where to start with that."

"I am sure that if you go to them, they will guide you through the process," Sandrine offered. "Would you like to leave and attend to that?"

"No," Dani said. "The diner is right across the street from a police station. I can stop in on my way there."

"*Bien*," Sandrine said. "I am sure you will feel a little better after you do that, knowing that he is being looked for by someone official."

Dani hoped her boss was right.

LIKE DANI, JAKE ARRIVED AT WORK AHEAD OF SCHEDULE, sitting at his desk in the squad room precisely at noon.

He hoped the extra three hours would help, and he promptly started calling other precincts in the city, trying to determine if there were any open cases matching the four that he and Frank were working.

Almost every attempt proved fruitless, but he did find two such crimes. One in Washington Heights from early July and one in the Bay Ridge section of Brooklyn a week after Gil McCandless' murder. He asked his counterparts at both precincts, the 33rd uptown and the 68th across the East River, to fax him copies of the files, and he promised to do the same with everything he had. No point in not sharing intel.

Frank arrived around two and assembled the officers he'd lined up to work the Wilson funeral. As he and Jake had discussed, all of them were black, four men and two women. With Frank, it was a detail of seven, which should be more than sufficient for their purposes. All were dressed appropriately for such a solemn occasion.

He briefed them on Wilson's case so, should another mourner ask how they knew the deceased, they could give believable answers.

"Frank?" It was Darryl Jackson, one of the youngest in the division. "If the vic was gay, doesn't it make sense that some of us would be too? You know, like his friends from going out and what-not?"

"Good point, Jackson," Frank said. "You work that out among yourselves, just keep it subtle. No swishing around." Some of the officers laughed.

Darryl Jackson was not among them. "Wouldn't do that anyway, sir," he said. "That's just disrespectful. Not to mention stereotypical, and I don't think I need to tell any you of what bullshit *that* is."

Jake had been listening in, since this was the first major operation they'd undertaken with the case. He wondered if he and Darryl Jackson might have more in common than their N.Y.P.D. shields.

"Okay," Frank concluded, "viewing starts at four. You all have the address, but I suggest you stagger your arrivals. And some of you pair up, people sometimes go together to pay their respects. You've all worked undercover before, so you should know the routine."

Everyone acknowledged their understanding and went about their business until it would be time to head uptown.

"Frank?" Jake said as the undercovers dispersed, talking among themselves. "I got some info you should know about."

Back at their desks, Jake shared what he'd learned about the two open homicides.

"Shit," Frank muttered. "If it's the same perp, our body count just went to six."

"I know," Jake concurred. "M.O.s sound the same, victim profiles too."

"Okay, nothing we can do about it 'til the faxes come in. And I've got a wake to attend."

"I'll be there too," Jake shared for the first time.

"You?" Frank asked, a puzzled look on his face. "I thought we agreed the undercovers should be black."

"I won't be undercover," Jake said. "I'm going as the detective working the case. And to offer my condolences to Owen Toussaint."

Frank eyed his partner. "You two friends or something?"

"Not really," Jake said. "I don't know. I just felt for him when we were at his office. And then what you said later about Loretta and how you'd feel in his shoes. We talked briefly when he called with the funeral arrangements. It just seems like it's the right thing to do."

"Well, then," Frank said, "trust your gut." He still looked vaguely suspicious. "Just don't blow my cover. And tell Toussaint to keep mum too."

"He already knows," Jake said. "I told him what to expect when he gave me the particulars on the arrangements."

Prentiss checked his watch—for some reason Jake never understood, he didn't trust the large, industrial clock on the wall of the squad room—and said, "Well, it's about time for me to head uptown. You coming?"

"In a few," Jake said. "I wanna decipher my notes on the two new cases first. Plus, we shouldn't show up at the same time anyway."

"Well, I'll see you there," Frank said, putting on his jacket. "Just don't say hello!"

Jake forced himself to chuckle as Frank left the squad room.

Sitting down, he dialed Brian at the *Voice*.

"Hey, it's me," he said.

"Hey, Jake," the reporter greeted him. "What's up?"

"I've got something you should know about. Are you going to be at the funeral home this afternoon?"

"I was just getting ready to leave the newsroom now," Brian told him. "I'm meeting Dmitri and we're heading uptown together."

"Oh?"

Brian laughed. "Yeah, he kinda never made it south of 23rd last night."

Jake had never gone in for the gossip Tommy often indulged with his friends. In fact, he found it tiresome. But Brian was *his* friend, and he was surprised at how his curiosity was suddenly piqued.

"Okay," Jake said, "we are *definitely* going to have to talk about that later. I'll see you at the wake."

They said their goodbyes and hung up.

Wow, Jake thought, shaking his head with a slight smile on his lips. *Didn't see that coming.*

CHAPTER TWENTY-SEVEN

THE HOLLOMAN FUNERAL HOME ON LENOX AVENUE was packed by the time Jake arrived at four-fifteen.

The room was filled with flowers, but Jake didn't bother looking for the arrangement he'd sent from himself and Tommy. Scanning the crowd, he assumed that many of the white mourners were work associates of Wilson's. He recognized a couple from their visit to the brokerage firm; the easily outraged Zachary Hoffman was not among them. Jake had had enough of their stuffy, entitled arrogance earlier in the week and avoided them completely.

How did Kenny deal with working among that every day? he wondered, before realizing that he did the same, just a different flavor.

Jake also noticed the receptionist from Owen's law firm. He assumed the three people she was talking to also worked at McCambridge & Blair. It made sense that they weren't out in force since, as far as they knew, their colleague had only lost a buddy.

He spotted Frank in a far corner, an excellent vantage point, engaged in conversation with Darryl Jackson. Jake could tell that his partner was steering clear of everyone they'd met earlier in the week. The other undercovers were scattered around the room, in pairs and singly.

Jake paid his respects at the casket. Despite the work that had been done by both Ruiz and then the undertaker, a silk scarf was still needed to conceal the fatal wound. Oddly, it provided a flash of personality to the otherwise sedate suit they'd put on the body.

Owen Toussaint was seated in the center of the front row of chairs and Jake approached him. The grieving boyfriend started to stand, but Jake gestured that he should remain seated. They shook hands.

"Owen, again, I'm so sorry for your loss," he said.

"Thank you, Jake," Owen replied. He turned to an elderly woman seated beside him. Jake recognized her from the mantlepiece photos. "Miss Thelma, this is a friend of mine," he said to her.

Jake was surprised to realize he was very happy to be described as such.

"His name's Jake Griffin," Owen continued, "he's the detective investigating Kenny's murder. Jake, this is Kenny's great aunt, Thelma Wilson. Kenny's father was her nephew."

Jake clasped the old lady's hand in both of his and said, "Ms. Wilson, I am so sorry for your loss. Owen's told me a lot of very nice things about Kenny."

"He was a good boy," Miss Thelma said.

Jake was surprised to note her stoicism since, as Owen had told him on the phone, she and Kenny were all that was left of their family.

"Do you mind if I have a word with Owen, ma'am?"

"Not at all, detective," she replied with quiet dignity. As soon as Owen stood and the men stepped away, she was joined by three women, all roughly her contemporaries.

Jake and Owen crossed to a nearby empty corner of the room. "She seems to be holding up well," he commented.

"Yes," Owen said. "Miss Thelma's a tough old bird. Seen a lot in her time and survived a lot too." He looked fondly in her direction. "Still, I imagine you can never really get used to losing a loved one, especially one so much younger."

"Well," Jake offered, "she's got you."

"She does," Owen said. "We've been leaning on each other a lot this week. I'm ashamed to admit that I did more leaning than she did."

"I'm guessing she knew about you and Kenny?"

"Oh, yeah, from the start. Never a problem for her," he said, the warmth evident in his voice, as well as his slight smile as he looked once again in her direction. "Kenny's parents were another story. They had serious issues when he came out to them in high school. Of course, that was long before he and I met, but he told me all about it. Always bothered him that they never made peace about it before the accident. That happened shortly after he was arrested at Stonewall."

Looking over Owen's shoulder, he saw Tommy and Steven enter the visitation parlor, followed by Brian and Dmitri. Jake was surprised to see that Cara had joined them. He realized that he couldn't recall having seen Tommy in a suit before, and had to admit he looked quite dapper.

Jake inclined his head in the direction of the new arrivals and Owen turned, offering a discreet wave.

The quintet joined them in the corner, each in turn hugging Owen and offering their condolences, including Cara whom Tommy introduced, along with the mention that she was a paralegal with the Public Defender's office.

"Owen's a tax attorney," he told his sister, as if that gave them something in common.

"Let's go pay our respects," Brian said to the others.

"There's someone I want you to meet first," Owen said, and led them to where Miss Thelma was sitting.

Jake noted Miss Thelma's expression as Owen introduced everyone. He surmised that he'd presented them as his friends as well, based on the warmth of the older woman's reaction as each shook her hand and, he assumed, offered their sympathy.

Seeing Jake by himself, Frank made his way over, looking casual if a bit awkward, as one might be in such circumstances.

"Anything?" Jake asked.

"Nothing," Frank replied. "But we've still got a few hours, and then the viewing tomorrow. Of course, perps are usually known to show up at the cemetery where they can keep their distance. That's what my money's on. If he shows at all, that is."

He looked across the room to where Darryl Jackson was engaged in a subdued conversation with two mourners, both young men and neither among the undercovers. "What's your take on him?" he asked.

"On who?"

"Jackson," Frank said. "He suggested pretending to be gay in the squad room and then got a little huffy when I told them not to swish. Now he's chatting up the vic's friends."

"I'm not sure I follow, Frank." Jake followed very well; he just wasn't going to take the bait without forcing Frank to spell it out. "Maybe he's just doing his job, finding out what he can."

"You think he's gay?"

"Hadn't given it any thought, really," Jake said. "It's none of my business if he is. He's a good cop. That's all that affects me."

"He is," Frank agreed. "A good cop, I mean. I was just wondering."

"And if he *was* gay?" Jake asked, trying not to let his annoyance seep into his tone. "What difference would it make? You said yourself he's a good cop. Isn't that all that really matters?"

Frank eyed his partner. It was the same look he'd given him before leaving the squad room earlier. "I suppose it is," he conceded. "I don't know, Griff, I guess I'm just old-school. When I was coming up, if a guy was that way, he kept it to himself and didn't make it everybody's business. Still not used to all these new ways of thinking." He scanned the crowded room. "Except for Wilson's Wall Street people and Toussaint's co-workers, I'm guessing a lotta the guys here are gay. Most of 'em look like you and me. Jesus, you'd never know it."

No, Jake thought with irritation, *you never would. And* you *clearly* don't. Then another thought occurred to him. *Or is he fishing?*

"Look, Frank" Jake said, "Toussaint introduced me to Wilson's aunt sitting there in the front row. She doesn't know about the undercovers, but she does know I'm the detective working the case. Maybe we shouldn't be seen talking to each other."

"Say no more," Prentiss agreed. "Thanks for the heads up on that. I'll go stand around with one of the others. Let me know later if you hear anything."

"Will do," Jake said. He offered his hand as if the two had only just met and bonded over their shared loss. Frank shook it before moving back across the room.

Owen and the others rejoined him when he was once again alone. After feeling his anger rise during his exchange with Frank, he didn't much care who his partner saw him talking to. Besides, he probably assumes that Cara is the mysterious "lady friend." *Typical.*

As much as he hated having to repeatedly lie to Frank, he hated being angry with him even more. Something was going to have to give, and soon.

"Okay," Steven said in a hushed, clandestine tone as the group returned to the corner. "I have an announcement to make." All eyes turned to him. "I want to be Miss Thelma when I grow up!"

"Oh, my god!" Dmitri said, eyes rolling. "Like you're ever gonna grow up!" The laughter they shared was subdued and respectful, but no less sincere and welcome.

Owen looked around the room, shaking his head. "It's funny," he said.

"What is?" asked Brian.

"All these people here were part of Kenny's life," he went on. "Friends, co-workers, gym buddies. And I knew a lot of them. A few are from my law firm." He turned his gaze back to their little grouping. "But with the exception of Miss Thelma, the five of you guys are the only ones here who really feel like friends of mine. And now you too, Cara."

"Why is that funny?" This was Dmitri.

"Because a week ago," Owen said, "I didn't know who any of you were."

Jake placed a reassuring hand on Owen's back. "I just wish Kenny had known you all," the attorney said as tears started to flow. The group instinctively formed a huddle around him, providing a comforting cocoon. *Fuck what Prentiss thinks about this*, Jake thought. *I'm done pretending.*

JAKE, TOMMY, AND THEIR FRIENDS STAYED UNTIL THE END OF THE VIEWING HOURS at eight, as did Prentiss and all the undercovers.

Frank and Jake had not intersected again after their initial conversation.

Before leaving the Holloman Funeral Home, Tommy said to Owen, "I don't know if you're gonna be up to it, but you're welcome to join all of us at Jake's place when you leave here." A flicker of concern darted through Owen's eyes. "Not to work," Tommy assured him. "Just to be among friends."

"Thanks," Owen said. "I think I'd like that very much."

This was the first Jake had heard of this, but he didn't mind in the least. In fact, he was happy that Tommy had taken the initiative. This little ragtag assortment was starting to feel like a family to Jake and he welcomed the emotions he was experiencing. Emotions he couldn't ever remember feeling among all the other Griffins.

"Work on what?" Cara asked.

Everyone else exchanged looks, and none of them were lost on her.

"Okay, give," she said. "Somebody tell me something."

As the unofficial ringleader, Jake felt all eyes on him. "Tommy'll fill you in later at my place. And I have a new piece of information." He glanced around. "As long as that's fine with everybody else."

Owen and Brian had only met Cara that afternoon but trusted the others' judgment on the matter.

"I suppose another legal mind can't hurt," Owen said.

"Alright," Jake said, "I still have a few hours left of my shift, so I should head back downtown. I'll see you all at home before midnight."

JAKE WAS BRACING HIMSELF FOR WHAT MIGHT AWAIT HIM BACK IN THE SQUAD ROOM.

He hadn't said anything to Frank before leaving the funeral home, but that was to avoid blowing his partner's cover, not a byproduct of his growing resentment.

As he drove south, navigating the usual cluster-fuck of midtown traffic, he found himself questioning that unpleasant emotion. It was natural to assume that he resented Frank. But why would he? He'd been the one lying, not his partner, both direct mistruths and lies of omission. Frank had merely been following the lead that Jake had established, not editing his thoughts, prejudicial though they might be.

If anything, Frank was being far more authentic than Jake.

Then it hit him.

He resented himself.

The disgust that had welled up since these murders began wasn't directed at his partner. Jake had dealt with anti-gay attitudes all his life, both the few directed at him and the many tossed off by those oblivious to his homosexuality, and he had managed to survive just fine.

No, this was *self*-disgust, born of his lack of courage to live his life truthfully. While coming out in the military would have gotten him a dishonorable discharge, doing so on the job would have no official repercussions. His union would ensure that. Granted, he might take a lot of harassment, disguised as "humor," but what's the worst that could happen? He was a good cop with a solid record. The respect he enjoyed in the squad room wasn't based on the assumption that he was straight; it was based on his work.

It took him almost an hour to reach the precinct lot and, by the time he pulled the parking brake on the Civic, he'd all but decided to come out to Frank tonight.

However, when he reached the squad room, he found his partner on the phone, a worried look on his face.

"Okay, okay," Frank said into the receiver. "I'll leave now. Don't worry. I'm on my way." He hung up.

"What's wrong?" Jake asked. "Please don't tell me there's another body."

"No," Frank said as he stood and pulled on his suit jacket. "Loretta had a fall."

"Shit," Jake said. "I'm sorry. Is she okay?"

"Not sure," he replied. "She's in the E.R. at Columbia-Presbyterian, the one in Queens. They're gonna run some X-rays. I gotta go be with her."

"Absolutely," Jake agreed. "Let me know if there's anything I can do."

"I'll call you at home tomorrow," Frank said as he left the squad room.

Jake glanced at the clock on the wall, seeing it was almost nine-thirty, and realized he hadn't eaten since lunch.

"Hey, Walt," he hollered, "I'm gonna grab some take-out from the Acropolis. I'll be back in fifteen or so."

"Gotcha," Detective Friedrich said.

"You want anything?" Jake asked.

"Nah," Walt replied. "I'm still belching from the dinner my wife packed me."

Across the street, Jake took a stool at the counter and ordered a cheeseburger platter to go, adding a bottle of Coke to the bill. Once the counter waitress took his order to the kitchen, Dani appeared in front of him.

"Detective," she said, "can I talk to you a minute?"

"Sure, Dani," Jake replied. "What's up? You seem upset."

"I am," she admitted. "Very. It's my friend, Iggy, the one I told you about the other night? He still hasn't turned up and nobody knows where he is. I wanted to know how I go about filing a missing-persons report across the street."

"Okay," Jake said, his tone understanding, "I'll be more than happy to show you who you'd need to talk to. It's not my department, you understand, but I can help. First tell me more details. Maybe I can start by helping you avoid making it official."

She told him about Iggy wanting to leave the diner when she quits and about their last conversation on Saturday night after work.

"He said he wanted to be alone and go to a bar," Dani informed him. "See, he was really upset. A guy he'd kinda been seeing got murdered on West 10th a week ago."

Jake's attention was suddenly on high alert. "Do you know the guy's name?" he asked. "The one Iggy was seeing."

"Lemme think," she said. "He always called him Rembrandt because the guy was an artist. I met him once when he guest-lectured at Parsons, that's when Iggy met him too. He told us about career options in advertising because that's where he worked."

Jake felt a dizzying sensation and his vision reminded him of the camera work in Hitchcock's "Vertigo." He cleared his throat and asked, "Dani, do you know if the guy's name was Cody Fischer?"

Recognition flashed across Dani's face. "Yes," she said, "that's it. Cody Fischer."

"And did Iggy say what bar he was going to last Saturday?"

"No," she said, "he didn't mention it. He was being really maudlin, not that I judge him for it. I mean, c'mon, who wouldn't be?" She paused and thought for a moment. "Knowing Ig, I wouldn't be surprised if he went someplace that he and Rem—I mean, Cody—used to go to together."

"Do you know what bars they frequented?"

"Only one I remember is a place called the Ninth Circle," she said. "It stuck in my head because of Dante, you know. The Nine Circles of Hell?"

"Okay, Dani, here's what I want you to do," he said. "Can you come over to the precinct when your shift ends? When is that? Midnight, right?"

"Yes," she said and then clarified. "Yes, it ends at midnight and yes, I can be there."

"Okay, come over and ask the desk sergeant for Sergeant Helen Olsen. Do you need to write that down?" Dani shook her head, so he continued. "She works the graveyard shift. I'll be gone by then, but I'll leave a message for her to expect you. She can walk you through filing the report.

"By the way," he added, sounding casual, "what's Iggy's last name?"

"Vance," she replied. "Why?"

"No reason," he deflected. "Just curious. Anyway, you'll be in safe hands with Sergeant Olsen."

"Thank you, detective," Dani said. Her relief was apparent.

"Why don't you start calling me Jake?"

She smiled. "Thank you, Jake."

Back in the squad room, Jake set his cheeseburger aside and located Cody Fischer's address book. As his stomach growled, he flipped to the pages marked "V-W."

CHAPTER TWENTY-EIGHT

TRAFFIC WAS LIGHT AND JAKE MADE IT HOME BY ELEVEN-THIRTY.

As he opened his front door, he could hear several voices engaged in subdued conversation. He hung his jacket on the rack in the hall, noticing an unfamiliar coat already there. He joined the rest in the living room.

Jake was surprised to find an unexpected guest—clearly the owner of the coat—seated in one of the wingback chairs, a cup of tea on the table beside it. "Miss Thelma," he said, taking her hand in both of his as he had done at the funeral home. "I'm glad you joined us."

"Thank you, detective," she said. "Going home to an empty house didn't suit me much, and Owen suggested I come with him. I hope I'm not intruding."

"Not at all," Jake assured her. "Being alone can be difficult at times like this, and I'm happy we can help." He gave her hand an affectionate squeeze and added, "And please call me Jake. We're pretty informal here."

"From what your boyfriend told us, Jake," she said, "you've been helping a *lot*."

Jake released her hand and looked at Tommy, but it was Brian who spoke.

"We were already going to tell Cara everything," he said, "and when Miss Thelma got here with Owen, it didn't feel right to keep her out of the loop. I checked with Owen first, and he said she can probably handle more truth than all of us combined." He paused. "So, I made a judgment call."

"Of course," Owen added, "I hadn't yet heard the whole story when he asked me. Just to be clear."

"Baby, wait 'til you hear some of what she told us," Tommy said.

He took this in. Choosing to trust the discretion of the group, he said, "Lemme get a drink and then I'm all ears."

Tommy leapt to his feet. "Sit," he said. "You must be tired, and I've already heard it." Looking to Miss Thelma, he added, "Although, I could listen to you share stories all night." With that, he was off to the dining room.

Jake sat in the other wingback, the one that Tommy had just vacated. Dmitri and Brian were side by side on the sofa, holding hands, and Owen was next to them at the end closest to Kenny's aunt. The others were seated on chairs which had been brought in from the dining room. Brian and Dmitri were sharing the crystal ashtray on the coffee table; Jake assumed Tommy had been as well.

"He's a keeper," Miss Thelma said when Tommy departed, an approving smile on her face.

"I got lucky," Jake replied.

"I say, you *both* got lucky, Jake," she corrected.

"Now, Miss Thelma," he continued, "what is it you told everyone?"

"Well, when Owen explained how the police department doesn't want to look at this as a serial killer, I couldn't help but think of all the times that police didn't investigate crimes committed against our people." She paused and sipped her tea. "They still don't, but that's another story for another day."

Owen and Steven exchanged looks that none of the others could begin to fully understand. They knew this, so they didn't try. They just respected it.

Tommy returned and handed Jake a Scotch, neat, and sat on the floor in front of him, snuggling in between his calves.

"Sometimes," Miss Thelma continued, "nice folks gotta pull some sneaky shenanigans to get good results. Lord knows, I've seen and heard of things in my time—some of those things I did *myself*—that I wouldn't necessarily talk about in church."

This was the second time Brian had heard this narrative. Ever the investigative journalist, his senses once again spiked. *There's a story in there*, he thought, promising himself that, when all this was behind them, he would get to know Miss Thelma better. Given her age, she'd lived through some remarkable changes in society and he wanted to write her story.

"So, if all of you young people are going behind the police department's back to stop a lunatic," Miss Thelma continued, "I say more power to you!"

"Before we go on," Jake said, "there's something you all should know." He told them about the two open cases he'd uncovered, the one in Washington Heights and the one in Bay Ridge.

"So that brings it to six," Brian said.

"Miss Thelma," Tommy said, "tell him about the stories you heard from your grandmother."

Brian interjected, giving Jake some context. "We started off telling them about how I got involved, shining a light on the serial killer angle. But when we got to the *strigoi* and what Margareta told us, that's when things got interesting."

"I gotta tell ya, Jake," Cara said. "When they brought that up, I thought I'd gone down the rabbit hole. Or was having a flashback from acid I dropped at Woodstock."

This inspired a laugh from everyone, including Miss Thelma, who seemed to get quite a kick out of it.

"This was the first I heard of it as well," Owen added. "I wasn't at Woodstock, but I know how Cara felt."

"Go on, Miss Thelma," Cara said. "I'm sorry for interrupting."

"Nothin' to be sorry for, sweetheart," the old lady said.

"But, Jake," she continued, "I just don't have it in me to tell it again. I wish I did, the good Lord *knows* I wish I did." Miss Thelma sighed, an exhalation that betrayed her spirit's fatigue. She looked Jake dead in the eye. "But I just don't. I'm fixing to bury the last of my kin and, as much as I want to help you catch his killer, I need to get myself on home.

"But I will tell you this," she continued. "'There are more things in heaven and earth, Horatio, than are dreamt of in your philosophies.'"

"Who's Horatio?" Tommy whispered, his head cocked back just enough for Jake to know that he was being addressed.

"It's Shakespeare," Jake whispered in reply, his eyes fixed on his elderly guest.

"What I'm saying," Miss Thelma went on, having drained her teacup, "is that not everything can be explained by science and what we call 'facts.' And tonight, when your friends here told us about the—what did you say it was called?" This last was to Brian.

"*Strigoi*," he said. "But I guess vampire works just as well."

"This *strigoi*," Miss Thelma continued, pronouncing the Romanian word flawlessly, "I said to myself, 'Thelma, you've heard some crazier tales in your day, and you heard 'em from your granny who never told you a lie.'"

She lifted her teacup and noted its emptiness. She set it back on the side table, and returned to the subject at hand. "So, what do all you young people have planned next?"

"We're still working that out, Miss Thelma," Jake said. "We're kind of making it up as we go. Brian had suggested leaking the serial angle to the local news stations, and I'm thinking he may be right. But other than that, I admit I'm at a loss.

"If we're dealing with some sort of creature—and I say '*if*'—we're up against something that all our combined training and experience hasn't prepared us for. And in the meantime, creature or human, we have to find a way to let people know that there's a very real danger out there."

"Well," she said, "it sounds like Brian here is taking care of that. And I agree with you about the television news. More folks watch the TV than read papers nowadays, I'm sad to say." She turned to Brian. "You can make that happen?"

"Easily, ma'am," he replied. "Especially now that we know there are other cases that no one shared info about."

She nodded thoughtfully. "Then you should," she stated firmly, then looked around the room. "If I get a vote, that is."

Everyone spoke at once, assuring her that she did indeed get a vote.

"And you did the research at the library about this *strigoi*?" she continued, still addressing Brian.

"Yes, ma'am."

"Do you have copies of it?" she asked. "I'd like to read about it. Granny's been dead for a dog's age, been a while since I had the jeepers scared outta me. I think I'm overdue."

"Miss Thelma," Cara said gently, "are you sure it's a good idea for you to read that? I mean, given your nephew and all."

"You're sweet to worry, honey, but when you've lived long as I have, you learn that most things in life aren't good ideas. Besides," she continued, her gaze fixed on her lap, "Kenny's gone and none of us can bring him back."

She looked up. "What we *can* do is stop whoever did it from doing it *again*. There's nothing in heaven and earth scary enough to keep me from *that*."

Miss Thelma turned to Owen. "Sweetheart, I think I should head on home."

Jake was shocked to see it was almost two in the morning. Everyone rose in unison, Owen assisting Miss Thelma to her feet. Tommy retrieved her lightweight coat from the hall and helped her into it. As she slipped her thin arms into the sleeves, she whispered to Jake, "A keeper."

Miss Thelma looked around at everyone. "Thank you all," she said. "Lord knows, this week's been a hard one. But people like you make the hard stuff possible to bear. Owen's right: I wish my Kenny had known all of you." At this, her eyes glistened. It was the first time any of them had seen the old woman's resolve give way, however slightly.

Brian pulled photocopies of his research from his leather messenger bag and handed them to Owen. "There's a set for you and a set for Miss Thelma," he said.

"Thank you, son," she answered for them both.

"Are you staying with her tonight?" Jake asked Owen in a whisper when the attorney stepped away from Miss Thelma to put his suit jacket back on.

"Yes," he said. "Like I told you, she's a tough old bird. But even tough old birds have their limits. I'm all she has left of Kenny, so I'll stay by her side until she doesn't need it anymore."

Everyone but Tommy made their exits at the same time. Jake slid up behind him in the entry hall and snaked his arms around his waist.

"I hope you're staying," Jake said.

"Of course," Tommy confirmed, turning in Jake's embrace to face him.

As they moved the empty glasses and coffee mugs, as well as Miss Thelma's teacup and saucer, to the kitchen, Jake said, "She likes you."

"Well, I like her too," Tommy replied.

"No," Jake said with emphasis, "she *likes* you. As in, she likes you for *me*."

Tommy smiled his love to Jake. "The world could learn a lot from her," he said, rinsing the dirties and putting them in the dishwasher. Jake was in the doorway, leaning against the frame. "She's probably the oldest person I know, and us being gay doesn't faze her in the least. Most of her life, it was a crime to be gay, people actually went to jail. But there she was, in a room full of all of us, and all she showed was love.

"And when you think of the loss she suffered this week," he continued, turning on the dishwasher. "All I can say is, she's pretty amazing."

"Know who else is amazing?" Jake asked. "You."

"Well, I studied under a master," he said, crossing to him.

As they linked their hands behind each other's waists, Jake said, "I decided to come out at work."

Tommy was stunned. "Wait! *What?!* Back up. When did you decide this?"

"On the drive from the funeral home to the precinct," he answered.

"This is huge, Jake," Tommy said. "What brought this on?"

"Everything," Jake said, shaking his head. "Frank, his comments, seeing Owen have to hide his feelings when we told him about Kenny, watching you and your friends. And that's another thing. Before this week, the only gay friends I had were *your* friends. But now I know Brian and Owen. I'm not being territorial, but they're *my* friends."

"I knew what you meant," Tommy said. "And it's made me happy to see you becoming friends with them."

Jake paused. "Like I said. Just … everything."

"Are you sure you're ready to take this step?" Tommy asked.

"No," his boyfriend replied matter-of-factly. "But I realized I'll never be ready. Some thing's you just gotta do, ready or not. I can't keep pretending. And I think Miss Thelma helped me see that truth."

"Do you have any idea how proud I am of you?"

"Yeah?" Jake asked teasingly, giving Tommy a peck on the lips. "Why don't we go upstairs and you show me?"

Tommy led him by the hand, neither of them bothering to turn off the lights as they went.

CHAPTER TWENTY-NINE

FRIDAY BEGAN AS MOST DAYS DO: the sun rose, the alarm sounded, and Jake flailed his arm to silence it.

He rolled over and looked at Tommy, still sleeping soundly. They hadn't made love the night before, despite their eagerness to get to the bedroom. Once they were naked, and in each other's arms, they'd shared an unspoken understanding that it was all they really needed after the events of the week prior.

They'd fallen asleep, holding one another closely.

Jake reached over and brushed an auburn curl off Tommy's brow and leaned in to kiss him, softly, where the forelock had been.

Tommy stirred.

"Shh," Jake whispered, his lips still against his lover's skin. "You sleep."

He slipped from beneath the sheet, pulled on a pair of gym shorts without underwear, and made his way downstairs.

Despite it being his day off, he wanted to get an early start. Rubbing sleep from his eyes, he got the coffeemaker going and poured himself a glass of orange juice. Standing at the kitchen counter, drinking his juice while the coffee dripped, he mentally mapped out his day.

His first order of business would be to call the squad room and find out if the faxes came in from the 33rd and the 68th. If they did, he'd want to swing by the precinct, photocopy them, drop a set off with Brian at the *Voice*, and bring the other set home to see if anything jumped out at him. If they hadn't arrived in the squad room, he'd just bide his time on that front.

Aside from that, he planned to touch base with Brian, either way. He wasn't going to disturb Owen, knowing he'd see him later at the viewing.

He heard a noise and turned. Barely awake, Tommy stood in the doorway to the kitchen, yawning and naked.

"Did I wake you?" Jake asked. "I tried to let you sleep."

"No," Tommy grumbled, his voice hoarse. "I had to pee. When I smelled the coffee, I knew where to find you." He yawned again. "Why're you up so early?"

"I have a lot I want to accomplish today," he replied, noticing that the coffee was ready. Nodding toward the pot, he asked, "You want some?"

"Please," Tommy said. "Lemme go put some clothes on. Be right back."

Jake watched Tommy retreat, admiring the curve of his buttocks. "You want any breakfast?" he called after him. "I've got English muffins, grapefruit, not sure what else."

"Sure," Tommy's voice echoed from the stairwell. "Whatever you're having."

Jake dropped muffins into the toaster and prepared the grapefruit. By the time Tommy returned, dressed in matching attire, breakfast was on the dining room table, including a second glass of juice.

They ate in silence, both still waking up as well as processing all they'd been through in the last eight days.

"Jake," Tommy said at last, his grapefruit and muffin only half-eaten. "There's something I need to talk to you about."

"Sure," Jake said. "What is it?"

Tommy got up and walked to the living room, returning with the crystal ashtray and his cigarettes. He lit one and closed his eyes.

"You want more coffee?" Jake asked, feeling a bit apprehensive about his boyfriend's out-of-character reticence.

"No," Tommy said, then thought again. "Yeah. I do, actually."

Jake went to the kitchen and brought back the pot, refilling both their mugs. Returning the carafe to its proper place, he sat back down at the table.

"What's up?" he asked.

"It's about last Friday," Tommy began tentatively. "When I went to the Eagle's Nest."

"Okay?"

"I told you I got some info from the bartender, Chris whatshisname."

"Albright."

"Yeah, him." He took a drag off his cigarette and swallowed a mouthful of coffee. "I didn't tell you everything."

"Go on," Jake said, liking the sound of this less and less. He could see Tommy was struggling with how to proceed. "Whatever it is, just say it."

Tommy looked Jake in the eyes, the first time he'd done so since broaching the topic. "See," he began, "we were talking at the bar, the one he was working, and he was giving me little bits of info. Then, he said he'd tell me more if I wanted to join him when he took his break."

"And?"

"Jake, I swear I only did it to find out more," Tommy said with emphasis.

Now Jake was concerned. "Did what?"

"He wouldn't tell me anything unless I fucked him," Tommy blurted out.

Jake sat there, immobile, silent, his expression inscrutable.

"Please say something," Tommy beseeched.

"Not sure what to say," was all Jake could manage. "Lemme get this straight. You took it upon yourself to go undercover and do *my* job, and then to get a witness talking, you fucked him? In the bar?"

"Please don't put it like that."

"How else should I put it?" Jake pushed away from the table and stalked into the kitchen, returning immediately without breaking his stride. "Is that why you were so into topping me Saturday night?"

"No," Tommy said, his voice almost inaudible.

"Is that how you think I get witnesses to talk?" Jake's voice had risen almost to the point of shouting. "Slip 'em my dick and see what they'll give up while they're coming?"

"Jake," Tommy begged, "it wasn't like that. I thought he just wanted to talk. Then I followed him to this back room—"

"You fucked him in a seedy *back room*?" Jake shouted. "Jesus Christ, it just keeps getting better!"

"Jake, please, let me finish."

"Not right now," Jake said. "I can't have this conversation right now."

"Jake, please, I need to."

"No," Jake yelled. "What you need is to let me process this shit before you dump even more on me." He strode into the kitchen, his anger evident in his gait. Tommy followed him.

"Baby—"

"*Don't!*" Jake said, whirling on him, making Tommy jump back. "You don't get to call me that. Not now." He turned his back on him and leaned the heels of his hands on the countertop to balance himself, his head hung forward. The world was spinning.

"Jake?" Tommy said softly.

Without turning or looking up, Jake said, his volume and tone restored to a more normal level, "Please. Just go."

"Are you breaking up with me?" He could tell Tommy had begun to cry.

He considered all the answers he might give. At last, he said, "No. I'm not. But this is too much for me to handle right now and I don't want to say something that would hurt you."

"Jake, I'm sorry," Tommy said. "I'm so sorry."

Jake took a deep breath to calm himself. "I know," he conceded. "But I need you to leave right now. I'm not breaking up, but I have to be alone. I'll call you tomorrow." With those words, he remembered what tomorrow was, a detail he'd forgotten with the unexpected drama. He could tell Tommy hadn't moved, so he asked, "Do you want me to pick you up for the cemetery?"

"I'm not gonna ask you to do that," Tommy said. "Not now. I'll go with Dmitri and the others." He paused. "I'll see you there?"

"Fine," Jake said, angling his head toward his shoulder, but not far enough to face his lover. "And Tommy?"

"Yeah?"

"I'm not okay with this, not by a long shot," he said, "but thank you for telling me."

Unsure how to respond, Tommy said, "You had a right to know."

Jake remained in the kitchen, leaning on the counter, until he heard Tommy come back downstairs five minutes later and leave by the front door.

AFTER TOMMY HAD LEFT, JAKE TOOK A SHOWER. Nothing was making any sense, so washing this morning off himself seemed like a good idea.

Once he was dressed in "day off" attire—jeans and a tee shirt—he collected his thoughts and called the precinct. After being transferred a few times, he learned that his contact at the 33rd had called and left a message, informing him that the case file was too voluminous to fax and that he'd photocopied it and was sending it with a department messenger. It should arrive that afternoon.

There'd been no word from the 68th.

He looked at the clock and saw it wasn't even eight yet. Not sure what to do with himself, he decided to change back into his shorts, this time with underwear, and go for a run in Central Park. If he had a heavy bag hanging in the basement, he'd beat the shit out of it. But he didn't so a run would have to do.

He arrived back at the brownstone shortly before ten and took another shower. Feeling only slightly better than before his exercise, he sprawled on the bed. His phone rang.

"Hello?" he said.

"Griff, it's me." It was Frank.

"How's Loretta?" Jake asked.

"Well, she's got a hairline fracture in one ankle and sprained the other one," he said. "But she'll be fine. Now at least I have ammunition when I tell her she should take it easy."

"I'm glad to hear she's gonna be okay. How are you?"

"Other than being in the E.R. damn near half the night, I'm dandy," Frank said. "At least I know she's alright. That's all I care about."

He went on to inform Jake that a neighbor would be staying with Loretta so he could be at the funeral home. "Are you gonna be there again?"

"I thought about it," Jake said, cursing himself for defaulting to ambiguity. "Yeah, I'll be there."

"Well, partner," Frank said. "I'll see you there. And don't wave."

This time Jake's laugh wasn't forced. He actually felt relief.

After hanging up, he dialed Brian's number.

"Newsroom, this is Brian Trent," he answered.

"Morning. It's me."

"Everything okay? You don't sound like yourself."

"Nothing to do with the case. Just something I'm dealing with."

"If you want a sounding board, you know where to find one."

"Thanks," Jake said, touched by the offer. "I'll work it out. Don't worry."

"So, what brings you to my phone this morning?"

He told Brian about the status of the case files from the other precincts, adding the promise to provide him with copies once they were in his hands. They both knew that Jake might have to redact certain things, but it wouldn't be anything necessary to what they were doing.

"Are you going to be at the funeral home later?" Jake asked.

"Absolutely," Brian assured him.

"Okay, I'll see you there."

"Jake?" Brian said before his friend could hang up.

"Yeah?"

"I mean it. Call me if you need."

"Appreciate that, buddy."

They rang off.

Jake headed down the two flights of stairs to the basement and took stock, deciding which beam would be the best from which to hang a heavy bag.

WHEN DANI ARRIVED AT GALERIE DELACROIX, she told Sandrine that she'd taken her advice and filed a missing-persons report on Iggy the night prior.

"Oh, Dani," Sandrine said, "I am so glad to hear that. *Et maintenant*, I am certain the police will find out something good."

Setting her purse on the corner of her desk, she asked her employer if there was an update on Colin's unfinished paintings.

"Nothing," Sandrine said.

Dani could tell from her expression that she should drop the subject. She'd known all along that the artist was temporarily living in one of the unfinished studios on the second floor and wondered why Sandrine hadn't used the proximity to assert a little more pressure on him. The ringing phone interrupted the thought.

THE SECOND DAY OF VIEWING AT THE HOLLOMAN FUNERAL HOME passed pretty much like the first, but with only about half the mourners.

All the undercovers were there, Frank included, but Jake didn't interact with them lest it rouse suspicion. With all that Miss Thelma had been told the night before, she was still unaware that her nephew's wake was being used as a stakeout. He didn't want to burden her with such information.

He sat with her and Owen in a comfortable silence. Nothing that might have needed to be said could be said there. And even so, it felt right to simply be together without conversation.

After he'd been there about an hour, Tommy showed up with Brian, Dmitri, and Steven, although Cara didn't accompany them. Jake excused himself so they could pay their respects to the other two without inserting the discomfort between him and Tommy into the moment.

It pained him to see Tommy, feeling as if he were looking at someone he didn't know. He'd tried, but he hadn't been able to make sense of it in the hours he spent pacing around the brownstone before dressing for the wake.

So he kept his distance, staying on the periphery of the room. He noticed a floral arrangement beside him and was disturbed to see it was the one he'd sent from the two of them. Keeping his cool, he positioned himself against the opposite wall.

Brian approached him. "Are you sure everything's okay with you?" he asked again.

Realizing that his conduct was glaringly obvious, he said, "Tommy and I had a fight this morning."

"Shit," Brian said. "Nothing serious, I hope."

"Remains to be seen," Jake replied. Seeing Brian's expression, he added, "One way or another, we'll work it out. But it's still unresolved and this isn't the place to try and make progress."

"Understandable," he said. "I thought it might be something like that. He was pretty quiet on the cab ride up, just said he had stuff on his mind. I did the math."

"Look," he continued. "I want to keep you up to date."

"Okay?" Jake said.

"I called my contacts at all the TV news stations this morning," Brian informed him. "Nobody was biting. They didn't say as much, but I'm certain it's because of the victim profile."

"And you're surprised?" Jake asked, his disgust apparent.

"I wish I were," Brian commiserated, "but, unfortunately, not one fucking bit."

"At least you tried," Jake offered, trite though he felt it to be.

Dmitri and Steven joined them, Tommy trailing behind sheepishly. Wanting to keep things smooth, Jake greeted them all warmly, even kissing Tommy on the cheek.

Tommy was taken aback. "Are you okay?" he asked in a hushed voice.

"No," Jake said. "But I will be. Can't think about all that at the moment, though. Right now, I'm here for Owen and Miss Thelma, and to do my job." He paused, awkward. "But I'm glad you came."

"Me too," Tommy said before Jake walked away from the group.

Finding a water cooler in the lobby, he filled a cup and drank it down.

"Okay, talk to me." Owen had followed him.

He was about to protest but thought better of it. "Tommy and I had a fight."

"About the case?" Owen asked.

"In a roundabout way, yeah. Don't worry about it. You've got enough on your shoulders right now." Deliberately changing the subject, he asked, "How is Miss Thelma really doing?"

Owen blew out a breath, his cheeks puffed. "I gotta tell ya, man," he said, "last night did her a lot of good *and* hit her pretty hard." The news wasn't surprising. "I don't think she slept much. I heard her walking a lot. I know *I* didn't. I skimmed Brian's research at her place after she went to bed. I kept thinking of Kenny being attacked like that. He must have been so terrified." His voice was strained with grief.

"Let's hope it was quick," was all Jake could manage.

Dmitri came up to the two of them. "Steven and I have to split and get ready for work," he told Owen. "Can't miss two nights in a row. Tommy's leaving with us and heading home, but I think Brian's gonna hang around for a while. He's meeting me at the club after he leaves here." He avoided making eye contact with Jake.

Tommy must have told him, he thought. *Unless he already knew.*

He pushed the thought from his mind, much as he'd just encouraged Owen to do with images of Kenny's death. Jake excused himself to use the restroom so he could sidestep an uncomfortable departure.

When he returned, the three had already left, and Brian was standing with Owen, each holding a cup from the water cooler.

"I'm sorry if that was awkward for you," Jake said to Owen.

"Not at all," Owen assured him. "I just hope everything works out for you two. I don't think Miss Thelma could handle that." The three shared a weary laugh, inappropriate though some might have thought it to be.

BRIAN LINGERED FOR ANOTHER NINETY MINUTES, leaving at about seven-thirty.

"I'm meeting Dmitri where he works," he informed Jake.

"I know," he replied. "He told us. Make sure you have plenty of singles." They chuckled, the subtle laughter giving way to Jake's smile at Brian. "I'm really happy you're having fun."

"So am I," he replied. "And you will too. *With* Tommy. I don't know what's going on, but I suspect you two will find a way to work through it." He hugged Jake. "And remember—call anytime you need." He paused. "Except tonight between three and dawn."

They both laughed and Brian made his exit just as Owen approached.

"Brian just left," Jake said.

"I know. He said goodbye to me and Miss Thelma inside." He looked a little uncomfortable.

"My turn to ask," Jake said. "You okay?"

"Even though I don't know what it is, I know you've got some heavy stuff on your mind right now. But I wondered if it would be okay if I came over for a little while? Miss Thelma has a church friend staying with her tonight, and I could use the company." Before Jake could answer, he added, "If it's not cool, I understand. I realize I'm not the only one dealing with shit here."

"Slow down," Jake said, a hand on Owen's shoulder. "It's perfectly okay. To be honest, I could use the company too."

"Thanks," Owen said, visibly relieved. "When I leave here, I'll take Miss Thelma home and then I'll be right over. You need me to pick up anything."

"We should be good," Jake assured him. "And if there's anything we want that I don't have, 72nd is only a few of blocks away. We can find it there."

Before heading out, Jake caught Frank's eye and the two met up in the men's room.

"Well?

"Same shit, different night," he said. With considerably fewer people paying their respects, there was much less chance that a perp would be among them, trying to blend in. "My money's still on the cemetery."

Jake told Frank what he'd learned about the case files from the other precincts. "I left a message with the desk to call my service as soon as the one from the 33rd gets there. I'm gonna check my service when I get home. I'll let you know when I hear something."

They staggered their exits from the men's room to avoid anyone seeing them together. Jake said goodnight to Miss Thelma and headed to the brownstone.

CHAPTER THIRTY

JAKE HAD ONLY BEEN BACK AT THE BROWNSTONE LESS THAN THIRTY MINUTES when Owen rang the bell.

He was still dressed in his three-piece suit, so Jake opted to remain in his own jacket and tie, not wanting his friend to feel uncomfortable. As they entered the living room, Jake asked, "What can I get you?"

"Something stronger than last night's coffee, I can tell you that," Owen replied, loosening the knot of his tie and sitting on the couch. "And I don't mean espresso either."

"Well," Jake said, "I'm a Scotch man myself, but I've got other options."

"Bourbon?" he asked.

"Bourbon it is," Jake said and headed into the dining room where he kept the liquor cabinet. "Rocks or neat?" he called out.

"Neat," Owen replied. "Only civilized way to drink whiskey."

Jake was relieved to hear a touch of normalcy had returned to Owen's demeanor. At least he assumed it was normal. He'd only been acquainted with the man for about ninety seconds before shattering his world with the news of Kenny's murder.

He poured the drinks and went back into the living room. Handing a glass to his guest, he said, "One bourbon," and then, raising his own, added, "One Scotch." With that he started to laugh, owing more to exhaustion that the thought that had just occurred to him.

Owen had a curious look on his face. "What?"

"One bourbon? One Scotch?" Jake said. "We'd have the George Thorogood song if Tommy was here." With that statement, his laughter dwindled immediately, and he sat down on the sofa.

"You doing okay?" Owen asked.

"I guess so," Jake said, looking into his glass. "Don't really know. I've got nothing to compare this to."

"How so?"

"Other than a short thing I had with a guy in Nam, guy in the Corps," he said, "this is the only real relationship I've ever had. It wasn't something I could ever make work with …"

"With having to stay closeted?" Owen finished for him when Jake let the thought hang uncompleted.

"Yeah," Jake said and took a drink.

"I can identify with that. It's not that Kenny was my first boyfriend, but he was the only one I ever really made an emotional investment in." He sipped his own drink. "The only one I thought was worth the trouble of making it work while keeping it a secret."

"Secrets," Jake echoed, distaste dripping from the two syllables. He drained his Scotch and offered his guest a refill.

Owen regarded his glass, still half full. "I'm good," he said.

Jake set his empty glass on the coffee table and headed into the dining room, returning almost immediately with the bottles of Johnny Walker Red and Jim Beam.

"Hey, look," he said, as he entered the room. "Johnny and Jim dropped by."

"The more the merrier," Owen said, a relaxed, if weary, smile on his face.

"Figured I'd save myself walking back and forth for every refill."

"Makes sense," Owen said. "Although, I don't know how many refills I'll have. I haven't gotten a lot of sleep the last few days, and I sure as hell haven't been eating as regularly as I should. And then I've gotta drive home."

"Shit," Jake said. "I just realized I never had dinner, and I'm guessing you didn't either."

"You guess right."

"Look, I know I've got stuff in the fridge, but whadda ya say we go find someplace quiet and grab a bite. You know, someplace that isn't here, where we can feel a little bit more normal."

"I like how you think, my friend," Owen said, raising his glass to Jake before draining it.

"You know what? Let's find someplace nice," Jake suggested. "We're both dressed for it. And we sure as hell both deserve it." As if to silently signal their agreement on the matter, they both retightened the knots of their ties.

"SOMEPLACE NICE" TURNED OUT TO BE SOMEPLACE *QUITE* NICE.

Feeling uncharacteristically spontaneous as they walked east toward the park on 72nd Street, Jake suggested Tavern on the Green, the iconic eatery at Central Park West and 67th.

"Isn't that a bit extravagant?" Owen asked. "You said, 'grab a bite,' not 'paint the town.'"

"I don't know about you," Jake said as they walked, "but I could really use the distraction of something completely out of the ordinary. And that place sure as hell ain't part of *my* ordinary."

Rather than take a table in the elegantly appointed Crystal Room, they opted for the much more subdued ambience of the Oak Room. Jake took it upon himself to order a Scotch and a bourbon, both neat, as they were handed their menus.

Having been there several times, Owen looked around the darkly paneled room as if anew, noting other men dressed pretty much as they were, and admitted to himself that they blended in very well. Like he assumed the others were, the two of them could easily be business associates ending the work week with a drink.

"This was a good idea," he acknowledged to Jake as their drinks were served.

Jake raised his glass and said, "To good ideas. And to friends."

Owen clinked his glass against Jake's and they drank.

Realizing how hungry they truly were, they both ordered steaks with baked potatoes. Having made short work of their salads, by the time their dinners arrived, they were ready for the refills—their seconds—the waiter offered.

They kept the conversation about themselves, avoiding the topics of Kenny, Tommy, and the case. Jake learned that his assumption had indeed been correct: he and Owen had a great deal in common when it came to staying in the closet professionally. They found many shared experiences in navigating that particular minefield, often nodding in commiseration as the other spoke.

As soon as the waiter had cleared their plates, saying he'd be right back with coffee and dessert menus, Jake said, "I've made a decision."

"What's that?"

"I'm coming out at work."

"Wow," Owen said matter-of-factly. "You're definitely the king of understatement tonight. Tavern on the Green is 'grab a bite,' and coming out at work is only *'a'* decision. Jake, as decisions go, that's fucking huge."

He paused as the waiter set down two cups of coffee and elegantly presented each with a leather-bound dessert menu, which they both promptly set aside. "How come you decided to do this?" Owen asked.

"You, in part."

"Me? Why is that?"

Jake shared his pain at watching how Owen had to handle their initial meeting in his office, going on to mention all the anti-gay jokes he regularly has to tolerate at work, and his overall disgust with himself at telling—and *living*—one lie after another.

"I made up my mind last night driving from the funeral home back to the precinct."

The waiter returned to take their dessert order, but they both declined, Owen requesting the check. When it was delivered in a discreet folder moments later, the attorney slipped his credit card into the pocket inside and handed it back to the waiter.

"What're you doing?" Jake asked. "I'm the one who suggested we," he paused, smiling, "'grab a bite.'"

"Please," Owen said. "Let me do this. I want to. It's important for me."

"Okay," Jake conceded, but not happily. "But I'm only agreeing for your benefit. Let's be clear on that."

AS THEY WALKED BACK TO THE BROWNSTONE, THE PARK ON THEIR RIGHT, Owen said, "I admire you, Jake. I really do."

"Oh?"

"I know from experience how difficult it can be to walk the tightrope that we have to at work," he said. "I also know how daunting—no, make that *terrifying*—it can be to consider changing that."

Jake was aware that he was feeling the four Scotches, the one at home and then three with dinner, and imagined the same might be true for Owen.

"The booze is just making you sappy," Jake said, hoping a joke would deflect the compliment, something he wasn't generally comfortable receiving.

"Well," Owen said with a chuckle, "I can't deny I'm feeling it. But I've been admiring you since we met and you went out of your way to offer me some sense of solidarity. You didn't have to do that, but you did, even though it meant taking something of a chance. My admiration only grew when you told me about the work you and Brian were doing to stop this nightmare.

"But this? Coming out at work? Man, what you're planning on doing requires balls of the highest order."

They were waiting for the light to change at Central Park West and 72nd and Jake took a moment to observe Owen.

"You look like it did you good to get out."

"It did," Owen admitted. "I feel a little guilty now, letting myself unwind in a fancy restaurant when Kenny's not even buried yet. But it just felt so fucking good to be a little closer to normal for a while."

"I know what you mean," Jake concurred. "The whole time, I hardly thought about the case." The light had changed. "Or Tommy."

In only five minutes they were back at the brownstone.

"Night cap?" Jake asked at the foot of the stone stairs.

Owen glanced at his watch. "Sure," he said, "why not?"

SEATED ONCE AGAIN ON THE SOFA, THEIR GLASSES FILLED, and their ties loosened, Owen asked, "Do you wanna talk about it? The thing with Tommy, I mean."

"No," Jake said, letting a weary sigh drag out the word. "Not that I don't feel comfortable sharing it with you," he added. "I just don't want to talk about it. Period. Net yet, anyway."

"I can respect that," he said, putting a comforting hand on Jake's shoulder.

Jake wasn't sure how he felt about the supportive gesture. Correction—he wasn't sure how he felt about his *reaction* to it.

Owen's touch had made something inside of him exhale, a release of tension of which he'd been unaware. And with that release came something else.

He realized that he wanted to kiss Owen.

"Ya know," he said, sounding a bit too chipper, "I didn't have room for dessert at the restaurant, but I think the walk gave me more of an appetite. Lemme go see what I got."

He topped off his drink and headed into the kitchen. Owen did the same.

Leaning in to examine the contents of his open refrigerator, Jake exclaimed, "I knew it! I was pretty sure I had some leftover cheesecake from Lindy's, and I was right." He pulled the box from the middle shelf and closed the refrigerator door.

Turning, he found Owen standing directly in front of him. The attorney took the box from him and set it on the counter of the island. He then placed a hand on either side of Jake's face and kissed him, a lingering communion of their slightly parted lips.

Jake did not resist.

It was Owen who pulled back. "I'm so sorry," he sputtered. "I had no right to do that." He picked up his glass from where he'd set it on the island and drank.

"It's okay," Jake said. "A little surprising, but completely okay."

He picked up his own glass and the two drank in silence for a moment, each trying to decipher what had just happened.

"You didn't mind?" Owen asked after a few minutes.

"Honestly?" Jake replied. "Not one bit."

"And it's not because you and Tommy are on the outs?"

"I could ask you a variation of the same thing where Kenny is concerned."

"Good point," Owen conceded. "But that had nothing to do with Kenny."

"And it had nothing to do with Tommy."

"Good."

"Then I guess that means it was about you and me," Jake said. This time it was he who initiated the kiss. Reaching up, he snaked his arms around Owen's well-muscled shoulders—the attorney had a good four inches on him—and brought their lips together. They took their time kissing, not hungrily making out like adolescents in back seats, but like grown men who weren't rushed by circumstance and repressed hormones.

Owen leaned against the counter and slid his strong arms around Jake's waist, pulling his body to him. Jake moaned into Owen's mouth when their erections pressed against the other.

Jake broke the kiss and asked, "Can we slow down just a bit?"

"Absolutely," Owen replied softly.

"This is just happening so fast," he picked up his glass and downed the rest of his Scotch.

Owen picked up his own glass and examined its contents, easily two shots of bourbon. He looked from the glass to Jake and maintained eye contact as he drained it.

"Why don't we go sit down before we fall down?" he suggested.

They returned to the living room, bringing their glasses but leaving the cheesecake on the counter.

As they sat, Owen refilled their drinks. Handing one to Jake, he asked, "And even if we're both on the rebound—granted, two different versions—is that so horrible?"

"That's not what this is for me."

"I'm just playing devil's advocate here," Owen said, reaching out and tracing Jake's jawline with a fingertip. "I think it's safe to say that we discovered a friendship this week, would you agree?"

"Without question."

"Well, friend," Owen said, "I have a strong sense that you're hurting."

"I am," Jake said.

"And I am too." He sipped his drink. "Is it a crime if we help each other hurt a little bit less?"

"Not one that I'd arrest us for."

"As opposed to this," Owen said, tipping his glass, taking another drink, and setting it on the coffee table. "I don't think it's a good idea for me to be driving tonight." He leaned in and kissed Jake once again, letting his body weight rest fully on him as they both laid back on the sofa.

This time, neither of them pulled away.

CHAPTER THIRTY-ONE

"DANI!" STAVROS KAROLIS BARKED FROM THE REGISTER. "You got visitor!"

Dani finished serving entrees to a two-top and approached the front of the diner. Seeing Sergeant Helen Olsen waiting at the counter, she braced herself, unsure of what she might hear. It was almost halfway her shift and a few hours before the start of Olsen's.

Despite his indignation at a waitress receiving a visitor, Stavros was sneaking lecherous glances at the cop. Sergeant Olsen was a pretty blonde of thirty-nine with an attractive figure that even her unflattering plainclothes outfit couldn't hide.

"Good evening, Sergeant Olsen," Dani said with trepidation. Uncertain of what to say next, she defaulted to her surroundings. "Would you like a table?"

"No, thank you, Dani," Olsen said, "the counter's fine. This is a 'two birds-one stone' visit. I can order my food to take across the street and follow up with you at the same time."

"Of course," Dani said. "Right this way." She led Olsen to the counter, taking her place behind it, pad in hand. The cop ordered a mushroom omelet and a side of toast to go, and waited for Dani to put the check on the carousel in the cook's window, sipping the water she'd been given.

When Dani returned, she looked at Olsen expectantly. "Since Griff asked me to give this my special attention," Helen began, "I red-flagged my report for the first and second shifts, basically asking them to see what they could find out in between their own cases."

"And?"

"And so far, we know that no one matching your friend's description visited an emergency room or was admitted to any hospitals in the city," she said. "Not last Saturday and not any day since then."

"That's good news, right?" Dani asked cautiously.

"It is and it isn't," the cop continued "Since we ruled out the hospitals, the next thing we have to do is check the morgue." She saw the color drain from Dani's face, and her heart went out to the girl. She could tell the night before when they first met that the kid had never been involved in anything like this.

"I don't have to *go* there, do I?" Dani asked, her fear apparent.

"No, no," Helen Olsen assured her. "We have a file of photos of all John Does. Jane Does too, but that doesn't apply here. All you have to do is sit down and go through the pictures." She took a sip of water. "I won't lie to you. You'll be looking at photographs of corpses, and some of them aren't pretty. But since your friend is black and in his twenties, we'll obviously spare you pictures of anyone who doesn't match that description. Plus, the streak you mentioned in his hair should also narrow down the process and make it fairly quick."

"When should I come over to do this?" Dani asked. "I'm guessing I'd do it across the street?"

Helen nodded. "What's your schedule like tomorrow? I can have someone ready to work with you."

"I work at the gallery from morning until I start here at four," she replied. "I'm sure my boss there would let me leave early, but I don't know. Our grand opening is a week from tonight, so we're pretty busy." A bell dinged, alerting Dani that her order was up. She retrieved it from the window and returned to the counter. "Would it be possible to come in after my shift tonight? I'd rather go without some sleep than miss time at the gallery tomorrow. Plus, I'd feel a lot better if you were there." Dani glanced at her watch. "Or I could come over on my break."

"That was actually going to be my next question," Olsen said, "but I'm glad you offered before I had to ask it. And I understand what you mean. A familiar face helps. I'll get on that as soon as I clock in so everything's all ready for you." She stood, taking her bag and the check. "Dani, I know this is scary for you, but with the department's resources, you'll have an answer, hopefully, a lot sooner than if you hadn't come to us." She offered a reassuring smile and said, "See you in a little while." With that, she headed to the front counter to pay Stavros before crossing the street for work.

THE SEX WAS ALMOST TRANSCENDENT FOR JAKE.

Not the slow, tender love-making he'd shared with Tommy in the shower only a little more than a week prior, nor the mind-blowing, unbridled passion of last Saturday night.

When he and Owen entered his bedroom and began undressing one another, they were removing more than clothes.

Each was knowingly helping the other to relieve himself of a multitude of burdens, and were giving each other permission to be completely vulnerable, both knowing that they could do so in total safety. Not surprisingly, while they enjoyed the prolonged encounter, each in turn had allowed himself to permit tears to flow as bits of pain and weariness left his spirit through the physical act. Also not surprisingly, when this occurred, the other one simply held him in a secure embrace without stopping what they were doing. Everything became part of the whole and there was beauty, sometimes bittersweet, in each component.

Jake had never experienced anything like it, least of all during sex.

After several rounds of intercourse, each taking turns in the dominant role, they lay in Jake's bed. Owen, having spied a pack of Tommy's cigarettes on the nightstand, lit one.

"I didn't know you smoked," Jake murmured beside him.

"Not regularly," Owen said as he exhaled a deep drag toward the ceiling, a look of peaceful contentment on his face despite the pain still evident in his dark eyes. "But after *that*? If there was ever a time for a cigarette, it's now." He took another deep drag, visibly enjoying it.

Jake reached over and took it from him, following suit.

"And *I* didn't know *you* smoked," Owen said.

"I quit after Nam," he informed him. "But you're right. If ever there was a time." He took another drag and handed it back to Owen. It wasn't lost on him that he'd never shared a cigarette with Tommy after any of the countless times they'd fucked in the last two years.

"I don't think I ever had sex like that," he admitted.

"So, it wasn't just me with that thought?" Owen asked.

"Nope." Jake lay fully on his back, looking upward. "Any regrets?"

"None," Owen said, almost too quickly, and Jake suspected that the statement wasn't entirely true. "You?"

"I'm fine," Jake assured him. He turned to Owen. "Can you stay?"

"I was hoping you'd ask," Owen replied. "I *do* have to wake up pretty early, though, so I can get home, get myself together, pick up Miss Thelma, and make it out to Queens before ten. Will that be a problem for you? I don't want to disrupt your morning routine."

"Not at all," Jake assured him. "I'm usually an early riser anyway."

"Then I guess I'm staying," Owen said.

Jake took the cigarette for another drag. Handing it back and reaching down to Owen's crotch, he asked, "Will it be a problem for *you* if we have another round before we call it a night? I don't want to disrupt your *sleep* routine."

Owen rested his head back on the pillows, eyes closed, and enjoyed the last of the cigarette while giving himself complete permission to also enjoy what Jake was doing. When Jake replaced his hand with his mouth, Owen stubbed out the butt and surrendered.

DURING HER BREAK FROM THE DINER, Dani was sitting in an interrogation room on the first floor of the 6th Precinct.

Sergeant Olsen had been waiting for her and, as she'd promised, there was a slim file folder on the table.

"Now," Olsen began, "I want you to be prepared. Some of these pictures might be upsetting to you, but I want you to focus on one thing and one thing only: are they Iggy or not. As soon as you can determine yes or no, just flip the photo and forget it. You think you can handle that?"

"Yes, sergeant," Dani said bravely. Olsen had brought her a can of Coke and she took a sip before beginning.

Dani flipped through the dozen photos rather quickly. "None of these are Iggy," she said. "Nobody has the blonde streak."

"I know," Olsen said. "But it's part of the process. Before moving on to the next phase, I have to notate in the file that you'd looked at John Doe photos. I'm aware that it was a little disturbing for you, but unfortunately, it's procedure. I just couldn't let you know that in advance because that might have prejudiced your examination of them. I hope you understand."

"Yes," Dani replied. "I do." She took another sip of soda. "You mentioned the next phase. What's that?"

Olson went on to explain, in civilian terms, that the search would now be expanded to officers visiting locations Iggy might have been that night and interviewing potential witnesses. She was up front with Dani, pointing out that it can be a hit-or-miss process. But she assured her that they'd do everything within their power to find out whatever information they could.

"Something I want you to consider," she added before Dani headed home. "You told me your friend was grieving the loss of his on-and-off boyfriend, correct?"

"Yes, that's right."

"Well, Dani," Olsen continued, "Iggy's twenty-two. I understand that it's out of character for him to abandon a job or to not inform you of his plans, but under the circumstances, it *is* possible that he just decided to take off and get away from the city after what happened to his friend."

"Is that a strong possibility?" Dani asked. "I mean, in your experience?"

"It's a possibility, that much I'll say. Whether it's strong or not remains to be seen. But since it *is* a possibility, I don't want you to rule it out. Promise?"

"I promise," Dani said. "And thank you so much, sergeant."

As soon as Dani had left the precinct, Helen Olsen dashed off a quick note and carried it up to Homicide, slipping it into Jake's mailbox.

"No John Does match description. You said you wanted to know as soon as I did, and now you do."

Per his request, she didn't sign it.

SANDRINE POURED HERSELF A COGNAC BEFORE BED.

With the opening only a week away, the day had been a long and busy one. But at least she'd been able to cross a major item off her list.

During the evening, she'd visited Colin in his studio and watched as he worked on one of the missing paintings. As he often did, he was painting in the nude, smears of pigment here and there on his fair skin. Another of his quirks which she attributed to his artist's temperament. The palette in his left hand and a cigarette dangling from his lips, he'd held the brush in his right, using the same hand to push his lank brown hair out of his eyes from time to time or flick ash onto the floor.

"How many more do you have left?" she'd asked from the doorway, no hint of pressure in her voice.

Without stopping his work or even looking at her, he'd said, "When I'm done with this, only two more. Lust and Gluttony. This one's Pride." Before she could ask, because he knew she would, he'd said, "The 'ole series will be ready for you to 'ang by Tuesday. Does that work, love?"

"It works fine," she'd said. "And thank you." She watched him continue to work for a few minutes. Before heading back downstairs to attend to some invoices, she'd asked, "Will you be painting through the night? Or going out?"

"Probably going out in a bit, soon as I'm 'appy with this. Need to unwind and blow off some steam, you know. Just like I always do."

Just like you always do, Sandrine had thought and shuddered.

"*Bien*," she had said and returned to the main level.

Standing in her dark apartment and looking out the large window at Houston Street, Sandrine sipped her cognac and wondered where Colin was blowing off steam.

And with whom.

"IT'S TEN P.M. DO YOU KNOW WHERE YOUR CHILDREN ARE?"

Her ubiquitous turban and heavy makeup removed, revealing a decidedly masculine shaved dome and face; a voluminous nightgown having replaced her flamboyant caftan, Fuchsia Lammé stood at the living room window of her apartment on Bleecker Street. A mug of steaming chamomile tea was clutched in both hands.

Hearing the ominous question, intoned nightly prior to the Channel 5 news, from the television behind her, Fuchsia looked out at the Village.

"No," she murmured, "I *don't* know where my children are." She sipped her tea. "But please, dear lord, keep my chickens safe tonight."

CHAPTER THIRTY-TWO

JAKE ARRIVED AT CALVARY CEMETERY FIFTEEN MINUTES before the graveside services were to begin.

Owen and Miss Thelma were already there, conferring with the pastor from her church who'd be officiating. Spotting Frank and the undercovers standing by a row of parked cars, Jake approached them.

"How's Loretta?" Jake asked his partner.

"Already complaining that she wants to move around," Frank said with a laugh. "Good indication that she's doing just fine, even with her injuries."

"You drove an unmarked today?" Jake asked, noticing Frank didn't have his old but beloved Impala.

"Yeah, my car's in the shop, so I took the subway to the precinct and picked this up."

"You took the subway from Flushing to Manhattan so you could drive back to Flushing?"

"I know," Frank said, laughing at himself, "sounds crazy. But I wanted the wheels for later, plus I had to meet with the undercovers since today's a little different."

It was a beautiful day and, mercifully, the humidity had taken some time off, allowing for the attendees to mourn in relative comfort.

"Think he'll show?" Jake asked Frank.

"I'm hoping so."

So am I, Jake thought, *and not for the same reasons*. He'd rationalized that if a perp attended the burial in broad daylight, that would put paid to all this *strigoi* nonsense. What he didn't admit to himself was that he was afraid no one suspicious would be there because their perp *was* a *strigoi*.

Frank pointed out two other burials about to begin, each some thirty yards from where Kenny Wilson would be reunited with his parents. "I'm sending some of them to the other graves, staying on the edges. That'll give 'em a broader field of vision and won't have them all clustered together here. Can't have 'em sticking out like sore thumbs."

"Sounds good," Jake agreed. "Speaking of sore thumbs, lemme get back over to Owen and Miss Thelma and not linger here with all of you."

"'Owen and Miss Thelma'?" Frank commented, looking a bit concerned. "Jake, I don't have to tell you that it's a bad idea to get personally involved in a case, do I?"

"No, you don't," he assured him, "and no, I'm not. Miss Thelma's actually been very helpful. Owen introduced me as the detective handling the case and she's offered to cooperate in any way she can. I think it helps her having me close by."

"Just be careful," Frank cautioned. "I can tell your getting pretty fond of her." Once again, he bore that suspicious look.

"No problem there, Frank."

Jake returned to the folding chairs that had been set up next to the grave and took the empty seat next to Owen.

"Everything okay with your partner?" he whispered.

"Yeah," Jake said, his voice equally soft. "He was just bringing me up to speed on how he's gonna position the undercovers."

Making sure none of the U.C.s were approaching the grave, Owen reached over and took Jake's hand.

While they were looking toward the cops by the cars, they failed to notice Tommy, Brian, and the others—Cara once again among them— approach the gravesite from the other direction.

"Morning," Brian said, his tone appropriately respectful of the occasion.

Jake and Owen turned and immediately disengaged hands, but not before Brian had noticed.

"Good morning," they both replied.

The group filed passed Miss Thelma, each leaning down to hug her and whispering their condolences. They all took seats in the third row, the second having been filled by Miss Thelma's church ladies.

"Owen," she said, "you've made some really nice friends through all this. I know Kenny would be happy." She cast a knowing look in Jake's direction. Knowing, if not entirely approving.

In addition to being a tough old bird, Jake thought, *she seems to be a pretty intuitive one too.*

The minister had prepared a beautiful service, despite not having known Kenny very well. Owen and Miss Thelma each offered a few words, sharing fond, sometimes amusing, remembrances of the young man. Everyone stood for the final prayer and, with the exception of Miss Thelma, remained standing as they each once again offered her their condolences. Jake noted that none of them offered their sympathies to Owen.

As Tommy passed Jake, he asked, "Can we talk later?"

Maintaining the appropriate decorum, Jake replied, "I'm not ready to do that yet. At least, not today. But I promise we will."

Tommy threw a glance in Owen's direction and looked as if he were about to speak but didn't. Jake assumed that he'd also seen them holding hands and wondered if he'd stopped himself from speaking because of the present circumstances or the risk of hypocrisy. Either way, he was grateful Tommy had opted for discretion.

Tommy left with the others, all of whom assured Miss Thelma they'd be at the repast to be hosted by her church in Harlem.

Jake excused himself and approached Frank, who'd rejoined the other undercovers by the cars.

"Anything?"

"Zip," Frank said and ran his hand over the top of his head.

"Shit," Jake muttered. "Well, you said it was no guarantee."

"I know, I know," his partner said, clearly not happy with the outcome.

No, you don't, Jake thought.

Frank continued. "It's just—"

He was cut off by the bark of the radio in the unmarked car next to them.

"Prentiss, come in," the voice crackling out of the speaker said.

Shaking his head, Frank opened the passenger door and leaned into the car, grabbing the microphone and pressing the button on the side.

"Prentiss here," he said. "Copy."

"Prentiss, Griff's guy at the six-eight just called. They found another body in Bay Ridge."

JAKE EXPLAINED HIS UNEXPECTED DEPARTURE TO OWEN without holding back any information. Not that he had that much to begin with.

To Miss Thelma, he only said that duty called and that he was sorry he wouldn't be able to join them at the church.

She patted his hand and said, "You have important work to do, Jake. I'd be upset with you if you missed *that*." Despite her obvious grief, her affection was sincere. "You and I will surely see each other soon."

Before leaving, he kissed her cheek. Standing back up, he just winked surreptitiously at Owen and said, "I'll call you later."

Jake followed Frank south in the Civic. Saturday traffic made the drive from Flushing to Bay Ridge twice as long as they had expected, but the crime scene was still active when they arrived.

Flashing their shields, they located Ralph Underwood, the detective with whom Jake had spoken a few days prior.

Extending his hand, Jake said, "Jake Griffin, Ralph."

"Good to meet you in person," Underwood said as they shook. Jake then introduced him to Frank.

The Brooklyn detective told them nothing they hadn't already encountered, four times in person and twice through the other precincts. The victim's name was Quentin Barstow, age thirty-two. Like all the others, he was well built, still in possession of his valuables, and missing the front of his throat.

"We already determined he was at a meat rack last night," Underwood said. "Had a piece of paper in his pocket with the bar's name and address and 'ten pm' written under it, along with some guy's name. Just the first name." He looked at his pad. "And not even a real name. Flip." He returned his attention to Jake and Frank. "That name come up in any of your cases?"

"That's a new one for us," Frank said.

"M.E.'s already come and gone," Underwood said. "We're gonna go check out the vic's apartment and this bar he went to. You're welcome to join us, but it ain't necessary."

The partners exchanged looks. Eager as they were to make headway, they knew they had no official jurisdiction here and would only be in the way.

"Thanks just the same, Ralph," Frank said, "but we're gonna head back to Manhattan. Be sure and let us know anything you find out."

"Count on it. And Jake? I'll have copies of all the files, this one included, sent over to you on Monday. Sorry it's taking so long, been a real shit show on this side of the river last few days."

"Understandable," Jake replied. "And Ralph? Have the M.E. check for traces of human saliva in the wound. Our guy spotted that on all the Manhattan vics."

"Human saliva?"

"Yeah, I know, man, we got some real crazies, don't we?" was all Jake said.

"This makes seven," Frank said to Jake once they were back where they'd parked their cars.

"So much for that number being lucky."

JAKE DROVE FROM BROOKLYN TO HARLEM AS FAST AS TRAFFIC WOULD ALLOW and arrived at the church's fellowship hall while the last of the guests were still there.

He was relieved to see that Tommy had already left, assuming he went directly to the Pot Shop. He found Brian and Dmitri sitting with Owen and Miss Thelma, empty plates in front of them. The remaining three dirty plates, Jake assumed, had belonged to the others.

"Jake," Miss Thelma said, clearly happy to see him. "Honey, the ladies cleared the buffet already, but I can have them make you a plate."

"Please don't trouble yourself," Jake said. "Or them. It's quite alright."

"Won't hear nothin' of the kind," she said, standing without assistance and heading into the adjoining kitchen.

"Owen told us you got a call," Brian said. "Was there another one?"

"Yeah," Jake replied before putting a hand over his mouth and exhaling through the fingers. They all exchanged troubled looks.

"I only told Brian and Dmitri," Owen assured him. "I didn't know how much you wanted said, so I kept it brief."

"Well," Jake said, "now that we know it's part of the overall case, we should all know everything there is to know."

He filled them in on what he'd learned at the scene.

"I've been to that bar," Dmitri said. "It's kinda a dive, no dancefloor. Just a pick-up joint, really."

Miss Thelma returned carrying a plate mounded with food, all of which smelled delicious. "There's coffee and soft drinks on the table over there," she said as she set the plate in front of Jake. "What would you like?"

Standing, he said, "What I'd like is for you to sit down, please. Will you do that? For me?"

She patted his cheek and did as he asked.

"Be right back," he told everyone and made his way to a table filled with pitchers of sweet tea and lemonade, a punch bowl, an ice bucket, and a large coffee urn.

He filled a cup with ice before pouring in some tea.

"Holding hands at the cemetery?"

He turned around to find Brian standing there, no judgment in his features.

"I saw you notice that," he said, chagrined.

"I'm not the only one."

"I was afraid of that."

"A rebound thing?" Brian asked, pouring himself some coffee from the urn and taking his time to add cream and sugar.

"No," Jake said. "For either of us. We just both found ourselves needing some comfort and ..."

"And one thing led to another," Brian said. "You don't have to tell me. Been down that road many a time, friend."

"What's Tommy told you? About our fight, I mean."

"Nothing. He's been as tight-lipped as you." He sipped his coffee, wincing at its heat. "I'm pretty sure Dmitri knows something. Steven too. But Dmitri hasn't brought it up and I haven't asked. I'm not opening the door to having to choose sides."

"And you shouldn't," Jake said. "What's between me and Tommy is between me and Tommy. It shouldn't have to affect anyone else."

"Including Owen?"

"What Owen and I did had nothing to do with Tommy or Kenny."

"And I'm not disputing that," he said, "but it had everything to do with you and Owen. If any feelings are starting to grow, how things play out with Tommy is gonna have an impact. There's no way around that."

Jake regarded him. "Wanna know how I can tell you're a good friend?"

"Sure, hit me with it."

"Because you tell me shit I don't wanna hear and I still manage to hear it loud and clear. *Without* getting pissed."

Brian laughed. "I'm sure you'll do the same for me when I fuck up," he said. "And trust me, I will."

They returned to the table and Jake dug into his plate of food. "Miss Thelma, this is amazing!"

"Don't tell me you never had soul food before," she said. "Jake, I'm gonna have to start feeding you on a regular basis."

"I won't say no to that," he assured her as he cleared his plate.

"Thelma, honey?" One of her church-lady friends had approached the table.

"I know, Addie, I know," she said, standing up again. "You boys are the last and I think the Lady's Board is fixin' to wrap things up. I hate to rush you, but I don't want to be a bother to them after they've done so much for me this week."

Assuring her that they completely understood, the four men helped clear the table, throwing out what was garbage and transporting what was not into the kitchen. That completed, they didn't resume their seats.

As Brian and Dmitri got their suit jackets from the vestibule, Owen asked, "Is this morning's call going to have you tied up the rest of the day?"

"Unless something remarkable turns up, no," Jake said. "Why?"

Owen looked around the room. The men from the church were breaking down the tables and chairs and stacking them against the wall. The ladies were carrying the beverages back into the kitchen.

"I'm sure I don't have to tell you what things are like now," he said, still surveying the room. "The leftovers get put away, the tables get folded up, the mourners go home. And then it's just you."

Jake embraced him, not out of passion, simply to impart the affection and support he felt for Owen. Releasing him, he asked, "Do you want to come over?"

"Do you mind?"

"Not in the least," Jake said, a firm grasp on Owen's shoulder and an understanding smile on his own face.

"I just don't want to be alone, that's all."

"You don't need to explain. You hear me?"

Owen smiled and nodded.

"What about Miss Thelma?" Jake asked. "Should you bring her too? She's in the same boat as you, and she's always welcome."

"Actually," Owen said, "she's in an entirely different boat. Miss Addie and the others are all going back to her place. I believe Miss Addie will be replacing me in the guest room tonight. And then they're all bringing her back here in the morning for church."

"Good," Jake said, satisfied that Miss Thelma's needs would be met.

They agreed that Owen would see Miss Thelma home and swing by his own place to change into more comfortable attire.

"While you're there," Jake said, "you might want to pack an overnight bag."

CHAPTER THIRTY-THREE

FUCHSIA LAMMÉ HEARD A CRASH FROM THE BACK ROOM and jumped.

"Lord, what has that chil' done now?" she said aloud to the empty shop.

Tommy had arrived for work still in his suit from the funeral, clearly worked up. She'd asked if it was because of his friend, knowing that he'd been another victim of this savage preying on her children.

"No," he'd said brusquely and headed into the back room to change. He'd dropped off less formal attire at the shop before heading out to Queens with his sister, Dmitri, and Steven. That was almost three hours ago and he'd barely said three words since returning. The crash was the first actual sound he'd made.

Fuchsia locked the front door and turned the "Closed" sign around, and went into the back, where she found Tommy kneeling on the floor among pieces of broken pottery, crying.

"Oh, honey," she said, squatting down next to him and enfolding him in the voluminous sleeves of her caftan. "Tell Mama all about it."

"I think he cheated on me," he sobbed in her arms.

"That nice detective?" she said, rocking him. "Why you think that, baby boy?"

"Because *I* cheated on *him*," he wailed.

"Oh, my goodness, chil'," she said. "Sounds like you done made a big ol' mess o' things. Shh," she comforted him, dabbing his eyes with her sleeve, thanking the good lord that he didn't wear makeup.

"You jus' calm yourself down and Mama gon' help you work it all out."

After about five minutes, Tommy had cried it out and was seated in a metal folding chair while Fuchsia used a broom to sweep the broken pottery aside.

"I don't know where to start, Fuchsia," he said, his voice still catching.

"The beginnin's always a good place." She sat in the other folding chair, which creaked under her weight.

"What about the shop?" he asked.

"Don' you worry nothin' 'bout the shop. If anybody want a pot that bad, they'll come back."

Tommy did indeed start at the beginning and, though he hadn't planned to, told her everything, ending with seeing Jake and Owen holding hands at the cemetery. Fuchsia remained silent until he looked at the pile of broken pottery, the latest casualty in the drama.

"Chil'," was all she could say, a look of utter disbelief etched into her expressive features.

"I know," he said. "It's all so crazy, and everything happened so fast."

"What's crazy is you playin' Sherlock Mothuhfuckin' Holmes and puttin' yourself in *danger*!" she scolded him. "How do you know this Chris boy wasn't the killer? He coulda kilt you *too*! And then where would yo' Mama be?! *Hmm*?!"

"Jake said pretty much the same thing," he said, unable to keep from chuckling despite his lingering sniffles. "Well, he left out the 'Mama' part."

"And he was right!" She handed him a tissue that could be thrown away and not require dry-cleaning. "You love him, donchu?" she asked with tenderness.

"How can you ask that, Fuchsia?" he protested. "You know I do."

"And I know he love you," she said. "One look at that boy and anybody can tell." She paused to redirect her own thoughts. "And you tol' him 'bout this bartender yesterday morning?"

"Uh huh," he said. "And he told me to leave."

"And he was okay at the wake that afternoon?"

"As okay as could be expected, I guess."

"Then why you so sure he done slep' with this lawyer? Because they was holdin' hands today?"

"Yeah," he said. "But I could tell. It was the vibe between them. I know how Jake looks after he's had sex."

"Okay, baby boy, I can't dispute that." She thought. "You think it was to get back at you?"

"No," Tommy said. "Jake's not spiteful like that."

"Then why else you think he mighta done the nasty with this Owen fella?"

Tommy chewed on this. "Maybe he was hurting? I don't know. Feeling alone?"

"Mmhmm," Fuchsia said nodding sagaciously, her turban adding emphasis to the gesture.

"And I know Owen's hurting. And alone."

This time Fuchsia rolled her eyes.

"Sounds like you done worked it all out," she said. "Now tell me more about this stromboli."

DANI WAS THRILLED WHEN SANDRINE TOLD HER the paintings would be done in time for the opening.

"And you're sure you can count on him?"

"*Mais oui,*" Sandrine said. "Colin and I have danced this tango many times before and it always ends the same way. He makes me wait and then delivers a masterpiece, knowing that I will forgive his transgressions."

Dani thought Sandrine looked ten years younger. The stress had really gotten to her over the last week and Dani was grateful that this burden had been lifted.

"Well, I can't wait to see them," she said. "You know I love all his other pieces, and these sound incredible."

"I am sure you will not be disappointed, *chérie*. In the meantime, I have a special project that is suited just to you."

With the positive response the invitations had gotten from the assorted art critics in the city, all of whom were eagerly awaiting the opening, it had occurred to Sandrine that, if each one brought a photographer, there would be no room for the patrons.

"*Alors*," she said, after explaining this to Dani, "I think we should have one photographer, maybe two, but they would be our own. The newspapers can print the photographs that they take. And, since you are a successful student at a prestigious art school," she added with pride in her protégé, "I thought that perhaps you could find our people."

Dani was thrilled to be entrusted with this task and set about calling fellow students from Parsons who were focused on photography.

Within an hour, she had two lined up.

About halfway through her shift at the gallery, the phone rang.

"Galerie Delacroix," Dani said cheerfully, still feeling the exhilaration of having accomplished her assignment to Sandrine's satisfaction. "How may I help you?"

"Dani Kramer, please."

"This is Dani."

"Dani, this is Helen Olsen."

"Hi, Sergeant Olsen," she said, suddenly nervous. From the background noise, she could tell the cop was in the precinct. "Are you still at work?"

"Unfortunately," Olsen said. "I'm covering for someone until relief can get here. I'll be able to get home soon, and then I'm off for two days."

"That's good," Dani said. "Is there anything new on Iggy?"

"I'm not sure," she replied. "Officer Iles, one of the second-shift guys here, spoke to someone last night, I think he said it was at the Ninth Circle. I know you'd mentioned that place. Anyway, this guy told Iles that he remembered seeing Iggy last Saturday. He didn't speak to him, only saw him from across the bar. He said that Iggy seemed agitated, but then he got talking to someone and appeared to calm down."

"Did he say who this other guy was?" Dani asked.

"He said he didn't know him. Mentioned that he may have seen him before, but wasn't certain," Olsen said. "But the important thing is that this witness places Iggy at the bar after you last saw him and said he was pretty sure that he left with this guy."

"Was he able to describe him?"

"Only the basics, and not very specific at that. Said he looked to be in his twenties, thin, brown hair. Wasn't too clear on anything else. Said it was dark and smoky and that he wasn't really paying much attention to them." Iles had given her more than that, but not enough to impart to Dani.

"At least it's something, right?"

"Well, it's more than we had."

"Thank you, Sergeant Olsen," she said. "You don't know how much I appreciate this."

After hanging up the phone, Helen Olsen went upstairs to Homicide. She'd promised to keep Griffin in the loop, and, seated at his desk, she wrote him a quick note about the break Iles had gotten at the Ninth Circle.

As she put the pad back in the pile where she'd found it, something caught her eye. Pulling a single sheet of paper from between two folders, she gazed at the composite sketch that Chris Albright had assisted with.

Olsen went to the Xerox machine and ran off half a dozen copies. Returning the sketch to Griffin's pile of work, she added an addendum to her note.

"I copied your composite sketch. I'm sending Iles back to the bar so he can ask his witness if it's the same guy. Will keep you posted."

Back at her own desk, she called Iles at home. "You may wanna get in here," she said.

"WHAT'S GOING ON WITH JAKE AND OWEN?"

Brian and Dmitri were lounging on Brian's bed smoking, naked, atop the sheet. Even with the air conditioning, they'd worked up quite a sweat.

"I thought we agreed we weren't going to discuss that," Brian said.

"I know," Dmitri groaned, prolonging the word. "But I'm curious."

"You mean, nosy," Brian said, tweaking his nose. "You can only be curious about stuff that isn't your business when you have my job." They both laughed. "Besides, if I tell you anything *I* know, and I'm not saying I know anything, you'll want to tell me what *you* know, and I'm *sure* you know *something*. Then where are we? Playing marriage counselors for our friends, and you know we'd wind up choosing sides."

"Why do you have to be such a grownup?" Dmitri asked.

"That's just it, D," Brian said. "We're all grownups here, including Jake, Tommy, and Owen. And grownups get to make their own choices, as well as their own mistakes. Our job, as grownup friends of the grownups, is to let them do that and be there for them when, and if, they need us."

"That means waiting," Dmitri groused, "and I hate waiting!"

Brian took a final drag and stubbed out his cigarette. Then he took Dmitri's cigarette and extinguished that as well. "I got something you don't have to wait for," he said rolling on top of his new boyfriend.

An hour later, they were once again sweaty and smoking.

"Fuck," Dmitri groaned.

"What?"

"I don't wanna get up, but I gotta get ready for work."

"You wanna shower here?"

"I could, but I'd still have to go home and get my dance gear," he said. "Besides, I told Steven I'd meet him for dinner." As he stood, Brian smacked his bare butt playfully. "You coming to the club tonight?"

"Can't," Brian said. "I'm hoping to get together with Jake and see what he can tell me about the body they found this morning."

"You two never stop working, do you?"

"'Fraid not, kiddo."

Once Dmitri had put his suit back on, albeit in a disheveled fashion, Brian got up and remained naked as he walked him to the door of his apartment. Kissing him, he said, "Dance your sneakers off and make lots of tips."

"Call me tomorrow?"

"Count on it."

"But not before noon, okay?"

"Not before noon," he said. "I know the rules."

Once Dmitri left, Brian padded into the kitchen and opened a beer before calling Jake.

"Hey, it's me," he said when the phone was answered. "What're you up to?"

"Owen's here," he said. "We were about to order some take-out. Why? What's up?"

"Umm," Brian hedged. "Is this a date?"

Jake laughed. "No, he just wanted some company after … well, everything. You wanna join us?"

"I'm not sure how to take that," Brian said, eliciting another laugh from his friend. "Actually, that's why I called. I was hoping you'd be free tonight to tell me whatever you know about this latest victim and then we could go over everything so far, see how this fits in."

"Hang on, lemme check." Brian could hear Jake place his hand over the receiver, which was pointless because he heard him ask Owen, "You up to Brian coming over?" He couldn't hear the reply, but Jake was back on the line, saying, "How fast can you get uptown? We'll wait on ordering until you're here."

AFTER STUFFING THEMSELVES ON CHINESE TAKEOUT and washing it down with the beer Brian had brought—this time a whole case— they got to work.

Rather than disrupt their digestions with talk of the case, Jake had brought Brian up to speed on his recent decision to come out at work, a choice the reporter heartily supported.

"Are you sure you're up to this?" Brian asked Owen as Jake cleared the table of the plates and empty cardboard cartons.

"Not sure I'm up to anything, but if I'm going to do *something*, it may as well be worthwhile."

Jake had had no follow-up reports from the 68th, so all he had to share was what he'd seen and heard at the crime scene, which was more extensive than what he'd imparted at the church.

"And there's no doubt in your mind that it's the same perp?" Brian asked.

"None," Jake said.

"I had a thought," Owen interjected. They both looked at him. "Do you know what this …" He looked at his notes. "Quentin Barstow did for a living?"

"No," Jake said. "Why?"

"Well, we already know that all the victims were gay men who'd been at a bar, but have we considered anything else they might have had in common?"

Jake and Brian exchanged intrigued looks and started rifling through their notes and files. In short order, they had a list compiled.

Victim number one, Gil McCandless, had been an unemployed actor, but an employed waiter working at the Four Seasons on East 52nd. Billy Curtis was a personal trainer putting clients through their paces at a gym in the West Village, but making home calls to an elite few. Cody Fischer, an artist at an ad agency. Kenny Wilson, stock trader.

Until he got the file from the 33rd and now two from the 68th, the only information Jake had on the others was their names and when they were killed: Arthur Noonan had been found in Bay Ridge on June second, Hector Quinones in Washington Heights July fifth, and now Quentin Barstow.

"I guess that wasn't all that helpful," Owen said.

"I'm not so sure," Jake pointed out. "We don't know anything about Noonan, Quinones, and Barstow, but look at the others. All of them had jobs that put them in regular contact with upper-income people. Is it possible that we're looking for a wealthy psychopath?"

"Or a wealthy *strigoi*," Brian interjected.

"Excuse me, guys," Owen said, rising from the table, "I gotta pee."

As he headed toward the front hall, Jake hollered, "It's the second door—"

"I know," Owen called back to him from the stairs.

"He knows," Brian teased him.

"Jesus," Jake said, looking mournfully toward the papers spread out before them. "I don't know how much more I can accomplish tonight." He went into the kitchen, opening another three bottles of beer. "I can't believe it's only been nine fucking days since we found Fischer. I didn't even know you then, not really. And Owen? Not at all." He drank several swallows from his bottle. "And since then, two more people are dead, we find out about two others we hadn't known about, Tommy sleeps with a fuckin' bartender, I wind up in bed with—"

"What?!" Brian exclaimed. "Is that what happened?"

Realizing he couldn't unring the bell, he said, "Yeah. The night he went 'undercover' at the Eagle's Nest. He fucked Chris Albright. Claims the idiot wouldn't give up info without getting some dick in return. First."

"And this is what has you all fucked up?" Brian asked.

"Yeah," Jake replied, giving his friend a quizzical look. "What else would it be?"

"Shit, man, I'm sorry," Brian said, choosing his words carefully.

"Sorry about what?" Owen had returned from the bathroom just in time to hear only the last comment.

Jake sighed. "Well, since I ran my mouth and told Brian, I may as well tell you too." He slid the third bottle to where Owen had been sitting and said, "Pull up a chair, it's story time with Uncle Jake."

When he'd finished, they were both shaking their heads.

"Didn't he realize the chance he was taking being alone with him?" Owen said.

"I think he believed he was helping," Jake said, sick of the story by now, having replayed it over and over in his head since Tommy had told him. Thinking about it, the only time that had stopped was when he'd been with Owen at the restaurant and then back at home.

"Well," Brian said, "he told you. Obviously, it was eating at him."

"Oh, I know it was," Jake said. "I could tell that while he was confessing. Doesn't mean it didn't piss me off."

Brian regarded Owen and Jake before speaking. "Jake," he began, the uncharacteristic caution audible in his tone, "I may be overstepping here, and if I am, let me know."

"Just ask it," Jake said.

"Have you and Tommy ever had an arrangement?"

"An 'arrangement?'"

Brian shared his awkwardness in silence with Owen, their exchanged look making it clear that they understood something to which their friend was not privy.

"Okay," Brian began with a slight, though not impatient, sigh. "Tommy's your first real relationship, right? I mean your first gay relationship."

"Yeah?" Jake replied, unsure of where this was heading.

"Well," Brian proceeded, "in our community—"

"Community?" Jake interrupted.

Owen reached over and took Jake's hand in reassurance.

"Yes," he said, "community."

"In our community," Brian resumed, "a lot of guys view monogamy as a concept of the straight world. I've been in several successful relationships that were open."

"Successful?" Jake balked. "Then how come you're not still in them?"

Sensing Jake's resistance to the shattering of long-held norms, Brian proceeded cautiously and with affection.

"Because ultimately we didn't want the same things," he said. "But fidelity, or monogamy, or whatever you want to call it—that was never an issue." He looked to Owen for backup.

"What Brian's talking about," he said, giving Jake's hand a squeeze, "was never my scene, but it was Kenny's"

Jake looked at him.

"Remember I told you that Kenny went out with friends when I had to work late?"

"Yeah?"

"Well, he didn't always come home alone."

Jake withdrew his hand from Owen's grasp. "And you were okay with this?"

Owen nodded. "I was. Because it had nothing to do with him and me."

Taking a chance, Brian added, "You do know, don't you, that Tommy saw you two at the cemetery?"

"Fuck," Owen groaned.

"I was pretty sure he had," Jake said. "But one has nothing to do with the other." He looked to Owen. "Even though you didn't know the details, we made that clear last night. I just needed to feel—"

"Normal?" Owen finished for him. "I know, Jake. I did too. I'm not doubting your motives."

"Look, I know you only just found out about the bartender," Brian said, "and in the middle of a shit storm to boot. And I know that what Owen and I have said are pretty new concepts to you. But what are you thinking?"

Jake considered his answer before offering it. "I'm thinking I can't trust him," he said. "It's not just that he fucked Albright. Part of it is why he was there in the first place. Remember when you told me you were afraid of secrets? That's all I seem to be dealing with lately. Making sense of the secrets I've been keeping from Frank is bad enough. I don't have the mental strength to deal with anyone else's, especially ones like this.

"Right now, if I can't trust him," he continued, "I can't be with him. Down the road, that might change, I don't know, maybe. But not now."

Brian was nodding. "I can't argue with that."

"Neither can I," added Owen supportively.

Jake drained his beer and said, "So there, everything's in the open. Now my two best friends know all about it."

"Your two best friends?" Brian asked.

Jake thought about what he'd said. "Yeah," he confirmed, "my two best friends."

"Well," Brian said, putting a hand on Jake's, "I've been called a lot worse."

CHAPTER THIRTY-FOUR

THE TRIO HAD PUT THE WORK ASIDE FOR THE NIGHT and settled onto the couch to see what HBO had to offer. They all, each for his own reasons, needed a break, a complete respite from thought.

And, furthermore, each was happy to help the other two achieve it.

By the second half of a double feature of mindless comedies, the coffee table was covered with empty beer bottles; rocks glasses were now among them, Johnny and Jim having joined the party. The crystal ashtray was overflowing. The stress and booze had taken their toll, prompting Jake and Owen to return to old habits, Jake having retrieved Tommy's almost-full pack from his nightstand.

When Jake had resumed his seat on the middle of the sofa and lit a cigarette, Owen put his arm around him, and had said, "You're a bad influence, detective," and kissed his cheek before lighting one of his own.

"Good lord," Brian had said, "I leave you two alone for twenty-four hours!"

After the movies, a tipsy Brian announced that he was heading home. It was just past ten o'clock.

"We could share a cab," he said to Owen, "unless ..."

Jake and Owen looked at each other. It was Jake who spoke first.

"You're certainly welcome to stay," he said to the attorney, "but after what I told you, I'd understand if you weren't comfortable doing that."

"Jake," he replied, "the only thing that's changed since last night is that you told me why you two fought. I trusted your motives then and I trust them now. Besides, I have no right to judge you.

"I guess the question is, do you *want* me to stay."

Had their bond not grown such suddenly deep roots, Brian would have felt awkward as hell bearing witness to this exchange. But not now.

"Yes," Jake said, "I want you to stay."

"Okay," Brian said gamely, "that's settled. I'm flying solo."

"Well," Jake said, reminding Brian of the joke he'd made on the phone, "you're welcome to stay too."

All three laughed. "Careful," Brian cautioned, "we don't know *all* of each other's secrets. I might like that."

"I might too," Owen said, looking directly at Brian.

"You serious?" Jake asked him. "I was just being a smart ass."

"I'm willing if you are," Owen told him. "After the unbelievable insanity of the last week—insanity none of us signed up for, I should add—something crazy that actually feels good, that we actually *chose*, might be what we all need."

"Well, you're right about one thing," Jake said, picking up his beer. "'Crazy' is the word for it."

Brian and Owen exchanged a look. The reporter's nose for undiscovered information caught a whiff of something. He sat in one of the wingbacks.

"You've never had a threesome," he asked Jake, with no hint of challenge in his tone, "have you?"

Jake looked at the other two men, feeling cornered. "No," he admitted begrudgingly. "I told you that my sex life has always been pretty conventional. I'm guessing you two *have*?"

They both nodded.

"Has the idea ever intrigued you at all?" Owen asked him. His tone was one of sincere interest, not temptation.

Jake looked at the two of them, but didn't see potential sex partners. He saw two of the closest friends he'd ever had, the two people in the world whom, at the present moment and in less than a week, he trusted and admired and respected more than anyone else.

He also saw two men about whom he'd come to care very deeply, and with whom he felt entirely safe.

"I wouldn't know what to do," he admitted.

Brian and Owen both laughed, but not unkindly, Brian moving from the chair to his prior seat on the other side of Jake. "You'd be surprised," he said.

"SURPRISED?"

Colin had heard Sandrine open the door to his studio and turned excitedly to greet her, unbridled exuberance in his voice. Once again, he was completely nude, palette in one hand, brush in the other. "Pride" leaned against the wall, the 4-by-6-foot canvas complete. On the easel behind Colin was another canvas, nearly finished. Based on the colors, Sandrine assumed it was "Lust."

"Not at all," Sandrine said impassively. "You have never left me with empty spaces on the walls." She crossed the room to examine the recently completed work. "You have not signed it."

"I'm waiting 'til all seven are done to sign 'em all," he informed her. He had moved directly behind Sandrine to join in her admiration of his work.

She turned and used one manicured finger to brush a lock of brown hair from his eyes. "Not going out tonight to … unwind?"

"No, love," he said, returning to his work in progress. "I'm in the 'omestretch now. No more nights out 'til we open." He added a broad stroke of deep crimson to the colors bursting from the all-black background.

"I am relieved to hear that," she said. "This week will be busy for us all and I do not want you to overdo it."

"No worries there, love," he said, still focused on the painting. "I've done all the unwinding I need for now."

And then what? she wondered as she left the studio.

HAVING SPOTTED THE EYEWITNESS AT THE FAR END OF THE BAR, Officer Patrick Iles sidled up next to the man in question.

Like the prior night, Iles was in plain-clothes, an effort to blend in, as well as to catch people off guard when he showed his badge. Tonight, he was wearing jeans, a pale blue Oxford button-down, and a light blazer.

Also like the prior night, the witness was dressed to attract. A tall, slim black man, his lithe body was encased in tight Levi's and an equally tight wifebeater, which showcased his lean, muscular arms.

"Can I talk to you for a minute, Mr. Chisholm?" Iles asked the man leaning there.

The guy gave him an irritated glance. "I already told you everything I know."

"It's about a composite sketch," Iles said.

"And I also told you I didn't see this guy well enough to help with that." Like his first, brief statement, this too carried the message that the conversation was over.

"I'm not asking you to help with it," Iles persisted, "just to look at one."

He eyed the cop impatiently. "Okay," he said, still clearly annoyed that his personal manhunt had been interrupted. "Lemme see it."

Iles withdrew a tri-folded piece of paper from his inside jacket pocket and handed it to the witness. The guy took it and stepped toward an adjacent wall where a light was mounted, unfolding the paper as he went. Anxious to get it over with, he said, "I told you, I didn't get a good look—"

He cut himself off. "Well, fuck," he said, his tone having changed to one of astonishment. "This is him. His hair's a little different, but everything else, especially the eyes, is spot on."

He returned to Iles and handed the paper back to him, having read what was written on it. "You think this is the motherfucker who's been hacking guys up?" he asked in a confidential tone.

"We're not sure yet," Iles said. "But you're certain that this is the man you saw with Iggy last Saturday night?"

"Yeah, for sure. Even with the dark and the smoke, those eyes stood out. Piercing, you know?"

"Thanks," Iles said. "See? You've been more help than you thought you'd be." He paused, sizing up the witness. "Can I buy you a drink? To thank you?"

Warming to the young officer, despite the cop's wedding band, he said, "Only if you join me."

The corners of Iles' mouth turned up slightly. "Afraid I can't. I'm on duty." The witness looked dejected. "But," Iles added, "I can have a soda. And I'm off the clock in about a half hour. Then I can do what I want." Raising one eyebrow, he added, "*Whatever* I want."

As the witness smiled knowingly, Iles caught the bartender's eye and ordered a refill for the man next to him and a Coke for himself.

Extending his hand, the cop said, "Patrick Iles, Mr. Chisholm."

"I know," the man said, smiling as he eyed him up and down. "I got your card." Pausing to light a Newport, he added, "But lose that 'Mister' shit. You can call me Kyle if you want, but most folks call me K.C."

"And I know that," Iles said. "I took notes last night." Their eyes locked, Iles took a sip of his Coke.

"I FEEL LIKE I'VE STEPPED INTO SOME PARALLEL UNIVERSE," Jake said as he poured Coke over ice.

He, Brian, and Owen were all standing in the kitchen, naked, at two-thirty in the morning, the only lights coming from the hood over the range and what was spilling in from the living room.

"I bet," Brian said. "I hope it's a good one."

Turning, his glass in hand, Jake said, "I think so?"

His introduction to multiple-partner sex had been revelatory. He'd had his fair share of casual one-night stands in the past, albeit probably far fewer than many other gay men his age in the city, but only one-on-one, never anything like this.

When he'd slept with Owen the night before, he'd done so on impulse, with an underlying curiosity as to what might come of it. But tonight was the first time he'd ever had sex with a friend whom he knew would remain a friend.

"So, this is what the whole 'free love' thing is all about, huh?" he asked.

"A version of it, I guess," Owen said, coming up beside him and sliding an arm around his waist. "Actually, it wasn't all that different from last night."

"How so?" Jake asked.

"Well, we all desperately needed some form of release," he said, "some oasis in the middle of all this shit. Our closeness, our trust, made that possible."

"And from what you've told me," Brian chimed in, "your experiences have been kinda limited."

Jake responded to the instinct to defend himself, but Brian raised a silencing hand before he could speak. "I'm not judging you," he asserted. "I totally get that you have your reasons and that they're all legit.

"I won't speak for Owen," he continued, "but casual, no-strings sex—sometimes even anonymous—is part of our world."

Jake did not need the first-person plural pronoun explained further.

"Well," he said, "it's not like I've never had one-night stands."

"Yeah," Brian countered, "but having one-night stands because you're afraid of being found out, and having them because they can be fun are two different things."

Jake chewed on this, and Owen saw the chance to interject. "I can't disagree with him."

As he looked from Brian to Owen, Jake seemed to them like a bird shoved from the nest by its mother, unsure of its first flight.

"And this is all part of what Tommy's world was like before me?"

Brian shot a momentary glace in Owen's direction to gauge his response to the mention of Tommy's name. He was relieved to find none.

"I can't answer that," he told Jake, "but the odds are better than not. Everybody's different."

"He's right," Owen concurred. "Random pick-ups were never my thing, but Kenny had quite a few notches on his bedpost."

"It's a lot to think about," Jake conceded.

Brian snaked a supportive arm around his shoulders. "I guess the big question," he said, "is, did you enjoy it?"

Jake looked at him. "Honest answer?"

Stepping to Jake's other side, Owen said, "Nothing but."

Jake shot them a tentatively mischievous smile. "Enough to hope we do it again."

He suspected that the others hoped the same thing. And he was right.

"SHE'S IN 'ER FLAT FOR THE NIGHT," Colin said, still working on his painting, having heard the high-heeled footsteps ascending the stairs to the fourth floor.

His tone and body language no longer bore the giddiness he'd feigned for Sandrine's benefit. They were somewhat darker, more focused, more carnal.

Without a sound, a slim figure emerged from the shadows. Colin didn't have to see him to sense he was there.

"You're not going out tonight?" he asked.

"I just told 'er that to mollify 'er," Colin said, adding more crimson. "I promised I'd take you out, didn't I, ducks?"

"Yes."

"Then that's what we'll do," he said, satisfied with his work for the night. "I'll wash up and put on clothes, then off we go."

"Where are we going?"

"I don't know," Colin said as he turned on the water in the large work sink. "I was thinking someplace new for both of us."

SHORTLY BEFORE DAWN, VIVVIE RESTIVO PUSHED HER SHOPPING CART into a protected area under the West Side Highway.

She was still several blocks away from the encampment she called home, but she needed a rest.

Sitting on a large block of cement, she looked down.

"Well, I'll be," she said, spying a sneaker next to a pile of refuse.

Hoping to find its mate and thereby acquire a new pair of shoes, Vivvie knelt down and began pushing aside the pile of detritus.

"Oh, shit," she said, uncovering a denim clad leg beyond the sneaker.

Hell, ya gotta do what ya gotta do, she mentally rationalized and continued searching. *If he's dead, he won't be needin' his sneakers no more*, she thought.

She found the second sneaker at the end of a bent leg, tucked under the first she'd spied. She pulled the shoes off the feet they'd been encasing and tossed them into her shopping cart. Unable to control her curiosity, Vivvie continued digging and, a minute later, she screamed and staggered back, landing on her rump.

Not wanting to draw attention, she covered her mouth with both hands, got back on her feet, and furtively looked in all directions. No one was approaching, and she released the breath she'd been holding in her lungs.

Looking down, Vivvie began to cry. *He's just a baby*, she thought.

Lying at Vivvie's feet was the body of a teenage boy. From the dirt on his clothes, Vivvie assumed he was one of the street kids, runaways trying to survive the best they could.

Who would do this to a little boy? she wondered, her heart aching.

The Hispanic youth lay on his back, his eyes wide and terrified. His throat had been savagely torn open.

Collecting her wits and not wanting to be found over a dead body, Vivvie pulled all the refuse she could find atop the boy, making sure no part of him was sticking out of the pile, and hurriedly pushed her shopping cart east toward her camp.

CHAPTER THIRTY-FIVE

UNLIKE OWEN, BRIAN HAD NOT BROUGHT AN OVERNIGHT BAG, but had stayed, nonetheless.

Jake had feared that, in the light of day, after sharing his queen-size bed in the nude, there might be unwelcome awkwardness, but, to his complete surprise, he was proven wrong. He, Owen, and Brian woke early and made breakfast together without a trace of discomfort. After eating, each went about the business of his day: Brian and Owen leaving for their respective apartments and Jake mentally preparing himself to report for work at three.

Jake found himself envious of his two friends and their ease with what had transpired between them. *Was this all part of being true to himself?* he wondered. Maybe he didn't need to be so on guard all the time. Unlike Brian, Owen wasn't out at work, but he was still infinitely more comfortable in his own skin than Jake was.

Food for thought.

He spent the morning reviewing what little they'd accomplished the night before, making special note to find out ASAP more specifics on Noonan, Quinones, and Barstow. He packed the paperwork into an attaché case he almost never used, and which had to be excavated from the back of a closet. That done, he made himself lunch before indulging in a long shower prior to dressing for work.

Jake arrived in the squad room fifteen minutes early, feeling more refreshed than he had in weeks. He wondered how much his recent sexual exploits had to do with the shift in his inner energy since, the last time he'd been in the precinct, he hadn't yet slept with either Owen or Brian. And he'd only just made the decision to come out.

A lot had changed since Thursday evening.

He set his attaché case next to his desk and picked up the note from Helen Olsen. He immediately called downstairs to Missing Persons, but was informed that Sergeant Olsen wouldn't be in until midnight the following evening. Jake asked if she could be reached at home and given a message to call him.

The officer on the other end of the line clearly didn't want to be bothered with that and told Jake to hang on. A moment later, he was back, reading Helen's home number into the phone.

Jake still left a message with him, leaving his home and service numbers, but then dialed Olsen at her apartment. He got no answer. *Shit*, he thought, as he updated his mental agenda to include reaching out to Olsen until she picked up, both at home and downstairs.

Jake's next order of business was to follow up with the other precincts. He left messages for Ralph Underwood at the 68th, and Oscar Jimenez, the homicide detective with whom he'd spoken at the 33rd, asking that they call him as soon as possible. In both cases, the detectives were off duty that day.

That done, he poured himself a cup of joe from the squad room's industrial coffeemaker and waited for Frank.

THE REST OF HIS SHIFT WAS AS UNEVENTFUL as the prior ten days had been turbulent.

Neither Underwood nor Jimenez returned his calls, which wasn't a surprise since they were both off. And his repeated attempts to reach Helen Olsen at home were unsuccessful.

No one contacted him or Frank with new information on any of the open cases and, fortunately, no new vics were found. That basically meant that they spent their Sunday doing paperwork.

At around eight, Jake asked, "You wanna go grab something to eat? We can let Friedrich know where to find us if we're needed."

"The Acropolis?" Frank asked.

"That's what I was thinking."

Frank heaved a sigh. "Ya know what, partner?" he said. "That actually sounds pretty damn good. Gimme five to hit the can and wash up."

Ten minutes later, they were seated in a booth by the front window, menus in hand.

"Hi, Jake."

He looked up to find a smiling Dani standing at the table.

"Hi, Dani," he said. "Nice to see you."

"Did Sergeant Olsen tell you? They may have a lead on Iggy."

The mention of an N.Y.P.D. officer from their precinct caught Frank's attention and he lowered his menu.

"Yeah," Jake said, aware that his partner was openly paying attention. "She left me a note. I'm really happy to hear that." He didn't add that Helen had seen the composite sketch and thought there might be a connection to the string of homicides. No use in upsetting the girl with speculation.

"Oh," she said, sounding a bit forlorn, "I forgot to tell you. Margareta quit."

"So soon?" he asked. "Did Stavros grab her butt once too often?"

Dani laughed. "No, but that's funny. Actually, it was because of the night she got so upset." She cast an uncertain glance in Frank's direction.

Alarms went off in Jake's head, knowing that Dani could easily mention his meeting with Brian and the presence of crime-scene photos.

"I'm sorry to hear that," he said, fishing for ways to avoid a potential train wreck. "I remember you telling me about it, some customer getting abusive because she's Italian?"

Dani picked up immediately on Jake's subterfuge and played along seamlessly.

"Yeah," she said. "Like I told you, he had her really upset. She said she couldn't work here anymore. Not with monsters like that."

"Well," he said, "please give her my best. It'd be nice to see her again outside of here."

"I'll do that," Dani assured him, feeling like a character in a spy movie. "Are you two ready to order?"

STEVEN AND DMITRI HAD DROPPED BY TOMMY'S APARTMENT around three, hoping to convince him to go to a movie or out for a drink.

He'd isolated himself the night before, coming home from work and going straight into his bedroom. When Steven had called Sunday morning, Cara had informed him of this, and he made up his mind an intervention was in order. He got right on the phone to Dmitri.

"Tommy," Cara said, knocking on his door. "D and Steven are here."

Her tone was gentle. Without having to be told, she knew something well out of the ordinary was troubling her little brother, and she wanted to help, not make it worse.

Tommy rolled onto his back and stared at the ceiling. After a moment, he said, "Tell 'em I'll be out in a minute."

When he emerged, Steven leapt to his feet. "Oh, honey, look at you!" he gasped. "You look like you haven't slept in days!"

"Way to make a guy feel better," Dmitri said.

"You hush," Steven admonished him before returning his full attention to Tommy. "You just come sit down with us, sweetie."

"Do I want to be privy to this?" Cara asked.

"You may as well be," Tommy said. "Everybody else is, it seems."

As Steven and Dmitri did their best to talk Tommy out of his funk, Cara was able to fit the pieces together.

"Just so I'm clear," she said in her usual no-nonsense tone, "you not only put yourself in danger by playing private detective, which, for the record, pissed me off royally when you mentioned it the other night at Jake's. But then you allowed yourself to be alone—and *vulnerable*, I might add—with a material witness who could just as easily have been the perp?"

"Uh, yeah," he said, feeling scolded.

"And if that wasn't bad enough, you jeopardized your *relationship*?"

"That about sums it up."

"You know I love you, right?"

"Yeah."

"Good. Then you won't be insulted when I say that you're a *fucking idiot*!" She stood. "You two clean up this mess. I don't have the stomach for it." She went into her bedroom.

She had no sooner gone than the phone rang.

"What if it's Jake?" Tommy asked them, looking terrified.

"Then you'll talk to him," Steven said, shooing him toward the phone.

"Hello?" Tommy said, his voice tentative.

At once, his face relaxed. "Yes, I can do that." He grabbed a pad and pen from the end table and began writing. "Yep, I've got it." He read back the details. "Okay, thanks, I look forward to it."

"What was that?" Dmitri asked when Tommy had hung up.

"I have a cater-waiter gig coming up, that's all," he said. "It sounds pretty cool. A gallery opening in SoHo this Friday. You two wanna come?"

ON MONDAY, *THE VOICE* HIT THE STREETS, featuring Brian's article about the "Cruising" protests.

Jake had gone out early to pick up a copy and was reading it over a late breakfast, happy for his friend that it made the front page.

Near the bottom of page three was Brian's follow-up on the "serial killer" speculation. He led off with his reporting of Kenny's murder, as well as the discovery of three other possibly related homicides in other precincts.

When Jake finished reading both articles, he called Brian.

"Great story on the protest," he said.

"Thanks, man," the reporter replied, sounding humbly pleased with the praise.

"But you know what?" Jake continued. "Something hit me."

"What's that?"

"Does it strike you as odd that gay guys turned out in droves to protest a movie," he said, "but none of them are protesting our own people being murdered?"

"The thought occurred to me when I was there covering it," Brian said. "But you wanna know what I think it is? Appearance."

"Go on," Jake said, intrigued.

"The movie's gonna be shown nationwide, and I think these guys see it as some sort of public-relations tool, like it's a commercial for being gay in New York or something. They're missing the point that A) it's a work of fiction, and B) it only shows one aspect of life here because that's what the story's about. But they don't see that. Bottom line, they don't like how it makes us look, and you know how obsessed gay men can be about looks.

"The murders, on the other hand, aren't getting any attention, so that subject drops down their list of priorities. The murders aren't making us look bad, so they're not as important."

"Jesus Christ," Jake said. "If that's the case, it's totally fucked up."

"You don't have to tell me."

"By the way, your piece on Kenny and the 'serial' follow-up was some solid reporting."

"Thank you. Again."

Jake was very relieved to note that absolutely nothing had changed about their friendship or its chemistry. Never having experienced what he had two nights before, he wasn't sure what would come next. He was glad to learn that the answer was, "Nothing."

He briefly informed Brian that he had no new information on the other three cases and they made tentative plans to have dinner later in the week, prompting Brian to remember something.

"Hey, I've been meaning to ask you but, with everything going on, I keep forgetting," he said. "What're you doing this Friday night? You and Owen, if that's not being presumptuous."

"I'm not doing anything," Jake said, "but I have no idea about him. Why?"

"My buddy here at the paper is covering the opening of this 'rather chic,' in his words, new art gallery in SoHo," he said. "I thought I might tag along. You know, offer him my support. I wondered if you two wanted to join me. Break the monotony with a little high-brow distraction and some free Champagne."

"I'll mention it to Owen," he replied, "but as for me, count me in."

HELEN OLSEN ARRIVED AT WORK AT FIVE MINUTES TO TWELVE on Monday night and found the messages Jake had left.

Since they all requested that she call at any time, she picked up her phone and dialed him at home.

"Griff?" she said when he answered. "Helen Olsen here. You called?"

"Yes," he said, not hiding his relief at finally being able to talk to her. "I got your note."

"Sorry I couldn't get back to you," she said. "I spent my days off with my sister on Long Island. Needed a break from the city."

Don't I know it, Jake thought.

"No worries," he assured her. "What can you tell me about this lead? You said you copied the composite? Anything come of that?"

In addition to the pink "While You Were Out" slips on her desk had been a note from Patrick Iles. She picked it up.

"Iles said his witness at the Ninth Circle I.D.ed the sketch. Told him it was the guy Dani's friend was talking to the night he disappeared. That's all I know so far. I'll have more after I can have a face-to-face with him. Does that help either of us?"

"Actually," Jake said, feeling his gut sink, "I hope it doesn't. If Dani's friend left with this guy, I have a feeling it's now my case and not yours."

"I was thinking the same thing," she said.

"Well," Jake concluded, "keep me posted, and I'll do the same. Between you and me, I don't have a good feeling about this, but let's hope I'm wrong."

"Already hoping that, Griff," she said before they ended their call.

THE WEEK WAS A WHIRLWIND FOR DANI, with the opening only days away.

The highlight, for her, in the midst of all the preparations, came on Tuesday afternoon when Colin's "Seven Deadly Sins" paintings were hung in the middle viewing space.

Each was four-by-six feet in size and were rendered vertically with a background so black it seemed to actually breathe when Dani looked at them. Onto that background, Colin had created an explosion of color that was so bold it was almost violent, reaching beyond the surface of the canvas and assaulting the viewer. For each of the sins, he'd chosen a different dominant color: green for "Envy," deep red for "Lust," a burning orange for "Wrath," et cetera.

Once they were hung on the blindingly white walls—under Sandrine's scrutinous supervision, naturally—the middle gallery had been transformed into a journey through the realms of depravity. Dani would have thought that the end result would have left her feeling disturbed, unsettled. But, to her surprise, she found it all rather seductive, almost an invitation to indulge in the sins displayed.

In her classes, she had learned that art is neither good nor bad; it can only be described as effective or ineffective. And this was enormously effective.

Each of the paintings had been signed in the lower-right corner—"Davenport"—in deep maroon, almost rust, that resembled slashes more than strokes of a paintbrush.

"You were right," she said to Sandrine once the workmen had left the gallery. "These are amazing. They pull you in, almost through the canvas into another dimension. I envy him."

"Don't," Sandrine said, her tone even but firm. "Do not envy Colin."

"Why not?"

"Look at these paintings, Dani," she said. "Look closely and let yourself feel."

Dani thought she had, but she followed Sandrine's guidance and opened herself up even more.

"Do you not feel it?" Sandrine asked softly. "The pain? The anger? The *violence*?"

"Yes," Dani said tentatively. "I thought that was the point. To feel the darkness of the sins."

"*Non*," Sandrine said. "He is trying to pull you into that darkness, into the darkest corners of his soul so he won't be alone with all this … torture."

If he still has a soul, she thought, though she would not give it voice.

"Do not envy Colin Davenport," she asserted once more. "He should envy you."

"HOW ARE YOU HOLDING UP?" Jake asked.

Owen sighed into the phone. "No clue," he conceded. "Like you said about your issues with Tommy, I've got nothing to compare this with."

It was Wednesday morning and Owen was in his office when Jake had called him. They'd spoken on the phone every day but hadn't seen each other since they'd all parted ways on Sunday.

"Well," Jake said, "whatever you need, you know I'm here for you."

"I know." The statement was simple but spoke volumes.

On Monday, their phone call had been focused on what, if anything, they were embarking on. Both readily acknowledged the inadvisability of either considering a serious involvement at the moment, Jake being on the rebound and Owen still, understandably, in mourning.

But the upthrust of that conversation, however, had been that, while both brought undeniable detractions to the situation, what they found themselves sharing seemed genuine and, in many ways, a blessing, a sort of emotional lifeboat after simultaneous shipwrecks.

They agreed to simply see where it led.

"Look," Jake broached, "I was wondering what you might have planned for Friday evening."

"Planned?" Owen replied. "Jake, I'm lucky if I can plan what I'll eat for my next meal." Jake laughed along with him; not a guffaw that said, "That's a good one!;" more a chuckle that imparted, "Brother, I know what you mean."

"Why?" Owen continued. "What's up?"

"Well," he said, "Brian told me he's going to the opening of an art gallery in SoHo and thought we might like to join him."

"We," Jake thought. The implication of the word had many levels, all of which he was surprised to find he enjoyed.

"Honestly," Owen said, "I can't predict from one day to the next how I'm gonna be feeling."

"I understand," Jake replied.

"*But,*" Owen continued, "as of now? I say I'm in. Life has to go on, right?"

"That it does," Jake said.

"GODAMMIT! I HAVE TO WORK!" Dmitri yelled, almost screamed. "Life *sucks!*"

"Honey, calm down," Steven soothed.

They were in Dmitri's living room on Barrow Street, having just called Uncle Charlie's to get their schedules for the week.

"Yeah," Dmitri protested, "but I *so* wanted to go with Brian to the opening! Especially since Tommy's gonna be working it."

"But what can you do?" Steven asked rhetorically. "You have to work. I'm sure—no, I *know*—that Brian will understand."

"It's not about what Brian understands," Dmitri ranted.

"I know, honey. It's about what you want," Steven said. "But we have to be grownups here."

"I fucking *hate* that word!"

"I know you do," Steven said. "And I have a feeling it hates you too."

"I *know* it does!"

"Here's an idea," Steven offered. "Tell Brian you have to work, but make plans with him for after. Then you can let him tell you all about the opening. He's a reporter. He *lives* to pass along news. Eat up every word. Then eat up *him!*"

Dmitri started to laugh. "See?" he said. "This is why I keep you around!"

"WHAT ARE YOU DOING AFTER WORK TOMORROW NIGHT?"

Dani was standing beside the booth Jake occupied, ready to take his order, but more eager to make plans.

"Are you propositioning me?" he asked, already laughing.

"You wish," she said. "But then again, I have a feeling you don't."

"Tomorrow's Thursday," he said. "That's my 'Friday.' Nothing. Why?"

"Because I told Margareta that you'd like to see her again," she said. "I thought I could bring her to … wherever, and you could talk to her. She said she'd be okay with that."

Jake's brain was suddenly running a mile a minute.

"Do you think Stavros would let me use the phone?" he asked.

"I don't know," she replied. "Want me to check?"

"Please."

She returned to the table a minute or two later and said, "Since it's you, he says it's fine."

He followed her to the front counter where she gestured to the wall-mounted phone. He dialed Brian at home from memory.

"Hey, it's me," he said when Brian answered.

"What's up?" Brian asked. "And don't tell me another body."

"No," Jake assured him. "Can you be at my place tomorrow at midnight?"

"Hungry for more?" Brian asked. It was a joke, not an offer, and both knew it.

"Not this time," Jake said. "Dani arranged for Margareta to meet with us. Can you be there?"

"Without question."

"Good," Jake said. "I'll see you then."

Having hung up the phone, he gave Dani his address and told her to confirm with Margareta.

CHAPTER THIRTY-SIX

THURSDAY BROUGHT A WELCOME RELIEF FROM THE HEAT WAVE in the form of a torrential thunderstorm, drenching the city from late afternoon until well into the night.

Jake had been at home for more than a half an hour when the doorbell rang.

It was Brian, holding an umbrella.

The reporter stepped through the door, his leather messenger bag slung over his shoulder, and kissed him passionately.

Once their lips had parted, Jake said, "What the hell was that?" His tone wasn't challenging, merely curious. This was still uncharted territory for him.

"Is it okay if I don't know?" Brian asked. "Everything's so fucking insane right now, kissing you seemed like the only sane thing I could think of."

Realizing at once that the connection had less to do with sex than it did with grabbing at meager vestiges of sanity, Jake smiled. "I get it," he said, and pressed his lips to Brian's. "I really get it."

They moved to the living room and had just seated themselves when the doorbell rang again. As Jake had expected, Dani and Margareta were waiting outside, each with an umbrella in hand, but still looking like two drowned kittens.

"Please," he said, "come in."

Having escorted them into the living room, he offered refreshments, listing the options.

"Refreshments would be good," Dani said. "I'm celebrating."

"Oh?" Jake asked. "What's the occasion?"

"Tonight was my last shift at the Acropolis. As of tomorrow, I'm officially employed in the New York art world!"

"Well," Jake said, "I guess congratulations are in order!"

"Indeed," Brian added. "Mazel tov!"

"I would like a cup of tea," Margareta said, sounding apologetic to have asked.

"Coming right up," Jake replied, hoping his tone was a bit more enthusiastic than hers had been, his aim to put her at ease. "Dani?" he added.

"Anything is fine," she said. Just as he'd turned, she spoke up. "Maybe something stronger than tea? I mean, I'm celebrating, right?"

"What's your pleasure?" Jake asked. "I'm a Scotch man, Brian drinks bourbon. I'm sure I've got you covered."

"Do you have any wine?" she asked.

I *don't, but* Tommy *does*, he thought, wishing he hadn't. "Red or white?"

"Red, if you have it."

He returned a few minutes later, bringing Margareta a mug of steeping tea and Dani a glass of cabernet. His second trip served up one Scotch and one bourbon and, if only for himself, a silent chuckle on behalf of George Thorogood.

"Margareta," Brian began once they were all served and Jake was seated, "I've done as much research as I can on the *strigoi*, but I'm hoping you can tell us more."

She sipped her tea with shaking hands, her eyes downcast, and asked, "What do you want to know?"

"Did your grandmother ever tell you how to stop them?" he asked.

"She only told me silver," Margareta said. "Silver and fire."

Brian looked at Jake. "Did she ever mention decapitation?" he asked the frightened girl.

"No," Margareta said, looking at Brian, bearing a confused expression. "She never say nothing about that."

With another brief glance at Jake, Brian said, "What I read mentions silver and fire, as well as decapitation. Silver will immobilize them, but fire and decapitation are the only ways to kill them. At least, from what I read. But I trust that you know more."

"She never say nothing about, how you say? Dee. Cap. Ih.Tay-tion?" Margareta said stiltedly. "What is this you speak of? I do not know this word."

"Cutting off the head," Brian told her.

"Oh!" Margareta said, suddenly animated. "Yes, you cut off the head! *Bunica mea*, she tell me about that. You cut off the head and the *strigoi* cannot hurt you. They are gone for good."

"Okay," Brian said, "silver, fire, and decapitation. Anything else? Did she tell you anything else that could stop the *strigoi*?"

"No," Margareta said, clutching her mug as if it were a life preserver. "Only that. Nothing else can stop them."

Brian looked at Jake. "Okay," he said. "I guess we know what our arsenal will be."

"*Promise me*?" Margareta beseeched, her words reeking of an imploring tone, tears spilling from her eyes. "Promise me you will stop the *strigoi*?"

"I promise," Brian said. He and Jake both wondered if that promise was hollow.

"TALK TO ME, JAKE," DANI SAID, SUDDENLY MORE BALLSY than he'd ever known her to be.

"I know I'm overstepping and it's not like we're buddies, but something's going on here, and now I'm part of it. I think I have a right to know."

They were standing in the dining room. Margareta had asked to use the bathroom and Brian was sorting through his notes on the sofa.

"I wish I knew what to tell you, Dani," he said. "You remember you told me about the guy your friend Iggy was seeing? The artist?"

"Yeah?" she replied.

"Well," he continued, "Brian and I think Cody is part of something bigger than random murders. We think it's a pattern. And what Margareta has told us has us thinking it may be something bigger than either of us has ever encountered."

"A *strigoi*?" she asked.

"I hate to admit it," he said, "but yes. Or, at least, a psycho who *thinks* he's a *strigoi*."

"Jesus," was all she could say.

"Obviously," Jake said, "keep all this to yourself."

"Without question," Dani assured him with no hesitation. "Besides. Who would believe me?"

"Exactly," he said.

She looked around the dining room and what was visible of the rooms beyond. "So, this is where you live, huh?" she asked.

"Yep," he said. "Humble though it is."

"And does Brian live here with you?" she asked.

"Uh, no," he said, sizing her up anew. "Why do you ask?"

Dani laughed. "C'mon, Jake," she said. "I'm an art student. You think I can't spot a gay guy from a mile off?"

"You knew?" he asked.

"Please!" she said. "The first time I served you coffee."

"Is it that obvious?"

"Obvious? No," she assured him. "Unless you know what to look for. Trust me," she added, already knowing what he was thinking, "your partner doesn't have a clue."

"Thank God for that," Jake said.

"Are you sure you're not with Mr. Handsome Reporter?"

"No," he said. "We're just friends."

"Uh huh," Dani said, with an air of "I know better than you."

Jake found himself wondering when the waitress from the diner across the street had also become a friend. Maybe he ought to open himself up more to what life was presenting to him.

Although he didn't know it, Dani was thinking the same thing.

"Listen," he said, finding a welcome opportunity to change the subject, "Sergeant Olsen may have a lead on Iggy. I'll keep you posted."

A mistake? Maybe. He wasn't sure. But it felt right.

"Thank you, Jake," she said, offering a warm smile.

Now he *knew* it was right.

CHAPTER THIRTY-SEVEN

THE SIDEWALK IN FRONT OF GALERIE DELAROIX resembled the premiere of a much-anticipated all-star movie.

Thanks to Dani's expert preparations, there were red velvet cordons strung between gold-toned posts bordering the requisite red carpet. And with the respite from the oppressive heat, the line of eager attendees was able to wait in comfort, a gentle summer breeze moving through the canyon of buildings.

In the window of one of the doors hung an elegant, gilt-edged sign. "Life & Death in the Abstract," it read, "The American premiere of Colin Davenport."

Guests had been lined up for thirty minutes before the doors opened, Jake, Brian, and Owen among them. Alex Mayhew, having been granted exclusive privilege, was already inside, ready to observe and interview the first arrivals to Galerie Delacroix. He clutched his notepad in trembling hands.

The brown paper had been removed from the windows, and Alex could see the patrons outside eagerly looking in, anxious to get a closer glimpse at the works adorning the walls.

"I've never been to anything like this," Jake said to Owen on the red carpet.

"You think I have?" Owen replied, reaching out and taking his hand.

Jake looked down. Except for brief and very random occasions with Tommy in the Village, he'd never held hands with another man in public before. And Owen was not letting go.

At promptly eight o'clock, the doors of Galerie Delacroix were unlocked and swung open wide. The crowd filtered in. The forward progression of guests was stalled by the reaction to "Mourning Become Electric," as Sandrine had planned. Gasps, "oohs," and "ahs" filled the gallery space as first-night patrons crossed the threshold. The line suddenly advanced quickly as those first through the doors moved further inside, hungry to see more.

Jake and Owen were still hand-in-hand when they entered and came face to face with Tommy, bearing a tray of canapés.

The waiter turned on his heel and headed into the back of the gallery. Owen attempted to disengage his hand, but Jake held firm.

"No," he said. "I'm here with you."

"Did you know he was working this event?" Owen asked.

"I found out when you did," Jake replied. "Would you rather leave?"

"I'm fine with it if you are," he said.

"Then let's get a drink and enjoy the artwork."

"Would you two sort this out away from the door," Brian cajoled from behind them. "You're holding up the line."

"Okay, okay," Jake said. The three moved to the bar set up in the front corner by the window.

"YOU'RE NOT NERVOUS, ARE YOU?"

Colin had been pacing in his studio, chain-smoking, his friend watching him stalk back and forth like a caged leopard at the zoo.

"Fuck, no," Colin said. "I'm never fucking nervous. I'm just impatient. I wanna get down there and enjoy the adulation."

"Okay," his friend said from his seat in a corner.

"They're never gonna forget tonight, ducks," Colin said, striding across the room. "Not a bloody one of 'em."

"I THINK IT'S GOING WELL," DANI SAID TO SANDRINE as they observed the first-night attendees move about the gallery.

Mixed in with the patrons of the arts were the critics they'd expected. They were easy to spot: all their faces were pointedly impassive, and they all held note pads into which they scribbled their thoughts.

Something Sandrine noted was that, in America, openings seemed to lack the bourgeois dilettantes she'd learned to tolerate in the south of France. The people currently circulating about her gallery seemed to truly appreciate the nuances of art. Sandrine felt gratified.

The harpist Dani had booked, a slender Asian woman in an elegant black gown, was in the corner of the front room opposite the bar, and her music wafted throughout the space like an enticing fragrance. Two Parsons students were circulating, taking copious photos of the artwork and the admiring patrons alike. Three waiters, all handsome young men, Tommy in their number, were discreetly moving among the guests, offering bite-sized samples of *haute cuisine*.

Sandrine could not have been more pleased.

"I *know* it is going well, *chérie*," she replied. "And thanks, in no small measure, to you." Sandrine put an arm around her young assistant's shoulders as they surveyed their mutual accomplishment. "This is as much your success as it is mine. *Merci mille fois, ma chère*."

"Would you like some Champagne?" Dani asked. "I think I'll have a glass. If that's okay."

"*D'accord, chérie*," Sandrine said. "*Et oui*, I would like that very much."

As Dani made her way through the crowd and approached the bar, Alex stepped beside Sandrine.

"Thank you so much, Ms. Delacroix," he gushed. "You have no idea what an honor it is to be the first reporter to feature the gallery. Not to mention getting to meet Mr. Davenport!"

"It is nothing, Monsieur Mayhew," Sandrine said. "The pleasure is truly mine. And your article was wonderful. *Merci* for that." She didn't mention her curiosity about Colin's wanting to meet Alex.

"Well," he said, finding himself at a loss for words, "back to work." He disappeared into the crowd.

Dani returned moments later, two flutes in hand, and gave one to Sandrine.

"To Galerie Delacroix," she said, raising her own glass.

"And to us," Sandrine added.

They delicately clinked their flutes and sipped the exquisite vintage.

"Dani?"

The young woman turned from Sandrine and was surprised to see Helen Olsen.

"Sergeant Olsen!" she said. "I didn't know you were coming."

"I thought I'd stop by before my shift," Olsen informed her. "You'd mentioned this event and I was curious." She assessed Dani's designer cocktail dress. "Quite a step up from your other work clothes."

Dani self-consciously looked down at herself. "Sandrine took me to Bergdorf's yesterday. I tried to tell her it wasn't necessary, but she insisted."

"*D'accord*," Sandrine said. "I wanted Dani to look as magnificent as the work she's done with me. *Et voila!* She may eclipse the paintings!"

"So, you're not here on business?" Dani asked Helen, wanting to steer the topic away from herself. "I mean, there's no new information?"

"Nothing since I told you that your friend had been seen at the Ninth Circle that night," Helen said. "I'm sorry I don't have better news."

"I understand," Dani said, her disappointment evident. "Oh, I'm sorry," she added. "Sandrine, this is Sergeant Helen Olsen. She's the one I filed the missing-persons report with. Sergeant Olsen, this is the gallery owner, Sandrine Delacroix."

As the two shook hands, Helen said, "This place is gorgeous. You must be so proud."

"*Merci*," Sandrine said. "And yes, I am. I am also very proud of Dani. I could not have done all this without her."

"I don't want to monopolize your time, Ms. Delacroix," Helen said. "I'm sure you have other people to greet. And I want to admire these beautiful paintings." She stepped away and became part of the crowd, but not before saying, "And Dani? You *do* look magnificent."

"I CAN'T BELIEVE HE'S HERE," TOMMY MUTTERED IN THE BACK ROOM as he refilled his tray with hors d'oeuvre from the portable warming cabinet.

"Who?" Mateo Aguilar asked. A fellow cater-waiter, he was beside Tommy, also refilling his tray.

"My fucking boyfriend," Tommy said. "At least, I *think* he's still my boyfriend."

"You're not sure?"

"We had this big fight last Friday, and now he's here with someone else."

"Rubbing it in your face?" Mateo asked.

"No," Tommy said, "that's not his style. I think he came with this reporter friend of his. That's my best guess, anyway. It's all just so fucked up."

"Honey," Mateo said, "just ignore them. Don't even serve them. Point them out to me and I'll take care of that. This way, you can just pretend they're not even here and you can concentrate on being your fabulous self and do your job."

"You're the best, Matty," Tommy said.

"I already know that," he replied with a winning grin.

JAKE, OWEN, AND BRIAN WERE IN THE MIDDLE GALLERY, admiring the "Seven Deadly Sins" series, when Helen Olsen joined them.

After Jake introduced her to the others, they all compared their thoughts on the abstract artwork surrounding them.

"Dani told me that the artist only finished these on Tuesday or Wednesday," Helen told Jake.

"Wow," Owen said. "Talk about cutting it down to the wire."

Jake glanced from one painting to the next and said to Helen, "Look at the signatures. All the paintings have a different color theme, but all the signatures are in the same color." He approached the nearest one. "Helen, come here."

She stepped to his side and looked at him inquiringly. "What is it?"

He pointed to the deep maroon name and asked, "Call me crazy, but what does that look like to you?"

Helen, who would be the first to admit her ignorance when it came to art, took a closer look. "I'd say it looks like dried blood. He's good, he mixed the colors perfectly."

"Creepy," was all Jake could say, unable to take his eyes off the lower right-hand corner of the canvas.

"Well," she said, "they *are* the Seven Deadly Sins."

Seven, his mind screamed. *Seven Deadly Sins. Seven paintings. Seven victims.*

Jake once again experienced the same sense of vertigo that had hit him in the diner the night Dani told him her missing friend had been dating Cody Fischer. Trying to remain inconspicuous, he turned in a full circle, taking in each of the seven paintings, his eye fixed on the seven blood-like signatures.

"I think I need a drink to cleanse me of all this sinful thinking," Brian said, interrupting Jake's transfixed state. "Who wants to join me?"

All four made their way to the bar in the front room, Jake bringing up the rear, moving slowly, his eyes still fixed on the seven paintings.

As they entered the main exhibit space, they passed a tray-bearing Tommy, and Jake's gaze followed him, something not lost on either Owen or Brian. The two shared a silent dialogue with their eyes as Helen continued on to the bar.

It was Owen who spoke.

"Jake?"

Rousing himself back into the present and turning his attention to Owen, Jake said, "Yeah?"

Pointedly looking first to Brian, Owen met Jake's eyes. "You should go talk to him. Whatever's in your heart that you need to say, you should say it. I support you whatever it is."

"And so do I," Brian added, taking a step toward Jake, his tone and body language endorsing Owen's suggestion.

The detective felt an uncharacteristic discomfort at being unsure of what to do next. He looked from Owen to Brian and back again, his eyes seeking guidance from his unexpected mentors in the strange new landscape.

Sensing Jake's uncertainty, Brian said, "Just do it."

Jake glanced at Owen, seeking his blessing, which he received by way of a slight smile, took a deep breath, and stepped back into the "Seven Deadly Sins" room.

Sidling up to Tommy, who'd just finished a professional service of shitake mushrooms to a trio of smartly dressed men, Jake said, "Can we talk please?"

Tommy turned at the sound of the familiar voice and searched Jake's face for a hint of what might be said. Finding none and fearing the worst, he muttered, "I'm working," and turned away.

Before Jake could stop him, he'd disappeared through the crowd and into the store room.

Jake made his way back to the others, who'd gathered at the bar.

"Well?" Owen asked. "That was pretty quick."

"He's working," was all Jake would say.

In a confidential tone, Brian advised, "Before the weekend is out, talk to him."

"I will," Jake assured his friend.

And he meant it.

SANDRINE HAD EXCUSED HERSELF AND GONE TO COLIN'S STUDIO. When she returned moments later, she asked Dani to have the harpist pause her playing.

"*Mesdames et messieurs*," Sandrine said in a warm but authoritative voice the moment the music had ceased, "*mes amis. Bienvenue au Galerie Delacroix!* Thank you all so much for making this evening *tres magnifique.* I hope you have all enjoyed the exhibit and are anxious to meet the talented artist responsible for it.

"I am honored to present, in his American debut, Colin Davenport."

The room erupted in appreciative applause as a sullen, lanky young man strode forward from the workroom, a lit cigarette dangling from his lips despite the "No Smoking" signs posted discreetly throughout the gallery, his dark brown hair hanging over his eyes. He made his way through the crowds until he reached Sandrine in the front.

Next to the bar, Helen turned to her fellow police officer. "He looks like the composite," she said.

"I was just thinking the same thing," Jake replied.

"Hey, doesn't he—" Brian began.

"That's just what we were saying," Jake answered, having known what Brian was about to ask. "But he also looks like Sid Vicious, minus the spiked hair. As well as more than half the guys in the bars tonight."

"Still," Brian said. "I think it's worth checking into."

"I intend to," Jake assured him. "Just not now, in the middle of all this. I doubt he's gonna head back to Europe and leave all the fawning behind. At least not right away."

Across the room, Colin whispered into Sandrine's ear. "'Ave your little lapdog fetch some champers, love."

"Do not call her that," Sandrine spat while maintaining a gracious smile. She turned to Dani and asked her to get two glasses of Champagne.

As Dani approached the bar, Jake caught her eye.

"Dani, do you know how long Mr. Davenport will be here in the States? And where he's staying?"

"I believe Sandrine said he'll be here for at least another month, possibly longer," she informed him. "And as for where he's staying, you're standing in it. He's been living out of a studio on the second floor." She picked up two Champagne flutes. "Why?"

"I was just curious," he dodged. "I may want to buy a painting."

Their attention was pulled to the other side of the room when Colin spoke up.

"Thank you all," he said. "This is pretty fucking exciting. There's somebody I want to introduce to you all, 'e's been my muse lately, and I think you should all meet 'im."

Sandrine's confusion was evident only to Dani. To the other guests, she appeared to be in complete control of the evening.

"Come on out, love," Colin called into the back.

As Colin's muse joined him, Dani gasped, dropping one of the flutes, which shattered at her feet, splashing them all with expensive Champagne.

"What's—" was all Jake could get out before Helen Olsen said, "Holy shit!"

Standing next to Colin Davenport was Iggy, resplendently dressed, such as Dani had never seen him, in black slacks and a royal purple silk shirt, a gold chain sparkling around his neck, his outfit resembling the large painting to his right. His Afro still sported the blonde stripe and he virtually glowed with pleasure at being by Colin's side.

Behind them, Sandrine allowed her composure to slip, and as she glared at the back of the artist's head, it was evident to anyone who took note of her that she was seething.

CHAPTER THIRTY-EIGHT

"GET OUT OF HERE," SANDRINE YELLED, "ALL OF YOU!"

The three waiters promptly vacated the workroom, leaving Sandrine alone with Colin. She shut the door behind them.

"What have you *done*?!" Her fury was a palpable force, a maelstrom sucking the oxygen from the room.

"Calm down, love," he said glibly. "Don't want the 'oi polloi to 'ear you."

She advanced on him, menacingly. "I do not care *who* hears me! How *dare* you turn that boy!"

"I wanted company," he said, popping a canapé into his mouth.

Sandrine swung an open palm toward his cheek, but he grabbed her wrist, his own arm moving so quickly that she did not see it until she was in his tight grasp.

"Don't you ever try to 'it me," he snarled. "Do you understand? *Love?*"

"Let go of my wrist." Her snarl was no less threatening than his. He did, flinging it from his grip.

"Has he been staying here? In my building?" she demanded.

"Where else? I wasn't gonna leave him out on the sidewalk, tied to a post like a pup."

"How dare you?!" she repeated.

"Do you think Dani's enjoying the reunion?" His smile showed his delight, however evil it may have been.

"You are a monster!" she yelled.

"Um," he said, "I think we both already knew that. Blimey, you've known that since you were Dani's age."

"I want him out of here," she stated. "And you back in Europe. I will make arrangements for a flight tomorrow."

"Not so fast, love," he said. "I'm thinkin' I might put down some roots 'ere." Knowing it would infuriate her further, he sang, "I love New York!" He ate another canapé and said, "Now, if you'll excuse me, I 'ave an adoring public to greet." He walked past her and opened the door. "Oh, and love? You might want to fix your 'air and touch up your makeup. You look a bleedin' *fright!*"

"WHERE THE HELL HAVE YOU *BEEN*?"

Sandrine had no sooner dragged Colin into the back when Dani cornered Iggy.

"Around," he said, looking at the crowd and not at her.

"You scared the *shit* outta me!" Much to her own surprise, she was managing to keep her volume at a reasonable level despite her anger. "And how the hell did you wind up with Colin?"

"We met at a bar," was all he said.

"You met at a bar?" she echoed. "And that's it?"

"And I've been staying here with him, okay?"

"No, it's not okay," she shot back. "Wait! *Here?* You've been here this whole time? Here, where I've been working every day? And you never once said anything? What the *hell*, Ig!"

"I just needed to be alone," he said. "Not deal with anyone or anything."

"Except Colin, apparently."

"Yes and no," Iggy said. "He mostly let me do my own thing. I've been sleeping most days anyway."

"This is not over," she said. "I have a job to do here. You've already distracted me from it too much."

She walked away from him and rejoined Helen Olsen near the bar. She felt like an idiot.

"IGGY!"

The moment Colin reemerged from the workroom, he bellowed. Ignoring the praise from the patrons he practically pushed aside, those that weren't stunned by his outburst, he walked straight to Iggy.

"C'mon, ducks," he said. "We're gettin' the fuck outta 'ere."

"Where are we going?" Iggy asked.

"Out," Colin spat. "I don't care where. I fucking *'ate* this place right about now."

"But what about—"

"*I said we're leaving!*" Colin roared at him, causing heads to turn in their direction. He grabbed Iggy by the wrist and stalked out the front door, pushing it open roughly and dragging Iggy into the night.

The hushed conversations in the room were suddenly not about art.

Sandrine had just entered the front gallery when they left, and Dani approached her.

"Are you okay, Sandrine?" she asked.

"That is what I want to ask you. I have been dealing with his childishness for years, but you have not yet built up the same tolerance."

"Well," Dani said, "I'm upset, I'm angry, I'm confused. But, to be honest, mostly I'm just relieved that he's okay." She chewed on her lower lip.

"What is it, Dani?"

"I don't know," she replied. "Something about him seemed wrong. Different. I can't put my finger on it."

I can, Sandrine thought. *And trust me,* ma cherie, *Colin will pay dearly this time.*

"WHAT WAS ALL THAT ABOUT?"

Alex had made a beeline to Brian when Colin had burst out of the back room, hoping his colleague had heard more between the artist and his surprise guest than he had.

"Your guess is as good as mine," Brian said. "Please tell me that you're not adding that to your review."

"No," Alex assured him. "I'm just being nosy."

"You know," Brian said, "I think you missed your calling. I hear that *Page Six* is looking for a gossip columnist."

"Funny," Alex said, "very funny."

"DID YOU HEAR WHAT SHE SAID TO YOUR FRIEND?"

Brian had pulled Jake aside after Alex went in search of gossip. He, Jake, and Owen had all witnessed Dani's embarrassment with Helen a few minutes earlier. Fortunately, the seasoned police vet had put the girl at ease, explaining that she'd done nothing wrong. At the moment, Owen and Helen were engaged in conversation.

"Which part?" Jake asked.

"The part about that kid, what's his name? Iggy? The part about Iggy seeming different. That it was like there was something wrong with him."

"Yeah," Jake said, wanting to hear where Brian was taking this before commenting further.

"Okay," Brian continued, "first Picasso over there is a dead ringer for the composite sketch, and then Iggy shows up after being missing for two weeks, and Dani says he seems totally different? I don't like this, Jake. I don't like any of it."

"Me either," he concurred. "I was doing the same math as you." Noticing that Owen had stepped away, leaving Helen alone, he said, "Hang tight. I wanna talk to Olsen."

He stepped to her. "What're your thoughts?" he asked.

"That the case just got closed," she said. "Since we're alone ..." She let the thought hang like one of the paintings.

"Yeah?" Jake said.

"This is totally none of my business, and you can tell me so," she began. "But I'm curious. Are you and Owen, I don't know. A thing?"

This was not at all what Jake thought she would say, and he was taken by such surprise that when he replied, "Uh, yeah," he didn't realize he'd just come out to his first fellow officer.

"Cool," she said. "I like him."

Jake was flabbergasted by how casually she took the revelation.

"Nobody at the precinct knows," he said.

"Don't worry, Griff," she assured him. "This stays between you and me."

"Now it's my turn to be curious," he said. "How did you know? About me, I mean."

"Well, I've kinda suspected for a while now."

"Christ, I hate that word. 'Suspected.' We suspect people of crimes and being gay isn't a crime."

"You forget yourself, detective," she said, teasing him slightly. "It wasn't all that long ago that it was."

"You know what I mean."

"Yeah," she said, "I'm just giving you shit. And I get your point. We really need a better word for it."

"We do," he said, relaxing into what felt like new skin.

"And Jake?" she added. "Thank you for trusting me with that."

"You're actually the first person on the force that I've come out to," he shared. "I made up my mind last Friday that I was done living in the shadows. Just haven't had the chance to tell Prentiss yet. I figured he'd be the first, but I guess not."

"Think of me as a dress rehearsal," she said, putting a friendly hand on his arm. "I'm gonna make sure Dani's okay and head to the precinct. I wanna leave enough time to grab a bite at the diner before my shift. Even though *my* case is closed, I'll let you know whatever Iles was able to turn up at the bar."

"I appreciate that," Jake said, although something in his gut told him that he already knew what that would be.

"WELL, THAT WAS BIZARRE."

"You'll have to be more specific," Brian said. "There seem to be floor shows left and right here."

Owen had returned from the men's room and was standing with the reporter when Jake rejoined them.

"Oh, no," Jake said, "not the drama, though that, too, has been pretty fuckin' bizarre." He picked up a glass of Champagne from the bar. "I was talking about my conversation with Helen."

"What was bizarre about it?" Owen inquired.

"She asked if you and I were a thing," he replied.

Owen and Brian exchanged looks before returning their attention to Jake.

"And you said …?" Brian queried.

"I believe my exact words were, 'Uh, yeah,'" he said. "I know, Mister Wordsmith, not exactly pithy, but hey, I hadn't prepared a speech."

Owen wrapped his arms around Jake and kissed him. "You did it!" he enthused. "You came out to somebody from work!"

"Good for you, man!" Brian had gotten behind Jake and embraced him as well, effectively creating a "hug sandwich."

"Can I join or is it by invitation only?"

They turned to find Steven standing there.

"Hey, wait 'til you hear this," Brian said by way of greeting him. "Jake just came out to a fellow cop!"

"Mazel tov, honey! Mazel tov!" It was Steven's turn to hug him, adding a kiss on each cheek.

Releasing Jake, he said, "I cannot *believe* how late I am! I just could *not* decide what to wear! I hope I didn't miss anything good."

The other three exchanged looks and began to laugh.

"SOUNDS LIKE I *DID* MISS THE GOOD STUFF!"

Even as Jake and the others were filling him in on all the evening's drama, Steven was clutching his invisible pearls. "I wonder what Tommy knows," he said and went in search of him.

"Whadda ya say we get outta here and head back to my place?" Jake said.

"Before you ask," Brian said, "I can't play junior G-man tonight."

"Actually, I wasn't going to," Jake said. "Aside from what we think we learned here, there's nothing new and I really don't want another night that feels like we haven't accomplished anything."

"Good," Brian said, "because I have a date with Dmitri when he's done dancing."

"Sounds fun," Owen said. "Going out or staying in?"

"Staying in," Brian said. "In *deep*, I hope."

Jake laughed. "I don't think you have to hope all that much." He glanced around the room and said, "Before we go, I want to check on Dani. I'll be right back."

He found her in the middle gallery, surrounded by sin and talking to Sandrine.

"Ms. Delacroix?" he said as he approached them. "We haven't met. I'm Jake Griffin, I'm a friend of Dani's."

Sandrine shook his offered hand and said, "My priceless jewel," making Dani blush.

"Tonight was wonderful," he said, "and your gallery is breathtaking. What can you tell me about the artist?"

Sandrine gave him her standard biographical information, which was mostly true with the omission of the fact that she'd known him for two decades. They'd met when she'd been working in a gallery in the south of France, where she'd curated his first exhibit in that country. From there, they'd traveled around the continent together, ultimately coming to the States.

"Fascinating," Jake said, not having learned anything useful. He turned to Dani and asked, "May I have a word before we leave?"

"Absolutely," she said.

He turned back to Sandrine. "Once again, thank you for having us. And congratulations on your success."

"*Merci,*" she said.

Dani led him into the workroom where the waiters were packing up. Seeing them, Tommy invented a reason to leave, telling Mateo he wanted to check the gallery space for anything he might have overlooked.

"How are you doing?" he asked Dani. "I know you had a pretty big shock."

"Honestly, Jake?" she said. "I wish I knew. Right now, all I can focus on is getting through tonight. Despite all the drama surrounding Colin and Iggy, it went really well, but my work isn't done until everyone's gone, and the doors are locked."

"Understandable," he said.

"Is it okay if I call you at home tomorrow?" she asked. "I'll have a better idea of what I'm thinking after I get some sleep."

"No problem," he told her. "I'm off, so any time is good."

Not having planned to do so, he gave her a hug and a friendly kiss on the cheek. "You really hit one outta the park tonight. I hope you're proud of yourself."

"I am, Jake," she said. "And thank you. For everything."

After leaving the gallery the trio headed west on Houston until they reached 7th Avenue, where they caught the Number One train heading north.

Brian got off in Chelsea, with Jake and Owen telling him to have fun and to give their love to Dmitri, and the train left the station, carrying them to the Upper West Side.

HARRY BRANDON, OR, AS HE WAS KNOWN PROFESSIONALLY, BRANDON HARRIS, ran his hands over his naked body.

Standing in front of a full-length mirror in the dressing room at Uncle Charlie's and having just stepped out of the shower, he liked what he saw. The remaining droplets of water clung to his well-defined pecs and abs, and, being of mixed race, his light brown skin glowed.

Yeah, he thought, *I'm lookin' fine.*

In the mirror's reflection, he saw movement behind him. "I'm hittin' some after-hours clubs down in the Village," he said. "You wanna come with?"

"Not tonight," Dmitri said. "I got me a date with a hunky journalist."

"For real?" Harry asked, running his hands over his torso, still looking in the mirror. "You two a thing?"

"I'm hopin' so," Dmitri replied, toweling himself off, having just emerged from his own shower.

"Well, you go, girl," Harry said. Having given his body his seal of approval, he removed the plastic shower cap and let his dreadlocks spill down his back.

Dmitri finished dressing, hoping his outfit would please Brian: tight satin basketball shorts and a torso-hugging tank top. After checking his hair in the mirror, he put his wallet and various accessories into his gym bag and slung the strap over one shoulder.

Once on the sidewalk in front of Uncle Charlie's, he and Brandon shared a hug and kissed each other on the cheek, one heading east to catch a cab, the other heading west. Since it was such a nice night, he was going to walk through the park and take a subway downtown.

CHAPTER THIRTY-NINE

THE HUMIDITY HAD NOT RETURNED ON SATURDAY MORNING, so, having risen early, Jake and Owen decided to go for a jog in Central Park.

After running for about ninety minutes, they left the park at 72nd Street and picked up health shakes at a neighborhood store. They returned to the park, hoping to find a bench off the beaten path to sit and enjoy their drinks.

Rounding a bend, they spotted about a dozen uniforms and a couple of plainclothesmen gathered within and around the telltale yellow tape.

"Holy shit," Jake said.

"What?"

"That's my partner," he replied. He handed Owen his shake and said, "You wait here."

As he approached the group, he called to Frank.

"Where the hell have you been?" Frank asked. "I've been calling you for more than an hour."

"Jogging with a buddy. What is it?" Jake asked, although Frank's presence in the 22nd Precinct told him all he needed to know.

"Another one," Frank said grimly.

"Goddammit," Jake muttered. "M.E. here yet?"

"Come and gone," Frank said. He and Jake advanced past the tape and approached the body, which was lying on its back, dressed in a tank top and short-shorts, both equally form-fitting. A gym bag lay on the ground about five feet from the corpse, an evidence tag planted in the dirt beside it.

"Jesus Christ," Jake gasped, staggering backward. "Oh, Jesus Christ, no!"

"What the hell?" Frank said. He'd never, in all their time together, seen his partner have a reaction to a crime scene even a quarter this strong.

"I— I know him," Jake said, looking almost as pale as the bloodless victim.

"You're shittin' me!"

"No," Jake said, unable to catch his breath. He was bent forward, his hands on his knees.

"How would you know somebody like this?"

"For God's sake, Frank, he's my boyfriend's buddy!"

"Your— your *what*?" Frank stammered.

"Oh, Jesus Christ, Frank," he yelled. "I'm gay, alright? Your partner's a, what did you call Fischer? Oh, yeah, your partner's a goddamn fruit loop!" His head was spinning. "I gotta get outta here."

"You're right," Frank agreed, no malice in his voice. "If you were friends with the vic, you shouldn't be here anyway."

Jake turned to walk away, but Frank gently put a hand on his shoulder and turned him back around.

"We can talk about this another time," he said, "but I want you to know we're fine. Nothing's changed. Okay?"

"Sure, whatever," Jake said, not dismissing his partner's gesture. He simply couldn't process anything.

Frank sensed this. "Well, you take care of whatever you have to. You know how to reach me."

"What was that all about?" Owen asked when Jake got back to him. He, along with all the cops present from the 22nd, had heard Jake's outburst.

"Jesus Christ, Owen," he said, almost crying. "It's Dmitri. That fucking sonofabitch killed Dmitri."

Owen dropped the cups and wrapped his arms around Jake, who let his tears fall.

From twenty feet off, Frank saw this and turned away discreetly, giving Jake a modicum of privacy. But not before noting that his partner was in the embrace of a material witness.

After a minute or two like that, Jake was struck by a horrible thought. "I gotta get to Tommy."

"Of course," Owen said. "Do you want me to come with you?"

Sniffling, Jake said, "No, I think I should go alone. Do me a favor though? Can you go to Brian's? He should hear this from a friend, and I can't be in two places at once."

"Absolutely," Owen assured him. "Are you fine going like this, or do you want to change?"

"I just wanna get there," Jake said, having collected himself enough to think a little.

"No problem," Owen said. "Let's get a cab."

OWEN GOT OUT AT 23ᴿᴰ STREET, STILL TRYING TO FIGURE OUT how to break the news to Brian.

About ten minutes later, Jake paid the driver and exited the taxi at 7ᵗʰ and Grove. By the time he walked the half block to the apartment Tommy and Cara shared, he'd begun to tremble.

Using the key Tommy had given him, he let himself in the street door, but knocked when he reached their third-floor apartment. Cara answered.

"Jake!" she said, clearly surprised to see him there. "How—" She stopped herself when she got a good look at his face. "What is it? You've been crying?" she asked as she pulled him into the apartment.

"I need to talk to Tommy," he said, his voice strained.

"Of course," she replied and hurried to his bedroom door.

"Tommy, get up," she called in as she knocked. "It's important." Jake heard her open the door but couldn't hear what she said once inside Tommy's room.

When Tommy came out moments later, it was obvious that she'd woken him. The fact that she'd woken him with the news that Jake was in the living room had left him wide awake.

"Jake?" he said. "What is it? What's wrong?"

Jake went to him and enfolded him in his arms. "Tommy, do me a favor and hold onto me, okay? Don't let go."

Clearly troubled by what was unfolding, Tommy said, "Alright?" and wrapped his arms around Jake.

"Another body was found this morning, this time in Central Park," Jake said. He could feel Tommy begin to shake all over and stiffen at the same time. "Baby, I'm so sorry. It was Dmitri."

Tommy unleashed a howl of anguish that Jake was sure he'd be hearing in nightmares for weeks. At first, he tried to push Jake away, but Jake held on to him tightly and let him break down. Cara had been standing within earshot and joined Jake in physically supporting her brother.

"Oh, my god," Tommy kept saying repeatedly between sobs. Jake and Cara moved him to the couch where they sat on either side of him, continuing to hold him. Still in denial, Tommy grabbed Jake's hand and begged, "Are you sure? Maybe there's a mistake. It's gotta be a mistake!" Desperation dripped from his voice as distinctly as the tears dripped from his cheeks.

"Tommy," Jake said gently, "I saw him. I was at the crime scene. There's no mistake. Baby, I wish there were." At this news, Tommy broke down again. Jake looked to Cara, feeling helpless. The expression on her face told him she did too.

"Tommy," Jake said, "I know you can't think right now, but do you want me to go to the shop and tell Fuchsia you won't be in?"

Through his sobs, Tommy was unable to speak, so he just nodded his head.

Jake kissed his hair and said, "You call me any time, any reason. And if I don't hear from you, I'll be showing up."

"I'll keep you posted, Jake," Cara said softly. "And thank you."

Jake kissed Tommy's hair again and stood up.

Tommy managed to collect himself enough to raise his head and say, "Yes. Thank you for coming to tell me, Jake. Especially under the circumstances."

"Hey," Jake said, "there are no circumstances right now. I didn't want you hearing it from anyone else."

"Well," Tommy managed, "thank you." He dissolved once again into tears, Cara holding him tightly. Jake let himself out.

AFTER BREAKING THE NEWS TO FUCHSIA LAMMÉ, who almost fainted, he asked to use the phone.

"Anything you need, honey," she said, seated in a chair and fanning herself with a large, garish scarf. For as melodramatic as Fuchsia often was, Jake recognized legitimate shock when he saw it.

Before picking up the phone, he asked, "Is there anything I can get you?"

"Darlin', there's a little fridge in the back," she said. "Could you get me some iced tea, sugar?"

"Right away," he said and retrieved the cold drink for her.

"Thank you," she said. "Oh, my good Lord, poor Tommy!" Fuchsia began to cry into her scarf.

Jake picked up the phone and dialed Brian's apartment. Owen answered, which didn't surprise him.

"How is he?" Jake asked.

"Upset, naturally," Owen replied, "but holding it together for the most part. How about Tommy?"

"A total mess," he said. "I'm at the Pot Shop now. I just told Fuchsia and let her know he won't be in for a few days. Cara's with Tommy and she said she'll keep me posted."

"Good," Owen said. "Jake? I'm glad it was you who told him. It says a lot about the man you are."

"I didn't want him to hear it from anyone else, except maybe Cara," he said. "I knew this would destroy him and he'd need someone there strong enough to support him."

"Still," Owen said, "don't minimize what you did."

Before hanging up the phone, Jake told him he'd catch a cab and join him at Brian's. When he turned, he saw Fuchsia flipping the sign on the door to "Closed."

"Closing up shop?" he asked.

"One of my chickens is in trouble," she said, "and a mama hen's gotta do what a mama hen's gotta do. I'm headin' over to Tommy's. If nothin' else, I'll make sure he gets some food in him."

Jake grabbed a pen and pad from the counter and dashed off the number of his answering service. "Here," he said, handing it to her. "Tommy already has it, but he won't be thinking clearly. Make sure Cara gets a copy. I might not be home for a while, but I'll check in regularly. Call if he needs *anything*, okay?"

"You're a sweetheart, you know that, Jake? If you wasn't taken, Miss Fuchsia would be tryin' to steal yo' heart."

They left the shop together, Fuchsia Lammé locking the door behind them.

OWEN HAD BEEN RIGHT: BRIAN WAS HOLDING IT TOGETHER RATHER WELL, all things considered.

"When he never showed up last night, I started to get worried," he said, shaking his head in disbelief. He was sitting in an easy chair, Jake and Owen were on the couch. Owen had made coffee and they each held a mug.

"But I just figured he went out after work with some of the dancers," Brian continued. "It surprised me that he'd do that without calling, but it was the only thing I could come up with that made any sense.

"But this?" he said. "This doesn't make a fucking bit of sense. What the hell was he doing in the park? The club is on the east side. Could he have been foolish enough to walk through there at that hour?"

"I have no idea, Brian," Jake said.

"And you're sure it's the *strigoi*?" Brian beseeched. "Lots of us have had the shit beat out of us near the Ramble." The Central Park location was a nature preserve by day, a gay cruising ground by night.

"He was found about seven blocks south of the Ramble," Jake said, self-aware that he was reverting to his "talking to the survivors" tone. "Besides," he added, hoping to sound more like Brian's friend and less like a cop, "the wounds were consistent."

"How the hell am I gonna write about this?" Brian asked, standing up and stalking about the living room. "'The deceased was a white male and a helluva good fuck'?"

Owen stood and went to him, putting an arm around him. "You'll do whatever you have to do," he said. "Even if that means handing it off to another reporter. Don't put yourself through more anguish than you're already feeling. Trust me, I know."

Brian looked at him curiously. "Oh, my fucking god," he said suddenly. "Owen, I'm so sorry. When you told me about D, everything went out of focus for me. Of *course*, you know. It was selfish of me to forget that."

"You're fine, Brian," he said. "It wasn't at all selfish. I'm still dealing with it, obviously, but that doesn't mean I can't be here for *you*."

Once again, Jake was struck by the fact that, three weeks ago, none of them knew each other, and yet here they were. To him, the bonds he was feeling in the room at the moment felt like they'd been forged years prior.

"What're you going to do with the rest of your day?" Jake asked. "I can't speak for Owen, but I'm off duty and I'd be happy to stay here. Or we could go back to my place if you want somewhere more neutral."

"I can be here too," Owen added.

"Thanks, guys," Brian said, "but I really want to get into the newsroom. If I write the story, and emphasize that this is a serial killer, I'll at least feel like I'm doing something useful."

"As long as you think you can handle that," Jake advised. "Like Owen said, there's no need to put yourself through any additional hell."

"And call us if you need anything," Owen added. "And I mean *anything*." He turned to Jake and said, "If it's okay with you, I'll spend the day at the brownstone so we're both in one place if Brian or Tommy call."

"That's fine," Jake said. "I was going to suggest that."

They waited while Brian changed into something other than the dirty sweatpants he'd pulled on when Owen arrived and they left together, Brian jumping on the Number One downtown to the Village, and Jake and Owen catching a cab to the Upper West Side. Before separating at the corner, Brian looked at Jake and said, "Human or not, let's nail this motherfucker to a goddamn cross."

BACK AT THE BROWNSTONE, JAKE CALLED THE PRECINCT and left a message for Frank. Having done that, he repeated the process with Loretta at their home in Flushing, making sure to ask about her recovery.

"I can't believe it's only just now noon," Owen said when Jake hung up the phone. "It feels like we've been up for days already."

"Tell me about it," Jake replied as he flopped onto the couch next to him. He fell silent, his brow furrowed.

"Talk to me," Owen gently prompted.

"I can't stop thinking about Tommy," he confessed.

"Well, c'mon," Owen replied, "that's completely natural. Do you want to call and check on him?"

"No," he said. "Cara has the number here, and I gave Fuchsia my service number in case it wasn't handy at the apartment. They'll call if they need anything." He was silent again for a few minutes. "I can't fucking believe it, Owen." He caught himself, as Brian had done earlier. "But I don't need to tell you that. I'm sorry."

"Like I told Brian," he assured him, "you have nothing to be sorry for. So much has happened to all of us in the last two weeks, Kenny's funeral feels like a lifetime ago." He took Jake's hand. "What do *you* need?"

Jake looked at him and simply said, "Hold me?"

Owen did.

CHAPTER FORTY

FRANK CALLED AROUND DINNERTIME.

"How're you holding up?" he asked. "I've never seen you like that before."

"I'm better than I was this morning," Jake replied. "Thanks for asking."

"Of course, I'd ask," Frank said. "You're my partner *and* my friend. Your welfare matters to me."

Although he didn't say it, Jake was also extremely appreciative that his unplanned and explosive revelation in the park didn't seem to have affected anything between them.

"About the other thing," Frank continued delicately. "I know I can say some stupid shit sometimes and I want to apologize for that. You're the first gay guy I've known this well, and what hurts you, hurts me. Doesn't matter to me who turns your head."

"You might be surprised, Frank," he said without judgment. "You didn't know I'm gay. You might know more and just not realize it."

"I hadn't thought of that," Frank said. Jake could picture his partner suddenly reassessing everyone he knew and worked with. Darryl Jackson immediately sprang to mind.

"Anyway," Jake went on, "apology completely accepted. Thank you for that."

"I won't keep you," Frank said. "The vic had I.D. on him. Dmitri Volkov, but you already knew that. Address on Barrow Street. I've already been there and nothing's out of the ordinary."

"Okay?" Jake said, wondering what the purpose of Frank's call was if ethics barred him from working this case directly.

"You mentioned he was close with your … boyfriend," Frank said. The hesitation indicated Frank's lingering discomfort, but the fact that he used the word at all was a good sign. "I don't want to pry, but are you talking about Owen Toussaint?" He left the ethical considerations unsaid, if not unimplied.

Jake understood the unasked question. "Frank, Owen and I are just friends. Yes, we met through this investigation, but no, he's not my boyfriend."

In the moment it took Frank to respond, Jake realized that, prior to all this, he *would* have considered Owen his boyfriend after all they'd shared in so short a time.

But no more.

"My boyfriend's name is Tommy. He lives in the Village. I went right there right from the park and told him about Dmitri. Why?"

"Well," Frank said, "it would save us a lot of time if your boyfriend knew how I could reach the vic's next of kin."

"Got it," Jake said. "Are you at home?"

"Indeed I am."

"Okay," Jake said. "You sit tight. I'll call Tommy and get right back to you."

"Thanks, Jake," Frank said. "Knew I could count on you."

Moments later, Cara answered the phone.

"How is he?" he asked right away.

"Better," she said, "but not much. I gave him half a phenobarb and Fuchsia made a big pot of gumbo. She said it's the Southern version of Jewish penicillin. I guess she's talking about chicken soup. I wouldn't know, I'm Italian. Steven's here too."

"Good," Jake said, not hiding his relief. He related Frank's phone call to her. "I don't want to disturb them, but could you see if Tommy or Steven has a home phone number or address for Dmitri's parents?"

"Sure," she said, "hang on." He heard her set the receiver on the end table, followed by her voice in the distance. He couldn't distinguish what she was saying, but a moment later, Steven was on the line.

"Hi, Jake," he said. Griffin had never heard him sound so understated, no hint of the usual flamboyance.

"Hi, Steven," he said. "How're you holding up?" He could tell Steven had been crying, and recently. He could imagine that the mood in their apartment was rather somber, but at least none of them were facing this alone.

"Still in shock," he replied. "By the way, thank you for coming down here to tell Tommy in person."

"Nothing to thank me for," Jake deflected.

"I have a phone number for D's parents, but not an address," he said. Jake heard the sound of papers being shuffled and assumed that Steven was rummaging around in his ubiquitous shoulder bag. "Here it is," he continued. He dictated a phone number with a seven-one-eight area code. "I don't know the address, only that it's in Brighton Beach where D grew up." The Brooklyn neighborhood was an enclave for Jewish immigrants, mostly Russian, which is what Dmitri's parents were on both counts.

"Thanks, Steven," Jake said. "This is a big help. My partner can get an address."

"Oh, and Jake?" Steven said. "D's folks are Jewish and it's the Sabbath 'til sunset. They're not Orthodox, so I don't know if it matters. Just thought you should know."

Jake thanked him. "How long will you be there?" he asked.

"I'm not going anywhere," he assured Jake. "I brought a bag. I already called the club, told them about D, said I won't be in for a few days. And in the meantime, I'm just gonna camp out here."

"Thanks," Jake said. "Call me if either of you need anything. Cara has all my numbers."

"We'll do that, Jake," Steven said. "Thanks for that too."

After hanging up, Jake called Frank at home and gave him the Volkovs' phone number, indicating that it was in Brighton Beach, along with the information about their being Jewish, but not Orthodox.

"I don't see that mattering," Frank said. "Probably won't get an address from Ma Bell before sunset anyway."

Before sunset, Jake thought, the two words sending a chill up his spine.

Before hanging up, Frank said, "Jake?"

"Yeah?"

"I'm not tellin' you what to do or anything," he said, "and you'd know best what you need. But why don't you think about taking a personal day or two. This one hit too close to home for you, and it sounds like there might be people who need you more than I do right now."

Jake was touched. "Thanks, Frank," he said. "I mean that. And I'll consider it. I will. I'll let you know in the morning what I decide."

They said goodnight and hung up.

Jake informed Owen that his next order of business was to call Brian and check on him.

"No," Owen said, pulling him into a comforting embrace, "your next order of business is to sit down and close your eyes. I'll call Brian."

Jake looked up at him, his expression weary, but warm. "I'm really glad you're here," he said.

"Jake," he replied, "for two weeks people have been making sure I was okay. Now let me do that for you. You *and* Brian." He gave him a kiss. "Now get on that couch."

Jake gladly complied. "His numbers are next to the phone," he said, his shoes already off and his feet up. "If you don't get him at home, try the *Voice*."

"I think I could have figured that out," Owen said. The smile on his face was audible in his words.

He reached Brian in the newsroom.

"How're you holding up?" he asked the reporter.

"Better than I would have thought, man" he said. "Working on this story has actually been pretty therapeutic."

"Good," Owen said. "I was afraid it might make you feel worse. I'm glad I was wrong."

"Have you heard how Tommy's doing?"

Owen related the information Jake had gotten from Cara when he called, adding that Steven would be staying there for the time being.

"Jake wanted you to know that Steven had a phone number for Dmitri's parents in Brooklyn," he said, "and that he passed it along to his partner. I guess he's going to tell them this evening."

"Thanks for letting me know," Brian said. "If you hear anything about the arrangements—"

"We'll let you know right away," Owen finished for him.

Brian was silent for a moment. "Listen," he said, "what're you two doing tonight?"

"I don't know," Owen replied. Lowering his volume, he said, "This kicked Jake's ass around the block. I know, it kicked yours too, but Jake found out by seeing the body. Not saying it's a competition."

"No, I get it," Brian assured him. "I don't envy him. I asked because I meant what I said on the sidewalk today. I think we should step it up and track down this sick fuck, and I'm not feeling too patient."

"What're you whispering about over there?" Jake asked from the sofa, his eyes still closed as he'd been instructed.

"Hang on," Owen said into the phone. He explained, in brief, Brian's request.

"Hell, yes," Jake said, sitting up, completely alert. "And I know where to start."

BRIAN ARRIVED AT THE BROWNSTONE AROUND SEVEN-THIRTY, having taken a cab directly from the *Voice*.

After calling the precinct to arrange for the personal days, Jake had remained on the couch, per Owen's orders. The attorney got busy in the kitchen and, timed perfectly to Brian's arrival, had a large bowl of spaghetti and one of salad on the dining room table. In addition, he'd selected a bottle of red from Jake's wine rack and was letting it breathe.

"Why is it that whenever somebody loses a loved one, people want to feed them?" Brian mused as they began their meal.

"Well," Owen posited, "having been on both sides of that equation recently, I assume it's because when you're grieving you either don't have the capacity to cook or you just don't care if you eat."

"I told you Fuchsia was heading to Tommy's, right?" Jake asked. "Well, according to Cara, the first thing she did was make a pot of gumbo."

"See?" Brian said.

Sensing that it was safe to broach the subject, Jake asked, "How did the article come out?"

"Pretty good, actually," Brian said. "Like I told Owen, it wound up being very therapeutic. I didn't dwell too heavily on Dmitri, only the basic info you gave me about the crime scene, just enough to underscore the whole serial angle. I didn't editorialize, but the subtext was pretty clear: 'How many more people have to die before someone official does something?'"

"Well," Owen said, "you seem a lot more together than you did when we were at your place."

"And I'll be even better when we do something about stopping this fucker once and for all."

THEY WORKED TOGETHER TO CLEAR THE TABLE AFTER DINNER.

"Okay," Brian said to Jake as they sat back down, "you said you know where to start. I have a pretty good idea where that is, but why don't you tell us?"

"The gallery," Jake answered succinctly. Brian's nod indicated that he'd predicted correctly.

"Let's start with some assumptions," he continued. "Assumption One: that our perp is, in fact, a *strigoi* and not a garden-variety psycho. Which leads us to Assumption Two: the *strigoi* is Colin Davenport. If we're working from those two assumptions, the *only* place to start is the gallery."

"Let's hope that's also where we finish," Brian said.

"How do you think the owner fits into all this?" Owen asked.

"Not sure," Jake admitted.

"I might have something," Brian said, pulling papers from his messenger bag. "Here it is," he said, a photocopied page in his hand. "According to several of the books, the *strigoi* need a mortal human to serve as something of a protector. It also says that the protector must always be nearby, especially during daylight hours. Didn't Dani tell you that Davenport has been living out of one of the studios there?"

"Yeah," Jake confirmed.

"And Delacroix lives on the top floor and works in the gallery all day," Brian said. "That fits. And from what the press kit said, she's been his mentor for some time now. I think she may be his protector, as well."

"If that's the case," Owen began, "how do we get past her?"

"That may not be an issue," Jake said, "I don't know what it was about, but she looked pretty pissed off at him last night. I don't know how protective she's feeling at the moment. Now might be the perfect time to strike."

"Her attitude seemed to shift when Davenport brought out Iggy," Owen recalled. Brian and Jake exchanged looks. At that particular moment the prior evening, their attention had been drawn downward by the sound of the shattering glass. They hadn't been focused on Sandrine. "Two things were clear to me. For one, Delacroix is very fond of Dani, and for another, Iggy's appearance had a huge impact on her. A very negative one. Perhaps Delacroix's protective instincts are transitioning from one protégé to another."

"That makes sense, given everything we witnessed after that," Brian said.

"Okay," Owen interjected, "so, we start at the gallery. Then what?"

Jake looked to Brian, with a nod toward his research. "I'll defer to you on that," he said. "You're the one who did the digging at the library."

Before Brian could answer, Jake's phone rang. They all shared an apprehensive look.

"Whadda ya think?" Jake asked. "Cara or Frank?"

"Let's hope neither," Owen said as Jake stood up to answer it.

"Hello?" he said into the kitchen phone. After only a moment, he continued, "Oh. Hi. I totally forgot you said you'd call." He covered the receiver with his hand and stage-whispered, "It's Dani."

Brian was immediately out of his chair. "Get her over here!" he said with urgency. "And see if she can bring Margareta!"

"Dani? Can you hang on a second?" Turning to Brian, his hand once again blocking their conversation, he asked, "Why?"

"Because we need them," Brian insisted. "Margareta knows the *strigoi*, Dani knows the gallery."

From behind him, still seated at the table, Owen said, "He's right. I hate to involve them, but they have information we don't."

Unable to refute what they'd said, Jake returned to the phone call. "Dani," he began, "we have a situation here and could really use your help. Is there any way you could come to the brownstone tonight?" He waited. Brian and Owen saw his expression change from one of hopeful anticipation to one of relief. "Thank you. Very much." He went on to ask if she could possibly get a hold of Margareta and bring her along. "Okay," he said, "I understand. We'll be expecting you."

"Well?" Brian demanded before Jake had even hung up.

"She's coming, but she's not sure about Margareta," he informed them. "She said she'd try."

"Okay," Brian said, "then we'll take it from there."

LESS THAN AN HOUR LATER, THE DOORBELL RANG.

Jake hurried to answer it and, to his relief, discovered that Dani had been able to bring along her former co-worker after all.

This time Jake showed them to the dining room table and not the homier environment of the living room. Dani sensed immediately that this was all business, and quite serious business at that.

Once they were seated and Owen had provided them with water, both declining anything stronger, Jake said, "Okay, what we're about to tell you is going to sound completely insane to you, Dani. I have a feeling that Margareta won't share your reaction, though."

Dani looked to her friend. Margareta was visibly shaken just being in the presence of Jake and Brian, knowing all too well what would be discussed.

Jake then presented everything their combined investigations had led them to believe, handing the narrative off to Brian when it reached the point of his research at the library.

"The night you two came here," Brian said, "everything you told us, Margareta, was exactly what I'd read in the books. Most of them were pretty old, but a couple were written within the last fifteen years, which suggests to me that these aren't simply ancient legends, but that the belief still persists."

"Still with us?" Jake asked Dani.

"You're right," she replied. "It sounds insane. But I'm with you so far."

Jake told them about Dmitri's murder in Central Park and their personal connection to him.

"Oh, my god," Dani said. "Jake, I'm so sorry. All of you. I can't imagine."

"Actually, you can," Brian said, "although you don't realize it yet."

"I don't understand," Dani said.

"That's okay," Jake offered. "You will.

"Right now," he continued, "we're operating on two assumptions. One is that these murders are being committed by a *strigoi*, crazy as that may sound."

"Not crazy," Margareta asserted.

"And the second," he said, "is that the *strigoi* is Colin Davenport." He slid a copy of the composite sketch toward Dani.

The color left her face, creating a deathly contrast to her dark brunette hair and brown eyes.

Jake reached out and took Dani's hand.

"And we're afraid that he's turned your friend into one, as well."

Dani pulled her hand away from his, as if doing so would negate what he'd just said. She was shaking her head in disbelief, unable to process all this information.

After everyone had left the gallery the night before, Dani had confronted Sandrine, asking if she'd known that Iggy had been on the premises. Understanding, and therefore forgiving, Dani's ire, Sandrine had assured her that she'd been completely ignorant of Colin having brought him there and had given Dani her word that she would make sure Colin regretted the pain he'd caused her assistant, once again omitting her belief that turning Iggy had been an attack on Dani.

If what they were saying was true, then Iggy was dead after all. At least a version of it.

"A witness at the Ninth Circle positively I.D.ed the composite sketch as the man Iggy left with the night he disappeared," Jake informed her.

"I think I need a drink," she said to him. It was Owen who rose to his feet.

"What do you want?" he asked. The wine was empty, but there were more bottles in the rack and the liquor cabinet was well stocked.

"I don't care," she said. "Something brown, no vodka or gin. And straight, not even ice."

He poured her a double bourbon, and she drank half of it at once.

"I knew something was horribly wrong last night," she said. "I *knew* it. I even told Sergeant Olsen and Sandrine."

She went on to recount her conversation with Sandrine after the gallery had closed, adding that her employer had informed her earlier that day that Colin and Iggy had not returned to the studio the night before after having stormed out of the opening.

Owen looked at Jake. "If they're not nesting there, how do we find them?"

Brian was looking at his papers again. "I don't think that'll be a problem," he said. "According to this, the *strigoi* can't be separated from the protector for very long. It makes them too vulnerable." He looked at Margareta. "Is that true?"

"Yes," she said. "*Strigoi* must be protected always."

"Wait," Dani said. "What're you talking about? Protector?" Then it hit her, and her eyes were filled with sorrow at the realization. "You don't mean Sandrine, do you? She can't be involved in all of this."

Jake looked at the other men and then at Dani. In a soft, understanding tone, he said, "We're afraid she might be." Seeing her face, he graphically recalled the sense of vertigo he'd experienced lately, and knew she was in the throes of her own version.

Dani's mind raced, recalling every anecdote Sandrine had shared about her history with Colin, praying something would stand out that would disprove what they were suggesting.

Nothing did.

Hoping that the next thing Jake or Brian said would add some clarity to the conversation, she asked, "How do Margareta and I fit in?"

Jake said, "The two of you know things that we don't. You, Dani, know both Sandrine and the gallery. And you," he said to Margareta, "you know the *strigoi*."

"I know *strigoi* must be killed!" Margareta's spirit was ignited by centuries-old passion and fervor that were encoded in her DNA. For as much as Dani had faltered over the last thirty minutes, Margareta had grown stronger. It was almost as if the two young women had exchanged roles.

"We're all in agreement on that," Jake said. "Now, how're we gonna do it?"

CHAPTER FORTY-ONE

THEY WORKED THROUGH THE NIGHT, OWEN REGULARLY MAKING MORE COFFEE.

"First things first," Jake had said as they got down to business. "Dani, is the gallery open on Sundays?"

"No," she replied. "It's our one day closed. Why?"

"Good," he said. "Because we'll want to act fast. And not after sunset either.

"Do you have Sandrine's number at home?" he continued.

"Yes."

"Call her now before it gets too late," he instructed. "Tell her that you're concerned about Iggy and wanted to know if they're back so you two could work out your differences. If they aren't, give her this number and tell her to call you here when they return. Tell her you're staying with me for a few days. Make up a reason she'll buy coming from you."

He paused, something new occurring to him. "You didn't tell her I'm a cop, did you?"

"No, just that you're a friend."

"Good," he said, "we don't want her getting suspicious until we have a better handle on where she stands."

"Where she stands?" Dani asked.

At Jake's prompting, Owen shared his observations at the opening.

Digesting this, Dani went into the kitchen and dialed Sandrine's phone number in the apartment.

"Sandrine?" she said. "I hope I'm not calling too late." Dani listened to her employer's response while everyone was fixated on her. "Oh, good," she said. "I'm calling because I was wondering if Colin and Iggy ever came back. I don't like how I left things with Ig and I really want to just work it out and move past it." Again, she listened.

Brian leaned toward Jake and whispered, "She's good."

"Oh, okay," Dani said, her disappointment evident. "Do you have something to write with?" Listening. "Okay, let me give you a number where you can reach me." Another brief pause. "No, I'm not. I'm staying for a few days with my friend Jake. You met him last night." A pause. "The neighbors are fumigating their apartment and I can't take the smell." Pause. "No, we're just friends." Her slight laugh sounded strained and forced to everyone at the table. "He's kinda like a big brother in a lot of ways. Ready for the number?"

She dictated Jake's home number and added, "It doesn't matter how late you call here. It's important that I know." She said goodbye and hung up.

"They're not back yet," she said as she returned to the dining room, "but you probably figured that out."

"You did really well," Jake assured her. "I know this can't be easy. Probably doesn't even seem real. But putting a stop to this without your help would be a lot harder, maybe even impossible."

"It's funny," Dani reflected, her gaze fixed on the table. "I never met him until last night, and the whole time we were preparing for the opening, I'd built up this image in my head, from his paintings, from Sandrine's stories.

"But then, last night, the minute I laid eyes on him, I felt this overwhelming feeling that I wanted nothing to do with him. On any level." She looked at each of them, Margareta included. "Isn't that weird?"

"Not at all," Jake said. "You've got a good gut. You should trust it. I'm sure Owen and Brian would agree. All three of us regularly have to trust those gut feelings. What you just described is routine in our lines of work."

"Okay," Owen said, "what next?"

"I'm guessing you have a key to the gallery?" Jake asked Dani.

"Yes, but not any of the rooms on the upper floors," she said.

"That could be a problem if Davenport is upstairs and Sandrine is uncooperative," Brian said.

"Any ideas?" Owen asked Jake.

"Considering what we're up against," he said, "if Sandrine won't cooperate, it means she's still protecting him. And if that's the case, then she's in our way. I'm not opposed to physically restraining her and taking the keys by force." Dani let out a tiny gasp. "I'm sorry, Dani. But if she's working with him, it can't be avoided."

"I understand," she said. "At least I think I do. This is all so fucked up."

Margareta placed a comforting hand on Dani's leg, eliciting a fragile smile from her.

"Of course," Jake went on, "everything hinges on whether or not they show back up there."

"They will," Margareta said with conviction. "They must in order to survive. Young one may not know this, but older one does."

"Alright," Brian said, "we're inside the gallery and have access to the studio. Now what?"

"We kill them," Jake said.

"Them?!" Dani cried. "Iggy too?!"

This time Margareta put her arms around Dani's shoulders.

"Dani," Jake said as gently as he could, "Iggy is already dead. Colin did that. I know it's hard—hell, almost impossible—to comprehend that, especially since you saw him last night walking and talking. But you sensed it then. Something was terribly wrong. It wasn't Iggy anymore."

"But …" She couldn't complete the thought, given that, despite the insanity of it all, she knew in her heart that Jake was right. She had sensed it. That person had not been the friend she'd loved. And had already lost.

"Nothing about this is going to be easy," Brian added, matching Jake's comforting tone. "Shit, it's probably going to be dangerous. But if we don't do it, Davenport will get away with everything he's done and more people will die."

"I know," she said, her voice faltering. "I know he has to be stopped. Especially after what he did to Iggy. And to your friend in the park. All of them. My brain just needs to catch up."

"I understand," Jake said. "We've been hashing this out for some time now, and I refused to believe any of it at first too."

"What changed your mind?" she asked.

"Two things," he said. "For one, the medical examiner detected traces of human saliva in all the wounds."

"What was the other?"

He looked to Owen, who shared an encapsulated version of Miss Thelma's visit to the brownstone the first night of the wake and all she'd told them about voodoo, tales she'd heard of her grandmother's time as a slave.

"Do you need some time by yourself?" Jake asked her.

"No," she said. "That won't help us stop him." She looked to Margareta and Brian. "Tell us again how we kill … them?"

AT SHORTLY AFTER THREE A.M., JAKE'S PHONE RANG.

Dani started to rise, but Jake said, "Let me get it. She already knows you're at my place." She followed him into the kitchen.

"Hello?" he said.

"Hello, is this Jake?" Sandrine asked. Despite her continental sophistication, he sensed an edge of apprehension in her voice.

"Yes, Ms. Delacroix," he said.

"Please, call me Sandrine," she offered.

"Okay, Sandrine," he replied. "Hang on, I'll get Dani."

He handed off the phone.

"Hello, Sandrine?" she said.

"Dani, they have come back," Sandrine informed her. "I am still too furious to speak to him, but I can hear them downstairs." Her tone was hushed, almost frightened.

"Thank you, Sandrine," Dani said, nodding to the others. Everyone else exchanged looks, ranging from relief to fear. "Can you let me know if they leave again?"

"*Certainement*," Sandrine assured her.

"If I don't hear from you, I'll assume they're still there in the morning," Dani said, wishing she had used a singular pronoun. No sense in indicating that Colin's presence mattered to her. "Is it okay with you if I use my key to let myself in?"

"*D'accord*," she replied. "And Dani? Please be prepared to fail in repairing your friendship. Colin can have a terrible hold on people. I've seen it happen before. I don't want him to cause you more pain."

"Thank you, Sandrine," she said. "I'm prepared." *For anything, I hope*, she thought. "Do you want me to call you before I come to the gallery tomorrow?"

"That is not necessary, *ma chère*," Sandrine said. "But do not hesitate to come to my apartment if they upset you. I will not stand for that. Not anymore. Colin has hurt enough people."

"Thank you, Sandrine," Dani said once again. "I'll remember that."

"*Bonne nuit*, Dani."

"Goodnight, Sandrine."

With the exception of Margareta, they all spoke up at once the moment Dani had hung up the phone.

She first informed them that Colin and Iggy had returned to the gallery, as Brian and Margareta had predicted they would. Dani went on to share the impression she'd gotten from her boss that Colin had transgressed for the final time and there would be no going back.

"She said, 'Colin has hurt enough people'," Dani related. "And that she was too furious to even speak to him."

The men looked at one another. "That sounds hopeful," Owen commented.

Jake had come to think of them as a task force and, as such, recognized that the time had come to plan their assault on the gallery.

"Dani," he began as they all resumed their seats, "I'm sorry, but I'm afraid you have to come along. I could take your keys, but you know the interior layout. I wish we could leave you out of it, but that's not possible.

"But you," he continued, addressing Margareta, "you're either going home or waiting here. I'm not putting you in danger when your role ends once we have the information you can give us."

"I would very much like to see *strigoi* die," she said, "but I do not wish to go with you."

"Brian, get your copies," he instructed. "Be very specific. What do we need to stop Davenport?"

"Like I—" He corrected himself, looking to Margareta. "*We* said the other night, silver immobilizes them but doesn't necessarily kill them. For that, it's either decapitation or fire."

"Okay, that limits our options, but also tells us what we need." He looked to the ladies. "Do you have any silver jewelry, preferably chains or necklaces?" Both answered in the affirmative. "Okay, we'll need to swing by your places and get whatever you have." As an aside, he added, "When we do that, Margareta, we can leave you there. We'll come by and get you when it's all over.

"How about you two?" he asked the men.

"I wear gold," Owen said.

Brian held up his bare hands and said, "Except for a wristwatch, I don't wear jewelry."

"Okay," Jake responded. "I don't have anything either."

"What about Tommy and Steven?" Brian asked. "Do you think it would be worth calling them?"

"I'm not calling at this hour and waking them," he said. "I can try in the morning, but I'm not sure how much time that will leave us."

"What about those?" Dani asked. She was pointing at a pair of silver candelabra on the sideboard, each adorned with a long spike centered between the four arms for the candles. They'd belonged to Jake's grandmother and had been there so long, he wasn't even aware of them anymore.

"Dani, you're a genius," he said, grabbing the pair and hurriedly tossing aside the candles. Holding them aloft, he asked Margareta, "Will these work?"

"Oh, yes," she said. "Chains are good, but this is better to break skin."

"What about the other parts of the process?" Brian asked. "I don't suppose you forgot you have a headsman's axe hanging on a wall."

His comment made Jake think of something. "No, but wait here."

Jake charged up the stairs, taking them two at a time despite his fatigue. He returned only a minute or two later bearing a shiny sword in its scabbard and attached to a belt.

"From my dress blues in the Corps," he said. "I ditched the uniform, but I kept this, thinking I might someday hang it up as art."

"Do you know how to use it?" Owen asked. "I mean, like we'll need tomorrow."

"Let's find out," he said, taking a few steps backward into the living room and checking that he had a clear range for a swing.

He pulled the sword from its scabbard and held it in both hands.

"Pretend it's a baseball bat," Brian said. "And swing for the fences."

Following his friend's guidance, Jake did just that. The sound of the blade slicing through the air startled all of them.

"You should keep taking practice swings," Brian said. "Swinging through empty space and looking into someone's eyes are gonna be two different things."

Jake knew this all too well, having been through basic and then on the ground in Nam, as well as firearms training with the force.

"That leaves fire," Owen said.

"Last resort," Dani said, a firmness in her tone that took them all by surprise. "If Sandrine is done protecting Colin, I don't want all her hard work destroyed."

"I can understand that, Dani," Jake said, returning the sword to the scabbard. "But, last resort or not, it still has to be an option. If I fail with the sword, Colin has to be stopped by whatever means necessary." He specifically didn't include Iggy, not wanting to further upset her on that matter.

"We'd need something flammable that we can easily carry," Owen said.

"Maybe not," Dani added, a hint of reluctance in her voice. "Colin works in oils. That means that there have to be cans of thinner in his studio. That's flammable and it's already there."

"What about igniting it?" Brian asked. "We can't stand there fucking around with a matchbook, and my Zippo's only good for one toss."

"I have road flares in my spare-tire well," Jake said, "in case I pass a collision when I'm off duty."

It was all coming together so quickly, so seamlessly, that Jake was worried. It almost felt too sure of a thing. He pushed aside his fears and moved ahead.

"Okay," he said, sounding like the commander of a squadron, a tone to which they all responded. "We have our arsenal. Now, let's map out our plan of attack."

CHAPTER FORTY-TWO

THREE DOORS DOWN THE STREET FROM GALERIE DELACROIX WAS AN ALLEY.

About twenty feet into the narrow passage, Jake and the others stood, huddled together. They'd dropped Margareta at home in transit and were about to enter the gallery. As Jake had learned in both the Corps and the department, it's always necessary to regroup immediately before a tactical operation.

Brian lit a cigarette and Jake was reminded of the custom in Nam.

"Could be a condemned man's last smoke," Larry used to say before they both lit up.

"Gimme one of them," he told Brian.

"Yeah," Owen added, "me too."

Although it was probably just understandable nerves, Jake wondered if Owen was thinking a variation of the memory he'd just had. He hoped not. God, he hoped not.

"Okay," he said. "Once we're in, we go to Sandrine's apartment to get the keys. And be prepared for anything." As he said this last, he looked at Dani, an unspoken question in his eyes.

She nodded.

"If she cooperates, great," he said. "If not, Brian, I need you to restrain her while Owen and I get the keys."

"Roger that," Brian said.

Jake was praying that it wouldn't be necessary. Brian was much more muscular than Owen and he needed his strength in a firefight.

"Then we proceed to the studio on the second floor," he continued.

"And then?" Brian asked.

"I wish to fuck I knew," Jake admitted. "Nothing in Nam or on the force has been like this."

Owen spoke up. "Silver immobilizes them," he said, "so that should be our first step." He glanced down at the large, canvas tote bag he carried with the two candle holders inside.

"Use the sword before fire," Dani said. "Please." Her desire to preserve the gallery and its contents was apparent to the three men.

Jake had strapped his Corps sword around his waist and absent-mindedly stroked the hilt with his fingertips.

"I say we take out Iggy first," Brian said. "Sorry, Dani, but he's the weaker one. It's gotta be that way."

"I know," she said reluctantly.

"If we need to use fire," Jake said, "Owen, I'm putting you on point to locate and splash any thinner you can find, got it?"

"I hear you," he said.

"Brian, you've got the flares."

Brian had loaded up his leather messenger bag from the wheel well in Jake's hatchback.

"Got it covered," he said.

"Okay," Jake said. "Let's roll."

As Owen and Dani headed toward the mouth of the alley, Jake put a hand on Brian's arm, holding him back. Reaching behind himself, he withdrew his department-issued sidearm from the waistband at the back of his jeans. "You know how to use this?" he asked.

"Like a camera," Brian said. "Point and shoot."

"If that's the best you've got to offer," Jake said, "I'll just hope it doesn't come to that." He handed Brian the gun and they followed Owen and Dani.

DANI USED HER KEY TO UNLOCK THE FRONT DOOR and, once inside the front gallery, Jake raised a hand, stopping them all in their tracks and silencing them at the same time.

He listened intently, but heard nothing.

"Of course, it's gonna be quiet," Brian whispered. "Look outside. The sun's up. They're asleep."

With the same, still upraised hand he'd used to hush them, Jake waved him off and pointed upward.

The quartet quietly made their way to the top floor, where Dani knocked on the door to Sandrine's apartment.

"Sandrine," she said, "it's Dani."

Almost immediately, Sandrine opened the door. Once it was opened, her expression turned from concern for her protégé to resigned recognition.

"I see you're not alone," she said, a chill in her voice. "Come in, Detective Griffin."

As the four entered the apartment and Sandrine shut the door, he said, "You know who I am." It was not a question.

"Yes, detective," she said. "When I saw you talking to Sergeant Olsen at the opening, I had a suspicion. Only a few phone calls the next day confirmed it." She moved into the room. "And if I know who you are, I assume that you know who I am."

"You're protecting Colin Davenport," he said.

"*D'accord*," she responded, her spirit deflated, self-loathing saturating her tone.

"Then you also know why we're here," he said.

"Do you mind?" she asked, as she poured herself a cognac, despite the hour. Jake couldn't help likening it to the cigarette ritual he'd recalled in the alley.

Taking a sip, she said, "I knew this day would come. For more than twenty years, I knew. Please believe me," she said, her tone not sharing the imploring nature of her words, "I never wanted any harm to come to anyone."

"Then why did you let it?" Dani asked, feeling betrayed.

"Oh, Dani," Sandrine said, setting her cognac down and approaching the girl. "You, least of all. If I had known, if I had any idea, I would have stopped him any way I could. But he resented you, he was jealous of my affection for you. That is why he targeted your friend."

Sandrine opened her arms and stepped toward Dani, intending to embrace her. Dani smacked her once-mentor's outstretched arms away, all her pain channeled into the act.

"You allowed him to kill people!" she screamed.

"Dani," Sandrine said, her voice feeble. "Please forgive me."

"The keys," Jake demanded in an even tone. "For the studio."

With a lingering, pained gaze on Dani, Sandrine moved to the counter where her purse lay and withdrew a large ring.

Approaching Jake, her hand outstretched, a single key gripped between two manicured fingers, she said, "Do what you must."

Jake snatched the keyring from her and left the apartment, followed by everyone else, the owner included.

In front of a door on the second-floor landing, he turned back. "This one?" he asked Sandrine. She nodded.

He carefully inserted the key into the lock and turned it, being cautious not to make more noise than was necessary.

He swung the door open and stepped inside quickly, moving with haste to avoid any potential assault. The windowless room was dark, the only light entering from the stairwell. Having assured himself that it was clear, he waved the others through.

The space wasn't large, and it took very little effort to determine that it was empty.

"Where else might they be?" he demanded of Sandrine.

"Colin sometimes uses the basement when he … sleeps," she replied.

"Okay," Jake said. "Let's go." Pointing toward the gallon-sized tins of paint thinner, he added, "Dani, Brian, grab those."

The group stealthily descended the stairs to the main level and, having moved into the workroom, Jake opened the door to the basement.

"Down here?" he asked Sandrine.

"*Oui*," she said.

He passed through the darkened doorway, the others behind him.

CHAPTER FORTY-THREE

AS WAS THE STUDIO, THE BASEMENT WAS WINDOWLESS and, it seemed, even darker.

Jake located a wall switch at the top of the stairs and flipped it. Below, a bare bulb suspended from the ceiling blazed to life, illuminating the steps before him.

Descending to the bottom, Jake held a hand aloft, signaling the others to wait for the "all clear." Once his feet were on the cement floor, he needed only a moment to take in his surroundings.

Several large, empty wooden crates—used to transport artwork, he assumed—were stacked against the far wall and, in the corner beyond them, lay a bare mattress. Atop it, Colin was prostrate on his back, Iggy curled into the bend of one arm. They were both … sleeping? Jake didn't know what word was appropriate.

With the same hand he'd used to halt them, Jake motioned the others down. Brian, bringing up the rear, was immediately behind Sandrine and, when she reached the bottom of the stairs, he sensed a change in her vibe, her spine stiffening as she sucked in a gasp and shivered.

"Dani," Jake whispered, "you take a candlestick. I want you armed."

Owen handed her one, taking the other for himself and tossing the tote bag aside. Dani and Brian had set the tins of thinner on the floor where they stood.

Jake withdrew his sword from its scabbard and stealthily approached the mattress.

"Colin!" Sandrine shrieked, responding to her ingrained nature, instincts that had governed her for two decades. The artist bolted upright without seeming to bend any of the joints in his body, jarring Iggy from his own slumber in the process.

On his feet atop the mattress, Colin focused on Jake. With a blood-curdling snarl, his features transformed. Extending all ten fingers to the extreme, his nails elongated into sharp claws, and his incisors, canines, and eye teeth lengthened into vicious fangs, filling his opened mouth with a row of deadly points. His eyes took on a reddish cast and his nostrils flared like those of a rabid animal.

Iggy, organically responding to the chemical message sent by his master, was also on his feet, having undergone the same hideous transformation.

Owen gasped and staggered backward, and Dani screamed, holding the candlestick in front of herself, instinctively warding off attack. Jake, who had mentally prepared himself for the inconceivable, stood firm, as did Brian, whose time in the library had given him a slight, if woefully insufficient, preview of what was unfolding before him.

Colin leapt from the mattress, his body seeming to move slowly as if he were flying, and landed on the cement floor directly in front of Jake. His eyes fixed on the detective, he held his ground, pointed a talon at Iggy, and flicked his finger to indicate Dani.

The youngling sprang forward and, before Owen could stop him, had pinned Dani to the stone wall.

"Kill her," Colin snarled, the corners of his mouth turning up in a delighted smile.

Iggy's lips pulled back on command, his lethal teeth exposed and glistening, his own mouth as mirthful as Colin's.

"I'm sorry, Iggy," Dani whimpered. "You know I loved you." With those words, she rammed the point of the candlestick she held into his chest.

Letting out a cry of agony, Iggy staggered backward and collapsed against the wooden crates, crashing to the floor. He instinctively grasped at the base of the candlestick and screamed, the metal searing his skin. The room was suddenly filled with the stench of burned flesh. Releasing the silver, he fell back. The only movement from him was his twitching hands and feet, and his eyes, darting left and right from within the prison of his paralyzed state.

"One down," Brian said with enthusiasm, ready to kick some ass. He'd turned his attention to Sandrine, prepared to stop any preemptive move she had up her designer sleeve.

Owen helped Dani to her feet. The two watched in terror as Jake and Colin faced off.

"The thinner!" Jake yelled as Colin recoiled from the sword. Owen unscrewed the cap from a tin and, using his foot, tipped it over, letting the contents run across the floor toward Colin. Dani was already unscrewing the caps on the other cans.

"No!" Sandrine screamed and lunged forward. Not wanting to resort to the gun tucked into the back of his jeans, Brian swung her around and landed a right hook on her face, sending her against the wall behind her.

"More!" Jake yelled, his left hand indicating the thinner, his right hand clutching the sword.

Dani grabbed a can and stepped closer, splashing its contents directly onto Colin and the wood behind him.

"You think you can stop me?" Colin snarled at Jake, his voice sounding inhuman. "You think you're the first to try?"

Any reply Jake could think of felt like a line from a bad movie, so he simply swung the sword, missing by a good six inches. He hated to admit to himself that he was scared shitless.

Owen's attention was caught by Sandrine, rousing herself from her stupor against the stone wall of the basement.

"Brian!" he called, alerting him.

Before Brian could act, Colin had lunged forward, wrapping his clawed hand around Jake's throat.

"No!" Owen screamed, even as Dani shrieked in terror.

Lifting Jake a good foot off the floor, Colin drew his other hand back and, using his claws, sliced open his midsection before flinging him violently aside.

Jake's body tumbled over Iggy's, dislodging the candlestick, and, in the process, dropping the sword. As Jake came to rest against the wall, Iggy rose up, blood dripping from his eyes like tears, his murderous gaze fixed on Dani.

"Owen!" Brian screamed. "The sword!"

Remembering the reporter's game-day instructions at the brownstone to swing for the fences, Owen hefted Jake's sword in both hands and channeled all his Little League memories into his rage.

Iggy's head spiraled through the air and landed at Colin's feet.

Her fury overtaking her, Dani grabbed a can of thinner and advanced on Colin, splashing him with its contents.

"You motherfucking piece of shit!" she screamed as she flailed her arms, soaking him and the wood behind him with the deadly liquid.

With a move so fast it was invisible to the mortal eyes in the room, Colin knocked the can from Dani's hands, sending it flying across the shadowy room. In an instant, he snaked his claws into her thick hair and yanked her head back, exposing the tender flesh of her throat.

"Don't any of you move!" he roared as he backed up, the girl held in front of him as a shield. Reaching the stacked crates, he used his free hand to fling them aside, revealing the opening to a tunnel in the stone wall.

Having regained her senses, Sandrine bent down and picked up the candlestick Owen had dropped.

"Get Jake out of here," she said to Owen, her tone chillingly calm. Turning to Brian, she said, "You stay."

She slowly advanced on Colin as Owen, stunned into action by Sandrine's command, carried Jake up the stairs, the sword returned to its scabbard.

Colin hissed at the Frenchwoman and yanked Dani's hair, causing her to cry out in pain and terror.

"You wouldn't dare," he threatened Sandrine. "You don't have the courage."

"You were right once," she said. "If I had courage, I would have turned you down twenty years ago when you offered me everything I wanted.

"But I have that courage now," she screamed as she lunged forward. In the blink of an eye, Colin and Dani were gone, having disappeared into the tunnel, leaving Sandrine standing in the empty space the pair had occupied a mere moment before.

"Use your lighter," she said to Brian. "Make it impossible for him to return." She retrieved the canvas tote and the candelabra, and moved to the stairs to wait for him.

Instead of his Zippo, Brian pulled a flare from the messenger bag and ignited it. Without giving second thoughts any berth, he tossed it into the pile of thinner-soaked crates.

The basement was instantly an inferno. "Hurry!" Sandrine yelled from behind him, and Brian raced for the stairs. Reaching the workroom, he slammed the door and said to the others, "We've gotta get outta here. *Now!*"

ONCE THEY WERE SAFELY BACK IN JAKE'S CIVIC, Brian, in the backseat with the car's owner, said, "He's bleeding bad." He had a rag pressed to Jake's midsection.

The sound of approaching sirens was already blaring behind them, New York's Bravest on their way to put out the fire at Galerie Delacroix. At the sound, Sandrine began to cry in the shotgun seat, but the others didn't know if the tears were for Dani, Jake, the gallery, or herself. Nor did they care.

His attention focused solely on Jake, Brian said, "We can't take him to an E.R. Not with a wound like this and him being a cop. Too many questions."

"I know," Owen said from the driver's seat. "Just keep pressure on the wound." He popped the car into first and squealed out, his expression fixed and confident.

"Where're we going?" Brian asked.

"Miss Thelma's."

CHAPTER FORTY-FOUR

MISS THELMA LIVED IN A BEAUTIFUL THREE-STORY HOUSE on Astor Row, the block of East 130th Street developed by John Jacob Astor and his grandson in the early 1880s.

Everyone was seated about Miss Thelma's living room, all except for Owen, Brian, and Frank, the cop pacing incessantly, and Fuchsia who was in the kitchen.

On the drive uptown, Jake had said, his cadence stilted between pained gasps, "Call Frank." Brian had assured him that they would. "When we get there, call Frank." He'd been emphatic. "His number's in my wallet. Have him call Ruiz."

"I will, Jake," he'd repeated. "You just stay calm." He could feel Jake's blood seeping through his fingers where he pressed the N.Y.P.D. polo shirt Owen had found in the hatchback.

"And call Tommy," he said. "Please."

Behind the wheel of the Civic, Owen was dodging traffic and shifting gears like a stunt driver.

"Did you get that?" Brian asked him.

"Call Frank, number in his wallet," he said from memory. "Have Frank call Ruiz. Call Tommy."

"You okay?" Brian asked Owen.

"I will be when we get him there," he replied, his hands white-knuckled on the steering wheel.

HAVING ARRIVED AT MISS THELMA'S AND SEEING JAKE CARRIED DOWNSTAIRS, Owen set about making the requested phone calls.

"You sit there and don't fucking move," Brian commanded Sandrine, pointing to one of the chairs in the living room with Jake's gun, a persuasive reminder to the woman that he wasn't kidding around.

Once Owen had explained the circumstances, Frank assured him he'd contact Ruiz and then head to their location.

Calling Tommy was a more delicate matter. Fortunately, it was Cara who answered the phone.

"Jake's been hurt," he said, after having told her who was calling. "He wants Tommy here. If he's able."

Cara assured him that they'd leave immediately. When she arrived, she had Tommy, Steven, and Fuchsia in tow.

Three hours later, they were all gathered in Miss Thelma's living room, awaiting word from below. It had fallen to Brian to apprise them all of everything that had transpired that day.

"And you're telling me that this Davenport is a fucking vampire?" Frank had asked. His incredulity was pushed to the limit and understood by everyone.

"In a nutshell," Brian had said, "yes."

"Do you have any idea how ridiculous that sounds?"

"Which is why there can't be an official report on it," Brian had responded.

The fire at Galerie Delacroix had summoned units from three firehouses and was still an ongoing scene. The various chemicals throughout the building only served to fuel the blaze. All three networks had the conflagration featured on the evening news.

Brian had then laid out their entire covert investigation, from the beginning, cross-referencing crime-scene photos with the copies he'd made from textbooks, mentioning Margareta's input and the traces of human saliva found in the wounds on the victims.

"So Griff was your anonymous source?"

"Unofficially," Brian admitted, "yes."

Frank looked at them all as if they were insane.

"Tell me you've never been forced to believe something you thought was impossible," Brian had challenged him.

Frank had thought back to the morning before last in Central Park when his partner had come out to him. He shook his head and ran his hand over the top of it.

"Will it help when you hear it from Jake?" Brian had asked, his volume lower and his tone less challenging.

"Yeah," Frank had conceded. "It'll help a lot." He had to admit to himself, though, that he was already convinced.

"And she was protecting him?" he asked, looking toward an immobile Sandrine with disgust.

"Until tonight," Brian replied. "Yes."

"What changed tonight?" Frank asked, addressing the Frenchwoman directly for the first time since he'd arrived.

"I am so sorry," she began.

"Save it!" Frank barked. "We don't give a shit how sorry you are. How do we stop this motherfucker?"

In a voice that was so calm it set everyone on edge, she said, "Colin has a new protector." The defeat in her voice was palpable, but its source was impossible to discern. "He must," she went on. "I felt his power over me release when we entered the basement. He would not do that without another protector doing his bidding." She went on to explain that, when she'd first met Colin, his protector at the time was David Armitage, a middle-aged, gay antiques dealer from Richmond, England. Upon taking Sandrine into his fold, Colin had slaughtered Armitage. "I guess I was lucky," she concluded.

"That remains to be seen," Frank said. "Any idea who this new protector might be?"

"Someone who desires success," she said. "That is what he promises in exchange for protection. Success in abundance. That is how he seduced me twenty years ago."

They were all distracted from the interrogation by the opening of the basement door.

MISS THELMA AND MIGUEL RUIZ EMERGED INTO THE LIVING ROOM in blood-smeared surgical gowns, pulling off their latex gloves.

Everyone leapt to their feet.

"Jake is going to be okay," Miss Thelma assured them, making her way to the nearest seat and lowering herself into it.

Ruiz reached under his gown and pulled out a pack of cigarettes. Looking to Miss Thelma, he asked, "Is this okay?"

"Honey," she said, "after the job you did downstairs, I don't care *what* you smoke in here."

Taking that as blanket permission, Brian pulled out his pack, and Owen grubbed one. Once they, along with Ruiz and Tommy, had lit up, Miss Thelma gave her report.

"The wound was deep," she said, "and he lost a lot of blood. But Miguel here was able to suture the deeper tissue and, together, we sewed him up. He should be in a hospital, but if he can't, he can't. He'll need fluids and antibiotics, but we can do that with an I.V. Owen, if you take him back home, I can come by every day to check on him."

"So can I," Miguel interjected. "I have a few contacts at some of the hospitals who can make sure we get the necessary meds, I.V. bags, and whole blood." At this, Frank shook his head in bewilderment, but let it ride.

Is everybody up to something? he wondered in dismay.

Miss Thelma took a deep breath. "Lord, it's been a dog's age since I was in an O.R." She looked to Tommy. "And next to Miguel, you were the real life-saver today. If we didn't have you, I don't know what we would have done."

Tommy, nestled lethargically between Cara and Steven on the couch, looked down at the bandage affixed to the bend of his right arm. Being the only one present with type O-negative blood, it had fallen to him to donate roughly a pint to be used during surgery.

"How did you know to bring him here?" Cara asked Owen.

Miss Thelma laughed, though it was weary and mirthless.

"Honey," she said, "do you remember me telling you that we all do things we keep secret?"

"Yes," Cara responded.

"Well, I didn't share it with you that night, but I spent my life being a doctor," Miss Thelma told her. "Almost all of it was the usual stuff, but downstairs, I helped out plenty of young women who found themselves in trouble and had no place to turn. This was all before 1973 and the Supreme Court finally wised up." She looked at Frank. "You didn't hear that," she said, her tone kind, but leaving no room for disagreement.

"I ain't heard nothin'," he said, glancing in Ruiz's direction. "From nobody."

"I knew about Miss Thelma's work and the operating room in her basement," Owen interjected. "When everything went down today, I knew this was the only place we could bring Jake."

"I'm glad you were there," Tommy said, his gaze at Owen conveying his sincerity.

"Could someone get me a glass of water, please?" Miss Thelma asked.

Steven said, "I'll get it," and dashed into the kitchen

Frank turned his gaze from Miss Thelma back to Sandrine.

"Now," he said, stern command in his tone, "about this new protector. You said Davenport would have seduced him or her with promises of success?"

"Holy shit," Brian muttered.

Everyone was distracted by Steven's return with Miss Thelma's water. Fuchsia followed him into the room.

"What, Brian?" Owen asked once Steven and Fuchsia were seated.

"You introduced Alex Mayhew to Colin, didn't you?" Brian asked Sandrine. "The day he interviewed you?"

"Yes," she answered feebly. "In the studio."

"And did you leave them alone?" he pressed.

"For a brief time," she said. "I thought it odd that he would speak to a reporter before the exhibit was unveiled. He has never done that. But he was adamant that day."

"And I saw them with their heads together at the opening," Brian shared with everyone. "Do you think Alex could be his new protector?" he asked Sandrine.

"Does Alex have ambitions?" She answered his question with one of her own.

"Absolutely."

"Then it is very likely."

"What about the kid?" Owen asked. "Dani's friend. Iggy."

"*Non*," Sandrine replied, the sorrow clear in her voice. "Colin turned Iggy merely to hurt Dani. He resented my affection for her."

"Do you think he's killed her too?" Owen inquired.

"I do not believe so," Sandrine posited. "She was his insurance when he fled the basement. He will keep her until he no longer needs that insurance. But we will have to act fast."

"We?" Frank asked. "Who said I'm letting you anywhere near this?"

"We need her," Owen pointed out.

"And if the new protector *is* Alex," Brian said, "then I know where they are."

TWO FLOORS BELOW STREET LEVEL AT *THE VILLAGE VOICE* was a sub-basement, a cavern to which Alex enjoyed escaping when he needed to think.

"He showed it to me as soon as he stumbled onto it," Brian said. While they had explored Alex's subterranean find, they'd discovered a doorway to a passage, something neither had investigated at the time owing to the apparent instability of the structure.

"I knows them," Fuchsia said. "Them tunnels runs all under them buildings. Rumor is they was part of the Underground Railroad back in the day."

"Do they connect to your shop?" Brian asked her.

"Sho nuf, baby," Fuchsia replied. "I gots me a sub-basement too. Tunnels 'n' all."

They all exchanged looks.

"Then we have a way in," Frank said.

"YOU'RE IN ON THIS?" BRIAN ASKED.

"I ain't saying I'm buying into all the vampire shit," Frank replied in Miss Thelma's kitchen. "But if whoever did that to my partner is down in those tunnels, then he's got me to deal with." He looked the reporter dead in the eye. "You believe all this?"

"I believe what I see, Frank," Brian said. "And you ain't seen the shit I seen today."

"Fair enough," Frank allowed. "Let's go bring this motherfucker down." He took a deep breath and let it out. "But first, there's something I gotta do."

FRANK ENTERED MISS THELMA'S UNDERGROUND OPERATING ROOM and approached the table on which his partner lay.

"How you doing, Griff?" he asked.

"Been better," he said, his voice gravelly from the anesthesia. "But we won this round, huh?"

"You won the battle," Frank said, "but not the war. We'll be heading out soon to finish it."

"We can't have any reports on this, you know that, right?"

"From what they all told me upstairs," Frank said, "I'm inclined to agree."

"You're okay with that?"

Frank put his hand on Jake's. "If a killer gets stopped and my partner cheats death stopping him," he said, "I don't think I could be more okay."

"Then we're good?"

"We're perfect." Frank glanced toward the door. "I think there's somebody else wants to talk to you before we leave." He raised Jake's hand and kissed the back of it. "Don't know what I'd do if I lost you, Griff."

Before the moment got awkward, he left and Tommy entered.

"Hey," he said. "How're you doing?"

"How do I look?" Jake asked.

"Like shit," Tommy said, "but you're alive."

"I'm sorry I didn't stop him before he got Dmitri," Jake said.

"I know," Tommy responded. "But he'll be stopped tonight. That's what matters most."

"How're you holding up?"

"I don't know," he said. "All this has made me think about a lot of shit."

"Us?" Jake asked.

"That too," Tommy admitted. "I don't want you to think I'm abandoning you when you're down, but I think I need some time to myself."

"I understand," Jake said. He did.

"Still friends?" Tommy asked.

"To the end," Jake assured him with a sincere smile.

"You want me to get Owen?"

Jake was moved by the offer and tears sparkled at the corners of his eyes.

"Please."

WHILE FRANK AND TOMMY WERE CHECKING ON THE PATIENT, Miss Thelma had taken Owen into the kitchen.

"You and Jake?" she asked him, her tone gentle, not challenging.

"I'm not sure how to answer that, Miss Thelma."

"With the truth, Owen," she said. "Whatever it is."

Without sharing graphic details, he told her about the rift between Jake and Tommy, and how he and Jake had reached out to one another for comfort after the second night of the wake. However, he discreetly omitted any mention of Brian.

"I realize the timing seems cold," he confessed.

"The timing is the timing, Owen," she said, "and that's something none of us gets to choose, leastways in matters of the heart. It's not my place to judge." She enfolded him in a loving embrace. "But it *is* my place to stick my two cents in. You two would be wise to move slowly. I don't want to see either of you getting hurt because you rushed into something."

"I just feel like I'm betraying Kenny," he said, his voice thickening with emotion.

"By being happy?" she asked. "Owen, do you think Kenny would want you to deny yourself that? For all we know, Kenny put in a word upstairs that nudged you and Jake closer.

"Jake's a good man," she went on, a hand gently placed on his cheek, "and so are you. As much as I'm still grieving Kenny, and probably always will, seeing you with Jake gives my heart some hope."

Before Owen could respond, Tommy entered the kitchen.

"I'm sorry to interrupt," he said, "but Jake's awake and wants to see you, Owen."

CHAPTER FORTY-FIVE

WITH FRANK AND BRIAN CALLING THE SHOTS, the squad that set out in Frank's Impala also included Owen, Sandrine, and Tommy, the last at his insistence despite still being somewhat weakened by his blood donation.

Fuchsia came along as well but only to offer access to her space and the sub-basement below. Once they'd all entered The Pot Shop and she'd provided keys to the store with instructions to lock up, she beat a hasty retreat, her caftan swirling behind her, as usual, as she made her way up Christopher Street.

"What can you tell us?" Frank demanded of Sandrine as they all descended the second flight of stairs below street level.

"Only that Alex will defend him to the death," she said. "As I would have done. But he is new," she continued. "His spirit will be weak. Use that."

Frank found himself, not for the first time that day, wanting to strangle the life out of this bitch. Her cool exterior, evident with everything she uttered, reminded him of the role she'd played in so many deaths, as well as his own partner's brush with the same.

The sub-basement beneath The Pot Shop was smaller than the one Brian had seen at *The Voice*, but was otherwise identical: low-ceilinged, walls of ancient bricks, a doorway framed by heavy beams leading to a dark passage. Also alike was that the room had been retrofitted with electricity, but navigating the passage would require the flashlights they'd tossed into the tote with the candlesticks.

As he had at the gallery, Owen carried the bag, but this time Jake's sword was belted around his waist as well. Frank and Brian were both armed with handguns.

"Let's do this," Frank said. Turning to Owen, he added, "Flashlights."

Once they'd been distributed to the men, Frank was the first into the passage, which led away from the front of the building and toward the center of the block. He paused to shine the light on the walls and ceiling of the tunnel. Turning back, he advised, "Doesn't look too unstable, but we're not gonna take any chances. Speak only if you have to and keep your voices down. And whatever you do, don't bump into the goddamn walls."

Owen followed Frank, with Tommy behind him. Brian brought up the rear, Jake's gun in his hand trained on Sandrine's back. After venturing about twenty feet in the claustrophobic space, the passage opened onto a slightly larger tunnel running perpendicular to the smaller one. Although a bit more spacious, this passageway appeared no less unstable. Brian thought it resembled a mineshaft with the large, square beams forming braces every fifteen feet or so.

"*The Voice* is in this direction," Frank stage-whispered before turning left and leading them onward.

"We must be under the middle of the block," Tommy whispered to Owen before advancing past him and falling in stride next to Frank. "*The Voice* should only be about fifty or sixty yards," he told him.

As they made their way, several rats scurried away from them and into the shadows, and at frequent intervals, they all had to brush cobwebs from their faces. The group noted several doorways, mostly on their left, leading to darker passages similar to the one they'd entered beneath the shop. Tommy had been counting them, referencing the ongoing tally with the number of storefronts between The Pot Shop and the newspaper.

He put a hand on Frank's shoulder, halting the cop. Behind them, the others also stopped.

"If each building on Christopher has one of these tunnels," Tommy whispered, but loudly enough for everyone to hear, "then we want the next one."

Brian made his way forward. "You two better prepare yourselves," he softly advised Frank and Tommy. "What you're gonna see in there is a total mind-fuck." He turned to Tommy. "Especially you. Try not to think about D."

Frank scanned the four faces behind him. "We ready?" he asked. Everyone either nodded or murmured their assent.

Like the tunnel through which they'd passed from the shop, the one they now entered was only about twenty feet long. The single hanging bulb in the sub-basement of *The Voice* created a vertical rectangle of illumination before them.

They all, without needing to be told, proceeded stealthily, careful to minimize the sounds of their footfalls on the brick floor. Just before the doorway, Frank raised a hand, as Jake had done at the foot of the basement stairs at the gallery, halting those behind him. He inched his head forward until he could see into the chamber.

Alex was seated on the floor in the near corner, his legs extended straight in front of him, his hands in his lap, his head hanging forward. Frank noted that he was breathing, but was unable to discern if he was unconscious, sleeping, or just lost in thought.

Beside the reporter, Colin Davenport was stretched out on the brick floor, facing the wall, nestled into the juncture where the two planes met.

Beyond Colin, seated on the floor in the corner opposite Alex, was Dani, her wrists and ankles bound, a strip of duct tape over her mouth. Unlike Alex, her head was not bowed and she immediately saw Frank. She remained silent and motionless, but her eyes screamed the terror she didn't dare utter.

Turning back, Frank pointed to Owen and then at the sword strapped to his waist, immediately raising the same finger to his lips. Owen slowly, noiselessly withdrew the weapon from its scabbard and gripped the hilt in both hands, handing off the tote bag to Tommy.

Next, Frank pointed to Brian and then to the gun in his own hand before shaking his head from side to side, silently saying, "Don't shoot," and then pointing to the ceiling.

Knowing the instability of the tunnel, Brian hadn't needed to be told.

Having communicated the marching orders, Frank stepped through the doorway.

At once, Alex's head snapped up, his eyes wide and frenzied. "Colin!" he shrieked, much as Sandrine had done only hours before in the basement of her now-gutted gallery.

In an instant, Davenport was on his feet and underwent the same hideous transformation Brian and Owen had witnessed earlier that day.

"What the fuck?!" Frank cried out, as, simultaneously, Tommy said, "Jesus Christ!'

Snarling through his frighteningly elongated teeth, Colin fixed a hateful gaze on Sandrine. "Good, you're 'ere, love," he growled. "Now I can enjoy making you watch your lapdog die."

Upon hearing this, Dani began to struggle against her restraints.

Alex had gotten to his feet and was looking frantically from Colin to the intruders and back again. Sandrine noted his ineptitude in his role.

Frank instinctively stepped forward, only to be met with a powerful backhand from Colin. Lifted from the floor by the blow, he crashed head-first against the far brick wall and fell to the ground as Sandrine rushed to Dani's side.

"You goddamn motherfucker!" Owen screamed and charged ahead.

With speed the human eye could not perceive, Colin spun him around and hurled him to the brick floor, rendering him semi-conscious. He yanked Owen's head back to expose his throat.

Before Brian could react, Tommy cried, "No!" and dropped the tote, the candlesticks inside clattering on the brick. He sprang forward, knocking Colin off Owen.

Rolling in each other's arms, they were stopped by the wall, Tommy beneath Colin's grasp. The *strigoi* reared his head and, in a mere moment, had shredded Tommy's throat. Without taking time to feed, Colin left his convulsing victim on the floor as blood gushed from the wound.

"I am so sorry, Dani," Sandrine beseeched, her tears and her regret flowing freely as she worked frantically to untie the knots binding her assistant.

With Tommy's blood dripping from his chin, Colin turned toward Brian. Unarmed with anything but a handgun, which he knew to be useless, Brian staggered backward, sure he would be Colin Davenport's next victim.

Simultaneously, two peripheral figures moved into action. Sandrine, to Brian's left, had risen, having untied Dani, who was attempting to rouse Frank; and Owen, to his right, had shaken off the blur of his head's impact with the floor in his tussle with Colin and was once again standing, his legs now unsteady and the sword clenched in both hands.

Sandrine had pulled a candelabra from the tote that Tommy had dropped. She made eye contact with Owen and they silently shared a plan of action.

"Colin!" Sandrine yelled, causing the murderous, inhuman artist to turn in her direction. Once he was fully facing her, she dove forward, sinking the sharp silver point into his chest.

As Colin staggered backward, his face registering his agony, as well as his arrogant disbelief at this turn of events, Owen lifted the sword. The heft of the weapon threw the injured attorney off balance. Seeing this, Brian rushed to his side, taking the sword from him and, in one smooth motion, swung.

While Davenport's head was still somersaulting through the air, his body crumpled to the floor.

Alex, who had been ineffectually cowering in the corner, saw his promise of success die before his eyes and screamed in anguish. At the sound, Brian noted for the first time that the volume of the confrontation had small motes of mortar dust falling from the ceiling.

Sandrine rushed to Dani and helped her assist Frank to his feet. Like Owen's, his head wound was bleeding. Sandrine grabbed the cop's gun and aimed the weapon at Alex, yelling, "All of you, go! Now! *Vite!*"

"What the fuck are you doing?!" Brian exclaimed. "You'll bring this whole fuckin' place down on top of us!"

"Not if you hurry!" she yelled back, bringing further mortar from above. "*Go!*"

Brian moved to Dani and helped her assist Frank toward the tunnel. Owen knelt beside Tommy. Unable to do anything for him, he reached down and closed his eyes. The three of them aided Frank into the passageway. Once they'd covered some ground, Sandrine taunted Alex.

"I lied," she said. "Your article was *merde*! Shit! You could never be what you dreamed, even *with* Colin's empty promises." She was backing into the tunnel, antagonizing an outraged Alex forward, his eyes betraying his insanity.

Once Sandrine was halfway between the sub-basement under *The Voice* and the main tunnel, she fired, sending a bullet through Alex Mayhew's skull and bringing the ancient passageway down on top of her.

Hearing the gunshot and the subsequent cave-in, Brian cried, "Run!" and the trio hoisted Frank into their arms. Behind them, the main tunnel was giving way, bricks, stones, and rotting support beams crashing down.

They emerged into the sub-basement beneath Fuchsia's shop, a plume of dust following them through the door.

"Up!" Brian commanded, and they dragged a half-conscious Frank up two flights, through the shop, and into the sunlight.

CHAPTER FORTY-SIX

WITH FRANK INJURED, BRIAN DROVE THE IMPALA away from Christopher Street.

From the front passenger seat, Prentiss said, "I gotta get to a phone fast. Harlem's too far."

"My place is on 23rd," Brian said. "We'll head there."

At Brian's apartment, Dani cleaned Owen's head wound while Frank got on the horn to the precinct.

"Friedrich, it's Prentiss," he said, having gotten his colleague on the line. "We got a situation."

While Frank talked to Walt Friedrich, Brian flipped on the TV. A special bulletin was already airing, alerting viewers to the collapse of a sinkhole in Greenwich Village. It was speculated that the torrential thunderstorm three days prior was the probable cause.

In short order, Frank ended his call. "I gotta get back to the scene," he told Brian. "See what damage control I can do before the bodies are found."

Brian glanced at the cop's head wound. "You sure you're up to that?"

Frank ran his hand over the top of his head and winced. "No choice," he said. "If nothing else, my gun's still down there."

"The guy you called," Brian said. "You can trust him?"

"Next to Jake," Frank replied, "there's nobody in the unit I trust more."

"Okay," Brian said, nodding. "I guess we'll drop you at Christopher and head uptown."

Owen and Dani emerged from the bathroom, the former holding a compress to the back of his crown. "How's the patient?" Frank asked.

"It wasn't as bad as it looked," Dani reported. "Head wounds always bleed a lot. They seem worse than they are." She looked at Frank's scalp. "Now your turn."

"No time," he protested, but Dani already had him by the arm, leading him toward the bathroom.

"*Meshuggeneh!*" she said. "You're not going anywhere looking like that!"

While Dani cleaned an impatient Frank's wound, Brian filled Owen in.

"Honestly?" Owen said. "I think I'd rather go dig bodies out of the tunnel than deliver this news."

"I know, man," Brian commiserated. "I know."

TWENTY MINUTES LATER, BRIAN WAS DRIVING THE IMPALA north on the West Side Highway.

Before they dropped him off at Christopher and 7th, Frank had given explicit instructions on what to tell Jake and Ruiz regarding his return to the tunnels and meeting Friedrich there. Brian, in turn, had told him to call from Fuchsia's shop with updates.

"How's the head?" Brian asked over his shoulder once they were on the highway.

"Better," Owen replied from beside Dani in the backseat. "Still hurts, but not as much. Whatever she found in your medicine cabinet is working overtime."

"Percodan," she added.

"I doubt you'll be feeling much of anything by the time we get there," Brian said, "which means I'll have to do all the debriefing."

"Sorry, man," Owen offered.

"No worries," he replied. "Just focus on that wound."

"How're you going to handle it?" Dani asked Brian.

"No fuckin' clue," he admitted. "When Owen told me about D, we'd only been a thing for less than two weeks, and a casual thing at that. But Tommy was Cara's brother and Jake's 'sort of' ex. I figure I'll break it as gently as possible to her and let Fuchsia and Miss Thelma take it from there. Their 'caregiver' skills are far superior to mine."

"I can help them with that," she volunteered. "How about Jake?"

"We'll tell him together," Owen said from beside her, his voice wearied by his injury and the painkiller.

They rode the rest of the way in silence. At 72nd Street, Brian merged onto the Henry Hudson Parkway and continued north, exiting at 125th and navigating a zig-zag pattern through the streets until he reached Astor Row.

AT MISS THELMA'S HOUSE, CARA DID THE MATH WHEN THE TRIO ENTERED without Tommy or Frank, and crumbled into Fuchsia's embrace.

While Brian explained, as delicately as he could, how things had unfolded beneath *The Voice*, Miss Thelma dispatched Miguel to the basement and escorted Owen into the kitchen. The M.E. returned from his assigned task and—after having administered mild sedatives to Cara, Steven, and Fuchsia—set about tending to Owen's injury.

"First-class cleaning," he said to Dani as she entered the kitchen to brew a large pot of tea. He was using a pocket flashlight to check Owen's pupils.

"Concussion?" Miss Thelma asked.

"Possibly a mild one," Miguel replied, still focused on the patient. "What'd you give him for pain?" he asked Dani as he flicked the light onto and away from Owen's eyes.

"Percodan."

"How many milligrams?"

"I didn't check," she admitted, feeling suddenly inept. "I only gave him one pill, though. I'm sorry."

"Nothing to be sorry for," he said. "You did a good job." He turned to Miss Thelma. "The Percodan might explain some of the delay in dilation. He'll need an X-ray as soon as possible."

"Not until we talk to Jake," Owen protested.

"Don't worry," Ruiz assured him. "Once we're done here, I'll take you to him. But then we're getting you straight to St. Luke's-Roosevelt." The hospital at 114th and Amsterdam was the closest to Astor Row. The M.E. knew who to call in order to avoid any record of Owen's visit. Pulling on a pair of latex gloves, he added, "Before any of that, though, you need a few stitches." He turned to Miss Thelma. "Doctor? Care to assist?"

Brian came into the kitchen just as they were finishing up.

"Dani's serving tea," he informed them, "but I could use something a little stronger, if you have it."

"All I've got is sherry," Miss Thelma replied. "You haven't had any medication, have you?"

"No," he told her. "Owen's the only one. Plus the three in the living room."

"Okay then," she said, removing her gloves and opening a cabinet.

"How's he doing?" Brian asked Miguel.

"Possible concussion," the M.E. informed him. "He'll need X-rays."

"But—!" Owen spoke up.

"I know," Ruiz interrupted with reassurance. "But first you need to see Jake."

Miss Thelma handed Brian a glass of sherry. "Sit tight for a few," he said to Owen. "I need *my* medicine first." Taking a seat next to his friend at the kitchen table, he lit a cigarette and downed the sherry.

Brian cast an inquiring glance at his hostess.

As she refilled hiss glass, she said, "Medicinal purposes."

BETWEEN THE INJURY AND THE MEDICATION, OWEN WAS STILL UNSTEADY on his feet, so Brian and Miguel assisted him down the stairs.

When they entered the small procedure room, Jake was sleeping. Miguel helped Owen into a chair beside the bed, checked Jake's pulse rate, and excused himself. Brian stood on the opposite side of the bed, and each gently took one of Jake's hands. The touch woke him.

Immediately alert despite his condition and the sedatives, he looked from one to the other and back again. "What happened?" he asked, his tone urgent.

"Davenport is dead," Brian said. "I think Alex and Delacroix are too." He and Owen exchanged looks. The moment did not go unnoticed by their friend.

"What aren't you telling me?" Jake pressed.

"Jake," Owen began, clasping his hand more securely. "Tommy didn't make it."

"What?!" Jake cried, attempting to sit up. They each placed a hand on his shoulders, simultaneously soothing him and easing him back down, even as he resisted their effort.

From just outside the door, Ruiz heard the outcry he'd anticipated and hurried in. Ignoring Jake's protests, he injected a sedative into the I.V. line, not enough to render him unconscious, but sufficient to calm him.

Once Jake had settled down somewhat, Miguel asked the other two, "Mind if I stay?"

Brian answered for them both. "Might be a good idea."

"Why didn't anyone tell me he was going with you?" Jake beseeched, his diction slurred by the injection and his own emotion. Tears had begun to flow down the sides of his face. "I would have stopped him. I should have protected him."

"You were in no condition to be part of the plan," Brian said. "He wanted to be there for Dmitri." He paused a moment. "And for you."

"What—?" Jake choked. "What happened?"

Brian looked to Owen.

"He saved my life," the attorney said, adopting, as had Brian, a tone he hoped would be soothing. "Davenport had me on the ground and was about to rip my throat open. Tommy tackled him off me. That's when Davenport killed him."

"He died a hero," Brian interjected, hoping it would provide some small measure of comfort.

"Like Larry?!" Jake spat, his bitterness as apparent as his grief.

"No," Brian said softly, lovingly brushing tears from his friend's cheek as he bent to kiss his hair. "Not like Larry."

"How can you say that?!"

"Because Owen's still here," he pointed out gently. "Tommy didn't die in vain."

Jake looked from Brian to Owen and surrendered to the grief. They bent over him and, together, held him as he sobbed. They also held each other.

Anything else Jake needed to be told could wait.

CHAPTER FORTY-SEVEN

FIVE DAYS LATER, OWEN ASSISTED JAKE TO THE DINING ROOM TABLE where Frank and Loretta were already seated.

Like Owen, Frank sported a small bandage on his head. Loretta's leg was still in its cast, a pair of crutches leaning against the wall behind her.

Easing himself into his chair with a grimace, Jake managed a strained, disheartened chuckle. "We look like a 'walking wounded' support group."

"At least we're walking," Frank commented, immediately regretting the seeming flippancy when he saw Jake's expression. Chagrined, he said, "Damn, Griff. I'm sorry."

Despite the sting he felt at his partner's comment, Jake waved off the apology. "Tommy wasn't the only one to die." He smiled. "But you were right the other day, Frank—you *do* say some shit."

The four sat in silence, which Jake broke after a moment, his tone solemn. "He's being buried tomorrow."

"Will you be there?" Frank asked.

"No." Jake recounted his conversation two days prior with Cara when she had visited to check on him.

In the immediate aftermath of Tommy's murder, the elder LaRosas had finally made their prejudices less important than their parental love, arranging for Tommy to be laid to rest in New Rochelle with his family.

"From what Cara says," he continued, "they're pretty broken up that they never made peace with it while he was alive."

Owen couldn't help thinking of Kenny and his version of the same regret.

The sound of the kitchen timer offered a welcome interruption and Owen excused himself.

"Brian told me that the Volkovs will be sitting *shiva* all week," Jake added. "Seems they've welcomed him into the family. Owen and I are gonna try and get down to Brighton Beach if I feel strong enough."

"Keep me posted on that," Frank said. "I wanna go with you."

"I got a bone to pick with you, Jake," Loretta said sternly. "Frank tells me you're gay."

"Um," Jake said, unsure of where this was heading. "Yeah."

"And how come we're only just now hearing about it?" she demanded. "You know you're family, and family shares these things! If you had a man, then he's family too! Why hasn't he been at my dinner table?"

"Speaking of which," Frank said, taking advantage of Owen's temporary absence. "At the park, you told me he wasn't your boyfriend."

"Well," Jake admitted, "on Saturday, he wasn't. But a lot can change in a few days."

"Ain't that the truth, partner," Frank said.

He brought Jake up to speed on the quick thinking and fancy footwork he and Ruiz had pulled off, with Friedrich's help, in order to tie up loose ends and avoid questions which had no believable answers.

In the end, the murders had been attributed to Alex Mayhew, with Sandrine Delacroix losing her life in the process of stopping him.

As for Colin Davenport, natural time had caught up with his unnatural existence, and decomposition reduced him to long-dead skeletal remains in a matter of minutes. When his body was unearthed from the rubble, it was assumed that the corpse had been in the subterranean tunnels for at least a century.

The resolution of the murders received no media attention, a sad echo of the crimes themselves.

"How's everything with Young?" Jake asked when Frank finished the debriefing.

"Nothing for you to worry about," he assured him. "He bought the story that you had an emergency appendectomy and moved on to the next item on his agenda. As for me, I took a tumble helping Loretta up the stairs."

"How about the case?" Jake pressed.

"What case?" Frank asked. "You know he wasn't losing sleep over it before. You think he noticed when it just stopped?"

"Good," Jake said.

"No," Frank interjected. "Not good. Not good at all."

Jake furrowed his brow. "Go on," he prompted.

"Before, it didn't hit home for me," Frank said. "But any one of those guys could have been you. Or Owen. Or any of your friends, who're now my friends. I take that shit personally."

Owen had returned with a freshly baked quiche, placed it in the center of the table, and taken his seat next to Jake.

"That means a lot, Frank," Jake said. "It really does."

"And I meant it. This whole thing has opened my eyes. You coming out to me the most." He took Loretta's hand. "We know what it's like to be hated for who we are, and that shit sucks. I'm guessing that you two know the same thing."

Jake and Owen exchanged understanding looks and joined hands like the other couple at the table.

"And what you told me about Miss Thelma hit a chord," Frank went on. "About how the cops don't investigate crimes against certain people. I know how she feels, but I never knew I was one of those cops." He took a drink of water. "It all just makes a man think."

"Well," Loretta said, her tone implying that the conversation had reached a satisfactory conclusion, "at least we know we've got the two of you working to make it better." She looked to Owen. "And what is this? It smells wonderful!"

HE KNOWS THE MOMENT HE ENTERS THE CROWDED, SHADOWY BAR in Greenwich Village that he'll score tonight.

He steps into the refreshing warmth and leaves the November chill outside. At night, the autumn months in New York City get even colder. Letting his eyes adjust to the dark, he takes in the lay of the land. The air is a haze of cigarette smoke, lending an ethereal, multi-hued glow to the flashing disco lights. Bodies undulate on the dance floor, each offering its own evocative interpretation of the flavor-of-the-month hit—Barbra Streisand and Donna Summer's "No More Tears," at the moment—every square inch of exposed flesh glazed with sweat despite the cold outside. He can smell the hunger in the room and savors the potent aroma. As usual, the music's volume is pumped so high that he feels the bass in his chest.

Or is that his heart? Difficult to tell. Being on the prowl always spikes his senses and his pulse rate. He never fails to delight in the rush.

He smiles—a cynical smile with self-aware amusement—noting that he could very well be in any gay club in New York. All over the city, this exact scene is playing itself out at this very moment, the only variations being the different actors portraying the same roles in the nightly tragic comedy.

But isn't that part of the allure? he asks himself. *Maybe the* whole *allure?* All the players know the script of this two-act farce by heart. Act One in the club, Act Two to be brought to life in some other, equally random setting. And after the curtain call, no cast party, no fond farewells, no promises to always stay in touch. Each will go his own way, secretly hoping not to cross paths again.

At least he knows the score, as well as why he is here. One coin, two sides. Not to mention, it's less obvious than the baths. He actually enjoys the façade of seemingly being out only for a drink, maybe a dance or two, and playing along with the false serendipity of leaving with someone. All part of a game he shamelessly relishes playing, especially since he plays it rather well.

As he makes his way through the clusters of men, he stealthily scans the crowd, waiting for his instincts to tell him he's found what he came for. Autumn nights in the Village offer a veritable smorgasbord; it's simply a matter of deciding which selection will satisfy his appetite. The bar is packed with men, many of them clones of one another: muscled torsos encased in form-fitting tank tops in an array of colors, bubble butts that had been poured into well-worn Levi's or equally snug leather pants, bulging biceps sporting the occasional leather armband, a rainbow of bandanas—color-coded to communicate assorted interests and predilections—hanging from back pockets, two out of every three guys proudly displaying a mustache identical to the one on the Winston man blowing smoke rings from the billboard above Times Square.

Yes, he thinks, *quite the delicious selection.*

He sidles up to the bar and orders a beer he has no intention of drinking, wanting only the prop as he continues his search. Bottle in hand, he finds a spot from which his vantage point allows him to take in the whole room, and he leans casually against a wall away from the entrance.

It isn't long before eye contact is made, and he immediately knows he's found what he's come looking for. Leaning against the opposite wall, in almost a mirror of his own faux-casual pose, is a man who appears to be in his mid-twenties: well-toned body, dark hair not unlike his own, piercing eyes that seem to defy the pervasive shadows.

He walks with a purpose as he crosses the room and leans against the wall next to the object of his desire. Without maintaining the eye contact that had been established from twenty feet away, he disinterestedly observes the dancing bodies.

"Crowded tonight," he says, as if to no one in particular.

"Yeah," replies the stranger, who, like himself, is idly watching the room as if still on the prowl.

"Wanna get outta here?" he asks. His tone implies that if he were answered in the negative, he wouldn't much care. Why should he? The place was packed with options, each as anonymous as the next.

Thus was the game of the hunt.

"Sure."

As they make their way to the door, he says, "At least those killings have stopped."

"Yeah," his nameless companion replies. "Now we can go back to fucking whoever we want without having to worry about it."

"Go back?" he asks. "Did we ever stop?"

"No," comes the reply. "I guess we didn't."

Without further conversation, they step back into the chilly night, each intent solely on satisfying his own desires.

THE END

Acknowledgements

Nothing worthwhile is accomplished in a vacuum, and the book you're holding is certainly no exception. I send my deep gratitude and appreciation to the people who helped make "Night Hunt" a reality:

My dear friend and mentor Frank Diggs, for providing his medical know-how and for sharing his memories of the NYC gay scene in the late 1970s; Jeff Ellis, one of the two "B'more Besties," for providing his military knowledge; the other "B'more Bestie," Martin Savage, my literary kindred spirit and the first eyes other than my own to read these pages—he keeps me honest; Jodi, Rachel, and Mrs. McDonald of the Walbrook Branch of Baltimore's Enoch Pratt Free Library (my second home and where much of the work on this novel took place), for providing invaluable references and resources, and for sharing in my excitement; my sister and brother-in-law, Debi and Chris Cacace, and dear friend Danielle Levitt—their unflagging love and support have put so many of my dreams within reach; Dr. Sharon Thomas-Parker, for challenging me to set ambitious goals; and most especially my life-partner, Casey Hampleton, who, from Day One where my writing is concerned, has been my loudest cheerleader and my sternest taskmaster—without him, *my* story would be sorely lacking.